Nora ...
of mo...
storyte... ...nd
poigna... ...s
earned her almost every award for excellence in her
field. The youngest of five children, Nora Roberts lives in
western Maryland. She has two sons.

Visit her web... ...hed on or before ... ...n.

... 2016

Nora Roberts

California Summer

MILLS &
BOON

This edition published in Great Britain 2014
by Mills & Boon, an imprint of Harlequin (UK) Limited,
Eton House, 18-24 Paradise Road, Richmond, Surrey, TW9 1SR

CALIFORNIA SUMMER © 2013 Harlequin Books S.A.

Once More With Feeling © 1983 Nora Roberts
Sullivan's Woman © 1984 Nora Roberts

ISBN: 978-0-263-90458-1

029-0613

Harlequin (UK) policy is to use papers that are natural, renewable and recyclable products and made from wood grown in sustainable forests. The logging and manufacturing processes conform to the legal environmental regulations of the country of origin.

Printed and bound by
CPI Group (UK) Ltd, Croydon, CR0 4YY

Once More
With Feeling

To Ran,
for all the songs yet unwritten,
for all the songs yet unsung.

Chapter 1

He stood out of view as he watched her. His first thought was how little she had changed in five years. Time, it seemed, hadn't rushed or dragged but had merely hung suspended.

Raven Williams was a small, slender woman who moved quickly, with a thin, underlying nervousness that was unaccountably appealing. She was tanned deep gold from the California sun, but at twenty-five her skin was as smooth and dewy soft as a child's. She pampered it when she remembered and ignored it when she forgot. It never seemed to make any difference. Her long hair was thick and straight and true black. She wore it simply, parted in the center. The ends brushed her hips and it swirled and floated as she walked.

Her face was pixielike, with its cheekbones well-defined and the chin slightly pointed. Her mouth smiled easily, but her eyes reflected her emotions. They were smoky gray and round. Whatever Raven felt would be reflected there. She had an overwhelming need to love and be loved. Her own need was one of the reasons for her tremendous success. The other was her voice—the rich, dark, velvet voice that had catapulted her to fame.

Raven always felt a little strange in a recording studio: insulated, sealed off from the rest of the world by the glass and the soundproofing. It had been more than six years since she had cut her first record, but she was still never completely comfortable in a studio. Raven was made for the stage, for the live audience that pumped the blood and heat into the music. She considered the studio too tame, too mechanical. When she worked in the studio, as she did now, she thought of it exclusively as a job. And she worked hard.

The recording session was going well. Raven listened to a playback with a single-mindedness that blocked out her surroundings. There was only the music. It was good, she decided, but it could be better. She'd missed something in the last song, left something out. Without knowing precisely what it was, Raven was certain she could find it. She signaled the engineers to stop the playback.

"Marc?"

A sandy-haired man with the solid frame of a light-weight wrestler entered the booth. "Problem?" he said simply, touching her shoulder.

"The last number, it's a little..." Raven searched for the word. "Empty," she decided at length. "What do you think?" She respected Marc Ridgely as a musician and depended on him as a friend. He was a man of few words who had a passion for old westerns and Jordan almonds. He was also one of the finest guitarists in the country.

Marc reached up to stroke his beard, a gesture, Raven had always thought, that took the place of several sentences. "Do it again," he advised. "The instrumental's fine."

She laughed, producing a sound as warm and rich as her singing voice. "Cruel but true," she murmured, slipping the headset back on. She went back to the microphone. "Another vocal on 'Love and Lose,' please," she instructed the engineers. "I have it on the best authority that it's the singer, not the musicians." She saw Marc grin before she turned to the mike. Then the music washed over her.

Raven closed her eyes and poured herself into the song. It was a slow, aching ballad suited to the smoky depths of her voice. The lyrics were hers, ones she had written long before. It had only been recently that she had felt strong enough to sing them publicly. There was only the music in her head now, an arrangement of notes she herself had produced. And as she added her voice, she knew that what had been missing before had been her emotions. She had restricted them on the other recordings, afraid to risk them. Now she let them out. Her voice flowed with them.

An ache passed through her, a shadow of a pain buried for years. She sang as though the words would bring her relief. The hurt was there, still with her when the song was finished.

For a moment there was silence, but Raven was too dazed to note the admiration of her colleagues. She pulled off the headset, suddenly sharply conscious of its weight.

"Okay?" Marc entered the booth and slipped his arm around her. He felt her tremble lightly.

"Yes." Raven pressed her fingers to her temple a moment and gave a surprised laugh. "Yes, of course. I got a bit wrapped up in that one."

He tilted her face to his, and in a rare show of public affection for a shy man, kissed her. "You were fantastic."

Her eyes warmed, and the tears that had threatened were banished. "I needed that."

"The kiss or the compliment?"

"Both." She laughed and tossed her hair behind her back. "Stars need constant admiration, you know."

"Where's the star?" a backup vocalist wanted to know.

Raven tried for a haughty look as she glanced over. "You," she said ominously, "can be replaced." The vocalist grinned in return, too used to Raven's lack of pretentions to be intimidated.

"Who'd carry you through the session?"

Raven turned to Marc. "Take that one out and shoot him," she requested mildly, then looked up at the booth. "That's a wrap," she called out before her eyes locked on the man now standing in full view behind the glass.

The blood drained from her face. The remnants of emotion from the song surged back in full force. She nearly swayed from the power of it. "Brandon." It was a thought to be spoken aloud but only in a whisper. It was a dream she thought had finally run its course. Then his eyes were on hers, and Raven knew it was real. He'd come back.

Years of performing had taught her to act. It was always an effort for her to slip a mask into place, but by the time Brand Carstairs had come down from the booth, Raven wore a professionally untroubled face. She'd deal with the storm inside later.

"Brandon, it's wonderful to see you again." She held out both hands and tilted her face up to his for the expected, meaningless kiss of strangers who happen to be in the same business.

Her composure startled him. He'd seen her pale, seen the shock in her eyes. Now she wore a façade she'd never had before. It was slick, bright and practiced. Brand realized he'd been wrong; she *had* changed.

"Raven." He kissed her lightly and took both her hands. "You're more beautiful than anyone has a right to be." There was the lightest touch of brogue in his speech, a mist of Ireland over the more formal British. Raven allowed herself a moment to look at him, really look at him.

He was tall and now, as always, seemed a bit too thin. His hair was as dark as her own but waved where hers was needle straight. It was thick and full over his ears and down to the collar of his shirt. His face hadn't changed; it was still the same face that drove girls and women to scream and swoon at his concerts. It was rawboned and tanned, more intriguing than handsome, as the features were not altogether even. There was some-

thing of the dreamer there, from his mother's Irish half.
Perhaps that was what drew women to him, though
they were just as fascinated by the occasional British
reserve. And the eyes. Even now Raven felt the pull of
his large, heavy-lidded aquamarine eyes. They were un-
settling eyes for as easygoing a man as Brand Carstairs.
The blue and green seemed constantly at odds. But it
was the charm he wore so easily that tilted the scales,
Raven realized. Charm and blatant sex appeal were an
irresistible combination.

"You haven't changed, have you, Brandon?" The
question was quiet, the first and only sign of Raven's
distress.

"Funny." He smiled, not the quick, flashing grin he
was capable of, but a slow, considering smile. "I thought
the same of you when I first saw you. I don't suppose
it's true of either of us."

"No." God, how she wished he would release her
hands. "What brings you to L.A., Brandon?"

"Business, love," he answered carelessly, though his
eyes were taking in every inch of her face. "And, of
course, the chance to see you again."

"Of course." Her voice was coldly polite, and the
smile never reached her eyes.

The sarcasm surprised him. The Raven he remembered hadn't known the meaning of the word. She saw
his brow lift into consideration. "I do want to see you,
Raven," Brand told her with his sudden, disarming sincerity. "Very much. Can we have dinner?"

Her pulse had accelerated at his change of tone. Just
reflex, just an old habit, she told herself and struggled

to keep her hands passive in his. "I'm sorry, Brandon," she answered with perfect calm. "I'm booked." Her eyes slipped past him in search of Marc, whose head was bent over his guitar as he jammed with another musician. Raven could have sworn with frustration. Brand followed the direction of her gaze. Briefly his eyes narrowed.

"Tomorrow, then," he said. His tone was still light and casual. "I want to talk to you." He smiled as to an old friend. "I'll just drop by the house awhile."

"Brandon," Raven began and tugged on her hands.

"You still have Julie, don't you?" Brand smiled and held on to her hands, unaware of—or ignoring—her resistance.

"Yes, I..."

"I'd like to see her again. I'll come by around four. I know the way." He grinned, then kissed her again, a quick, friendly brushing of lips before he released her hands, turned and walked away.

"Yes," she murmured to herself. "You know the way."

An hour later Raven drove through the electric gates that led to her house. The one thing she hadn't allowed Julie or her agent to thrust on her was a chauffeur. Raven enjoyed driving, having control of the low, sleek foreign car and indulging from time to time in an excess of speed. She claimed it cleared her head. It obviously hadn't done the job, she thought as she pulled up in front of the house with a short, peevish squeal of the brakes. Distracted, she left her purse sitting on the seat beside her as she sprang from the car and jogged up the three stone steps that led to the front door. It was locked. Her frustration only mounted when she was forced to go back and rip the keys from the ignition.

Slamming into the house, Raven went directly to the music room. She flung herself down on the silk-covered Victorian sofa and stared straight ahead without seeing anything. A gleaming mahogany grand piano dominated the room. It was played often and at odd hours. There were Tiffany lamps and Persian rugs and a dime-store flowerpot with a struggling African violet. An old, scarred music cabinet was filled to overflowing. Sheet music spilled onto the floor. A priceless Fabergé box sat next to the brass unicorn she had found in a thrift shop and had fallen in love with. One wall was crowded with awards: Grammys, gold and platinum records, plaques and statues and the keys to a few cities. On another was the framed sheet music from the first song she had written and a breathtaking Picasso. The sofa on which she sat had a bad spring.

It was a strange hodgepodge of cultures and tastes and uniquely Raven's own. She would have thought *eclectic* a pretentious word. She had allowed Julie her exacting taste everywhere else in the house, but here she had expressed herself. Raven needed the room the same way she needed to drive her own car. It kept her sane and helped her remember exactly who Raven Williams was. But the room, like the drive, hadn't calmed her nerves. She walked to the piano.

She pounded out Mozart fiercely. Like her eyes, her music reflected her moods. Now it was tormented, volatile. Even when she'd finished, anger seemed to hover in the air.

"Well, I see you're home." Julie's voice, mild and unruffled, came from the doorway. Julie walked into the room as she had walked into Raven's life: poised and confident. When Raven had met her nearly six years before, Julie had been rich and bored, a party-goer born into old money. Their relationship had given them both something of importance: friendship and a dual dependence. Julie handled the myriad details attached to Raven's career. Raven gave Julie a purpose that the glittery world of wealth had lacked.

"Didn't the recording go well?" Julie was tall and blond, with an elegant body and that exquisitely casual California chic.

Raven lifted her head, and the smile fled from Julie's face. It had been a long time since she'd seen that helpless, ravaged look. "What happened?"

Raven let out a long breath. "He's back."

"Where did you see him?" There was no need for Julie to ask for names. In all the years of their association only two things had had the power to put that look on Raven's face. One of them was a man.

"At the studio." Raven combed her fingers through her hair. "He was up in the booth. I don't know how long he'd been there before I saw him."

Julie pursed her lightly tinted lips. "I wonder what Brand Carstairs is doing in California."

"I don't know." Raven shook her head. "He said business. Maybe he's going to tour again." In an effort to release the tension, she rubbed her hand over the back of her neck. "He's coming here tomorrow."

Julie's brows rose. "I see."

"Don't turn secretary on me, Julie," Raven pleaded. She shut her eyes. "Help me."

"Do you want to see him?" The question was practical. Julie, Raven knew, was practical. She was organized, logical and a stickler for details—all the things Raven wasn't. They needed each other.

"No," Raven began almost fiercely. "Yes..." She swore then and pressed both hands to her temples. "I don't know." Now her tone was quiet and weary. "You know what he's like, Julie. Oh, God, I thought it was over. I thought it was finished!"

With something like a moan, she jumped from the stool to pace around the room. She didn't look like a star in jeans and a simple linen blouse. Her closet held everything from bib overalls to sables. The sables were for the performer; the overalls were for her.

"I'd buried all the hurts. I was so sure." Her voice was low and a little desperate. It was still impossible for her to believe that she had remained this vulnerable after five years. She had only to see him again, and she felt it once more. "I knew sooner or later that I'd run into him somewhere." She ran her fingers through her hair as she roamed the room. "I think I'd always pictured it would be in Europe—London—probably at a party or a benefit. I'd have expected him there; maybe that would have been easier. But today I just looked up and there he was. It all came back. I didn't have any time to stop it. I'd been singing that damn song that I'd written right after he'd left." Raven laughed and shook her head. "Isn't that wild?" She took a deep breath and repeated softly, wonderingly, "Isn't that wild?"

The room was silent for nearly a full minute before Julie spoke. "What are you going to do?"

"Do?" Raven spun back to her. Her hair flew out to follow the sudden movement. "I'm not going to *do* anything. I'm not a child looking for happy-ever-after anymore." Her eyes were still dark with emotion, but her voice had grown gradually steadier. "I was barely twenty when I met Brandon, and I was blindly in love with his talent. He was kind to me at a time when I badly needed kindness. I was overwhelmed by him and with my own success."

She lifted a hand to her hair and carefully pushed it behind her shoulders. "I couldn't cope with what he wanted from me. I wasn't ready for a physical relationship." She walked to the brass unicorn and ran a fingertip down its withers. "So he left," she said softly. "And I was hurt. All I could see—maybe all I wanted to see—was that he didn't understand, didn't care enough to want to know why I said no. But that was unrealistic." She turned to Julie then with a frustrated sigh. "Why don't you say something?"

"You're doing fine without me."

"All right, then." Raven thrust her hands in her pockets and stalked to the window. "One of the things I've learned is that if you don't want to get hurt, you don't get too close. You're the only person I've never applied that rule to, and you're the only one who hasn't let me down." She took a deep breath.

"I was infatuated with Brandon years ago. Perhaps it was a kind of love, but a girl's love, easily brushed aside. It was a shock seeing him today, especially right after I finished that song. The coincidence was…" Raven pushed the feelings away and turned back from the window. "Brandon will come over tomorrow, and he'll say whatever it is that he has to say, then he'll go. That'll be the end of it."

Julie studied Raven's face. "Will it?"

"Oh, yes." Raven smiled. She was a bit weary after the emotional outburst but more confident. She had regained her control. "I like my life just as it is, Julie. He's not going to change it. No one is, not this time."

Chapter 2

Raven had dressed carefully, telling herself it was because of the fittings she had scheduled and the luncheon meeting with her agent. She knew it was a lie, but the smart, sophisticated clothes made her feel confident. Who could feel vulnerable dressed in a St. Laurent?

Her coat was white silk and full cut with batwing sleeves that made it seem almost like a cape. She wore it over matching pants with an orchid cowlneck blouse and a thick, gold belt. With the flat-brimmed hat and the carefully selected earrings, she felt invulnerable. You've come a long way, she had thought as she had studied herself in the bedroom mirror.

Now, standing in Wayne Metcalf's elaborate fitting room, she thought the same thing again—about both of them. Wayne and Raven had started the rise to fame together, she scratching out a living singing in seamy clubs and smoky piano bars and he waiting tables and sketching designs no one had the time to look at. But Raven had looked and admired and remembered.

Wayne had just begun to eke out a living in his trade when plans had begun for Raven's first concert tour. The first professional decision she made without advice was the choice of her costume designer. She had never regretted it. Like Julie, Wayne was a friend close enough to know something about Raven's early personal life. And like Julie, he was fiercely, unquestionably loyal.

Raven wandered around the room, a much plusher room, she mused, than the first offices of Metcalf Designs. There'd been no carpet on that floor, no signed lithographs on laquered walls, no panoramic view of Beverly Hills. It had been a cramped, airless little room above a Greek restaurant. Raven could still remember the strange, heavy aromas that would seep through the walls. She could still hear the exotic music that had vibrated through the bare wood floor.

Raven's star had not risen with that first concert tour, it had rocketed. The initial taste of fame had been so heady and so quick, she had hardly had the time to savor it all: tours, rehearsals, hotel rooms, reporters, mobs of fans, unbelievable amounts of money and impossible demands. She had loved it, although the traveling had sometimes left her weak and disoriented and the fans could be as frightening as they were wonderful. Still she had loved it.

Wayne, deluged with offers after the publicity of that first tour, had soon moved out of the one-room office above the *moussaka* and *souvlaki*. He'd been Raven's designer for six years, and although he now had a large staff and a huge workload, he still saw to every detail of her designs himself.

While she waited for him, Raven wandered to the bar and poured herself a ginger ale. Through all the years of luncheon meetings, elegant brunches and recording sessions, she had never taken more than an occasional drink. In this respect, at least, she would control her life.

The past, she mused, was never very far away, at least not while she still had to worry about her mother. Raven shut her eyes and wished that she could shut off her thoughts as easily. How long had it been that she had lived with that constant anxiety? She could never remember a life without it. She had been very young when she had first discovered that her mother wasn't like other mothers. Even as a little girl, she had hated the oddly sweet smell of the liquor on her mother's breath that no mints could disguise, and she had dreaded the flushed face, the first slurred, affectionate, then angry tones that had drawn mocking stares or sympathetic glances from friends and neighbors.

Raven pressed her fingers against her brow. So many years. So much waste. And now her mother had disappeared again. Where was she? In what sordid hotel room had she holed herself up in to drink away what was left of her life? Raven made a determined effort to push her mother out of her mind, but the terrible images, the frightful scenes, played on in her mind.

It's my life! I have to get on with it, Raven told herself, but she could feel the bitter taste of sorrow and guilt rise in her throat. She started when the door across swung open and Wayne walked in.

He leaned against the knob. "Beautiful!" he said admiringly, surveying her. "Did you wear that for me?"

She made a sound that was somewhere between a laugh and a sob as she moved across the room to hug him. "Of course. Bless you!"

"If you were going to dress up for me, you might at least have worn something of mine," he complained but returned the embrace. He was tall, a thin reed of a man who had to bend over to give her the quick kiss. Not yet thirty, he had a scholarly attractive face with hair and eyes the same rich shade of brown. A small white scar marred his left eyebrow and gave him, he preferred to think, a rakish profile.

"Jealous?" Raven grinned and drew away from him. "I thought you were too big for that."

"You're never too big for that." He released her, then made his way across to the bar. "Well, at least take off your hat and coat."

Raven obliged, tossing them aside with a carelessness that made Wayne wince. He gazed at her for a long moment as he poured out a Perrier. She grinned again and did a slow model's turn. "How am I holding up?" she demanded.

"I should have seduced you when you were eighteen." He sighed and drank the sparkling water. "Then I wouldn't be constantly regretting that you slipped through my fingers."

She came back for her ginger ale. "You had your chance, fella."

"I was too exhausted in those days." He lifted his scarred brow in a practiced gesture that always amused her. "I get more rest now."

"Too late," she told him and touched her glass to his. "And you're much too busy with the model-of-the-week contest."

"I only date all those skinny girls for the publicity." He reached for a cigarette and lit it elegantly. "I'm basically a very retiring man."

"The brilliance of the pun I could make is terrifying, but I'll pass."

"Wise," he concluded, then blew out a delicate trail of smoke. "I hear Brand Carstairs is in town."

Raven's smile fled, then returned. "He never could keep a low profile."

"Are you okay?"

She shrugged her shoulders. "A minute ago I was beautiful, now you have to ask if I'm okay?"

"Raven." Wayne laid a hand on top of hers. "You folded up when he left. I was there, remember?"

"Of course I remember." The teasing note left her voice. "You were very good to me, Wayne. I don't think I would have made it without you and Julie."

"That's not what I'm talking about, Raven. I want to know how you feel now." He turned her hand over and laced his fingers through hers. "I could renew my offer to go try to break all his bones, if you like."

Touched and amused, she laughed. "I'm sure you're a real killer, Wayne, but it isn't necessary." The straightening of her shoulders was unconscious, a gesture of pride that made Wayne smile. "I'm not going to fold this time."

"Are you still in love with him?"

She hadn't expected such a direct question. Dropping her gaze, she took a moment to answer. "A better question is, Did I ever love him?"

"We both already know the answer to that one," Wayne countered. He took her hand when she would have turned away. "We've been friends a long time. What happens to you matters to me."

"Nothing's going to happen to me." Her eyes were back on his, and she smiled. "Absolutely nothing. Brandon is the past. Who knows better than I that you can't run away from the past, and who knows better how to cope with it?" She squeezed his hand. "Come on, show me the costumes that are going to make me look sensational."

After a quick, final glance at her face, Wayne walked over to a gleaming Chippendale table and pushed the button on an intercom. "Bring in Ms. Williams's designs."

Raven had approved the sketches, of course, and the fabrics, but still the completed designs took her by surprise. They had been created for the spotlights. She knew she'd sparkle on stage. It felt odd wearing blood red and silver sequins in Wayne's brightly lit, elegant room with mirrors tossing her image back at her from all angles. But then, she remembered, it was an odd business.

Raven stared at the woman in the mirrors and listened with half an ear to Wayne's mumbling as he tucked and adjusted. Her mind could not help but wander. Six years before, she'd been a terrified kid with an album shooting off the top of the charts and a whirlwind concert tour to face. It had all happened so fast: the typical overnight success—not counting the years she had struggled in smoke-choked dives. Still, she'd been young to make a name for herself and determined to prove she wasn't a one-shot fluke. The romance with Brand Carstairs, while she had still been fresh, hot news, hadn't hurt her career. For a brief time it had made her the crown princess of popular music. For more than six months their faces appeared on every magazine cover, dominating the newsstands. They'd laughed about it, Raven remembered, laughed at the silly, predictable headlines: "Raven and Brand Plan Love Nest"; "Williams and Carstairs Make Their Own Music."

Brand had complained about his billing. They had ignored the constant flare and flash of cameras because they had been happy and saw little else but each other. Then, when he had gone, the pictures and headlines had continued for a long time—the cold, cruel words that flashed the intimacies of private hurts for the public eye. Raven no longer looked at them.

Over the months and years, she had grown from the crown princess to a respected performer and celebrity in her own right. That's what's important, she reminded herself. Her career, her life. She'd learned about priorities the hard way.

Raven slipped into the glistening black jumpsuit and

found it fit like a second skin. Even her quiet breathing sent sequins flashing. Light streaked out from it at the slightest movement. It was, she decided after a critical survey, blisteringly sexy.

"I'd better not gain a quarter of an ounce before the tour," she remarked, turning to view her slim, sleek profile. Thoughtfully, she gathered her hair in her hand and tossed it behind her back. "Wayne..." He was kneeling at her feet, adjusting the hem. His answer was a grunt. "Wayne, I don't know if I have the nerve to wear this thing."

"This thing," he said mildly as he rose to pluck at the sleeve, "is fantastic."

"No artistic snub intended," she returned and smiled as he stepped back to survey her up and down in his concentrated, professional gaze. "But it's a bit..." She glanced at herself again. "Basic, isn't it?"

"You've got a nice little body, Raven." Wayne examined his creation from the rear. "Not all my clients could wear this without a bit of help here and there. Okay, take it off. It's perfect just as it is."

"I always feel like I've been to the doctor when I've finished here," she commented as she slipped back into her white slacks and orchid blouse. "Who knows more about our bodies' secrets than our dressmakers?"

"Who else knows more about *your* secrets, darling?" he corrected absently as he made notes on each one of the costumes. "Women tend to get chatty when they're half-dressed."

"Oh, what lovely gossip do you know?" Fastening her belt, Raven walked to him, then leaned companionably on his shoulder. "Tell me something wonderfully indiscreet and shocking, Wayne."

"Babs Curtin has a new lover," he murmured, still intent on his notes.

"I said shocking," Raven complained. "Not predictable."

"I've sworn an oath of secrecy, written in dressmaker's chalk."

"I'm very disappointed in you." Raven left his side to fetch her coat and hat. "I was certain you had feet of clay."

"Lauren Chase just signed to do the lead in *Fantasy*."

Raven stopped on her way to the door and whirled. "What?" She dashed back across the room and yanked the notebook from Wayne's hand.

"Somehow I thought that would get your attention," Wayne observed dryly.

"When? Oh, Wayne," she went on before he could answer. "I'd give several years of my young life for a chance to write that score. Lauren Chase…oh, yes, she's so right for it. Who's doing the score, Wayne?" Raven gripped his shoulders and closed her eyes. "Go ahead, tell me, I can take it."

"She doesn't know. You're cutting off the circulation, Raven," he added, disengaging her hands.

"Doesn't know!" she groaned, crushing the hat down on her head in a way that made Wayne swear and adjust it himself. "That's worse, a thousand times worse! Some faceless, nameless songwriter who couldn't possibly know what's right for that fabulous screenplay is even now sitting at a piano making unforgivable mistakes."

"There's always the remote possibility that whoever's writing it has talent," he suggested and earned a lethal glare.

"Whose side are you on?" she demanded and flung the coat around her shoulders.

He grinned, grabbed her cheeks and gave her a resounding kiss. "Go home and stomp your feet, darling. You'll feel better."

She struggled not to smile. "I'm going next door and buy a Florence DeMille," she threatened him with the name of a leading competitor.

"I'll forgive you that statement," Wayne said with a hefty sigh. "Because along with my feet of clay I've a heart of gold."

She laughed and left him with her rack of costumes and his notebook.

The house was quiet when Raven returned. The faint scent of lemon oil and pine told her that the house had just been cleaned. As a matter of habit, she peeked into her music room and was satisfied that nothing there had been disturbed. She liked her disorganization just as it was. With the idle thought of making coffee, Raven wandered toward the kitchen.

She had bought the house for its size and rambling openness. It was the antithesis of the small, claustrophobic rooms she had grown up in. And it smelled clean, she decided. Not antiseptic; she would have hated that, but there was no lingering scent of stale cigarettes, no sickly sweet odor of yesterday's bottle. It was her house, as her life was hers. She'd bought them both with her voice.

Raven twirled once around the room, pleased with herself for no specific reason. I'm happy, she thought, just happy to be alive.

Grabbing a rose from a china vase, she began to sing as she walked down the hall. It was the sight of Julie's long, narrow bare feet propped up on the desk in the library that stopped her.

Raven hesitated, seeing Julie was on the phone, but was quickly gestured inside.

"I'm sorry, Mr. Cummings, but Ms. Williams has a strict policy against endorsements. Yes, I'm sure it's a marvelous product." Julie lifted her eyes from her pink-tinted toenails and met Raven's amused grin. She rolled her eyes to the ceiling, and Raven settled cross-legged in an overstuffed leather chair. The library, with its warm, mahogany paneling and stately furnishings, was Julie's domain. And, Raven thought, snuggling down more comfortably, it suited her.

"Of course, I'll see she gets your offer, but I warn you, Ms. Williams takes a firm stand on this." With one last exasperated glance at the ceiling, Julie hung up. "If you didn't insist on being nice to everybody who calls you, I could have thought of a few different words for that one," Julie snapped.

"Trouble?" Raven asked, sniffing her rose and smiling.

"Get smart and I'll tell them you'll be thrilled to endorse his Earth Bubble Shampoo." She laced her fingers behind her head as she made the threat.

"Mercy," Raven pleaded, then kicked off her elegant, orchid-toned shoes. "You look tired," she said, watching Julie stretch her back muscles. "Been busy?"

"Just last-minute nonsense to clear things for the tour." A shrug dismissed the complications she had handled. "I never did ask you how the recording went. It's finished, isn't it?"

"Yeah." Raven took a deep breath and twirled her rose by the stem. "It went perfectly. I haven't been happier with a session since the first one. Something just clicked."

"You worked hard enough on the material," Julie remarked, thinking of the endless nights Raven had spent writing and arranging.

"Sometimes I still can't believe it." She spoke softly, the words hardly more than thoughts. "I listen to a playback, and it's all there, the strings, the brass, the rhythm and backups, and I can't believe it's me. I've been so incredibly lucky."

"Talented," Julie corrected.

"Lots of people have talent," Raven reminded her. "But they're not sitting here. They're still in some dreary piano bar, waiting. Without luck, they're never going to be anywhere else."

"There are also things like drive, perseverance, guts." Raven's persistent lack of self-confidence infuriated Julie. She'd been with her almost from the beginning of Raven's start in California six years before. She'd seen the struggles and the disappointments. She knew about the fears, insecurities and work behind the glamour. There was nothing about Raven Williams that Julie didn't know.

The phone interrupted her thoughts on a lecture on self-worth. "It's your private line," she said as she pressed the button. "Hello." Raven tensed but relaxed when she saw Julie smile. "Hi, Henderson. Yes, she's right here, hold on. Your illustrious agent," Julie stated as she rose. She slipped her feet back into her sandals. Raven got up from her chair just as the doorbell chimed.

"I guess that's Brandon." With admirable ease, she flopped into the chair that Julie had just vacated. "Would you tell him I'll be along in a minute?"

"Sure." Julie turned and left as Raven's voice followed her down the hall.

"I left it where? In your office? Henderson, I don't know why I ever bother carrying a purse."

Julie smiled. Raven had a penchant for losing things: her purse, her shoes, her passport. Vital or trivial, it simply didn't matter. Music and people filled Raven's thoughts, and material objects were easily forgotten.

"Hello, Brand," Julie said as she opened the front door. "Nice to see you again." Her eyes were cool, and her mouth formed no smile.

"Hello, Julie."

There was warmth in his greeting. She sensed it and ignored it. "Come in," she invited. "Raven's expecting you; she'll be right out."

"It's good to be here again. I've missed this place."

"Have you?" Her tone was sharp.

His grin turned into a look of appraisal. Julie was a long-stemmed woman with a sleek cap of honey-blond hair and direct brown eyes. She was closer to Brand's age than Raven's and was the sort of woman he was usually attracted to: smart, sophisticated and coolly sexy. Yet, there could never have been anything between them but friendship. She was too fiercely devoted to Raven. Her loyalty, he saw, was unchanged.

"Five years is a long time, Julie."

"I'm not sure it's long enough," she countered. Old resentments came simmering back to the surface. "You hurt her."

"Yes, I know." His gaze didn't falter at the confession, and there was no plea for understanding in his eyes. The lack of it touched off respect in Julie, but she dismissed it. She shook her head as she looked at him.

"So," she said softly, "you've come back."

"I've come back," he agreed, then smiled. "Did you think I wouldn't?"

"She didn't," Julie retorted, annoyed with herself for warming to him. "That's what matters."

"Julie, Henderson's sending over my purse." Raven came down the hall toward them in her quick, nervous stride. "I told him not to bother; I don't think there's anything in it but a comb and an expired credit card. Hello, Brandon." She offered her hands as she had at the recording studio, but now she felt more able to accept his touch.

She hadn't bothered to put her shoes back on or to repaint her mouth. Her smile was freer, more as he remembered it. "Raven." Brand brought her hands to his lips. Instantly she stiffened, and Brand released her.

"Can we talk in the music room?" His smile was easy, friendly. "I was always comfortable in there."

"Of course." She turned toward the doorway. "Would you like something to drink?"

"I'd have some tea." He gave Julie his quick, charming grin. "You always made a good cup of tea."

"I'll bring it in." Without responding to the grin, Julie moved down the hall toward the kitchen. Brand followed Raven into the music room.

He touched her shoulder before she could cross to the sofa. It was a gesture that asked her to wait. Turning her head, Raven saw that he was giving the room one of his long, detailed studies. She had seen that look on his face before. It was a curious aspect of what seemed like a casual nature. There was an intensity about him at times that recalled the tough London street kid who'd once fought his way to the top of his profession. The key to his talent seemed to be in his natural gift for observation. He saw everything, remembered everything. Then he translated it into lyric and melody.

The fingers on her shoulder caressed once, almost absently, and brought back a flood of memories. Raven would have moved away, but he dropped the hand and turned to her. She had never been able to resist his eyes.

"I remember every detail of this room. I've pictured it from time to time when I couldn't do anything but think of you." He lifted his hand again to brush the back of it against her cheek.

"Don't." She shook her head and stepped away.

"It's difficult not to touch you, Raven. Especially

here. Do you remember the long evenings we spent here? The quiet afternoons?"

He was moving her—with just his voice, just the steady spell of his eyes. "It was a long time ago, Brandon."

"It doesn't seem so long ago at the moment. It could be yesterday; you look the same."

"I'm not," she told him with a slight shake of her head. He saw her eyes darken before she turned away. "If I had known this was why you wanted to see me, I wouldn't have let you come. It's over, Brandon. It's been over for a long time."

"Is it?" Raven hadn't realized he was so close behind her. He turned her in his arms and caught her. "Show me, then," he demanded. "Just once."

The moment his mouth touched hers, she was thrown back in time. It was all there—the heat, the need, the loving. His lips were so soft, so warm; hers parted with only the slightest pressure. She knew how he would taste, how he would smell. Her memory was sharper than she had thought. Nothing was forgotten.

He tangled his fingers in the thickness of her hair, tilting her head further back as he deepened the kiss. He wanted to luxuriate in her flavor, in her scent, in her soft, yielding response. Her hands were trapped between their bodies, and she curled her fingers into the sweater he wore. The need, the longing, seemed much too fresh to have been dormant for five years. Brand held her close but without urgency. There was a quiet kind of certainty in the way he explored her mouth. Raven responded, giving, accepting, remembering. But when she felt the pleasure drifting toward passion, she resisted. When she struggled, he loosened his hold but didn't release her. Raven stared up at him with a look he well remembered but had never been able to completely decipher.

"It doesn't seem it's altogether finished after all," he murmured.

"You never did play fair, did you?" Raven pushed out of his arms, furious and shaken. "Let me tell you something, Brandon. I won't fall at your feet this time. You hurt me before, but I don't bruise so easily now. I have no intention of letting you back into my life."

"I think you will," he corrected easily. "But perhaps not in the way you mean." He paused and caught her hair with his fingers. "I can apologize for kissing you, Raven, if you'd like me to lie."

"Don't bother. You've always been good at romance. I rather enjoyed it." She sat down on the sofa and smiled brightly up at him.

He lifted a brow. It was hardly the response he had expected. He drew out a cigarette and lit it. "You seem to have grown up in my absence."

"Being an adult has its advantages," Raven observed. The kiss had stirred more than she cared to admit, even to herself.

"I always found your naiveté charming."

"It's difficult to remain naive, however charming, in this business." She leaned back against the cushion, relaxing deliberately. "I'm not wide-eyed and twenty anymore, Brandon."

"Tough and jaded are you, Raven?"

"Tough enough," she returned. "You gave me my first lesson!"

He took a deep drag on his cigarette, then considered the glowing tip of it. "Maybe I did," he murmured. "Maybe you needed it."

"Maybe you'd like me to thank you," she tossed back, and he looked over at her again.

"Perhaps." He walked over, then dropped down beside her on the sofa. His laugh was sudden and unexpected. "Good God, Raven, you've never had this bloody spring fixed."

The tension in her neck fled as she laughed with him. "I like it that way." She tossed her hair behind her back. "It's more personal."

"To say nothing of uncomfortable."

"I never sit on that spot," she told him.

"You leave it for unsuspecting guests, I imagine." He shifted away from the defective spring.

"That's right. I like people to feel at home."

Julie brought in a tea tray and found them sitting companionably on the sofa. Her quick, practiced glance found no tension on Raven's face. Satisfied, she left them again.

"How've you been, Brandon? Busy, I imagine." Raven crossed her legs under her and leaned over to pour the tea. It was a move Brandon had seen many times. Almost savagely, he crushed out his cigarette.

"Busy enough." He understated the five albums he had released since she'd last seen him and the three grueling concert tours. There'd been more than twenty songs with his name on the copyright in the past year.

"You've been living in London?"

"Mostly." His brow lifted, and she caught the gesture as she handed him his tea.

"I read the trades," she said mildly. "Don't we all?"

"I saw your television special last month." He sipped his tea and relaxed against the back of the sofa. His eyes were on her, and she thought them a bit more green than blue now. "You were marvelous."

"Last month?" She frowned at him, puzzled. "It wasn't aired in England, was it?"

"I was in New York. Did you write all the songs for the album you finished up yesterday?"

"All but two." Shrugging, she took up her own china cup. "Marc wrote 'Right Now' and 'Coming Back.' He's got the touch."

"Yes." Brand eyed her steadily. "Does he have you, too?" Raven's head whipped around. "I read the trades," he said mildly.

"That comes under a more personal heading." Her eyes were dark with anger.

"More bluntly stated, none of my business?" he asked, sipping again.

"You were always bright, Brandon."

"Thanks, love." He set down his cup. "But my question was professional. I need to know if you have any entanglements at the moment."

"Entanglements are usually personal. Ask me about my dancing lessons."

"Later, perhaps. Raven, I need your undivided devotion for the next three months." His smile was engaging. Raven fought his charm.

"Well," she said and set her cup beside his. "That's bluntly stated."

"No indecent proposal at the moment," he assured her. Settling back in the hook of the sofa's arm, he sought her eyes. "I'm doing the score for *Fantasy*. I need a partner."

Chapter 3

To say she was surprised would have been a ridiculous understatement. Brand watched her eyes widen. He thought they were the color of peat smoke. She didn't move but simply stared at him, her hands resting lightly on her knees. Her thoughts had been flung in a thousand different directions, and she was trying to sit calmly and bring them back to order.

Fantasy. The book that had captured America's heart. A novel that had been on the bestseller list for more than fifty weeks. The sale of its paperback rights had broken all records. The film rights had been purchased as well, and Carol Mason, the author, had written the screenplay herself. It was to be a musical; *the* musical of the nineties. Speculation had been buzzing for months on both coasts as to who would write the score. It would be the coup of the decade, the chance of a lifetime. The plot was a dream, and the reigning box-office queen had the lead. And the music... Raven already had half-formed songs in her head. Carefully she reached back and poured more tea. Things like this don't just fall in your lap, she reminded herself. Perhaps he means something entirely different.

"You're going to score *Fantasy,*" she said at length, cautiously. Her eyes met his again. His were clear, confident, a little puzzled. "I just heard that Lauren Chase had been signed. Everywhere I go, people are wondering who's going to play Tessa, who's going to play Joe."

"Jack Ladd," Brand supplied, and the puzzlement in Raven's eyes changed to pure pleasure.

"Perfect!" She reached over to take his hands. "You're going to have a tremendous hit. I'm very happy for you."

And she was. He could see as well as hear the absolute sincerity. It was typical of her to gain genuine pleasure from someone else's good fortune, just as it was typical of her to suffer for someone else's misfortune. Raven's feelings ran deep, and he knew she'd never been afraid to show emotion. Her unaffectedness had always been a great part of her appeal. For the moment, she had forgotten to be cautious with Brand. She smiled at him as she held his hands.

"So that's why you're in California," she said. "Have you already started?"

"No." He seemed to consider something for a moment, then his fingers interlaced with hers. Her hands were narrow-boned and slender, with palms as soft as a child's. "Raven, I meant what I said. I need a partner. I need you."

She started to remove her hands from his, but he tightened his fingers. "I've never known you to need anyone, Brandon," she said, not quite succeeding in making her tone light. "Least of all me."

His grip tightened quickly, causing Raven's eyes to widen at the unexpected pain. Just as quickly, he released her. "This is business, Raven."

She lifted a brow at the temper in his voice. "Business is usually handled through my agent," she said. "You remember Henderson."

He gave her a long, steady look. "I remember everything." He saw the flash of hurt in her eyes, swiftly controlled. "Raven," his tone was gentler now. "I'm sorry."

She shrugged and gave her attention back to her tea. "Old wounds, Brandon. It does seem to me that if there was a legitimate offer, Henderson would have gotten wind of it."

"There's been an offer," Brand told her. "I asked him to let me speak to you first."

"Oh?" Her hair had drifted down, curtaining her face, and she flipped it behind her back. "Why?"

"Because I thought that if you knew we'd be working together, you'd turn it down."

"Yes," she agreed. "You're right."

"And that," he said without missing a beat, "would be incredibly soft-headed. Henderson knows that as well as I do."

"Oh, does he?" Raven rose, furious. "Isn't it marvelous the way people determine my life? Did you two decide I was too feeble-brained to make this decision on my own?"

"Not exactly." Brand's voice was cool. "We did agree that left to yourself, you have a tendency to be emotional rather than sensible."

"Terrific. Do I get a leash and collar for Christmas?"

"Don't be an idiot," Brand advised.

"Oh, so now I'm an idiot?" Raven turned away to pace the room. She had the same quicksilver temper he remembered. She was all motion, all energy. "I don't know how I've managed all this time without your pretty compliments, Brandon." She whirled back to him. "Why in the world would you want an emotional idiot as a collaborator?"

"Because," Brandon said and rose, "you're a hell of a writer. Now shut up."

"Of course," she said, seating herself on the piano bench. "Since you asked so nicely."

Deliberately he took out another cigarette, lit it and blew out a stream of smoke, all the while his eyes resting on her face. "This is an important project, Raven," he said. "Let's not blow it. Because we were once very close, I wanted to talk to you face to face, not through a mediator, not through a bloody telephone wire. Can you understand that?"

She waited a long moment before answering. "Maybe."

Brand smiled and moved over to her. "We'll add stubborn to those adjectives later, but I don't want you mad again."

"Then let me ask you something before you say anything I'll have to get mad about." Raven tilted her head and studied his face. "First, why do you want a collaborator on this? Why share the glory?"

"It's also a matter of sharing the work, love. Fifteen songs."

She nodded. "All right, number two, then. Why me, Brandon? Why not someone who's scored a musical before?"

He answered her by walking around her and slipping down on the piano bench beside her. Without speaking, he began to play. The notes flooded the room like ghosts. "Remember this?" he murmured, glancing over and into her eyes.

Raven didn't have to answer. She rose and walked away. It was too difficult to sit beside him at the same piano where they had composed the song he now played. She remembered how they had laughed, how warm his eyes had been, how safe she had felt in his arms. It was the first and only song they had written and recorded together.

Even after he had stopped playing, she continued to prowl the room. "What does 'Clouds and Rain' have to do with anything?" she demanded. He had touched a chord in her; he heard it in the tone of her voice. He felt a pang of guilt at having intentionally peeled away a layer of her defense.

"There's a Grammy over there and a gold record, thanks to that two minutes and forty-three seconds, Raven. We work well together."

She turned back to look at him. "We did once."

"We will again." Brand stood and came to her but

this time made no move to touch her. "Raven, you know how important this could be to your career. And you must realize what you'd be bringing to the project. *Fantasy* needs your special talents."

She wanted it. She could hardly believe that something she wanted so badly was being offered to her. But how would it be to work with him again, to be in constant close contact? Would she be able to deal with it? Would she be sacrificing her personal sanity for professional gain? But I don't love him anymore, she reminded herself. Raven caught her bottom lip between her teeth in a gesture of indecision. Brand saw it.

"Raven, think of the music."

"I am," she admitted. "I'm also thinking of you—of us." She gave him a clear, candid look. "I'm not sure it would be healthy for me."

"I can't promise not to touch you." He was annoyed, and his voice reflected it in its crisp, concise tone. "But I can promise not to push myself on you. Is that good enough?"

Raven evaded the question. "If I agreed, when would we start? I've a tour coming up."

"I know, in two weeks. You'll be finished in six, so we could start the first week in May."

"I see." Her mouth turned up a bit as she combed her fingers through her hair. "You've looked into this thoroughly."

"I told you, it's business."

"All right, Brandon," she said, conceding his point. "Where would we work? Not here," she said quickly.

There was a sudden pressure in her chest. "I won't work with you here."

"No, I thought not. I have a place," he continued when Raven remained silent. "It's in Cornwall."

"Cornwall?" Raven repeated. "Why Cornwall?"

"Because it's quiet and isolated, and no one, especially the press, knows I have it. They'll be all over us when they hear we're working together, especially on this project. It's too hot an item."

"Couldn't we just rent a small cave on the coast somewhere?"

He laughed and caught her hair in his hand. "You know how poor the acoustics are in a cave. Cornwall's incredible in the spring, Raven. Come with me."

She lifted a hand to his chest to push back, not certain if she was about to agree or decline. He could still draw too much from her too effortlessly. She needed to think, she decided; a few days to put it all in perspective.

"Raven."

She turned to see Julie in the doorway. "Yes?"

"There's a call for you."

Vaguely annoyed, Raven frowned at her. "Can't it wait, Julie? I…"

"It's on your private line."

Brand felt her stiffen and looked down curiously. Her eyes were completely blank.

"I see." Her voice was calm, but he detected the faintest of tremors.

"Raven?" Without thinking, he took her by the shoulders and turned her to face him. "What is it?"

"Nothing." She drew out of his arms. There was something remote about her now, something distant that puzzled him. "Have some more tea," she invited and smiled, but her eyes remained blank. "I'll be back in a minute."

She was gone for more than ten, and Brand had begun to pace restlessly through the room. Raven was definitely no longer the malleable young girl she had been five years before; he knew that. He wasn't at all certain she would agree to work with him. He wanted her—for the project and yes, for himself. Holding her, tasting her again, had stirred up much more than memories. She fascinated him and always had. Even when she had been so young, there had been an air of secrecy about her. There still was. It was as if she kept certain parts of herself locked in a closet out of reach. She had held him off five years before in more than a physical sense. It had frustrated him then and continued to frustrate him.

But he was older, too. He'd made mistakes with her before and had no intention of repeating them. Brand knew what he wanted and was determined to get it. Sitting back at the piano, he began to play the song he had written with Raven. He remembered her voice, warm and sultry, in his ear. He was nearly at the end when he sensed her presence.

Glancing up, Brand saw her standing in the doorway. Her eyes were unusually dark and intense. Then he realized it was because she was pale, and the contrast accentuated the gray of her irises. Had the song disturbed her that much? He stopped immediately and rose to go to her.

"Raven..."

"I've decided to do it," she interrupted. Her hands were folded neatly in front of her, her eyes direct.

"Good." He took her hands and found it chilled. "Are you all right?"

"Yes, of course." She removed her hands from his, but her gaze never faltered. "I suppose Henderson will fill me in on all the details."

Something about her calm disturbed him. It was as if she'd set part of herself aside. "Let's have dinner, Raven." The urge to be with her, to pierce her armor, was almost overwhelming. "I'll take you to the Bistro; you always liked it there."

"Not tonight, Brandon, I...have some things to do."

"Tomorrow," he insisted, knowing he was pushing but unable to prevent himself. She looked suddenly weary.

"Yes, all right, tomorrow." She gave him a tired smile. "I'm sorry, but I'll have to ask you to leave now, Brandon. I didn't realize how late it was."

"All right." Bending toward her, he gently kissed her. It was an instinctive gesture, one that demanded no response. He felt the need to warm her, protect her. "Seven tomorrow," he told her. "I'm at the Bel-Air; you only have to call me."

Raven waited until she heard the front door shut behind her. She pressed the heel of her hand to her brow and let the tide of emotions rush through her. There were no tears, but a blinding headache raged behind her eyes. She felt Julie's hand on her shoulder.

"They found her?" Julie asked, concerned. Automatically she began kneading the tension from Raven's shoulders.

"Yes, they found her." She let out a long, deep breath. "She's coming back."

Chapter 4

The sanitarium was white and clean. The architect, a good one, had conceived a restful building without medical overtones. The uninformed might have mistaken it for an exclusive hotel snuggled in California's scenic Ojai. It was a proud, elegantly fashioned building with several magnificent views of the countryside. Raven detested it.

Inside, the floors were thickly carpeted, and conversation was always low-key. Raven hated the controlled silence, the padded quiet. The staff members wore street clothes and only small, discreet badges to identify themselves, and they were among the best trained in the country, just as the Fieldmore Clinic was the best detoxification center on the west coast. Raven had made certain of its reputation before she had brought her mother there for the first time over five years before.

Raven waited in Justin Karter's paneled, book-lined, tasteful office. It received its southern exposure through a wide, thick-paned window. The morning sunlight beamed in on a thriving collection of leafy green plants. Raven wondered idly why her own plants seemed always to put up only a halfhearted struggle for life, one they usually lost. Perhaps she should ask Dr. Karter what his secret was. She laughed a little and rubbed her fingers on the nagging headache between her brows.

How she hated these visits and the leathery, glossy smell of his office. She was cold and cupped her elbows, hugging her arms across her midriff. Raven was always cold in the Fieldmore Clinic, from the moment she walked through the stately white double doors until long after she walked out again. It was a penetrating cold that went straight to the bone. Turning away from the window, she paced nervously around the room. When she heard the door open, she stopped and turned around slowly.

Karter entered, a small, youthful man with a corn-colored beard and healthy pink cheeks. He had an earnest face, accentuated by tortoise-rimmed glasses and a faint smattering of freckles. Under other circumstances, Raven would have liked his face, even warmed to it.

"Ms. Williams." He held out a hand and took hers in a quick, professional grip. It was cold, he realized, and as fragile as he remembered. Her hair was pinned up at the nape of her neck, and she looked young and pale in the dark tailored suit. This woman was far different from the vibrant, laughing entertainer he had watched on television a few weeks before.

"Hello, Dr. Karter."

It always amazed him that the rich, full-toned voice belonged to such a small, delicate-looking woman. He had thought the same years before when she had been hardly more than a child. He was an ardent fan but had never asked her to sign any of the albums in his collection. It would, he knew, embarrass them both.

"Please sit down, Ms. Williams. Could I get you some coffee?"

"No, please." She swallowed. Her throat was always dry when she spoke to him. "I'd like to see my mother first."

"There are a few things I'd like to discuss with you."

He watched her moisten her lips, the only sign of agitation. "After I've seen her."

"All right." Karter took her by the arm and led her from the room. They walked across the quiet, carpeted hallway to the elevators. "Ms. Williams," he began. He would have liked to have called her Raven. He thought of her as Raven, just as the rest of the world did. But he could never quite break through the film of reserve she slipped on in his presence. It was, Karter knew, because he knew her secrets. She trusted him to keep them but was never comfortable with him. She turned to him now, her great, gray eyes direct and expressionless.

"Yes, Doctor?" Only once had Raven ever broken down in his presence, and she had promised herself she would never do so again. She would not be destroyed by her mother's illness, and she would not make a public display of herself.

"I don't want you to be shocked by your mother's

appearance." They stepped into the elevator together, and he kept his hand on her arm. "She had made a great deal of progress during her last stay here, but she left prematurely, as you know. Over the past three months, her condition has…deteriorated."

"Please," Raven said wearily, "don't be delicate. I know where she was found and how. You'll dry her out again, and in a couple of months she'll leave and it'll start all over. It never changes."

"Alcoholics fight a continuing battle."

"Don't tell me about alcoholics," she shot back. The reserve cracked, and the emotion poured through. "Don't preach to me about battles." She stopped herself, then, shaking her head, pressed her fingers to the concentrated source of her headache. "I know all about alcoholics," she said more calmly. "I haven't your dedication or your optimism."

"You keep bringing her back," he reminded Raven softly.

"She's my mother." The elevator doors slid open, and Raven walked through them.

Her skin grew colder as they moved down the hallway. There were doors on either side, but she refused to think of the people beyond them. The hospital flavor was stronger here. Raven thought she could smell the antiseptic, the hovering medicinal odor that always made a hint of nausea roll in her stomach. When Karter stopped in front of a door and reached for a knob, Raven laid a hand on top of his.

"I'll see her alone, please."

He sensed her rigid control. Her eyes were calm, but

he had seen the quick flash of panic in them. Her fingers didn't tremble on his hand but were stiff and icy. "All right. But only a few minutes. There are complications we need to discuss." He took his hand from the knob. "I'll wait for you here."

Raven nodded and twisted the knob herself. She took a moment, struggling to gather every ounce of strength, then walked inside.

The woman lay in a hospital bed on good linen sheets, dozing lightly. There was a tube feeding liquid into her through a needle in her arm. The drapes were drawn, and the room was in shadows. It was a comfortable room painted in soft blue with an ivory carpet and a few good paintings. With her fingers dug into the leather bag she carried, Raven approached the bed.

Raven's first thought was that her mother had lost weight. There were hollows in her cheeks, and her skin had the familiar unhealthy yellow cast. Her dark hair was cropped short and streaked liberally with gray. It had been lovely hair, Raven remembered, glossy and full. Her face was gaunt, with deathly circles under the eyes and a mouth that seemed dry and pulled in. The helplessness stabbed at Raven, and for a minute she closed her eyes against it. She let them fall while she looked down on the sleeping woman. Without a sound, without moving, the woman in bed opened her eyes. They were dark and gray like her daughter's.

"Mama." Raven let the tears roll freely. "Why?"

By the time Raven got to her front door, she was exhausted. She wanted bed and oblivion. The headache was still with her, but the pain had turned into a dull, sickening throb. Closing the door behind her, she leaned back on it, trying to summon the strength to walk up the stairs.

"Raven?"

She opened her eyes and watched Julie come down the hall toward her. Seeing Raven so pale and beaten, Julie slipped an arm around her shoulders. Her concern took the form of a scolding. "You should have let me go with you. I should never have let you go alone." She was already guiding Raven up the stairs.

"My mother, my problem," Raven said tiredly.

"That's the only selfish part of you," Julie said in a low, furious voice as they entered Raven's bedroom. "I'm supposed to be your friend. You'd never let me go through something like this alone."

"Please, don't be angry with me." Raven swayed on her feet as Julie stripped off the dark suit jacket. "It's something I feel is my responsibility, just mine. I've felt that way for too long to change now."

"I am angry with you." Julie's voice was tight as she slipped the matching skirt down over Raven's hips. "This is the only thing you do that makes me genuinely angry with you. I can't stand it when you do this to yourself." She looked back at the pale, tired face. "Have you eaten?" Raven shook her head as she stepped out of the skirt. "And you won't," she concluded, brushing Raven's fumbling hands away from the buttons of the white lawn blouse. She undid them herself, then pushed the material from Raven's shoulders. Raven stood, unresisting.

"I'm having dinner with Brandon," Raven murmured, going willingly as Julie guided her toward the bed.

"I'll call him and cancel. I can bring you up something later. You need to sleep."

"No." Raven slipped between the crisp, cool sheets. "I want to go. I need to go," she corrected as she shut her eyes. "I need to get out; I don't want to think for a while. I'll rest now. He won't be here until seven."

Julie walked over to pull the shades. Even before the room was darkened, Raven was asleep.

It was some minutes past seven when Julie opened the door to Brandon. He wore a stone-colored suit with a navy shirt open at the throat. He looked casually elegant, Julie thought. The nosegay of violets was charming rather than silly in his hands. He lifted a brow at the clinging black sheath she wore.

"Hello, Julie. You look terrific." He plucked one of the violets out of the nosegay and handed it to her. "Going out?"

Julie accepted the flower. "In a little while," she answered. "Raven should be down in a minute. Brand..." Hesitating, Julie shook her head, then turned to lead him into the music room. "I'll fix you a drink. Bourbon, isn't it? Neat."

Brand caught her arm. "That isn't what you were going to say."

She took a deep breath. "No." For a moment longer she hesitated, then began, fixing him with her dark brown eyes. "Raven's very important to me. There aren't many like her, especially in this town. She's genuine, and though she thinks she has, she hasn't really developed any hard edges yet. I wouldn't like to see her hurt, especially right now. No, I won't answer any questions," she said, anticipating him. "It's Raven's story, not mine. But I'm going to tell you this: She needs a light touch and a great deal of patience. You'd better have them both."

"How much do you know about what happened between us five years ago, Julie?" Brandon asked.

"I know what Raven told me."

"One day you ought to ask me how I felt and why I left."

"And would you tell me?"

"Yes," he returned without hesitation. "I would."

"I'm sorry!" Raven came dashing down the stairs in a filmy flutter of white. "I hate to be late." Her hair settled in silky confusion over the shoulders of the thin voile dress as she stopped at the foot of the stairs. "I couldn't seem to find my shoes."

There was a becoming blush of color on her cheeks, and her eyes were bright and full of laughter. It passed through Brand's mind quickly, and then was discarded, that she looked a little too bright, a little too vibrant.

"Beautiful as ever." He handed her the flowers. "I've never minded waiting for you."

"Ah, the golden Irish tongue," she murmured as she buried her face in the violets. "I've missed it." Raven held the flowers up to her nose while her eyes laughed at him over them. "And I believe I'll let you spoil me tonight, Brandon. I'm in a mood to be pampered."

He took her free hand in his. "Where do you want to go?"

"Anywhere. Everywhere." She tossed her head. "But dinner first. I'm starving."

"All right, I'll buy you a cheeseburger."

"Some things do stay the same," she commented before she turned to Julie. "You have fun, and don't worry about me." She paused a moment, then smiled and kissed her cheek. "I promise I won't lose my key. And say hello to…" She hesitated as she walked toward the door with Brandon. "Who is it tonight?"

"Lorenzo," Julie answered, watching them. "The shoe baron."

"Oh, yes." Raven laughed as they walked into the cool, early spring air. "Amazing." She tucked her arm through Brandon's. "Julie's always having some millionaire fall in love with her. It's a gift."

"Shoe baron?" Brand questioned as he opened the car door for Raven.

"*Mmm*. Italian. He wears beautiful designer suits and looks as though he should be stamped on the head of a coin."

Brand slid in beside her and in an old reflex gesture brushed the hair that lay on her shoulder behind her back. "Serious?"

Raven tried not to be moved by the touch of his fingers. "No more serious than the oil tycoon or the perfume magnate." The leathery smell of the upholstery reminded her abruptly of Karter's office. Quickly she pushed away the sensation. "What are you going to feed me, Brandon?" she asked brightly—too brightly. "I warn you, I'm starving."

He circled her throat with his hand so that she had no choice but to meet his eyes directly. "Are you going to tell me what's wrong?"

He'd always seen too much too quickly, she thought. It was one of the qualities that had made him an exceptional songwriter.

Raven placed her hand on top of his. "No questions, Brandon, not now."

She felt his hesitation. Then he turned his hand over and gripped hers. Slowly, overriding her initial resistance, he brought her palm to his lips. "Not now," he agreed, watching her eyes. "I can still move you," he murmured and smiled as though the knowledge pleased him. "I can feel it."

Raven felt the tremors racing up her arms. "Yes." She drew her hand from his but kept her eyes steady. "You can still move me. But things aren't the same anymore."

He grinned, a quick flash of white teeth, then started the engine. "No, things aren't the same anymore."

As he pulled away, she had the uncomfortable impression that they had said the same words but meant two different things.

Dinner was quiet and intimate and perfect. They ate in a tiny old inn they had once discovered by chance. Here, Brand knew, there would be no interruptions for autographs, no greetings and drinks from old acquaintances. Here there would be just the two of them, a man and a woman amidst candlelight, wine, fine food, and an intimate atmosphere.

As the evening wore on, Raven's smile became more spontaneous, less desperate, and the unhappiness he had seen deep in her eyes before now faded. Though he noticed the transition, Brand made no comment.

"I feel like I haven't eaten in a week," Raven managed between bites of the tender roast beef that was the house speciality.

"Want some of mine?" Brand offered his plate.

Raven scooped up a bit of baked potato; her eyes seemed to laugh at him. "We'll have them wrap it up so I can take it home. I want to leave room for dessert. Did you see that pastry tray?"

"I suppose I could roll you to Cornwall," Brand considered, adding some burgundy to his glass.

Raven laughed, a throaty sound that appealed and aroused. "I'll be a bag of bones by the time we go to Cornwall," she claimed. "You know what those whirlwind tours can do." She shook her head as he offered her more wine.

"One-night stands from San Francisco to New York." Brand lifted his glass as Raven gave him a quizzing look. "I spoke to Henderson." He twirled a strand of her hair around his finger so absently, Raven was certain he was unaware of the gesture. She made no complaint. "If it's agreeable with you, I'll meet you in New York at the end of the tour. We'll fly to England from there."

"All right." She took a deep breath, having finally reached her fill of the roast beef. "You'd better set it up with Julie. I haven't any memory for dates and times. Are you staying in the States until then?"

"I'm doing a couple of weeks in Vegas." He brushed his fingers across her cheek, and when she would have resisted, he laid his hand companionably over hers. "I haven't played there in quite a while. I don't suppose it's changed."

She laughed and shook her head. "No. I played there, oh, about six months ago, I guess. Julie won a bundle at the baccarat table. I was a victim of the slots."

"I read the reviews. Were you as sensational as they said?" He smiled at her while one finger played with the thin gold bracelet at her wrist.

"Oh, I was much more sensational than they said," she assured him.

"I'd like to have seen you." His finger drifted lazily to her pulse. He felt it jump at his touch. "It's been much too long since I've heard you sing."

"You heard me just the other day in the studio," she pointed out. She took her hand from his to reach for her wine. He easily took her other one. "Brandon," she began, half-amused.

"I've heard you over the radio as well," he continued, "but it's not the same as watching you come alive at a concert. Or," he smiled as his voice took on that soft, intimate note she remembered, "listening to you when you sing just for me."

His tone was as smooth as the burgundy she drank. Knowing how easily he could cloud her brain, she vowed to keep their conversation light. "Do you know what I want right now?" She lowered her own voice as she leaned toward him, but he recognized the laughter in her eyes.

"Dessert," he answered.

"You know me so well, Brandon." She smiled.

She wanted to go dancing. By mutual consent, when they left the restaurant they avoided the popular, trendy spots in town and found a crowded, smoky hole-in-the-wall club with a good band, much like the dozens they had both played in at the beginnings of their respective careers. They thought they wouldn't be recognized there. For almost twenty minutes they were right.

"Excuse me, aren't you Brand Carstairs?" The toothy young blond stared up at Brand in admiration. Then she glanced at Raven. "And Raven Williams."

"Bob Muldroon," Brand returned in a passable Texas drawl. "And my wife Sheila. Say howdy, Sheila," he instructed as he held her close and swayed on the postage-sized dance floor.

"Howdy," Raven said obligingly.

"Oh, Mr. Carstairs." She giggled and thrust out a cocktail napkin and a pencil. "Please, I'm Debbie. Could you write, 'To my good friend Debbie'?"

"Sure." Brand gave her one of his charming smiles and told Raven to turn around. He scrawled quickly, using her back for support.

"And you, too, Raven," Debbie asked when he'd finished. "On the other side."

It was typical of her fans to treat her informally. They thought of her as Raven. Her spontaneous warmth made it difficult for anyone to approach her with the awe normally reserved for superstars. Raven wrote on her side of the napkin when Brand offered his back. When she had finished, she noted that Debbie's eyes were wide and fixed on Brand. The pulse in her throat was jumping like a jackhammer. Raven knew what fantasies were dancing in the girl's mind.

"Here you are, Debbie." She touched her hand to bring the girl back to reality.

"Oh." Debbie took the napkin, looked at it blankly a moment, then smiled up at Brand. "Thanks." She looked at Raven, then ran a hand through her hair as if she had just realized what she had done. "Thanks a lot."

"You're welcome." Brand smiled but began to edge Raven toward the door.

It was too much to expect that the incident had gone unnoticed or that no one else would recognize them. For the next fifteen minutes they were wedged between the crowd and the door, signing autographs and dealing with a barrage of questions. Brand made certain they weren't separated from each other as he slowly maneuvered a path through the crowd.

They were jostled and shoved a bit but he judged the crowd to be fairly civilized. It was still early by L.A. standards, and there hadn't been too much drinking yet. Still he wanted her out. This type of situation was notoriously explosive; the mood could change abruptly. One overenthusiastic fan and it could all be different. And ugly. Raven signed and signed some more while an occasional hand reached out to touch her hair. Brand felt a small wave of relief as he finally drew her out into the fresh air. Only a few followed them out of the club, and they were able to make their way to Brand's car with just a smattering of extra autographs.

"Damn it. I'm sorry." He leaned across her to lock her door. "I should have known better than to have taken you there."

Raven took a long breath, combing her hair back from her face with her fingers as she turned to him. "Don't be silly; I wanted to go. Besides, the people were nice."

"They aren't always," he muttered as the car merged with Los Angeles traffic.

"No." She leaned back, letting her body relax. "But I've been pretty lucky. Things have only gotten out of hand once or twice. It's the hype, I suppose, and it's to be expected that fans sometimes forget we're flesh and blood."

"So they try to take little chunks of us home with them."

"That," Raven said dryly, "can be a problem. I remember seeing a film clip of a concert you gave, oh, seven or eight years ago." She leaned her elbow on the back of the seat now and cupped her cheek in her palm. "A London concert where the fans broke through the security. They seemed to swallow you whole. It must have been dreadful."

"They loved me enough to give me a couple of broken ribs."

"Oh, Brandon." She sat up straight now, shocked. "That's terrible. I never knew that."

He smiled and moved his shoulders. "We played it down. It did rather spoil my taste for live concerts for a while. I got over it." He turned, heading toward the hills. "Security's tighter these days."

"I don't know if I'd be able to face an audience after something like that."

"Where else would you get the adrenaline?" he countered. "We need it, don't we? That instant gratification of applause." He laughed and pulled her over beside him. "Why else do we do it, Raven? Why else are there countless others out there scrambling to make it? Why did you start up the road, Raven?"

"To escape," she answered before she had time to think. She sighed and relaxed against his shoulder when he didn't demand an explanation. "Music was always something I could hold on to. It was constant, dependable. I needed something that was wholly mine." She turned her head a bit to study his profile. "Why did you?"

"For most of the same reasons, I suppose. I had something to say, and I wanted people to remember I said it."

She laughed. "And you were so radical at the start of your career. Such pounding, demanding songs. You were music's bad boy for some time."

"I've mellowed," he told her.

"'Fire Hot' didn't sound mellow to me," she commented. "Wasn't that the lead cut on your last album?"

He grinned, glancing down at her briefly. "I have to keep my hand in."

"It was number one on the charts for ten consecutive weeks," she pointed out. "That isn't bad for mellow."

"That's right," he agreed as if he'd just remembered. "It knocked off a little number of yours, didn't it? It was kind of a sweet little arrangement, as I recall. Maybe a bit heavy on the strings, but…"

She gave him an enthusiastic punch on the arm.

"Raven," Brand complained mildly. "You shouldn't distract me when I'm driving."

"That sweet little arrangement went platinum."

"I said it was sweet," he reminded her. "And the lyrics weren't bad. A bit sentimental, maybe, but…"

"I like sentimental lyrics," she told him, giving him another jab on the arm. "Not every song has to be a blistering social commentary."

"Of course not," he agreed reasonably. "There's always room for cute little ditties."

"Cute little ditties," Raven repeated, hardly aware that they had fallen back into one of their oldest habits by debating each other's work. "Just because I don't go in for showboating or lyrical trickery," she began. But when he swung off to the side of the road, she narrowed her eyes at him. "What are you doing?"

"Pulling over before you punch me again." He grinned and flicked a finger down her nose. "Showboating?"

"Showboating," she repeated. "What else do you call that guitar and piano duel at the end of 'Fire Hot'?"

"A classy way to fade out a song," he returned, and though she agreed with him, Raven made a sound of derision.

"I don't need the gadgetry. My songs are…"

"Overly sentimental."

She lifted a haughty brow. "If you feel my music is overly sentimental and cute, how do you imagine we'll work together?"

"Perfectly," he told her. "We'll balance each other, Raven, just as we always did."

"We're going to have terrible fights," she predicted.

"Yes, I imagine we will."

"And," she added, failing to suppress a smile, "you won't always win."

"Good. Then the fights won't be boring." He pulled her to him, and when she resisted, he cradled her head on his shoulder again. "Look," he ordered, pointing out the window, "why is it cities always look better at night from above?"

Raven looked down on the glittering Los Angeles skyline. "I suppose it's the mystique. It makes you wonder what's going on and you can't see how fast it's moving. Up here it's quiet." She felt his lips brush her temple. "Brandon." She drew away, but he stopped her.

"Don't pull away from me, Raven." It was a low, murmured request that shot heat up her spine. "Don't pull away from me."

His head lowered slowly, and his lips nibbled at hers, hardly touching, but the hand at the back of her neck was firm. He kept her facing him while he changed the angle of the kiss. His lips were persuasive, seductive. He kissed the soft, dewy skin of her cheeks, the fragile, closed eyelids, the scented hair at her temple. She could feel herself floating toward him as she always had, losing herself to him.

Her lips parted so that when his returned, he found them inviting him to explore. The kiss deepened, but slowly, as if he savored the taste of her on his tongue. Her hand slid up his chest until she held him and their bodies touched. He murmured something, then pressed his mouth against the curve of her neck. Her scent rose and enveloped him.

She moaned when he took her breast, a sound of both hunger and protest. His mouth came back to hers, plundering now as he responded to the need he felt flowing from her. She was unresisting, as open and warm as a shaft of sunlight. Her body was yearning toward him, melting irresistibly. She thought his hand burned through the thin fabric of her dress and set fire to her naked skin. It had been so long, she thought dizzily, so long since she had felt anything this intensely, needed anything this desperately. Her whole being tuned itself to him.

"Raven." His mouth was against her ear, her throat, the hollow of her cheek. "Oh, God, I want you." The kiss was urgent now, his hands no longer gentle. "So long," he said, echoing her earlier thought. "It's been so long. Come back with me. Let me take you back with me to the hotel. Stay with me tonight."

Passion flooded her senses. His tongue trailed over her warmed skin until he came again to her mouth. Then he took possession. The heat was building, strangling the breath in her throat, suffocating her. There was a fierce tug of war between fear and desire. She began to struggle.

"No." She took deep gulps of air. "Don't."

Brand took her by the shoulders and with one quick jerk had her face turned back up to his. "Why?" he demanded roughly. "You want me, I can feel it."

"No." She shook her head, and her hands trembled as

she pushed at his chest. "I don't. I can't." Raven tried
to deepen her breathing to steady it. "You're hurting
me, Brandon. Please let me go."

Slowly he relaxed his fingers, then released her. "The
same old story," he murmured. Turning away from her,
he carefully drew out a cigarette and lit it. "You still
give until I'm halfway mad, then pull away from me."
He took a long, deep drag. "I should have been better
prepared for it."

"You're not fair. I didn't start this; I never wanted…"

"You wanted," he tossed back furiously. "Damn it,
Raven, you wanted. I've had enough women to know
when I'm holding one who wants me."

She stiffened against the ache that was speeding
through her. "You're better off with one of your many
women, Brandon. I told you I wouldn't fall at your feet
this time, and I meant it. If we can have a professional
relationship, fine." She swallowed and straightened the
hair his fingers had so recently caressed. "If you can't
work with things on that level, then you'd best find another partner."

"I have the one I want." He tossed his cigarette
through the open window. "We'll play it your way for
a while, Raven. We're both professionals, and we both
know what this musical's going to do for our careers."
He started the engine. "I'll take you home."

Chapter 5

Raven hated to be late for a party, but there was no help for it. Her schedule was drum tight. If it hadn't been important that she be there, to rub elbows with Lauren Chase and a few other principals from the cast and crew of *Fantasy,* she'd have bowed out. There were only two days left before the start of her tour.

The truth was, Raven had forgotten about the party. Rehearsals had run over, then she had found herself driving into Beverly Hills to window shop. She hadn't wanted to buy anything but had simply wanted to do something mindless. For weeks there had been nothing but demand after demand, and she could look forward only to more of the same in the weeks to come. She would steal a few hours. She didn't want to think about her mother and the clean white sanitarium or song lists and cues or her confusion over Brand as she browsed through the treasures at Neiman-Marcus and Gucci. She looked at everything and bought nothing.

Arriving home, she was met by a huge handwritten note from Julie tacked on her bedroom door.

Party at Steve Jarett's. I know—you forgot. IMPORTANT! Get your glad rags together, babe, and go. Out with Lorenzo for dinner, we'll see you there. J.

Raven swore briefly, rebelled, then capitulated before she stalked to the closet to choose an outfit. An hour later she was cruising fast through the Hollywood Hills. It was important that she be there.

Steve Jarett was directing *Fantasy*. He was, at the moment, the silver screen's boy wonder, having just directed three major successes in a row. Raven wanted *Fantasy* to be his fourth as much as he did.

The party would be crowded, she mused, and looked wistfully at the open, star-studded sky. And noisy. Abruptly she laughed at herself. Since when did a noisy, crowded party become a trial by fire? There had been a time when she had enjoyed them. And there was no denying that the people who haunted these parties were fascinating and full of incredible stories. Raven could still be intrigued. It was just that… She sighed, allowing herself to admit the real reason she had dragged her feet. Brandon would be there. He was bound to be.

Would he bring a date? she wondered. Why wouldn't he? She answered herself shortly, downshifting as she took a curve. Unless he decided to wait and take his pick from the women there. Raven sighed again, seeing the blaze of lights that told her she was approaching Jarett's house. It was ridiculous to allow herself to get tied up in knots over something that had ended years before.

Her headlights caught the dull gleam of sturdy iron gates, and she slowed. The guard took her name, checked his list, then admitted her. She could hear the music before she was halfway up the curving, palm-lined drive.

There was a white-jacketed teenager waiting to hand her out of the Lamborghini. He was probably a struggling actor or an aspiring screenwriter or cinematographer, Raven thought as she smiled at him.

"Hi, I'm late. Do you think I can slip in without anybody noticing?"

"I don't think so, Ms. Williams, not looking like that."

Raven lifted her brows, surprised that he had recognized her so quickly in the dim light. But even if he had missed the face and hair, she realized, he would never have mistaken the voice.

"That's a compliment, isn't it?" she asked.

"Yes, ma'am," he said so warmly that she laughed.

"Well, I'm going to do my best, anyway. I don't like entrances unless they're on stage." She studied the sprawling, white brick mansion. "There must be a side door."

"Around to the left." He pointed. "There's a set of glass doors that lead into the library. Go through there and turn left. You should be able to slip in without being noticed."

"Thanks." She went to take a bill out of her purse, discovered she had left it in the car and leaned in the window to retrieve it. After a moment's search, she found a twenty and handed it to him.

"Thank *you!* Raven," he enthused as she turned away. Then he called to her, "Ms. Williams?" Raven turned back with a half smile. "Would you sign it for me?"

She tossed back her hair. "The bill?"

"Yeah."

She laughed and shook her head. "A fat lot of good it would do you then. Here." She dug into her bag again and came up with a slip of paper. One side was scrawled on, a list of groceries Julie had given her a few weeks before, but the other side was blank. "What's your name?" she demanded.

"Sam, Sam Rheinhart."

"Here, Sam Rheinhart," she said. Dashing off a quick line on the paper, she gave him the autograph. He stared after her, the twenty in one hand and the grocery list in the other, as she rushed off.

Raven found the glass doors without trouble. Though they were closed, the sounds of the party came clearly through. There were groups of people out back listening to a very loud rock band and drifting around by the pool. She stayed in the shadows. She wore an ankle-length skirt and a dolman-sleeve pullover in a dark plum color with silver metallic threads running through which captured the moonlight. Entering through the library, she gave herself a moment to adjust to the darkness before groping her way to the door.

There was no one in the hall immediately outside. Pleased with herself, Raven stepped out and gravitated slowly toward the focus of noise.

"Why, Raven!" It was Carly Devers, a tiny blond fluff of an actress with a little-girl voice and a rapier sharp talent. Though they generally moved in different circles, Raven liked her. "I didn't know you were here."

"Hi, Carly." They exchanged obligatory brushes of the cheek. "Congratulations are in order, aren't they? I heard you were being signed as second lead in *Fantasy.*"

"It's still in the working stage, but it looks like it. It's a gem of a part, and of course, working with Steve is *the* thing to do these days." As she spoke, she gave Raven a piercing look with her baby blue eyes. "You look fabulous," she said. Raven knew she meant it. "And of course, congratulations are in order for you as well, aren't they?"

"Yes, I'm excited about doing the score."

Carly tilted her head, and a smile spread over her face. "I was thinking more about Brand Carstairs than the score, darling." Raven's smile faded instantly. "Oops." Carly's smile only widened. "Still tender." There was no malice in her amusement. She linked her arm with Raven's. "I'd keep your little collaboration very tight this time around, Raven. I'm tempted to make a play for him myself, and I guarantee I'm not alone."

"What happened to Dirk Wagner?" Raven reminded herself to play it light as they drew closer to the laughter and murmurs of the party.

"Old news, darling, do try to keep up." Carly laughed, a tinkling bell of a sound that Raven could not help but respond to. "Still, I don't make it a habit to tread on someone else's territory."

"No signs posted, Carly," Raven said carelessly.

"Hmm." Carly tossed back a lock of silver-blond hair. A waiter passed by with a tray of glasses, and she neatly plucked off two. "I've heard he's a marvelous lover," she commented, her eyes bright and direct on Raven's.

Raven returned the look equably and accepted the offered champagne. "Have you? But then, I imagine that's old news, too."

"Touché," Carly murmured into her glass.

"Is Brandon here?" she asked, trying to prove to herself and her companion that the conversation meant nothing.

"Here and there," Carly said ambiguously. "I haven't decided whether he's been trying to avoid the flocks of females that crawl around him or if he's seeking them out. He doesn't give away much, does he?"

Raven uttered a noncommittal sound and shrugged. It was time, she decided, to change the subject. "Have you seen Steve? I suppose I should fight my way through and say hello."

It was a typical enough party, Raven decided. Clothes ranged from Rive Gauche to Salvation Army. There was a steady drum beat from the band by the pool underlying the talk and laughter. The doors to the terrace were open wide, letting out the clouds of smoke and allowing the warm night air to circulate freely. The expansive lawns were ablaze with colored lights. Raven was more interested in the people but gave the room itself a quick survey.

It was decorated stunningly in white—walls, furniture, rugs—with a few vivid green accents slashed here and there. Raven decided it was gorgeous and that she couldn't have lived in it in a million years. She'd never be able to put her feet up on the elegant, free-form glass coffee table. She went back to the people.

Her eyes sought out Julie with her handsome Italian millionaire. She spotted Wayne with one of his bone-thin models hanging on his arm. Raven decided that the rumors that he would design the costumes for *Fantasy* must be true. There were others Raven recognized: producers, two major stars whom she had watched countless times in darkened theaters, a choreographer she knew only by face and reputation, a screenwriter she had met before socially and several others whom she knew casually or not at all. She and Carly were both drawn into the vortex of the party.

There were dozens of greetings to exchange, along with hand-kissing and cheek-brushing, before Raven could begin to inch her way back toward the edges. She was always more comfortable with one or two people at a time than with a crowd, unless she was onstage. At a touch on her arm, she turned and found herself facing her host.

"Well, hello." Raven smiled, appreciating the chance for a tête-à-tête.

"Hi. I was afraid you weren't going to make it."

Raven realized she shouldn't have been surprised that he had noticed her absence in the crowds of people.

Steve Jarett noticed everything. He was a small, slight man with a pale, intense face and dark beard who looked ten years younger than his thirty-seven years. He was considered a perfectionist, often a pain when shooting, but the maker of beautiful films. He had a reputation for patience—enough to cause him to shoot a scene over and over and over again until he got precisely what he wanted. Five years before, he had stunned the industry with a low-budget sleeper that had become the unchallenged hit of the year. His first film had received an Oscar and had opened all the doors that had previously been firmly shut in his face. Steve Jarett held the keys now and knew exactly which ones to use.

He held both of her hands and studied her face. It was he who had insisted on Brand Carstairs as the writer of the original score for *Fantasy* and he who had approved the choice of Raven Williams as collaborator. *Fantasy* was his first musical, and he wasn't going to make any mistakes.

"Lauren's here," he said at length. "Have you met her?"

"No, I'd like to."

"I'd like you to get a real feel for her. I've copies of all of her films and records. You might study them before you begin work on the score."

Raven's brow rose. "I don't think I've missed any of her movies, but I'll watch them again. She is the core of the story."

He beamed suddenly, unexpectedly. "Exactly. And you know Jack Ladd."

"Yes, we've worked together before. You couldn't have picked a better Joe."

"I'm making him work off ten pounds," Jarett said, plucking a canape from a tray. "He has some very unflattering things to say about me at the moment."

"But he's taking off the ten pounds," Raven observed.

Jarett grinned. "Ounce by ounce. We go to the same gym. I keep reminding him Joe's a struggling writer, not a fulfilled hedonist."

Raven gave a low, gurgling laugh and popped a bite of cheese into her mouth. "Overweight or not, you're assembling a remarkable team. I don't know how you managed to wrangle Larry Keaston into choreographing. He's been retired for five years."

"Bribes and perseverance," Jarett said easily, glancing over to where the trim, white-haired former dancer lounged in a pearl-colored armchair. "I'm talking him into doing a cameo." He grinned at Raven again. "He's pretending dignified reluctance, but he's dying to get in front of the cameras again."

"If you can even get him to do a time step on film, you'll have the biggest coup of the decade," Raven observed and shook her head. And he'd do it, she thought. He has the touch.

"He's a big fan of yours," Jarett remarked and watched Raven's eyes widen.

"Of mine? You're joking."

"I am not." He gave Raven a curious look. "He wants to meet you."

Raven stared at Jarett, then again at Larry Keaston. Such things never ceased to amaze her. How many times, as a child, had she watched his movies on fuzzy black and white TV sets in cramped rooms while she had waited for her mother to come home? "You don't have to ask me twice," she told Jarett. She linked her arm in his.

Time passed quickly as Raven began enjoying herself. She talked at length with Larry Keaston and discovered her girlhood idol to be personable and witty. He spoke in a string of expletives delivered in his posh Boston accent. Though she spoke briefly with Jack Ladd, she had yet to meet Lauren Chase when she spotted Wayne drinking quietly in a corner.

"All alone?" she asked as she joined him.

"Observing the masses, my dear," he told her, sipping lightly from his whiskey and soda. "It's amazing how intelligent people will insist on clothing themselves in inappropriate costumes. Observe Lela Marring," he suggested, tilting his head toward a towering brunette in a narrow, pink minidress. "I have no idea why a woman would care to wear a place mat in public."

Raven suppressed a giggle. "She has very nice legs."

"Yes, all five feet of them." He swerved his line of vision. "Then, of course, there's Marshall Peters, who's trying to start a new trend. Chest hair and red satin."

Raven followed the direction of his gaze and this time did giggle. "Not everyone has your savoir-faire, Wayne."

"Of course not," he agreed readily and took out one of his imported cigarettes. "But surely, taste."

"I like the way you've dressed your latest protégée,"

Raven commented, nodding toward the thin model speaking to a current hot property in the television series game. The model was draped in cobwebby black and gold filigree lace. "I swear, Wayne, she can't be more than eighteen. What do you find to talk about?"

He gave Raven one of his long, sarcastic looks. "Are you being droll, darling?"

She laughed in spite of herself. "Not intentionally."

He gave her a pat on the cheek and lifted his glass again. "I notice Julie has her latest conquest with her, a Latin type with cheekbones."

"Shoes," Raven said vaguely, letting her eyes drift around the room. They rested in disbelief on a girl dressed in skin-tight leather pants and a spangled sweatshirt who wore heart-shaped glasses over heavily kohl-darkened eyes. Knowing Wayne would be horrified, she started to call his attention to her when she spotted Brand across the room.

His eyes were already on hers. Raven realized with a jolt that he had been watching her for some time. It had been at just such a party that they had first met, with noise and laughter and music all around them. Their eyes had found each other's then also.

It had been Raven's first Hollywood party, and she had been unashamedly overwhelmed. There had been people there whom she had known only as voices over the radio or faces on the screen. She had come alone then, too, but in that case it had been a mistake. She hadn't yet learned how to dodge and twist.

She remembered she had been cornered by an actor, though oddly she couldn't recall his name or his face.

She hadn't had the experience to deal with him and was slowly being backed against the wall when her eyes had met Brand's. Raven remembered how he had been watching her then, too, rather lazily, a half smile on his mouth. He must have seen the desperation in her eyes, because his smile had widened before he had started to weave his way through the crowd toward her. With perfect aplomb, Brand had slid between Raven and the actor, then had draped his arm over her shoulders.

"Miss me?" he had asked, and he had kissed her lightly before she could respond. "There're some people outside who want to meet you." He had shot the actor an apologetic glance. "Excuse us."

Before another word could be exchanged, he had propelled Raven through the groups of people and out to a terrace. She could still remember the scent of orange blossoms that had drifted from an orchard nearby and the silver sprinkle of moonlight on the flagstone.

Of course Raven had recognized him and had been flustered. She had managed to regain her poise by the time they were alone in the shadows on the terrace. She had brushed a hand through her hair and smiled at him. "Thanks."

"You're welcome." It had been the first time he had studied her in his direct, quiet fashion. She could still remember the sensation of gentle intrusion. "You're not quite what I expected."

"No?" Raven hadn't known exactly how to take that.

"No." He'd smiled at her. "Would you like to go get some coffee?"

"Yes." The agreement had sprung from her lips before she had given it a moment's thought.

"Good. Let's go." Brand had held out his hand. After a brief hesitation, Raven had put hers into it. It had been as simple as that.

"Raven...Raven."

She was tossed back into the present by the sound of Wayne's voice and his hand on her arm.

"Yes...what?" Blandly Raven looked up at him.

"Your thoughts are written all over your face," he murmured. "Not a wise move in a room full of curious people." Taking a fresh glass of champagne from a tray, he handed it to her. "Drink up."

She was grateful for something to do with her hands and took the glass. "I was just thinking," she said inadequately, then made a sound of frustration at Wayne's dry look. "So," she tried another tactic, "it seems we'll be working on the same project."

"Old home week?" he said with a crooked grin.

She shot him a direct look. "We're professionals," she stated, aware that they both knew whom she was speaking of.

"And friends?" he asked, touching a finger to her cheek.

Raven inclined her head. "We might be; I'm a friendly sort of person."

"Hmm." Wayne glanced over her shoulder and watched Brand approach. "At least he knows how to dress," he murmured, approving of Brand's casual but perfectly cut slate-colored slacks and jacket. "But are you sure Cornwall's necessary? Couldn't you try Sausalito?"

Raven laughed. "Is there anything you don't know?"

"I certainly hope not. Hello, Brand, nice to see you again."

Raven turned, smiling easily. The jolt of the memory had passed. "Hello, Brandon."

"Raven." His eyes stayed on her face. "You haven't met Lauren Chase."

With an effort Raven shifted her eyes from his. "No." She smiled and looked at the woman at his side.

Lauren Chase was a slender wisp of a woman with a thick mane of dark, chestnut hair and sea-green eyes. There was something ethereal about her. Perhaps, Raven thought, it was that pale, almost translucent skin or the way she had of walking as though her feet barely touched the ground. She had a strong mouth that folded itself in at the corners and a long, slender neck that she adorned with gold chains. Raven knew she was well into her thirties and decided she looked it. This was a woman who needn't rely on dewy youth for her beauty.

She had been married twice. The first divorce had become an explosive affair that had received a great deal of ugly press. Her second marriage was now seven years old and had produced two children. Raven recalled there was little written about Lauren Chase's current personal life. Obviously, she had learned to guard her privacy.

"Brand tells me you're going to put the heart in the music." Lauren's voice was full and rich.

"That's quite a responsibility." Raven shot Brand a

glance. "Generally Brand considers my lyrics on the sentimental side; often I consider him a cynic."

"Good." Lauren smiled. "Then we should have a score with some meat in it. Steve's given me final word on my own numbers."

Raven lifted a brow. She wasn't altogether certain if this had been a warning or a passing remark. "Then I suppose we should keep you up to date on our progress," she said agreeably.

"By mail and phone," Lauren said, slanting a glance at Brand, "since you're traipsing off halfway around the world to write."

"Artistic temperament," Brand said easily.

"No question, he has it," Raven assured her.

"You should know, I suppose." Lauren lifted a shoulder. Abruptly she fixed Raven with a sharp, straight look. "I want a lot out of this score. This is the one I've been waiting for." It was both a challenge and a demand.

Raven met the look with a slow nod. Lauren Chase was, she decided, the perfect Tessa. "You'll get it."

Lauren touched her upper lip with the tip of her tongue and smiled again. "Yes, I do believe I will at that. Well," she said, turning to Wayne and linking her arm through his, "why don't you get me a drink and tell me about the fabulous costumes you're going to design for me?"

Raven watched them move away. "That," she murmured, toying with the stem of her glass, "is a woman who knows what she wants."

"And she wants an Oscar," Brand remarked. Raven's

eyes came back to his. "You'll remember she's been nominated three times and edged out three times. She's determined it isn't going to happen again." He smiled then, fingering the dangling amethyst Raven wore at her ear. "Wouldn't you like to bag one yourself?"

"That's funny, I'd forgotten we could." She let the thought play in her mind. "It sounds good, but we'd better get the thing written before we dream up an acceptance speech."

"How're rehearsals going?"

"Good. Very good." She sipped absently at her champagne. "The band's tight. You leave for Vegas soon, don't you?"

"Yes. Did you come alone?"

She glanced back at him, confused for a moment. "Here? Why, yes. I was late because I'd forgotten about it altogether, but Julie left me a note. Did she introduce you to Lorenzo?"

"No, we haven't crossed paths tonight." As she had begun to search the crowd for Julie, Brand took her chin to bring her eyes back to his. "Will you let me take you home?"

Her expression shifted from startled to wary. "I have my car, Brandon."

"That isn't an answer."

Raven felt herself being drawn in and struggled. "It wouldn't be a good idea."

"Wouldn't it?" She sensed the sarcasm before he smiled, bent down and kissed her. It was a light touch—a tease, a promise or a challenge? "You could be right." He touched her earring again and set it swinging. "I'll see you in a few weeks," he said with a friendly grin, then turned and merged back into the crowd.

Raven stared after him, hardly realizing she had touched her lips with her tongue to seek his taste.

Chapter 6

The theater was dark and quiet. The sound of Raven's footsteps echoed, amplified by the excellent acoustics. Very soon the quiet would be shattered by stagehands, grips, electricians, all the many backstage people who would put together the essential and hardly noticed details of the show. Voices would bounce, mingling with hammering and other sounds of wood and metal. The noise would have a hollow, empty tone, almost like her footsteps. But it was an important sound, an appealing sound, which Raven had always enjoyed.

But she enjoyed the quiet, too and often found herself roaming an empty theater long before she was needed for rehearsals, hours before the fans started to line up outside the main doors. The press would be there then, with their everlasting, eternal questions. And Raven wasn't feeling too chummy with the press at the moment. Already she'd seen a half dozen different stories about herself and Brandon—speculation about their pending collaboration on *Fantasy* and rehashes of their former relationship. Old pictures had been dredged up and reprinted. Old questions were being asked again. Each time it was like bumping the same bruise.

Twice a week she put through a call to the Fieldmore Clinic and held almost identical conversations with Karter. Twice a week he transferred her to her mother's room. Though she knew it was foolish, Raven began to believe all the promises again, all the tearful vows. She began to hope. Without the demands of the tour to keep her occupied and exhausted, she knew she would have been an emotional wreck. Not for the first time in her life, she blessed her luck and her voice.

Mounting the stage, Raven turned to face an imaginary audience. The rows of seats seemed to roll back like a sea. But she knew how to navigate it, had known from the first moment of her first concert. She was an innate performer, just as her voice was natural and untrained. The hesitation, the uncertainty she felt now, had to do with the woman, not the singer. The song had hovered in her mind, but she still paused and considered before bringing it into play. Memories, she felt, could be dangerous things. But she needed to prove something to herself, so she sang. Her voice lifted, drifting to the far corners of the theater; her only accompaniment was her imagination.

Through the clouds and the rain
You were there,
And the sun came through to find us.

Oversentimental? She hadn't thought so when the words had been written. Now Raven sang what she hadn't sung in years. Two minutes and forty-three seconds that bound her and Brand together. Whenever it had played on the radio, she had switched it off, and never, though the requests had been many, had she ever incorporated it in an album or in a concert. She sang it now as a kind of test, remembering the drifting, almost aching harmony of her own low tones combined with Brand's clean, cool voice. She needed to be able to face the memory of working with him if she was to face the reality of doing so. The tour had reached its halfway point. There were only two weeks remaining.

It didn't hurt the way she had been afraid it would; there was no sharp slap across the face. There was more of a warm ache, almost pleasant, somehow sexual. She remembered the last time she had been in Brand's arms in the quiet car in the hills above L.A.

"I've never heard you sing that."

Caught off-guard, Raven swung around to stage right, her hand flying in quick panic to her throat. "Oh, Marc!" On a laugh, she let out a long breath. "You scared the wits out of me. I didn't know anyone was here."

"I didn't want you to stop. I've only heard the cut you and Carstairs made of that." He came forward now out of the shadows, and she saw he had an acoustic guitar slung over his shoulder. It was typical; she rarely saw him without an instrument in his hands or close by. "I've always thought it was too bad you never used it

again; it's one of your best. But I guess you didn't want
to sing it with anyone else."

Raven looked at him with genuine surprise. Of
course, that had been the essential reason, but she
hadn't realized it herself until that moment. "No, I guess
I didn't." She smiled at him. "I guess I still don't. Did
you come here to practice?"

"I called your room. Julie said you'd probably be
here." He walked to her, and since there were no chairs,
he sat on the floor. Raven sat with him. She crossed
her legs in the dun-colored trousers and let her hair fall
over the soft shoulders of her topaz angora sweater.
She was relaxed with him, ready to talk or jam like
any musician.

Raven smiled at Marc as he went through a quick,
complicated lick. "I'm glad you came by. Sometimes I
have to get the feel of the theater before a performance.
They all begin to run together at this part of a tour."
Raven closed her eyes and tilted her head, shaking her
hair back. "Where are we, Kansas City? God, I hate the
thought of getting back on that airplane. Shuttle here,
shuttle there. It always hits me like this at the halfway
point. In a couple of days I'll have my second wind."

Marc let her ramble while he played quick, quiet runs
on the guitar. He watched her hands as they lay still
on her knees. They were very narrow, and although
they were tanned golden brown, they remained fragile. There was a light tracing of blue vein just under
the skin. The nails were not long but well-shaped and
painted in some clear, hardening polish with a blush of
pink. There were no rings. Because they were motion-

less, he knew she was relaxed. Whatever nerves he had sensed when he had first spoken to her were stilled now.

"It's been going well, I think," she continued. "The Glass House is a terrific warm-up act, and the band's tight, even though we lost Kelly. The new bass is good, don't you think?"

"Knows his stuff," Marc said briefly. Raven grinned and reached over to tug his beard.

"So do you," she said. "Let me try."

Agreeably Marc slipped the strap over his head, then handed Raven his guitar. She was a better-than-average player, although she took a great deal of ribbing from the musicians in her troupe whenever she attempted the guitar. Periodically she threatened them with a bogus plan to incorporate her semiskillful playing into the act.

Still she liked to make music with the six strings. It soothed her. There was something intimate about holding an instrument close, feeling its vibrations against your own body. After hitting the same wrong note twice, Raven sighed, then wrinkled her nose at Marc's grin.

"I'm out of practice," she claimed, handing him back his Gibson.

"Good excuse."

"It's probably out of tune."

He ran quickly up and down the scales. "Nope."

"You might be kind and lie." She changed position, putting her feet flat on the floor and lacing her hands over her knees. "It's a good thing you're a musician. You'd have made a lousy politician."

"Too much traveling," he said as his fingers began to move again. He liked the sound of her laughter as it echoed around the empty theater.

"Oh, you're right! How can anyone remain sane going from city to city day after day? And music's such a stable business, too."

"Sturdy as a crap table."

"You've a gift for analogy," she told him, watching the skill of his fingers on the strings. "I love to watch you play," she continued. "It's so effortless. When Brandon was first teaching me, I..." but the words trailed off. Marc glanced up at her face, but his fingers never faltered. "I—it was difficult," she went on, wondering what had made her bring up the matter, "because he was left-handed, and naturally his guitar was, too. He bought me one of my own, but watching him, I had to learn backwards." She laughed, pleased with the memory. Absently she lifted a hand to toy with the thick, dangling staff of her earring. "Maybe that's why I play the way I do. I'm always having to twist it around in my head before it can get to my fingers."

She lapsed into silence while Marc continued to play. It was soothing and somehow intimate with the two of them alone in the huge, empty theater. But his music didn't sound lonely as it echoed. She began to sing with it quietly, as though they were at home, seated on a rug with the walls close and comforting around them.

It was true that the tour had tired her and that the

midway point had her feeling drained. But the interlude here was lifting her, though in a different way than
the audience would lift her that night. This wasn't the
quick, dizzying high that shot endurance back into her
for the time she was on stage and in the lights. This was
a steadying hand, like a good night's sleep or a home-
cooked meal. She smiled at Marc when the song was
over and said again, "I'm glad you came."

He looked at her, and for once his hands were silent on the strings. "How long have I been with you,
Raven?"

She thought back to when Marc had first become
a semiregular part of her troupe. "Four—four and a
half—years."

"Five this summer," he corrected. "It was in August,
and you were rehearsing for your second tour. You had
on baggy white pants and a T-shirt with a rainbow on
it. You were barefoot. You had a lost look in your eyes.
Carstairs had gone back to England about a month before."

Raven stared at him. She had never heard him make
such a long speech. "Isn't it strange that you would remember what I was wearing? It doesn't sound very
impressive."

"I remember because I fell in love with you on the
spot."

"Oh, Marc." She searched for something to say and
found nothing. Instead, she reached up and took his
hand. She knew he meant exactly what he said.

"Once or twice I've come close to asking you to live with me."

Raven let out a quick breath. "Why didn't you?"

"Because it would have hurt you to have said no and it would have hurt me to hear it." He laid the guitar across his lap and leaning over it, kissed her.

"I didn't know," she murmured, pressing both of his hands to her cheeks. "I should have. I'm sorry."

"You've never gotten him out of your head, Raven. It's damn frustrating competing with a memory." Marc squeezed her hands a moment, then released them. "It's also safe. I knew you'd never make a commitment to me, so I could avoid making one to you." He shrugged his well-muscled shoulders. "I think it always scared me that you were the kind of woman who would make a man give everything because you asked for nothing."

Her brows drew together. "Am I?"

"You need someone who can stand up to you. I'd never have been able to. I'd never have been able to say no or shout at you or make crazy love. Life's nothing without things like that, and we'd have ended up hurting each other."

She tilted her head and studied him. "Why are you telling me all this now?"

"Because I realized when I watched you singing that I'll always love you but I'll never have you. And if I did, I'd lose something very special." He reached across to touch her hair. "A fantasy that warms you on cold nights and makes you feel young again when you're old. Sometimes might-have-beens can be very precious."

Raven didn't know whether to smile or to cry. "I haven't hurt you?"

"No," he said so simply she knew he spoke the truth. "You've made me feel good. Have I made you uncomfortable?"

"No." She smiled at him. "You've made me feel good."

He grinned, then rose and held out a hand to her. "Let's go get some coffee."

Brand changed into jeans in his dressing room. It was after two in the morning, but he was wide-awake, still riding on energy left over from his last show. He'd go out, he decided, and put some of it to use at the blackjack table. He could grab Eddie or one of the other guys from the band and cruise the casinos.

There'd be women. Brand knew there'd be a throng of them waiting for him when he left the privacy of his dressing room. He could take his pick. But he didn't want a woman. He wanted a drink and some cards and some action; anything to use up the adrenaline speeding through his system.

He reached for his shirt, and the mirror reflected his naked torso. It was tight and lean, teetering on being thin, but there were surprising cords of muscles in the arms and shoulders. He'd had to use them often when he'd been a boy on the London streets. He always wondered if it had been the piano lessons his mother had insisted on that had saved him from being another victim of the streets. Music had opened up something for him. He hadn't been able to get enough, learn enough. It had been like food, and he had been starving.

At fifteen Brand had started his own band. He was tough and cocky and talked his way into cheap little dives. There had been women even then; not just girls, but women attracted by his youthful sexuality and arrogant confidence. But they'd only been part of the adventure. He had never given up, though the living had been lean in the beer-soaked taverns. He had pulled his way up and made a local reputation for himself; both his music and his personality were strong.

It had taken time. He had been twenty when he had cut his first record, and it had gone nowhere. Brand had recognized that its failure had been due to a combination of poor quality recording, mismanagement and his own see-if-I-care attitude. He had taken a few steps back, found a savvy manager, worked hard on arrangements and talked himself into another recording session.

Two years later he had bought his family a house in the London suburbs, pushed his younger brother into a university and set off on his first American tour.

Now, at thirty, there were times he felt he'd never been off the merry-go-round. Half his life had been given over to his career and its demands. He was tired of wandering. Brand wanted something to focus his life, something to center it. He knew he couldn't give up music, but it wasn't enough by itself anymore. His family wasn't enough, and neither was the money or the applause.

He knew what he wanted. He had known five years

before, but there were times he didn't feel as sure of himself as he had when he had been a fifteen-year-old punk talking his way past the back door of a third-rate nightclub. A capacity crowd had just paid thirty dollars a head to hear him, and he knew he could afford to take every cent he made on that two-week gig and throw it away on one roll of the dice. He had an urge to do it. He was restless, reckless, running on the same nerves he had felt the night he'd taken Raven home from their dinner date. He'd only seen her once after that—at Steve Jarett's house. Almost immediately afterward he had flown to Las Vegas to begin polishing his act.

It was catching up with him now—the tension, the anger, the needs. Not for the first time, Brand wondered whether his unreasonable need for her would end if he could have her once, just once. With quick, impatient movements, he thrust the tail of his shirt into the waist of his jeans. He knew better, but there were times he wished it could be. He left the dressing room looking for company.

For an hour Brand sat at the blackjack table. He lost a little, won a little, then lost it again. His mind wasn't on the cards. He had thought the noise, the bright lights, the rich smell of gambling was what he had wanted. There was a thin, intense woman beside him with a huge chunk of diamond on her finger and sapphires around her neck. She drank and lost at the same steady rhythm. Across the table was a young couple he pegged as honeymooners. The gold band on the girl's finger looked brilliantly new and untested. They were giddy with winning what Brand figured was about thirty dol-

lars. There was something touching in their pleasure
and in the soft, exchanged looks. All around them came
the endless chinkity-chink of the slots.

Brand found himself as restless as he had been an
hour before in his dressing room. A half-empty glass
of bourbon sat at his elbow, but he left it as he rose. He
didn't want the casino, and he felt an enormous surge
of envy for the man who had his woman and thirty dollars worth of chips.

When he entered his suite, it was dark and silent, a
sharp contrast to the world he had just left. Brand didn't
bother hitting the switches as he made his way into
the bedroom. Taking out a cigarette, he sat on the bed
before lighting it. The flame made a sharp hiss and a
brief flare. He sat with the silence, but the adrenaline
still pumped. Finally he switched on the small bedside
lamp and picked up the phone.

Raven was deep in sleep, but the ringing of the phone
shot panic through her before she was fully awake. Her
heart pounded in her throat before the mists could clear.
She'd grown up with calls coming in the middle of the
night. She forgot where she was and fumbled for the
phone with a sense of dread and anticipation.

"Yes...hello."

"Raven, I know I woke you. I'm sorry."

She tried to shake away the fog. "Brandon? Is something wrong? Are you all right?"

"Yes, I'm fine. Just unbelievably inconsiderate."

Relaxing, Raven sank back on the pillows and tried
to orient herself. "You're in Vegas, aren't you?" The dim
light told her it was nearing dawn. He was two hours

behind her. Or was it three? She couldn't for the life of her remember what time zone she was in.

"Yes, I'm in Vegas through next week."

"How's the show going?"

It was typical of her, he mused, not to demand to know why the hell he had called her in the middle of the night. She would simply accept that he needed to talk. He drew on the cigarette and wished he could touch her. "Better than my luck at the tables."

She laughed, comfortably sleepy. The connection was clean and sharp; he didn't sound hundreds of miles away. "Is it still blackjack?"

"I'm consistent," he murmured. "How's Kansas?"

"Where?" He laughed, pleasing her. "The audience was fantastic," she continued, letting her mind wander back to the show. "Has been straight along. That's the only thing that keeps you going on a tour like this. Will you be there in time for the show in New York? I'd love you to hear the warm-up act."

"I'll be there." He lay back on the bed as some of the superfluous energy started to drain. "Cornwall is sounding more and more appealing."

"You sound tired."

"I wasn't; I am now. Raven…"

She waited, but he didn't speak. "Yes?"

"I missed you. I needed to hear your voice. Tell me what you're looking at," he demanded, "what you see right now."

"It's dawn," she told him. "Or nearly. I can't see any buildings, just the sky. It's more mauve than gray and the light's very soft and thin." She smiled; it had been a long time since she had seen a day begin. "It's really lovely, Brandon. I'd forgotten."

"Will you be able to sleep again?" He had closed his eyes; the fatigue was taking over.

"Yes, but I'd rather go for a walk, though I don't think Julie would appreciate it if I asked her to come along."

Brand pried off his shoes, using the toe of one foot, then the other. "Go back to sleep, and we'll walk on the cliffs one morning in Cornwall. I shouldn't have woken you."

"No, I'm glad you did." She could hear the change; the voice that had been sharp and alert was now heavy. "Get some rest, Brandon. I'll look for you in New York."

"All right. Good night, Raven."

He was asleep almost before he hung up. Fifteen hundred miles away, Raven laid her cheek on the pillow and watched the morning come.

Chapter 7

Raven tried to be still while her hair was being twisted and knotted and groomed. Her dressing room was banked with flowers; they had been arriving steadily for more than two hours. And it was crowded with people. A tiny little man with sharp, black eyes touched up her blusher. Behind her, occasionally muttering in French, was the nimble-fingered woman who did her hair. Wayne was there, having business of his own here in New York. He'd told Raven that he'd come to see his designs in action and was even now in deep discussion with her dresser. Julie opened the door to another flower delivery.

"Have I packed everything? You know, I should have told Brandon to give me an extra day in town for shopping. There're probably a dozen things I need." Raven turned in her seat and heard the swift French oath as her partially knotted hair flew from the woman's fingers. "Sorry, Marie. Julie, did I pack a coat? I might need one." Slipping the card from the latest arrangement of flowers, she found it was from a successful television producer with whom she'd worked on her last TV special. "They're from Max.... There's a party tonight. Why don't you go?" She handed the card to Julie and allowed her lip liner to be straightened by the finicky makeup artist.

"Yes, you packed a coat, your suede, which you could need this early in the spring. And several sweaters," Julie said distractedly, checking her list. "And maybe I will."

"I can't believe this is it, the last show. It's been a good tour, hasn't it, Julie?" Raven turned her head and winced at the sharp tug on her hair.

"I can't remember you ever getting a better response or deserving one more...."

"And we're all glad it's over," Raven finished for her.

"I'm going to sleep for a week." Julie found space for the flowers, then continued to check off things in her notebook. "Not everyone has your constant flow of energy."

"I love playing New York," she said, tucking up her legs to the despair of her hairdresser.

"You must hold still!"

"Marie, if I hold still much longer, I'm going to explode." Raven smiled at the makeup artist as he fussed around her face. "You always know just what to do. It looks perfect; I feel beautiful."

Recognizing the signal, Julie began nudging people

from the room. Eventually they went, and soon only Julie and Wayne were left. The room quieted considerably; now the walls hummed gently with the vibrations of the warm-up act. Raven let out a deep sigh.

"I'll be so glad to have my face and body and hair back," she said and sprawled in the chair. "You should have seen what he made me put all over my face this morning."

"What was it?" Wayne asked absently as he smoothed the hem of one of her costumes.

"Green," she told him and shuddered.

He laughed and turned to Julie. "What are you going to do when this one takes off to the moors?"

"Cruise the Greek Islands and recuperate." She pushed absently at the small of her back. "I've already booked passage on the ninth. These tours are brutal."

"Listen to her." Raven sniffed and peered at herself critically in the glass. "She's the one who's held the whip and chair for four weeks. He certainly makes me look exotic, doesn't he?" She wrinkled her nose and spoiled the effect.

"Into costume," Julie commanded.

"See? Orders, orders." Obediently Raven rose.

"Here." Wayne lifted the red and silver dress from the hanger. "Since I nudged your dresser along, I'll be your minion."

"Oh, good, thanks." She stepped out of her robe and into the dress. "You know, Wayne," she continued as he zipped her up, "you were right about the black number. It gets a tremendous response. I never know if they're applauding me or the costume after that set."

"Have I ever let you down?" he demanded as he tucked a pleat.

"No." She turned her head to smile at him over her shoulder. "Never. Will you miss me?"

"Tragically." He kissed her ear.

There was a brief, brisk knock at the door. "Ten minutes, Ms. Williams."

She took a long breath. "Are you going to go out front?"

"I'll stay back with Julie." He glanced over at her, lifting a brow in question.

"Yes, thanks. Here, Raven, don't forget these wonderfully gaudy earrings." She watched Raven fasten one. "Really, Wayne, they're enough to make me shudder, but they're fabulous with that dress."

"Naturally."

She laughed, shaking her head. "The man's ego," she said to Raven, "never ceases to amaze me."

"As long as it doesn't outdistance the talent," he put in suavely.

"New York audiences are tough." Raven spoke quickly, her voice jumping suddenly with nerves and excitement. "They scare me to death."

"I thought you said you loved playing New York." Wayne took out a cigarette and offered one to Julie.

"I do, especially at the end of a tour. It keeps you sharp. They're really going to know if I'm not giving them everything. How do I look?"

"The dress is sensational," Wayne decided. "You'll do."

"Some help you are."

"Let's go," Julie urged. "You'll miss your cue."

"I never miss my cue." Raven fussed with the second earring, stalling. He'd said he'd be here, she told herself. *Why isn't he?* He could have gotten the time mixed up, or he could be caught in traffic. Or he could simply have forgotten that he'd promised to be here for the show.

The quick knock came again. "Five minutes, Ms. Williams."

"Raven." Julie's voice was a warning.

"Yes, yes, all right." She turned and gave them both a flippant smile. "Tell me I'm wonderful when it's over, even if I wasn't. I want to end the tour feeling marvelous."

Then she was dashing for the door and hurrying down the hall where the sounds of the warm-up band were no longer gentle; now they shook the walls.

"Ms. Williams, Ms. Williams! Raven!"

She turned, breaking the concentration she'd been building and looked at the harried stage manager. He thrust a white rose into her hand.

"Just came back for you."

Raven took the bud and lifted it, wanting to fill herself with the scent. She needed no note or message to tell her it was from Brand. For a moment she simply dreamed over it.

"Raven." The warm-up act had finished; the transition to her own band would take place on the darkened stage quickly. "You're going to miss your cue."

"No, I'm not." She gave the worried stage manager a kiss, forgetful of her carefully applied lipstick. Twirling the rose between her fingers, she took it with her. They were introducing her as she reached the wings.

Big build-up; don't let the audience cool down. They were already cheering for her. *Thirty seconds; take a breath.* Her band hit her introduction. Music crashed through the cheers. *One, two, three!*

She ran out, diving into a wave of applause.

The first set was hot and fast, staged to keep the audience up and wanting more. She seemed to be a ball of flame with hundreds of colored lights flashing around her. Raven knew how to play to them, play with them, and she pumped all her energy into a routine she had done virtually every night for four weeks. Enthusiasm and verve kept it fresh. It was hot under the lights, but she didn't notice. She was wrapping herself in the audience, in the music. The costume sizzled and sparked. Her voice smoked.

It was a demanding forty minutes, and when she rushed offstage during an instrumental break, she had less than three minutes in which to change costumes. Now she was in white, a brief, shimmering top covered with bugle beads matched with thin harem pants. The pace would slow a bit, giving the audience time to catch their breath. The balance was in ballads, the slow trembling ones she did best. The lighting was muted, soft and moody.

It was during a break between songs, when she traditionally talked to the audience, that someone in the audience spotted Brand in their midst. Soon more people knew, and while Raven went on unaware of the disturbance, the crowd soon became vocal. Shielding

her eyes, she could just make out the center of the com-
motion. Then she saw him. It seemed they wanted him
up on stage.

Raven was a good judge of moods and knew the
value of showmanship. If she didn't invite Brand on
stage, she'd lose the crowd. They had already taken the
choice out of her hands.

"Brandon." Raven spoke softly into the mike, but her
voice carried. Though she couldn't see his eyes with the
spotlight in her own, she knew he was looking at her.
"If you come up and sing," she told him, lightly, "we
might get you a refund on your ticket." She knew he'd
grin at that. There was an excited rush of applause and
cheers as he rose and came to the stage.

He was all in black: trim, well-cut slacks and a casual
polo sweater. The contrast was striking as he stood beside her. It might have been planned. Smiling at her, he
spoke softly, out of the range of the microphone. "I'm
sorry, Raven, I should have gone backstage. I wanted
to watch you from out front."

She tilted her head. It was, she discovered, more
wonderful to see him than she had imagined. "You're
the one being put to work. What would you like to do?"

Before he could answer, the demands sprang from
the crowd. Once the idea formed, it was shouted over
and over with growing enthusiasm. Raven's smile
faded. "Clouds and Rain."

Brand took her wrist and lifted the rose she held.
"You remember the words, don't you?"

It was a challenge. A stagehand rushed out with a
hand mike for Brand.

"My band doesn't know it," she began.

"I know it." Marc shifted his guitar and watched them. The crowd was still shouting when he gave the opening chords. "We'll follow you."

Brand kept his hand on Raven's wrist and lifted his own mike.

Raven knew how it needed to be sung: face to face, eye to eye. It was a caress of a song, meant for lovers. The audience was silent now. Their harmony was close, intricate. Raven had once thought it must be like making love. Their voices flowed into each other. And she forgot the audience, forgot the stage and for a moment forgot the five years.

There was more intimacy in singing with him than she had ever allowed in any other aspect of their relationship. Here she could not resist him. When he sang to her, it was as if he told her there wasn't anyone else, had never been anyone else. It was more moving than a kiss, more sexual than a touch.

When they finished, their voices hung a moment, locked together. Brand saw her lips tremble before he brought her close and took them.

They might have been on an island rather than on stage, spotlighted for thousands. She didn't hear the tumultuous applause, the cheers, the shouting of their names. Her arms went around him, one hand holding the mike, the other the rose. Cameras flashed like fireworks, but she was trapped in a velvet darkness. She lost all sense of time; her lips might have moved on his for hours or days or only seconds. But when he drew her away, she felt a keener sense of loss than any she had ever known before. Brand saw the confusion in her eyes, the dazed desire, and smiled.

"You're better than you ever were, Raven." He kissed her hand. "Too bad about those sentimental numbers you keep sticking into the act."

Her brows rose. "Try to boost your flagging career by letting you sing with me, and you insult me." Her balance was returning as they took a couple of elaborate bows, hands linked.

"Let's see if you can carry the rest on your own, love. I've warmed them back up for you." He kissed her again, but lightly now, on the cheek, before he waved to the audience and strolled offstage left.

Raven grinned at his back, then turned to her audience. "Too bad he never made it, isn't it?"

Raven should have been wrung dry after the two hours were over. But she wasn't. She'd given them three encores, and though they clamored for more, Brand caught her hand as she hesitated in the wings.

"They'll keep you out there all night, Raven." He could feel the speed of her pulse under his fingers. Because he knew how draining two hours onstage could be, he urged her back down the hall toward her dressing room.

There were crowds of people jammed in together in the hallway, congratulating her, touching her. Now and then a reporter managed to elbow through to shoot out a question. She answered, and Brandon tossed off remarks with quick charm while steering her determinedly toward her dressing room. Once inside, he locked the door.

"I think they liked me," she said gravely, then laughed and spun away from him. "I feel so good!" Her eyes lit on the bucket of ice that cradled a bottle. "Champagne?"

"I thought you'd need to console yourself after a flop like that." Brand moved over and drew out the bottle. "You'll have to open the door soon and see people. Do try to put on a cheerful front, love."

"I'll do my best." The cork popped, and the white froth fizzed a bit over the mouth of the bottle.

Brand poured two glasses to the rim and handed her one. "I meant it, Raven." He touched his glass to hers. "You were never better."

Raven smiled, bringing the glass to her lips. Again, he felt the painful thrust of desire. Carefully Brand took the glass from her, then set both it and his own down again. "There's something I didn't finish out there tonight."

She was unprepared. Even though he drew her close slowly and took his time bringing his mouth to hers, Raven wasn't ready. It was a long, deep, kiss that mingled with the champagne. His mouth was warm on hers, seeking. His hands ran over her hips, snugly encased in the thin black jumpsuit, but she could sense he was under very tight control.

His tongue made a thorough, lengthy journey through the moist recesses of her mouth, and she responded in kind. But he wanted her to do more than give; he wanted her to want more. And she did, feeling the pull of need, the flash of passion. She could feel the texture of his long, clever fingers through the sheer material of her costume, then flesh to flesh as he brought them up to caress the back of her neck.

Her head was swimming with a myriad of sensations: excitement and power still clinging from her performance; the heady, heavy scent of mixed flowers which crowded the air; the firm press of his body against her; and desire, more complex, more insistent than she had been prepared for.

"Brandon," she murmured against his lips. She wanted him, wanted him desperately, and was afraid.

Brand drew her away, then carefully studied her face. Her eyes were like thin glass over her emotions. "You're beautiful, Raven, one of the most beautiful women I know."

She was unsteady and tried to find her balance without clinging to him. She stepped back, resting her hand on the table that held their glasses. "One of the most?" she challenged, lifting her champagne.

"I know a lot of women." He grinned as he lifted his own glass. "Why don't you take that stuff off your face so I can see you?"

"Do you know how long I had to sit still while he troweled this stuff on?" Moving to the dressing table, she scooped up a generous glob of cold cream. Her blood was beginning to settle. "It's supposed to make me glamorous and alluring." She slathered it on.

"You make me nervous when you're glamorous, and you'd be alluring in a paper sack."

She lifted her eyes to his in the mirror. His expression was surprisingly serious. "I think that was a compliment." She smeared the white cream generously over her face and grinned. "Am I alluring now?"

Brand grinned back, then slowly let his eyes roam down her back to focus on her snugly clad bottom. "Raven, don't fish. The answer is obvious."

She began to tissue off the cream and with it the stage makeup. "Brandon. It was good to sing with you again." After removing the last of the cream from her face, Raven toyed with the stem of her champagne glass. "I always felt very special when I sang with you. I still do." He watched her chew for a moment on her bottom lip as if she was unsure about what she should say. "I imagine they'll play up that duet in the papers. They'll probably make something else out of it, especially—especially with the way we ended it."

"I like the way we ended it." Brand came over and laid his hands on her shoulders. "It should always be ended that way." He kissed the back of her neck while his eyes smiled into hers in the glass. "Are you worried about the press, Raven?"

"No, of course not. But, Brandon..."

"Do you know," he interrupted, brushing the hair away from her neck with the back of his hand, "no one else calls me that but my mother. Strange." He bent, nuzzling his lips into the sensitive curve of her neck. "You affect me in an entirely different way."

"Brandon..."

"When I was a boy," he continued, moving his lips up to her ear, "and she called me Brandon, I knew that was it. Whatever crime I'd committed had been found out. Justice was about to strike."

"I imagine you committed quite a few crimes." She forced herself to speak lightly. When she would have moved away, he turned her around to face him.

"Too many to count." He leaned to her, but instead of the kiss she expected and prepared for, he caught her bottom lip between his teeth. She clutched at his shirt as she struggled for breath and balance. Their eyes were open and on each other's, but his face dimmed, then faded, as passion clouded her vision.

Brand released her, then gave her a quick kiss on the nose. Raven ran a hand through her hair, trying to steady herself. He was tossing her back and forth too swiftly, too easily.

"Do you want to change before we let anyone in?" he asked. When she could focus again, Raven saw he was drinking champagne and watching her. There was an odd look on his face, as if, she thought, he were a boxer checking for weaknesses, looking for openings.

"I —yes." Raven brought herself back. "Yes, I think I would, but..." She glanced around the dressing room. "I don't know what I did with my clothes."

He laughed, and the look was gone from his face. Relieved, Raven laughed with him. They began to search through the flowers and sparkling costumes for her jeans and tennis shoes.

Chapter 8

It was late when they arrived at the airport. Raven was still riding on post-performance energy and chattered about everything that came into her head. She looked up at a half-moon as she and Brand transferred from limo to plane. The private jet wasn't what she had been expecting, and studying the comfortably lush interior of the main cabin helped to allay the fatigue of yet one more flight.

It was carpeted with a thick, pewter-colored shag and contained deep, leather chairs and a wide, plush sofa. There was a padded bar at one end and a doorway at the other which she discovered led into a tidy galley. "You didn't have this before," she commented as she poked her head into another room and found the bath, complete with tub.

"I bought it about three years ago." Brand sprawled

on the sofa and watched her as she explored. She looked different than she had a short time before. Her face was naked now, and he found he preferred it that way. Makeup seemed to needlessly gloss over her natural beauty. She wore faded jeans and sneakers, which she immediately pried off her feet. An oversize yellow sweater left her shapeless. It made him want to run his hands under it and find her. "Do you still hate to fly?"

Raven gave him a rueful grin. "Yes. You'd think after all this time I'd have gotten over it, but..." She continued to roam the cabin, not yet able to settle. If she had to, Raven felt she could give the entire performance again. She had enough energy.

"Strap in," Brand suggested, smiling at the quick, nervous gestures. "We'll get started, then you won't even know you're in the air."

"You don't know how many times I've heard that one." Still she did as he said and waited calmly enough while he told the pilot they were ready. In a few minutes they were airborne, and she was able to unstrap and roam again.

"I know the feeling," Brand commented, watching her. She turned in silent question. "It's as though you still have one last burst of energy to get rid of. It's the way I felt that night in Vegas when I called and woke you up."

She caught back her hair with both hands. "I feel I should jog for a few miles. It might settle me down."

"How about some coffee?"

"Yes." She wandered over to a porthole and pressed her nose against it. It was black as pitch outside the glass. "Yes, coffee would be nice, then you can tell me what marvelous ideas you have forming for the score. You've probably got dozens of them."

"A few." She heard the clatter of cups. "I imagine you've some of your own."

"A few," she said, and he chuckled. Turning away from the dark window, she saw him leaning against the opening between the galley and the main cabin. "How soon do you think we'll start to fight?"

"Soon enough. Let's wait at least until we're settled into the house. Is Julie going back to L.A., or have you tied up all your loose ends there?"

A shadow visited her face. Raven thought of the one brief visit she had paid to her mother since the start of the tour. They had had a day's layover in Chicago, and she had used the spare time to make the impossible flight to the coast and back. There had been the inevitable interview with Karter and a brief, emotional visit with her mother. Raven had been relieved to see that the cast had gone from her mother's skin and that there was more flesh to her face. There had been apologies and promises and tears, just as there always were, Raven thought wearily. And as she always did, she had begun to believe them again.

"I never seem to completely tie up the loose ends," she murmured.

"Will you tell me what's wrong?"

She shook her head. She couldn't bear to dwell on unhappiness now. "No, nothing, nothing really." The kettle sang out, and she smiled. "Your cue," she told him.

He studied her for a moment while the kettle spit

Nora Roberts

peevishly behind him. Then, turning, he went back into the galley to fix the coffee. "Black?" he asked, and she gave an absent assent.

Sitting on the sofa, Raven let her head fall back while the energy began to subside. It was almost as if she could feel it draining. Brand recognized the signs as soon as he came back into the room. He set down her mug of coffee, then sipped thoughtfully from his own as he watched her. Sensing him, Raven slowly opened her eyes. There was silence for a moment; her body and her mind were growing lethargic.

"What are you doing?" she murmured.

"Remembering."

Her lids shuttered down, concealing her eyes and their expression. "Don't."

He drank again, letting his eyes continue their slow, measured journey over her. "It's a bit much to ask me not to remember, Raven, isn't it?" It was a question that expected no answer, and she gave it none. But her lids fluttered up again.

He didn't have her full trust, nor did he believe he had ever had it. That was the root of their problems. He studied her while he stood and drank his coffee. There was high, natural color in her cheeks, and her eyes were dark and sleepy. She sat, as was her habit, with her legs crossed under her and her hands on her knees. In contrast to the relaxed position, her fingers moved restlessly.

"I still want you. You know that, don't you?"

Again Raven left his question unanswered, but he saw the pulse in her throat begin to thump. When she

spoke, her voice was calm. "We're going to work together, Brandon. It's best not to complicate things."

He laughed, not in mockery but in genuine amusement. She watched his eyes lose their brooding intensity and light. "By all means, let's keep things simple."
After draining his coffee, he walked over and sat beside
her. In a smooth, practiced move, he drew her against
his side. "Relax," he told her, annoyed when she resisted. "Give me some credit. I know how tired you
are. When are you going to trust me, Raven?"

She tilted her head until she could see him. Her look
was long and eloquent before she settled into the crook
of his shoulder and let out a long sigh. Like a child, she
fell asleep quickly, and like that of a child, the sleep was
deep. For a long moment he stayed as he was, Raven
curled against his side. Then he laid her down on the
sofa, watching as her hair drifted about her.

Rising, Brand switched off the lights. In the dark he
settled into one of the deep cabin chairs and lit a cigarette. Time passed as he sat gazing out at a sprinkle of
stars and listening to Raven's soft, steady breathing.
Unable to resist, he rose, and moving to her, lay down
beside her. She stirred when he brushed the hair from
her cheek, but only to snuggle closer to him. Over the
raw yearning came a curiously sweet satisfaction. He
wrapped his arm around her, felt her sigh, then slept.

It was Brand who awoke first. As was his habit, his
mind and body came together quickly. He lay still and
allowed his eyes to grow accustomed to the darkness.
Beside him, curled against his chest, Raven slept on.

He could make out the curve of her face, the pixie

sharp features, the rain straight fall of hair. Her leg was bent at the knee and had slipped between his. She was soft and warm and tempting. Brand knew he had experience enough to arouse her into submission before she was fully awake. She would be drowsy and disoriented.

The hazy gray of early dawn came upon them as he watched her. He could make out her lashes now, a long sweep of black that seemed to weigh her lids down. He wanted her, but not that way. Not the first time. Asleep, she sighed and moved against him. Desire rippled along his skin. Carefully Brand shifted away from her and rose.

In the kitchen he began to make coffee. A glance at his watch and a little arithmetic told him they'd be landing soon. He thought rather enthusiastically about breakfast. The drive from the airport to his house would take some time. He remembered an inn along the way where they could get a good meal and coffee better than the instant he was making.

Hearing Raven stir, he came to the doorway and watched her wake up. She moaned, rolled over and unsuccessfully tried to bury her face. Her hand reached out for a pillow that wasn't there, then slowly, on a disgusted sigh, she opened her eyes. Brand watched the stages as her eyes roamed the room. First came disinterest, then confusion, then sleepy understanding.

"Good morning," he ventured, and she shifted her eyes to him without moving her head. He was grinning at her, and his greeting was undeniably cheerful. She had a wary respect for cheerful risers.

"Coffee," she managed and shut her eyes again.

"In a minute." The kettle was beginning to hiss behind him. "How'd you sleep?"

Dragging her hands through her hair, she made a courageous attempt to sit up. The light was still gray but now brighter, and she pressed her fingers against her eyes for a moment. "I don't know yet," she mumbled from behind her hands. "Ask me later."

The whistle blew, and as Brand disappeared back into the galley, Raven brought her knees up to her chest and buried her face against them. She could hear him talking to her, making bright, meaningless conversation, but her mind wasn't yet receptive. She made no attempt to listen or to answer.

"Here, love." As Raven cautiously raised her head, Brand held out a steaming mug. "Have a bit, then you'll feel better." She accepted with murmured thanks. He sat down beside her. "I've a brother who wakes up ready to bite someone's—anyone's—head off. It's metabolism, I suppose."

Raven made a noncommittal sound and began to take tentative sips. It was hot and strong. For some moments there was silence as he drank his own cream-cooled coffee and watched her. When her cup was half empty, she looked over and managed a rueful smile.

"I'm sorry, Brandon. I'm simply not at my best in the morning. Especially early in the morning." She tilted her head so that she could see his watch, made a brave stab at mathematics, then gave up. "I don't suppose it matters what time it actually is," she decided, going back to the coffee. "It'll take me days to adjust to the change, anyway."

"A good meal will set you up," he told her, lazily sipping at his own coffee. "I read somewhere where drinking yeast and jogging cures jet lag, but I'll take my chances with breakfast."

"Yeast?" Raven grimaced into her mug, then drained it. "I think sleep's a better cure, piles of it." The mists were clearing, and she shook back her hair. "I guess we'll be landing soon, won't we?"

"Less than an hour, I'd say."

"Good. The less time I spend awake on a plane, the less time I have to think about being on one. I slept like a rock." With another sigh, Raven stretched her back, letting her shoulders lift and fall with the movement. "I made poor company." Her system was starting to hum again, though on slow speed.

"You were tired." Over the rim of his cup he watched the subtle movements of her body beneath the oversize sweater.

"I turned off like a tap," she admitted. "It happens that way sometimes after a concert." She lifted one shoulder in a quick shrug. "But I suppose we'll both be better today for the rest. Where did you sleep?"

"With you."

Raven closed her mouth on a yawn, swallowed and stared at him. "What?"

"I said I slept with you, here on the couch." Brand made a general gesture with his hand. "You like to snuggle."

She could see he was enjoying her dismayed shock.

His eyes were deep blue with amusement as he lifted his cup again. "You had no right…" Raven began.

"I always fancied being the first man you slept with," he told her before draining his cup. "Want some more coffee?"

Raven's face flooded with color; her eyes turned dark and opaque. She sprang up, but Brand managed to pluck the cup from her hand before she could hurl it across the room. For a moment she stood, breathing hard, watching him while he gave her his calm, measuring stare.

"Don't flatter yourself," she tossed out. "You don't know how many men I've slept with."

Very precisely, he set down both coffee cups, then looked back up at her. "You're as innocent as the day you were born, Raven. You've barely been touched by a man, much less been made love to."

Her temper flared like a rocket. "You don't know anything about who I've been with in the last five years, Brandon." She struggled to keep from shouting, to keep her voice as calm and controlled as his. "It's none of your business how many men I've slept with."

He lifted a brow, watching her thoughtfully. "Innocence isn't something to be ashamed of, Raven."

"I'm not…" She stopped, balling her fists. "You had no right to—" She swallowed and shook her head as fury and embarrassment raced through her. "—While I was asleep," she finished.

"Do what while you were asleep?" Brandon demanded, lazing back on the sofa. "Ravish you?" His humor shimmered over the old-fashioned word and made her feel ridiculous. "I don't think you'd have slept through it, Raven."

Her voice shook with emotion. "Don't laugh at me, Brandon."

"Then don't be such a fool." He reached over to the table beside him for a cigarette, then tapped the end of it against the surface without lighting it. His eyes were fixed on hers and no longer amused. "I could have had you if I'd wanted to, make no mistake about it."

"You have colossal nerve, Brandon. Please remember that you're not privy to my sex life and that you wouldn't have had me because I don't want you. I choose my own lovers."

She hadn't realized he could move so fast. The indolent slouch on the sofa was gone in a flash. He reached up, seizing her wrist, and in one swift move had yanked her down on her back, trapping her body with his. Her gasp of surprise was swallowed as his weight pressed down on her.

Never, in all the time they had spent together past and present, had Raven seen him so angry. An iron taste of fear rose in her throat. She could only shake her head, too terrified to struggle, too stunned to move. She had never suspected he possessed the capacity for violence she now read clearly on his face. This was far different from the cold rage she had seen before and which she knew how to deal with. His fingers bit into her wrist while his other hand came to circle her throat.

"How far do you think I'll push?" he demanded. His voice was harsh and deep with the hint of Ireland more pronounced. Her breathing was short and shallow with fear. Lying completely still, she made no answer. "Don't throw your imaginary string of lovers in my face, or, by God, you'll have a real one quickly enough whether you want me or not." His fingers tightened slightly around her throat. "When the time comes, I won't need to get you drunk on champagne or on exhaustion to have you lie with me. I could have you now, this minute, and after five minutes of struggle you'd be more than willing." His voice lowered, trembling along her skin. "I know how to play you, Raven, and don't you forget it."

His face was very close to hers. Their breathing mixed, both swift and strained, the only sound coming from the hum of the plane's engines. The fear in her eyes leaped out, finally penetrating his fury. Swearing, Brand pushed himself from her and rose. Her eyes stayed on his as she waited for what he would do next. He stared at her, then turned sharply away, moving over to a porthole.

Raven lay where she was, not realizing she was massaging the wrist that throbbed from his fingers. She watched him drag a hand through his hair.

"I slept with you last night because I wanted to be close to you." He took another long, cleansing breath. "It was nothing more than that. I never touched you. It was an innocent and rather sweet way to spend the night." He curled his fingers into a fist, remembering the frantic flutter of her pulse under his hand when he had circled it around her throat. It gave him no pleasure to know he had frightened her. "It never occurred to me that it would offend you like this. I apologize."

Raven covered her eyes with her hand as the tears

began. She swallowed sobs, not wanting to give way to them. Guilt and shame washed over her as fear drained. Her reaction to Brand's simple, affectionate gesture had been to slap his face. It had been embarrassment, she knew, but more, her own suppressed longing for him that had pushed her to react with anger and spiteful words. She'd tried to provoke him and had succeeded. But more, she knew now she had hurt him. Rising from the sofa, she attempted to make amends.

Though she walked over to stand behind him, Raven didn't touch him. She couldn't bear the thought that he might stiffen away from her.

"Brandon, I'm so sorry." She dug her teeth into her bottom lip to keep her voice steady. "That was stupid of me, and worse, unkind. I'm terribly ashamed of the way I acted. I wanted to make you angry; I was embarrassed, I suppose, and..." The words trailed off as she searched for some way to describe the way she had felt. Even now something inside her warmed and stirred at the knowledge that she had lain beside him, sharing the intimacy of sleep.

Raven heard him swear softly, then he rubbed a hand over the back of his neck. "I baited you."

"You're awfully good at it," she said, trying to make light of what had passed between them. "Much better than I am. I can't think about what I'm saying when I'm angry."

"Obviously, neither can I. Look, Raven," Brand began and turned. Her eyes were huge, swimming with restrained tears. He broke off what he had been about to say and moved to the table for his cigarettes. After lighting one, he turned back to her. "I'm sorry I lost my temper. It's something I don't do often because it's a nasty one. And you've got a good aim with a punch, Raven, and it reminded me of the last time we were together five years ago."

She felt her stomach tighten in defense. "I don't think either of us should dwell on that."

"No." He nodded slowly. His eyes were calm again and considering. Raven knew he was poking into her brain. "Not at the moment, in any case. We should get on with today." He smiled, and she felt each individual muscle in her body relax. "It seems we couldn't wait until we settled in before having a fight."

"No." She answered his smile. "But then I've always been impatient." Moving to him, Raven rose on her toes and pressed her lips tightly to his. "I'm really sorry, Brandon."

"You've already apologized."

"Yes, well, just remember the next time, it'll be your turn to grovel."

Brand tugged on her hair. "I'll make some more coffee. We should have time for one more cup before we have to strap in."

When he had gone into the galley, Raven stood where she was a moment. The last time, she thought, five years ago.

She remembered it perfectly: each word, each hurt. And she remembered that the balance of the fault then had also been hers. They'd been alone; he'd wanted her. She had wanted him. Then everything had gone wrong. Raven remembered how she had shouted at him, near hysteria. He'd been patient, then his patience had snapped, though not in the way it had today. Then, she remembered, he'd been cold, horribly, horribly cold. Comparing the two reactions, Raven realized she preferred the heat and violence to the icy disdain.

Raven could bring the scene back with ease. They'd been close, and the desire had risen to warm her. Then it was furnace hot and she was smothering, then shouting at him not to touch her. She'd told him she couldn't bear for him to touch her. Brand had taken her at her word and left her. Raven could easily remember the despair, the regret and confusion—and the love for him outweighing all else.

But when she had gone to find him the next morning, he had already checked out of his hotel. He had left California, left her, without a word. And there'd been no word from him in five years. No word, she mused, but for the stories in every magazine, in every newspaper. No word but for the whispered comments at parties and in restaurants whenever she would walk in. No word but for the constant questions, the endless speculation in print as to why they were no longer an item—why Brand Carstairs had begun to collect women like trophies.

So she had forced him out of her mind. Her work, her talent and her music had been used to fill the holes he had left in her life. She'd steadied herself and built a life with herself in control again. That was for the best, she had decided. Sharing the reins was dangerous. And, she mused, glancing toward the galley, it would still be dangerous. *He* would still be dangerous.

Quickly Raven shook her head. Brandon was right, she told herself. It was time to concentrate on today. They had work to do, a score to write. Taking a deep breath, she walked to the galley to help him with the coffee.

Chapter 9

Raven fell instantly in love with the primitive countryside of Cornwall. She could accept this as the setting for Arthur's Camelot. It was easy to imagine the clash of swords and the glint of armor, the thundering gallop of swift horses.

Spring was beginning to touch the moors, the green blooms just now emerging. Here and there was the faintest touch of pink from wild blossoms. A fine, constant drizzling mist added to the romance. There were houses, cottages really, with gardens beginning to thrive. Lawns were a tender, thin green, and she spotted the sassy yellow of daffodils and the sleepy blue of wood hyacinths. Brand drove south toward the coast and cliffs and Land's End.

They had eaten a country breakfast of brown eggs, thick bacon and oat cakes and had set off again in the little car Brand had arranged to have waiting for them at the airport.

"What's your house like, Brandon?" Raven asked as she rummaged through her purse in search of something to use to secure her hair. "You've never told me anything about it."

He glanced at her bent head. "I'll let you decide for yourself when you see it. It won't be long now."

Raven found two rubber bands of differing sizes and colors. "Are you being mysterious, or is this your way of avoiding telling me the roof leaks."

"It might," Brand considered. "Though I don't recall being dripped on. The Pengalleys would see to it; they're quite efficient about that sort of thing."

"Pengalleys?" Raven began to braid her hair.

"Caretakers," he told her. "They've a cottage a mile or so off from the house. They kept an eye on the place, and she does a bit of housekeeping when I'm in residence. He does the repairs."

"Pengalley," she murmured, rolling the name over on her tongue.

"Cornishmen, tried and true," Brand remarked absently.

"I know!" Raven turned to him with a sudden smile. "She's short and a bit stout, not fat, just solidly built, with dark hair pulled back and a staunch, rather disapproving face. He's thinner and going gray, and he tipples a bit from a flask when he thinks she's not looking."

Brand quirked a brow and shot her another brief glance. "Very clever. Just how did you manage it?"

"It had to be," Raven shrugged as she secured one braid and started on the next, "if any gothic novel I've ever read had a dab of truth in it. Are there any neighbors?"

"No one close by. That's one of the reasons I bought it."

"Antisocial?" she asked, smiling at him.

"Survival instinct," Brand corrected. "Sometimes I have to get away from it or go mad. Then I can go back and slip into harness again and enjoy it. It's like recharging." He felt her considering look and grinned. "I told you I'd mellowed."

"Yes," she said slowly, "you did." Still watching him, Raven twisted the rubber band around the tip of the second braid. "Yet you've still managed to put out quite a bit. All the albums, the double one last year; all but five of the songs were yours exclusively. And the songs you wrote for Cal Ripley—they were the best cuts on his album."

"Did you think so?" he asked.

"You know they were," she said, letting the rubber band snap into place.

"Praise is good for the ego, love."

"You've had your share now." She tossed both braids behind her back. "What I was getting at was that for someone who's so mellow, you're astonishingly productive."

"I do a lot of my writing here," Brand explained. "Or at my place in Ireland. More here, actually, because I've family across the channel, so there's visiting to be done if I'm there."

Raven gave him a curious look. "I thought you still lived in London."

"Primarily, but if I've serious work or simply need to be alone, I come here. I've family in London as well."

"Yes." Raven looked away again out into the misty landscape. "I suppose large families have disadvantages."

Something in her tone made him glance over again, but her face was averted. He said nothing, knowing from experience that any discussion of Raven's family was taboo. Occasionally in the past, he had probed, but she had always evaded him. He knew that she had been an only child and had left home at seventeen. Out of curiosity, Brand had questioned Julie. Julie knew all there was to know about Raven, he was certain, but she had told him nothing. It was yet another mystery about Raven which alternately frustrated and attracted Brand. Now he put the questions in the back of his mind and continued smoothly.

"Well, we won't be troubled by family or neighbors. Mrs. Pengalley righteously disapproves of show people, and will keep a healthy distance."

"Show people?" Raven repeated and turning back to him, grinned. "Have you been having orgies again, Brand?"

"Not for at least three months," he assured her and swung onto a back road. "I told you I'd mellowed. But she knows about actors and actresses, you see, because as Mr. Pengalley tells me, she makes it her business to read everything she can get her hands on about them.

And as for musicians, *rock* musicians, well…" He let the sentence trail off meaningfully, and Raven giggled.

"She'll think the worst, I imagine," she said cheerfully.

"The worst?" Brand cocked a brow at her.

"That you and I are carrying on a hot, illicit love affair."

"Is that the worst? It sounds rather appealing to me."

Raven colored and looked down at her hands. "You know what I meant."

Brand took her hand, kissing it lightly. "I know what you meant." The laugh in his voice eased her embarrassment. "Will it trouble you to be labeled a fallen woman?"

"I've been labeled a fallen woman for years," she returned with a smile, "every time I pick up a magazine. Do you know how many affairs I've had with people I've never even spoken to?"

"Celebrities are required to have overactive libidos," he murmured. "It's part of the job."

"Your press does yours credit," she observed dryly.

Brand nodded gravely. "I've always thought so. I heard about a pool going around London last year. They were betting on how many women I'd have in a three-month period. The British," he explained, "will bet on anything."

Raven allowed the silence to hang for a moment. "What number did you take?"

"Twenty-seven," he told her, then grinned. "I thought it best to be conservative."

She laughed, enjoying him. He would have done it,

too, she reflected. There was enough of the cocky street kid left in him. "I don't think I'd better ask you if you won."

"I wish you wouldn't," he said as the car began to climb up a macadam drive.

Raven saw the house. It was three stories high, formed of sober, Cornish stone with shutters of deep, weathered green and a series of stout chimneys on the roof. She could just make out thin puffs of smoke before they merged with the lead-colored sky.

"Oh, Brandon, how like you," she cried, enchanted. "How like you to find something like this."

She was out of the car before he could answer. It was then that she discovered the house had its back to the sea. There were no rear doors, she learned as she dashed quickly to the retaining wall on the left side. The cliff sheared off too close to the back of the house to make one practical. Instead, there were doors on the sides, set deep in Cornish stone.

Raven could look down from the safety of a waist-high wall and watch the water foam and lash out at jagged clumps of rock far below. The view sent a thrill of terror and delight through her. The sea roared below, a smashing fury of sound. Raven stood, heedless of the chill drizzle, and tried to take it all in.

"It's fabulous. Fabulous!" Turning, she lifted her face, studying the house again. Against the stone, in a great tangle of vines, grew wild roses and honeysuckles. They were greening, not yet ready to bloom, but she could already imagine their fragrance. A rock garden had been added, and among the tender green shoots was an occasional flash of color.

"You might find the inside fabulous, too," Brand ventured, laughing when she turned her wet face to him. "And dry."

"Oh, Brandon, don't be so unromantic." She turned a slow circle until she faced the house again. "It's like something out of *Wuthering Heights*."

He took her hand. "Unromantic or not, mate, I want a bath, a hot one, and my tea."

"That does have a nice sound to it," she admitted but hung back as he pulled her to the door. She thought the cliffs wonderfully jagged and fierce. "Will we have scones? I developed a taste for them when I toured England a couple years ago. Scones and clotted cream— why does that have to sound so dreadful?"

"You'll have to take that up with Mrs. Pengalley," Brand began as he placed his hand on the knob. It opened before he could apply any pressure.

Mrs. Pengalley looked much as Raven had jokingly described her. She was indeed a sturdily built woman with dark hair sternly disciplined into a sensible bun. She had dark, sober eyes that passed briefly over Raven, took in the braids and damp clothing, then rested on Brandon without a flicker of expression.

"Good morning, Mr. Carstairs, you made good time," she said in a soft, Cornish burr.

"Hullo, Mrs. Pengalley, it's good to see you again. This is Ms. Williams, who'll be staying with me."

"Her room's ready, sir. Good morning, Miss Williams."

"Good morning, Mrs. Pengalley," said Raven, a trifle

daunted. This, she was sure, was what was meant by "a formidable woman." "I hope I haven't put you to too much trouble."

"There's been little to do." Mrs. Pengalley's dark eyes shifted to Brand again. "There be fires laid, and the pantry's stocked, as you instructed. I've done you a casserole for tonight. You've only to heat it when you've a mind to eat. Mr. Pengalley laid in a good supply of wood; the nights're cool, and it's been damp. He'll be bringing your bags in now. We heard you drive up."

"Thanks." Brand glanced over, seeing that Raven was already wandering around the room. "We're both in need of a hot bath and some tea, then we should do well enough. Is there anything you want in particular, Raven?"

She glanced back over at the sound of her name but hadn't been attentive to the conversation. "I'm sorry. What?"

He smiled at her. "Is there anything you'd like before Mrs. Pengalley sees to tea?"

"No." Raven smiled at the housekeeper. "I'm sure everything's lovely."

Mrs. Pengalley inclined her head, her body bending not an inch. "I'll make your tea, then." As she swept from the room, Raven shot Brand a telling glance. He grinned and stretched his back.

"You continually amaze me, Brandon," she murmured, then went back to her study of the room.

It was, Raven knew, the room in which they would be doing most of their work over the next weeks. A grand piano, an old one which, she discovered on a quick testing run, had magnificent tone, was set near a pair of narrow windows. Occasional rag rugs dotted the oak-planked floor. The drapes were cream-colored lace and obviously handworked. Two comfortable sofas, both biscuit-colored, and a few Chippendale tables completed the furniture.

A fire crackled in the large stone fireplace. Raven moved closer to examine the pictures on the mantel.

At a glance, she could tell she was looking at Brand's family. There was a teenage boy in a black leather jacket whose features were the same as Brand's though his dark hair was a bit longer and was as straight as Raven's. He wore the same cocky grin as his brother. A woman was next; Raven thought her about twenty-five and astonishingly pretty with fair hair and slanted green eyes and a true English rose complexion. For all the difference in coloring, however, the resemblance to Brand was strong enough for Raven to recognize his sister. She was in another picture along with a blond man and two boys. Both boys had dark hair and the Carstairs mischief gleaming in their eyes. Raven decided Brand's sister had her hands full.

Raven studied the picture of Brand's parents for some time. The tall, thin frame had been passed down from his father, but it seemed only one of the children had inherited his fair, English looks. Raven judged it to be an old snapshot—twenty, perhaps twenty-five, years old. It had been painstaking staged, with the man and woman dead center, standing straight in their Sunday best. The woman was dark and lovely. The man looked a bit self-conscious and ill at ease having to pose, but the woman beamed into the camera. Her eyes bespoke mischief and her mouth a hint of the cockiness so easily recognized in her children.

There were more pictures: family groups and candid shots, with Brand in several of them. The Carstairses were very much a family. Raven felt a small stir of envy. Shaking it off, she turned back to Brand and smiled.

"This is quite a group." She flicked her fingers behind her toward the mantel. "You're the oldest, aren't you? I think I read that somewhere. The resemblance is remarkable."

"Sweeney genes from my mother's side," Brand told her, looking beyond her shoulder at the crowded grouping of frames. "The only one they slipped up on a bit was Alison." He ran a hand through his damp hair and came to stand beside her. "Let me take you upstairs, love, and get you settled in. The grand tour can wait until we're dry." He slipped an arm around her. "I'm glad you're here, Raven. I've never seen you with things that are mine before. And hotel rooms, no matter how luxurious, are never home."

Later, lounging in a steaming tub, Raven thought over Brand's statement. It was part of the business of being an entertainer to spend a great many nights in hotel rooms, albeit luxury suites, in their positions, but they were hotel rooms nonetheless. Home was a place for between concerts and guest appearances, and to her, it had become increasingly important over the years. It seemed the higher she rose, the more she needed a solid base. She realized it was the same with Brand.

They'd both been on the road for several weeks. He

was home now, and somehow Raven knew already that she, too, would be at home there. For all its age and size, there was something comforting in the house. Perhaps, Raven mused as she lazily soaped a leg, it's the age and size. Continuity was important to her, as she felt she'd had little of it in her life, and space was important for the same reason.

Raven had felt an instant affinity for the house. She liked the muffled roar of the sea outside her window and the breathtaking view. She liked the old-fashioned porcelain tub with the curved legs and the oval, mahogany-framed mirror over the tiny pedestal sink.

Rising from the tub, she lifted a towel from the heated bar. When she had dried herself, she wrapped a thick, buff-colored towel around her before letting down her hair. The two braids fell from where she had pinned them atop of her head. Absently, as she wandered back into the bedroom, she began to undo them.

Her luggage still sat beside an old brass chest, but she didn't give much thought to unpacking. Instead she walked to the window seat set in the south wall and knelt on the padded cushion.

Below her the sea hurled itself onto the rocks, tossed up by the wind. There was a sucking, drawing sound before it crashed back onto the shingles and cliffs. Like the sky, they were gray, except for where the waves crested in stiff, white caps. The rain drizzled still, with small drops hitting her window to trail lazily downward. Placing her arms on the wide sill, Raven rested her chin on them and lost herself in dreamy contemplation of the scene below.

"Raven."

She heard Brand's call and the knock and answered both absently. "Yes, come in."

"I thought you might be ready to go downstairs," he said.

"In a minute. What a spectacular view this is! Come look. Does your room face the sea like this? I think I could sit here watching it forever."

"It has its points," he agreed and came over to stand behind her. He tucked his hands into his pockets. "I didn't know you had such a fondness for the sea."

"Yes, always, but I've never had a room where I felt right on top of it before. I'm going to like hearing it at night." She smiled over her shoulder at him. "Is your house in Ireland on the coast, too?"

"No, it's more of a farm, actually. I'd like to take you there." He ran his fingers through her hair, finding it thick and soft and still faintly damp. "It's a green, weepy country, and as appealing as this one, in a different way."

"That's your favorite, isn't it?" Raven smiled up at him. "Even though you live in London and come here to do work, it's the place in Ireland that's special."

He returned the smile. "If it wasn't that there'd have been Sweeneys and Hardestys everywhere we looked, I'd have taken you there. My mother's family," he explained, "are very friendly people. If the score goes well, perhaps we can take a bit of a vacation there when we're done."

Raven hesitated. "Yes…I'd like that."

"Good." The smile turned into a grin. "And I like your dress."

Puzzled, Raven followed his lowered glance. Stunned, she gripped the towel at her breasts and scrambled to her feet. "I didn't realize...I'd forgotten." She could feel the color heating her cheeks. "Brandon, you might have said something."

"I just did," he pointed out. His eyes skimmed down to her thighs.

"Very funny," Raven retorted and found herself smiling. "Now, why don't you clear out and let me change?"

"Must you? Pity." He hooked his hand over the towel where it met between her breasts. The back of his fingers brushed the swell of her bosom. "I was just thinking I liked your outfit." Without touching her in any other way, he brought his mouth down to hers.

"You smell good," he murmured, then traced just the inside of her mouth with his tongue. "Rain's still in your hair."

A roaring louder than the sea began in her brain. Instinctually she was kissing him back, meeting his tongue with hers, stepping closer and rising on her toes. Though her response was quick and giving, he kept the kiss light. She sensed the hunger and the strength under tight control.

Under the towel, his finger swept over her nipple, finding it taut with desire. Raven felt a strong, unfamiliar ache between her thighs. She moaned with it as each muscle in her body went lax. He lifted his face and waited until her eyes opened.

"Shall I make love to you, Raven?"

She stared at him, aching with the churn of rising needs. He was putting the decision in her hands. She should have been grateful, relieved, yet at that moment she found she would have preferred it if he had simply swept her away. For an instant she wanted no choice, no voice, but only to be taken.

"You'll have to be sure," he told her quietly. Lifting her chin with his finger, he smiled. His eyes were a calm blue-green. "I've no intention of making it easy for you."

He dropped his hand. "I'll wait for you downstairs, though I still think it's a pity you have to change. You're very attractive in a towel."

"Brandon," she said when he was at the door. He turned, lifting a brow in acknowledgment. "What if I'd said yes?" Raven grinned, feeling a bit more steady with the distance between them. "Wouldn't that have been a bit awkward with Mrs. Pengalley still downstairs?"

Leaning against the door, he said lazily, "Raven, if you'd said yes, I wouldn't give a damn if Mrs. Pengalley and half the country were downstairs." He shut the door carefully behind him.

Chapter 10

Both Raven and Brand were anxious to begin. They started the day after their arrival and soon fell into an easy, workable routine. Brand rose early and was usually finishing up a good-sized breakfast by the time Raven dragged herself downstairs. When she was fortified with coffee, they started their morning stretch, working until noon and Mrs. Pengalley's arrival. While the housekeeper brought in the day's marketing and saw to whatever domestic chores needed to be seen to, Brand and Raven would take long walks.

The days were balmy, scented with sea spray and spring. The land was rugged, even harsh, with patches of poor ground covered with heather not yet in bloom. The pounding surf beat against towering granite cliffs. Hardy birds built their nests in the crags. Their cries could be heard over the crash of the waves. Standing high, Raven could see down to the village with its neat rows of cottages and white church spire.

They'd work again in the afternoon with the fire sizzling in the grate at their backs. After dinner they went over the day's work. By the end of the week they had a loosely based outline for the score and the completed title song.

They didn't work without snags. Both Raven and Brand felt too strongly about music for any collaboration to run smoothly. But the arguments seemed to stimulate both of them; and the final product was the better for them. They were a good team.

They remained friends. Brand made no further attempt to become Raven's lover. From time to time Raven would catch him staring intently at her. Then she would feel the pull, as sensual as a touch, as tempting as a kiss. The lack of pressure confused her and drew her more effectively than his advances could have. Advances could be refused, avoided. She knew he was waiting for her decision. Underneath the casualness, the jokes and professional disagreements, the air throbbed with tension.

The afternoon was long and a bit dreary. A steady downpour of rain kept Raven and Brand from walking the cliffs. Their music floated through the house, echoing in corners here and there and drifting to forgotten attics. They'd built the fire high with Mr. Pengalley's store of wood to chase away the dampness that seemed to seep through the windows. A tray of tea and biscuits that they had both forgotten rested on one of the Chippendale tables. Their argument was reaching its second stage.

"We've got to bring up the tempo," Raven insisted. "It just doesn't work this way."

"It's a mood piece, Raven."

"Not a funeral dirge. It drags this way, Brandon. People are going to be nodding off before she finishes singing it."

"Nobody falls asleep while Lauren Chase is singing," Brand countered. "This number is pure sex, Raven, and she'll sell it."

"Yes, she will," Raven agreed, "but not at this tempo." She shifted on the piano bench so that she faced him more directly. "All right, Joe's fallen asleep at the type-writer in the middle of the chapter he's writing. He's already believing himself a little mad because of the vivid dreams he's having about his character Tessa. She seems too real, and he's fallen in love with her even though he knows she's a product of his own imagina-tion, a character in a novel he's writing, a fantasy. And now, in the middle of the day, he's dreaming about her again, and this time she promises to come to him that night."

"I know the plot, Raven," Brand said dryly.

Though she narrowed her eyes, Raven checked her temper. She thought she detected some fatigue in his voice. Once or twice she'd been awakened in the middle of the night by his playing. "'Nightfall' is hot, Brandon. You're right about it being pure sex, and your lyrics are fabulous. But it still needs to move."

"It moves." He took a last drag on his cigarette before crushing it out. "Chase knows how to hang on to a note."

Raven made a quick sound of frustration. Unfortunately he was usually right about such things. His instincts were phenomenal. This time, however, she was certain that her own instincts—as a songwriter and as a woman—were keener. She knew the way the song had to be sung to reap the full effect. The moment she had read Brand's lyrics, she had known what was needed. The song had flowed, completed, through her head.

"I know she can hang on to a note, and she can handle choreography. She'll be able to do both and still do the song at the right tempo. Let me show you." She began to play the opening bars. Brand shrugged and rose from the bench.

Raven moved the tempo to *andante* and sang to her own accompaniment. Her voice wrapped itself around the music. Brand moved to the window to watch the rain. It was the song of a temptress, full of implicit, wild promises.

Raven's voice flowed over the range of notes, then heated when it was least expected until Brand felt a tight knot of desire in the pit of his stomach. There was something not quite earthy in the melody she had created. The quicker tempo made a sharp contrast, much more effective than the pace Brand had wanted. She ended abruptly in a raspy whisper without any fade-out. She tossed her hair, then shot him a look over her shoulder.

"Well?" There was a half smile on her face.

He had his back to her and kept his hands tucked

into his pockets. "You have to be right now and again, I suppose."

Raven laughed, spinning around on the bench until she faced the room. "You've a way with compliments, Brandon. It sets my heart fluttering."

"She doesn't have your range," he murmured. Then, making an impatient movement, he wandered over to the teapot. "I don't think she'll get as much out of the low scale as you do."

"Mmm." Raven shrugged as she watched him pour out a cup of tea. "She's got tremendous style, though; she'll milk every ounce out of it." He set the tea down again without touching it and roamed to the fire. As she watched him, a worried frown creased Raven's brow. "Brandon, what's wrong?"

He threw another log on the already roaring fire. "Nothing, just restless."

"This rain's depressing." She rose to go to the window. "I've never minded it. Sometimes I like a dreary, sleepy day. I can be lazy without feeling guilty. Maybe that's what you should do, Brandon, be lazy today. You've got that marvelous chessboard in the library. Why don't you teach me to play?" She lifted her hands to his shoulders and feeling the tension, began to knead absently. "Of course, that might be hard work. Julie gave up playing backgammon with me. She says I haven't any knack for strategy."

Raven broke off when Brand turned abruptly around and removed her hands from his shoulders. Without speaking, he walked away from her. He went to the liquor cabinet and drew out a bottle of bourbon. Raven watched as he poured three fingers into a glass and drank it down.

"I don't think I've the patience for games this afternoon," he told her as he poured a second drink.

"All right, Brandon," she said. "No games." She walked over to stand in front of him, keeping her eyes direct. "Why are you angry with me? Certainly not because of the song."

The look held for several long moments while the fire popped and sizzled in the grate. Raven heard a log fall as the one beneath it gave way.

"Perhaps it's time you and I talked," Brandon said as he idly swirled the remaining liquor in the glass. "It's dangerous to leave things hanging for five years; you never know when they're going to fall."

Raven felt a ripple of disquiet but nodded. "You may be right."

Brand gave her a quick smile. "Should we be civilized and sit down or take a few free swings standing up?"

She shrugged. "I don't think there's any need to be civilized. Civilized fighting never clears the air."

"All right," he began but was interrupted by the peal of the bell. Setting down his glass, Brand shot her a last look, then went to answer.

Alone, Raven tried to control her jitters. There was a storm brewing, she knew, and it wasn't outside the windows. Brand was itching for a fight, and though the reason was unclear to her, Raven found herself very willing to oblige him. The tension between them had been glossed over in the name of music and peace.

Now, despite her nerves, she was looking forward to shattering the calm. Hearing his returning footsteps, she walked back to the tea tray and picked up her cup.

"Package for you." Brand gestured with it as he came through the doorway. "From Henderson."

"I wonder what he could be sending me," she murmured, already ripping off the heavy packing tape. "Oh, of course." She tossed the wrappings carelessly aside and studied the album jacket. "They're sample jackets for the album I'm releasing this summer." Without glancing at him, Raven handed Brand one of the covers, then turned to another to read the liner notes.

For the next few minutes Brand studied the cover picture without speaking. Again, a background of white, Raven sitting in her habitual cross-legged fashion. She was looking full into the camera with only a tease of a smile on her lips. Her eyes were very gray and very direct. Over her shoulders and down to her knees, her hair spilled—a sharp contrast against the soft-focused white of the background. The arrangement appeared to be haphazard but had been cleverly posed nonetheless. She appeared to be nude, and the effect was fairly erotic.

"Did you approve this picture?"

"Hmm?" Raven pushed back her hair as she continued to read. "Oh, yes, I looked over the proofs before I left on tour. I'm still not completely sure about this song order, but I suppose it's a bit late to change it now."

"I always felt Henderson was above packaging you this way."

"Packaging me what way?" she asked absently.

"As a virgin offering to the masses." He handed her the cover.

"Brandon, really...how ridiculous."

"I don't think so," he said. "I think it's an uncannily apt description: virgin white, soft focus, and you sitting naked in the middle of it all."

"I'm not naked," she retorted indignantly. "I don't do nudes."

"The potential buyer isn't supposed to know that, though, is he?" Brand leaned against the piano and watched her through narrowed eyes.

"It's provocative, certainly. It's meant to be." Raven frowned down at the cover again. "There's nothing wrong with that. I'm not a child to be dressed up in Mary Janes and a pink pinafore, Brandon. This is business. There's nothing extreme about this cover. And I'm more modestly covered than I would be on a public beach."

"But not more decently," he said coldly. "There's a difference."

Color flooded her face, now a mixture of annoyance and embarrassment. "It's not indecent. I've never posed for an indecent picture. Karl Straighter is one of the finest photographers in the business. He doesn't shoot indecent pictures."

"One man's art is another's porn, I suppose."

Her eyes widened as she lowered the jackets to the piano bench. "That's a disgusting thing to say," she whispered. "You're being deliberately horrible."

"I'm simply giving you my opinion," he corrected, lifting a brow. "You don't have to like it."

"I don't need your opinion. I don't need your approval."

"No," he said and crushed out his cigarette. "You bloody well don't, do you? But you're going to have it in any case." He caught her by the arm when she would have turned away. The power of the grip contrasted the cool tone and frosty eyes.

"Let go of me," Raven demanded, putting her hand on top of his and trying unsuccessfully to pry it from her arm.

"When I'm finished."

"You have finished." Her voice was abruptly calm, and she stopped her frantic attempts to free herself. Instead she faced him squarely, emotion burning in her eyes. "I don't have to listen to you when you go out of your way to insult me, Brandon. I won't listen to you. You can prevent me from leaving because you're stronger than I am, but you can't make me listen." She swallowed but managed to keep her voice steady. "I run my own life. You're entitled to your opinion, certainly, but you're not entitled to hurt me with it. I don't want to talk to you now; I just want you to let me go."

He was silent for so long, Raven thought he would refuse. Then, slowly, he loosened his grip until she could slip her arm from his fingers. Without a word she turned and left the room.

Perhaps it was the strain of her argument with Brand or the lash of rain against the windows or the sudden

fury of thunder and lightning. The dream formed out
of a vague montage of childhood remembrances that
left her with impressions rather than vivid pictures.
Thoughts and images floated and receded against the
darkness of sleep. There were rolling sensations of
fear, guilt, despair, one lapping over the other while
she moaned and twisted beneath the sheets, trying to
force herself awake. But she was trapped, caught fast
in the world just below consciousness. Then the thunder seemed to explode inside her head, and the flash
of lightning split the room with a swift, white flash.
Screaming, Raven sat up in bed.

The room was pitch dark again when Brand rushed
in; he found his way to the bed by following the sounds
of Raven's wild weeping. "Raven. Here, love." Even
as he reached her, she threw herself into his arms and
clung. She was trembling hard, and her skin was icy.
Brand pulled the quilt up over her back and cuddled
her. "Don't cry, love, you're safe here." He patted and
stroked as he would for a child frightened of a storm.
"It'll soon be over."

"Hold me." She pressed her face into his bare shoulder. "Please, just hold me." Her breathing was quick,
burning her throat as she struggled for air. "Oh, Brandon, such an awful dream."

He rocked her and laid a light kiss on her temple.
"What was it about?" The telling, he recalled from
childhood, usually banished the fear.

"She'd left me alone again," Raven murmured, shuddering so that he drew her closer in response. The words
came out as jumbled as her thoughts, as tumbled as the

Nora Roberts

dream. "How I hated being alone in that room. The only light was from the building next door—one of those red neon lights that blinks on and off, on and off, so that the dark was never still. And so much noise out on the street, even with the windows closed. Too hot...too hot to sleep," she murmured into his shoulder. "I watched the light and waited for her to come back. She was drunk again." She whimpered, her fingers opening and closing against his chest. "And she'd brought a man with her. I put the pillow over my head so I wouldn't hear."

Raven paused to steady her breath. It was dark and quiet in Brand's arms. Outside, the storm rose in high fury.

"She fell down the steps and broke her arm, so we moved, but it was always the same. Dingy little rooms, airless rooms that smelled always of gin no matter how you scrubbed. Thin walls, walls that might as well not have existed for the privacy they gave you. But she always promised that this time, this time it'd be different. She'd get a job, and I'd go to school...but always one day I'd come home and there'd be a man and a bottle."

She wasn't clinging any longer but simply leaning against him as if all passion were spent. Lightning flared again, but she remained still.

"Raven." Brand eased her gently away and tilted her face to his. Tears were still streaming from her eyes, but her breathing was steadier. He could barely make out the shape of her face in the dark. "Where was your father?"

He could see the shine of her eyes as she stared at

him. She made a soft, quiet sound as one waking. He knew the words had slipped from her while she had been vulnerable and unaware. Now she was aware, but it was too late for defenses. The sigh she made was an empty, weary sound.

"I don't know who he was." Slowly she drew out of Brand's arms and rose from the bed. "She didn't, either. You see, there were so many."

Brand said nothing but reached into the pocket of the jeans he had hastily dragged on and found a pack of matches. Striking one, he lit the bedside candle. The light wavered and flickered, hardly more than a pulse beat in the dark. "How long," he asked and shook out the match, "did you live like that?"

Raven dragged both hands through her hair, then hugged herself. She knew she'd already said too much for evasions. "I don't remember a time she didn't drink, but when I was very young, five or six, she still had some control over it. She used to sing in clubs. She had big dreams and an average voice, but she was very lovely...once."

Pausing, Raven pressed her fingers against her eyes and wiped away tears. "By the time I was eight, she was...her problem was unmanageable. And there were always men. She needed men as much as she needed to drink. Some of them were better than others. One of them took me to the zoo a couple of times...."

She trailed off and turned away. Brand watched the candlelight flicker over the thin material of her nightgown.

"She got steadily worse. I think part of it was from

the frustration of having her voice go. Of course, she abused it dreadfully with smoking and drinking, but the more it deteriorated, the more she smoked and drank. She ruined her voice and ruined her health and ruined any chance she had of making something of herself. Sometimes I hated her. Sometimes I know she hated herself."

A sob escaped, but Raven pushed it back and began to wander the room. The movement seemed to make it easier, and the words tumbled out quicker, pressing for release. "She'd cry and cling to me and beg me not to hate her. She'd promise the moon, and more often than not, I'd believe her. 'This time'—that was one of her favorite beginnings. It still is." Raven let out a shaky sigh. "She loved me when she wasn't drinking and forgot me completely when she was. It was like living with two different women, and neither one of them was easy. When she was sober, she expected an average mother-and-daughter relationship. Had I done my homework? Why was I five minutes late getting home from school? When she was drunk, I was supposed to keep the hell out of her way. I remember once, when I was twelve, she went three months and sixteen days without a drink. Then I came home from school and found her passed out on the bed. She'd had an audition that afternoon for a gig at this two-bit club. Later she told me she'd just wanted one drink to calm her nerves. Just one..." Raven shivered and hugged herself tighter. "It's cold," she murmured.

Brand rose and stooped in front of the fire. He added kindling and logs to the bed of coals in the grate. Raven walked to the window to watch the fury of the storm over the sea. Lightning still flashed sporadically, but the violence of the thunder and the rain were dying.

"There were so many other times. She was working as a cocktail waitress in this little piano bar in Houston. I was sixteen then. I always came by on payday so I could make certain she didn't spend the money before I bought food. She'd been pretty good then. She'd been working about six weeks straight and had an affair going with the manager. He was one of the better ones. I used to play around at the piano if the place was empty. One of my mother's lovers had been a musician; he'd taught me the basics and said I had a good ear. Mama liked hearing me play." Her voice had quieted. Brand watched her trail a finger down the dark pane of window glass.

"Ben, the manager, asked me if I wanted to play during the lunch hour. He said I could sing, too, as long as I kept it soft and didn't talk to the customers. So I started." Raven sighed and ran a hand over her brow. Behind her came the pop and crackle of flame. "We left Houston for Oklahoma City. I lied about my age and got a job singing in a club. It was one of Mama's worst periods. There were times I was afraid to leave her alone, but she wasn't working then, and..." She broke off with a sound of frustration and rubbed at an ache in her temple. She wanted to stop, wanted to block it all out, but she knew she had come too far. Pressing her brow against the glass, she waited until her thoughts came back into order.

"We needed the money, so I had to risk leaving her

at night. I suppose we exchanged roles for a time," she murmured. "The thing I learned young, but consistently forgot, was that an alcoholic finds money for a bottle. Always, no matter what. One night during my second set she wove her way into the club. Wayne was working there and caught onto the situation quickly. He managed to quiet her down before it got too ugly. Later he helped me get her home and into bed. He was wonderful: no lectures, no pity, no advice. Just support."

Raven turned away from the window again and wandered to the fire. "But she came back again, twice more, and they let me go. There were other towns, other clubs, but it was the same then and hardly matters now. Just before I turned eighteen I left her." Her voice trembled a bit, and she took a moment to steady it. "I came home from work one night, and she was passed out at the kitchen table with one of those half-gallon jugs of wine. I knew if I didn't get away from her I'd go crazy. So I put her to bed, packed a bag, left her all the money I could spare and walked out. Just like that." She covered her face with her hands a moment, pressing her fingers into her eyes. "It was like being able to breathe for the first time in my life."

Raven roamed back to the kitchen. She could see the vague ghost of her own reflection. Studying it, listening to the steady but more peaceful drum of rain, she continued. "I worked my way to L.A., and Henderson saw me. He pushed me. I'm not certain what my ambition was before I signed with him. Just to survive, I think. One day and then the next. Then there were contracts and recording sessions and the whole crazy circus. Doors started opening. Some of them were trap doors, I've always thought." She gave a quick, wondering laugh. "God, it was marvelous and scary and I don't believe I could ever go through those first few months again. Anyway, Henderson got me publicity, and the first hit single got me more. And then I got a call from a hospital in Memphis."

Raven turned and began to pace. The light silk of her nightgown clung, then swirled, with her movements. "I had to go, of course. She was in pretty bad shape. Her latest lover had beaten her and stolen what little money she had. She cried. Oh, God, all the same promises. She was sorry; she loved me. Never again, never again. I was the only decent thing she'd ever done in her life." The tears were beginning to flow again, but this time Raven made no attempt to stop them. "As soon as she could travel, I brought her back with me. Julie had found a sanitarium in Ojai and a very earnest young doctor. Justin Randolf Karter. Isn't that a marvelous name, Brandon?" Bitterness spilled out with the tears. "A marvelous name, a remarkable man. He took me into his tasteful, leather-bound office and explained the treatment my mother would receive."

Whirling, Raven faced Brand, her shoulders heaving with sobs. "I didn't want to know! I just wanted him to do it. He told me not to set my hopes too high, and I told him I hadn't any hopes at all. He must have found me cynical, because he suggested several good organizations I could speak to. He reminded me that alcoholism is a disease and that my mother was a victim. I said the hell she was; *I* was the victim!" Raven forced the words out as she hugged herself tightly. "*I* was the victim; *I* had had to live with her and deal with her lies and her sickness and her men. It was so safe, so easy, for him to be sanctimonious and understanding behind that tidy white coat. And I *hated* her." The sobs came in short, quick jerks as she balled her hands and pressed them against her eyes. "And I loved her." Her breath trembled in and out as everything she had pent up over the weeks of her mother's latest treatment poured through her. "I still love her," she whispered.

Weary, nearly spent, she turned to the fire, resting her palms on the mantel. "Dr. Karter let me shout at him, then he sat with me when I broke down. I went home, and they started her treatment. Two days later I met you."

Raven didn't hear him move, didn't know he stood behind her, until she felt his hands on her shoulders. Without speaking she turned and went into his arms. Brand held her, feeling the light tremors while he stared down at the licking, greedy flames. Outside, the storm had become only a patter of rain against the windows.

"Raven, if you had told me, I might have been able to make things easier for you."

She shook her head, then buried her face against his chest. "No, I didn't want it to touch that part of my life. I just wasn't strong enough." Taking a deep breath, she pulled back far enough to look in his eyes. "I was afraid that if you knew you wouldn't want anything to do with me."

"Raven." There was hurt as well as censure in his voice.

"I know it was wrong, Brandon, even stupid, but you have to understand: everything seemed to be happening to me at once. I needed time. I needed to sort out how I was going to live my life, how I was going to deal with my career, my mother, everything." Her hands gripped his arms as she willed him to see through her eyes. "I was nobody one day and being mobbed by fans the next. My picture was everywhere. I heard myself every time I turned on the radio. You know what that's like."

Brand brushed her hair from her cheek. "Yes, I know what that's like." As he spoke, he could feel her relax with a little shudder.

"Before I could take a breath, Mama walked back into my life. Part of me hated her, but instead of realizing that it was a normal reaction and dealing with it, I felt an unreasonable guilt. And I was ashamed. No," she shook her head, anticipating him, "there's no use telling me I had no need to be. That's an intellectual statement, a practical statement; it has nothing to do with emotion. I don't expect you to understand that part of it. You've never had to deal with it. She's my mother. It isn't possible to completely separate myself from that, even knowing that the responsibility for her problem isn't mine." Raven gave him one last, long look before turning away. "And on top of everything that was happening to me, I fell in love with you." The flames danced and snapped as she watched. "I loved you," she murmured so quietly he strained to hear, "but I couldn't be your lover."

Brand stared at her back, started to reach for her, then dropped his hands to his sides. "Why?"

Only her head turned as she looked over her shoulder at him. Her face was in shadows. "Because then I would be like her," she whispered, then turned away again.

"You don't really believe that, Raven." Brand took her shoulders, but she shook her head, not answering. Firmly he turned her to face him, making a slow, thorough study of her. "Do you make a habit of condemning children for their parents' mistakes?"

"No, but I…"

"You don't have the right to do it to yourself."

She shut her eyes on a sigh. "I know, I know that, but…"

"There're no buts on this one, Raven." His fingers tightened until she opened her eyes again. "You know who you are."

There was only the sound of the sea and the rain and fire. "I wanted you," she managed in a trembling voice, "when you held me, touched me. You were the first man I'd ever wanted." She swallowed, and again he felt the shudder course through her. "Then I'd remember all those cramped little rooms, all those men with my mother…." She broke off and would have turned away again if his hands hadn't held her still.

Brand removed his hands from her arms, then slowly, his eyes still on hers, he used them to frame her face. "Sleeping with a stranger is different from making love with someone you care for."

Raven moistened her lips. "Yes, I know that, but..."

"Do you?" The question stopped her. She could do no more than let out a shaky breath. "Let me show you, Raven."

Her eyes were trapped by his. She knew he would release her if she so much as shook her head. Fear was tiny pinpoints along her skin. Need was a growing warmth in her blood. She lifted her hands to his wrists. "Yes."

Again Brand gently brushed the hair away from her cheeks. When her face was framed by his hands alone, he lowered his head and kissed her eyes closed. He could feel her trembling in his arms. Her hands still held his wrists, and her fingers tightened when he brought his mouth to hers. His was patient, waiting until her lips softened and parted.

The kisses grew deeper, but slowly, now moister until she swayed against him. His fingers caressed, his mouth roamed. Firelight flickered over them in reds and golds, casting its own shadows. Raven could feel the heat from it through the silk she wore, but it was the glow inside of her which built and flamed hot.

Brand lowered his hands to her shoulders, gently massaging as he teased her lower lip with his teeth. Raven felt the gown slip down over her breasts, then cling briefly to her hips before it drifted to the floor. She started to protest, but he deepened the kiss. The thought spiraled away. Down the curve of her back, over the slight flare of her hips, he ran his hands. Then he picked her up in his arms. With her mind spinning, she sank into the mattress. When Brand joined her, the touch of his naked body against hers jolted her, bringing on a fresh surge of doubts and fears.

"Brandon, please, I..." The words were muffled, then died inside his mouth.

Easily, his hands caressed her, stroking without hurry. Somewhere in the back of her mind she knew he held himself under tight control. But her mind had relaxed, and her limbs were heavy. His mouth wandered to her throat, tasting, giving pleasure, arousing by slow, irresistible degrees. He worked her nipple with his thumb, and she moaned and moved against him. Brand allowed his mouth to journey downward, laying light, feathering kisses over the curve of her breast. Lightly, very lightly, he ran his tongue over the tip. Raven felt the heat between her thighs, and tangling her fingers in his hair, pressed him closer. She arched and shuddered not from fear but from passion.

Heat unlike anything she had ever known or imagined was building inside her. She was still aware of the flicker of the fire and candlelight on her closed lids, of the soft brush of linen sheets against her back, of the faint, pleasant smell of woodsmoke. But these sensations were dim, while her being seemed focused on the liquefying touch of his tongue over her skin, the feathery brush of his fingers on her thighs. Over the hiss of rain and fire, she heard him murmur her name, heard her own soft, mindless response.

Her breath quickened, and her mouth grew hungry. Suddenly desperate, she drew his face back to hers. She wrapped her arms around him tightly as the pressure of the kiss pushed her head deep into the pillow.

Brand lay across her, flesh to flesh, so that her breasts yielded to his chest. Raven could feel the light mat of his hair against her skin.

His hand lay on her stomach and drifted down as she moved under him. There was a flash of panic as he slid between her thighs, then her breath caught in a heady rush of pleasure. He was still patient, his fingers gentle and unhurried as they gradually increased her rhythm.

For Raven, there was no world beyond the firelit room, beyond the four-poster bed. His mouth took hers, his tongue probing deeply, then moving to her ear, her throat, her neck and back to her lips. All the while, his hands and fingers were taking her past all thought, past all reason.

Then he was on top of her, and she opened for him, ready to give, to receive. She was too steeped in wonder to comprehend his strict, unwavering control. She knew only that she wanted him and urged him to take her. There was a swift flash of pain, dulled by a pleasure too acute to be measured. She cried out, but the sound was muffled against his mouth, then all was lost on wave after wave of delight.

Chapter 11

With her head in the curve of Brand's shoulder, Raven watched the fire. Her hand lay over his heart. She could feel its quick, steady rhythm under her palm.

The room was quiet, and outside, the rain had slackened to a murmur. Raven knew she would remember this moment every time she lay listening to rain against windows. Brand's arm was under her, curled over her back with his hand loosely holding her arm. Since he had rolled from her and drawn her against his side, he had been silent. Raven thought he slept and was content to lie with him, watching the fire and listening to the rain. She shifted her head, wanting to look at him and found he wasn't asleep. She could see the sheen of his eyes as he stared at the ceiling. Raven lifted a hand to his cheek.

"I thought you were asleep."

Brand caught her hand and pressed it to his lips. "No, I..." Looking down at her, he broke off, then slowly brushed a tear from her lash with his thumb. "I hurt you."

"No." Raven shook her head. For a moment she buried her face in the curve of his neck, where she could feel his warmth, smell his scent. "Oh, no, you didn't hurt me. You made me feel wonderful. I feel...free." She looked up at him again and smiled. "Does that sound foolish?"

"No." Brand ran his fingers through the length of her hair, pushing it back when it would have hidden her face from him. Her skin was flushed. In her eyes he could see the reflected flames from the fire. "You're so beautiful."

She smiled again and kissed him. "I've always thought the same about you."

He laughed, drawing her closer. "Have you?"

She lay half across him, heated flesh to heated flesh. "Yes, I always thought you'd make a remarkably lovely girl, and I see by your sister's picture that I was right."

He lifted a brow. "Strange, I never realized the direction of your thoughts. Perhaps it's best I didn't."

Raven gave one of her low, rich chuckles and pressed her lips against the column of his throat. She loved the way his tones could become suddenly suavely British. "I'm sure you make a much better man."

"That's comforting," he said dryly as he began to stroke her back, "under the circumstances." His fingers lingered at her hip to caress.

"I'm sure I like you much better this way." Raven

kissed the side of his throat again, working her way to his ear. Under her breast she felt the sudden jump and scramble of his heartbeat. "Brandon..." She sighed, nuzzling his ear. "You're so good to me, so kind, so gentle."

She heard him groan before he rolled over, reversing their positions. His eyes were heated and intense and very green, reminding her of the moment he had held her like this on the plane. Now again her pulse began to hammer, but not with fear.

"Love isn't always kind, Raven," he said roughly. "It isn't always gentle."

His mouth came down on hers crushingly, urgently, as all the restraints he had put on himself snapped. There was no patience in him now, only passion. Where before he had taken her up calmly, easily, now he took her plummeting at a desperate velocity. Her mouth felt bruised and tender from his, yet she learned hunger incited hunger. Raven wanted more, and still more, so she caught him closer.

Demanding, possessing, he took his hands over her. "So long," she heard him mutter. "I've wanted you for so long." Then his teeth found the sensitive area of her neck, and she heard nothing. She plunged toward the heat and the dark.

Brand felt her give and respond and demand. He was nearly wild with need. He wanted to touch all of her, taste all of her. He was as desperate as a starving man and as ruthless. Where before, responding to her innocence, he had been cautious, now he took what he had wanted for too many years. She was his as he had dreamed she would be: soft and yielding, then soft and hungry beneath him.

He could hear her moan, feel the bite of her fingernails in his shoulders as he took his mouth down the curve of her breast. The skin of her stomach was smooth and quivered under his tongue. He slipped a hand between her thighs, and she strained against him so that he knew she was as desperate as he. Yet he wouldn't take her, not yet. He felt an impossible greed. His tongue moved to follow the path of his hands. All the years he'd wanted her, all the frustrated passion, burst out, catching them both in the explosion. Not knowing the paths, Raven went where he led her and learned that desire was deeper, stronger, than anything she had known possible.

He was pulling her down—down until the heat was too intense to bear. But she wanted more. His hands were rough, bruising her skin. But she craved no gentleness. She was steeped in passion too deep for escape. She called out for him, desperately, mindlessly, for him to take her. She knew there couldn't be more; they'd gone past all the rules. Pleasure could not be sharper; passion could not be darker than it was at that moment.

Then he was inside her, and everything that had gone before paled against the color and the heat.

His mouth was buried at her neck. From far off he heard her gasps for breath merge with his own. They moved together like lightning, so that he could no longer think. There was only Raven. All passion intensified, concentrated, until he thought he would go mad from it. The pain of it shot through him, then flowed from him, leaving him weak.

They lay still, with Brand over her, his face buried in her hair. His breathing was ragged, and he gave no thought to his weight as he relaxed completely. Beneath him Raven shuddered again and again with the release of passion. She gripped his shoulders tightly, not wanting him to move, not wanting to relinquish the unity. If he had shown her the tenderness and compassion of loving the first time, now he had shown her darker secrets.

A log fell in the grate, scattering sparks against the screen. Brand lifted his head and looked down at her. His eyes were heavy, still smoldering, as they lowered to her swollen mouth. He placed a soft kiss on them, then, shifting his weight, prepared to rise.

"No, don't go." Raven took his arm, sitting up as he did.

"Only to bank the fire."

Bringing her knees to her chest, Raven watched as Brand stacked the fire for the night. The light danced over his skin as she stared, entranced. The ripple of muscles was surprising in one so lean. She saw them in his shoulders, his back, his thighs. The passion in the cool, easygoing man was just as surprising, but she knew the feel of it now, just as she knew the feel of the muscles. He turned and looked at her with the fire leaping at his back. They studied each other, both dazed by what had passed between them. Then he shook his head.

"My God, Raven, I want you again."

She held her arms out to him.

* * *

There was a brilliant ribbon of sunlight across Raven's eyes. It was a warm, red haze. She allowed her lids to open slowly before turning to Brand.

He slept still, his breathing deep and even. She had to suppress the urge to brush his hair away from his face because she didn't want to wake him. Not yet. For the first time in her life she woke to look at her lover's face. She felt a warm, settled satisfaction.

He *is* beautiful, she thought, remembering how he had been faintly distressed to hear her say so the night before. *And I love him.* Raven almost said the words aloud as she let herself think them. I've always loved him, right from the beginning, all through the years in between—and even more now that we're together. But no mistakes this time. She closed her eyes tight on the sudden fear that he could walk out of her life again. *No demands, no pressures.* We'll just be together; that's all I need.

She dropped her eyes to his mouth. It had been tender in the night, she remembered, then hungry, almost brutal. She hadn't realized how badly he had wanted her, or she him, until the barriers had shattered. *Five years, five empty years!* Raven pushed the thought away. There was no yesterday, no tomorrow; only the present.

Suddenly she smiled, thinking of the enormous breakfasts he habitually ate. She would usually stumble into the kitchen for coffee as he was cleaning off a plate. Cooking wasn't her best thing, she mused, but it would be fun to surprise him. His arm was tossed around her waist, holding her against him so that their bodies had warmed each other even in sleep. Carefully Raven slipped out from under it. Padding to the closet, she found a robe, then left Brand sleeping to go downstairs.

The kitchen was washed in sunlight. Raven went straight to the percolator. First things first, she decided. Strangely, she was wide-awake, there was none of the drowsy fogginess she habitually used coffee to chase away. She felt vital, full of energy, very much the way she felt when finishing a live concert, she realized as she scooped out coffee. Perhaps there was a parallel. Raven fit the lid on the pot, then plugged it in. She had always felt that performing for an audience was a bit like making love: sharing yourself, opening your emotions, pulling down the barriers. That's what she had done with Brand. The thought made her smile, and she was singing as she rummaged about for a frying pan.

Upstairs, Brand stirred, reached for her and found her gone. He opened his eyes to see that the bed beside him was empty. Quickly he pushed himself up and scanned the room. The fire was still burning. It had been late when he had added the last logs. The drapes were open to the full strength of the sun. It spilled across the bed and onto the floor. Raven's nightgown lay where it had fallen the night before.

Not a dream, he told himself, tugging a hand through his hair. They'd been together last night, again and again until every ounce of energy had been drained. Then they had slept, still holding each other, still clinging. His eyes drifted to the empty pillow beside him again. *But where—where the devil is she now?* Feeling a quick flutter of panic, he rose, tugged on his jeans and went to find her.

Before Brand reached the bottom of the stairs, her voice drifted to him.

Every morning when I wake,
I'll see your eyes.
And there'll only be the love we make,
No more good-byes.

He recognized the song as the one he had teased her about weeks before when they had sat in his car in the hills above Los Angeles. The knot in his stomach untied itself. He walked down the hall, listening to the husky, morning quality of her voice, then paused in the doorway to watch her.

Her movements suited the song she sang: cheerful, happy. The kitchen was filled with morning noises and scents. There was the popping rhythm of the percolator as the coffee bubbled on the burner, the hiss and sizzle of the fat sausage she had frying in a cast-iron skillet, the clatter of crockery as she searched for a platter. Her hair was streaming down her back, still tumbled from the night, while the short terry robe she wore rode high up on her thighs as she stretched to reach the top shelf of a cupboard.

Raven stopped singing for a moment to swear good-naturedly about her lack of height. After managing to get a grip on the platter, she lowered her heels back to the floor and turned. She gave a gasp when she spotted Brand, dropped the fork she held and just managed to save the platter from following it.

"Brandon!" Raven circled her throat with her hand a moment and took a deep breath. "You scared me! I didn't hear you come down."

Brand didn't answer her smile. He didn't move but only looked at her. "I love you, Raven."

Her eyes widened, and her lips trembled open, then shut again. The words, she reminded herself, mean so many different things. It was important not to take a simple statement and deepen its meaning. Raven kept her voice calm as she stooped to pick up the fork. "I love you, too, Brandon."

He frowned at the top of her head, then at her back as she turned away to the sink. She turned on the tap to rinse off the fork. "You sound like my sister. I've already two of those; I don't need another."

Raven took her time. She turned off the tap, composed her face into a smile, then turned. "I don't think of you as a brother, Brandon." The tension at the back of her neck made it difficult to move calmly back to the cupboard for cups and saucers. "It isn't easy for me to tell you how I feel. I needed your support, your compassion. You helped me last night more than I can say."

"Now you make me sound like a bloody doctor. I said I love you, Raven." There was a snap of anger in the words this time. When Raven turned back to him, her eyes were eloquent.

"Brandon, you don't have to feel obligated..." She broke off as his eyes flared. Storming into the room, he flicked off the gas under the smoking sausage, then yanked the percolator cord from the wall. Coffee continued to pop for a few moments, then subsided weakly.

"Don't tell me what I have to do!" he shouted. "I know what I have to do." He grabbed her by the shoulders and shook her. "I *have* to love you. It's not an obligation, it's a fact, it's a demand, it's a terror."

"Brandon…"

"Shut up," he commanded. He pulled her close, trapping the dishes she held between them before he kissed her. She tasted the desperation, the temper. "Don't tell me you love me in that calm, steady voice." Brand lifted his head only to change the angle of the kiss. His mouth was hard and insistent before it parted from hers. "I need more than that from you, Raven, much more than that." His eyes blazed green into hers. "I'll have more, damn it!"

"Brandon." She was breathless, dizzy, then laughing. This was no dream. "The cup's digging a permanent hole in my chest. Please, let me put the dishes down." He said something fierce about the dishes, but she managed to pull away from him enough to put them on the counter. "Oh, Brandon!" Immediately Raven threw her arms around his neck. "You have more; you have everything. I was afraid—and a fool to be afraid—to tell you how much I love you." She placed her hands on his cheeks, holding his face away from her so that he could read what was in her eyes. "I love you, Brandon."

Quick and urgent, their lips came together. They clung still when he swept her up in his arms. "You'll have to do without your coffee for a while," he told her as she pressed a kiss to the curve of his neck. She only murmured an assent as he began to carry her down the hall.

"Too far," she whispered.

"Mmm?"

"The bedroom's much too far away."

Brand turned his head to grin at her. "Too far," he agreed, taking a sharp right into the music room. "Entirely too far." They sank together on a sofa. "How's this?" He slipped his hands beneath the robe to feel her skin.

"We've always worked well together here." Raven laughed into his eyes, running her fingers along the muscles of his shoulders. It was real, she thought triumphantly, kissing him again.

"The secret," Brand decided, then dug his teeth playfully into her neck, "is a strong melody."

"It's nothing without the proper lyric."

"Music doesn't always need words." He switched to the other side of her neck as his hand roamed to her breast.

"No," she agreed, finding that her own hands refused to be still. They journeyed down his back and up again. "But harmony—two strong notes coming together and giving a bit to each other."

"Melding," he murmured. "I'm big on melding." He loosened the belt of her robe.

"Oh, Brandon!" she exclaimed suddenly, remembering. "Mrs. Pengalley…she'll be here soon."

"This should certainly clinch her opinion of show people," he decided as his mouth found her breast.

"Oh, no, Brandon, stop!" She laughed and moaned and struggled.

"Can't," he said reasonably, trailing his lips back up to her throat. "Savage lust," he explained and bit her ear. "Uncontrollable. Besides," he said as he kissed her, then moved to her other ear, "it's Sunday, her day off."

"It is?" Raven's mind was too clouded to recall trivial things like days of the week. "Savage lust?" she repeated as he pushed the robe from her shoulders. "Really?"

"Absolutely. Shall I show you?"

"Oh, yes," she whispered and brought his mouth back to hers. "Please do."

A long time later Raven sat on the hearth rug and watched Brand stir up the fire. She had reheated the coffee and brought it in along with the sausages. Brand had pulled a sweater on with his jeans, but she still wore the short, terry robe. Holding a coffee cup in both hands, she yawned and thought that she had never felt so relaxed. She felt like a cat sitting in her square of sunlight, watching Brand fix a log onto snapping flames. He turned to find her smiling at him.

"What are you thinking?" He stretched out on the floor beside her.

"How happy I am." She handed him his coffee, leaning over to kiss him as he took it. It all seemed so simple, so right.

"How happy?" he demanded. He smiled at her over the rim of the cup.

"Oh, somewhere between ecstatic and delirious, I

think." She sought his hand with hers. Their fingers linked. "Bordering on rapturous."

"Just bordering on?" Brand asked with a sigh. "Well, we'll work on it." He shook his head, then kissed her hand. "Do you know you nearly drove me mad in this room yesterday?"

"Yesterday?" Raven tossed her hair back over her shoulder with a jerk of her head. "What are you talking about?"

"I don't suppose you'll ever realize just how arousing your voice is," he mused as he sipped his coffee and studied her face. "That might be part of the reason—that touch of innocence with a hell-smoked voice."

"I like that." Raven reached behind her to set down her empty cup. The movement loosened the tie of her robe, leaving it open to brush the curve of her breasts. "Do you want one of these sausages? They're probably awful."

Brand lifted his eyes from the smooth expanse of flesh that the shift of material had revealed. He shook his head again and laughed. "You make them sound irresistible."

"A starving man can't be picky," she pointed out. Raven plucked one with her fingers and handed it over. "They're probably greasy."

He lifted a brow at this but took a bite. "Aren't you going to have one?"

"No. I know better than to eat my own cooking." She handed him a napkin.

"We could go out to eat."

"Use your imagination," she suggested, resting her

hands on her knees. "Pretend you've already eaten. It always works for me."

"My imagination isn't as good as yours." Brand finished off the sausage. "Maybe if you tell me what I've had."

"An enormous heap of scrambled eggs," she decided, narrowing her eyes. "Five or six, at least. You really should watch your cholesterol. And three pieces of toast with that dreadful marmalade you pile on."

"You haven't tried it," he reminded her.

"I imagined I did," she explained patiently. "You also had five slices of bacon." She put a bit of censure in her voice, and he grinned.

"I've a healthy morning appetite."

"I don't see how you could eat another bite after all that. Coffee?" Raven reached for the pot.

"No, I imagine I've had enough."

She laughed and leaning over, linked her arms around his neck. "Did I really drive you mad, Brandon?" She found the taste of her own power delicious and sweet.

"Yes." He rubbed her nose with his. "First it was all but impossible to simply be in the same room with you, wanting you as I did. Then that song." He gave a quiet laugh, then drew back to look at her. "Music doesn't always soothe the savage beast. And then that damn album jacket. I had to be furious, or I'd have thrown you down on the rug then and there."

He saw puzzlement, then comprehension, dawn in her eyes. "Is that why you..." She stopped, and the smile grew slowly. Raven tilted her head and ran the tip of her tongue over her teeth. "I suppose that now that you've had your way with me, I won't drive you mad anymore."

"That's right." He kissed her lightly. "I can take you or leave you." Brand set down his empty cup, then ruffled her hair, amused by her wry expression. "It's noon," he said with a glance at the clock. "We'd best get to it if we're going to get any work done today. That novelty number we were toying with, the one for the second female lead—I'd an idea for that."

"Really?" Raven unhooked her hands from behind his neck. "What sort of idea?"

"We might bounce up the beat, a bit of early forties jive tempo, you know. It'd be a good contrast to the rest of the score."

"Hmmm, could be a good dance number." Raven slipped her hands under his sweater and ran them up his naked chest. She smiled gently at the look of surprise that flickered in his eyes. "We need a good dance number there."

"That's what I was thinking," Brand murmured. The move had surprised him, and the light touch of her fingers sent a dull thud of desire hammering in his stomach. He reached for her, but she rose and moved to the piano.

"Like this, then?" Raven played a few bars of the melody they had worked with, using the tempo he had suggested. "A little boogie-woogie?"

"Yes." He forced his attention to the bouncing, repetitive beat but found his blood beating with it. "That's the idea."

She looked back over her shoulder and smiled at him. "Then all we need are the lyrics." She experimented a moment longer, then went to the coffeepot. "Cute and catchy." Raven drank, smiling down at Brand. "With a chorus."

"Any ideas?"

"Yes." She set down the cup. "I have some ideas." Raven sat down beside him, facing him, and thoughtfully brushed the hair back from his forehead. "If they're going to cast Carly, as it appears they're going to do, we need something to suit that baby-doll voice of hers. Her songs should be a direct foil for Lauren's." She pressed her lips lightly to his ear. "Of course, the chorus could carry the meat of it." Again she slipped a hand under his sweater, letting her fingertips toy with the soft mat of hair on his chest. She slid her eyes up to his. "What do you think?"

Brand took her arm and pulled her against him, but she turned her head so that the kiss only brushed her cheek. "Raven," he said after a laughing moan. But when she trailed her finger down to his stomach, she felt him suck in air. Again he moaned her name and crushed her against him.

Raven tilted her head back for the kiss. It was deep and desperate, but when he would have urged her down, she shifted so that her body covered his. She buried her mouth at his neck and felt the pulse hammering against her lips. Her hands were still under his sweater so that she was aware of the heating of his skin. He tugged at her robe, but she only pressed harder against him, lodging the fabric between them. She nipped at the cord of his neck.

"Raven." His voice was low and husky. "For God's sake, let me touch you."

"Am I driving you mad, Brandon?" she murmured, nearly delirious with her own power. Before he could answer, she brought her lips to his and took her tongue deep into his mouth. Slowly she hiked up his sweater, feeling the shudders of his skin as she worked it over his chest and shoulders. Even as she tossed it aside, Raven began journeying down his chest, using her lips and tongue to taste him.

It was a new sensation for her: the knowledge that he was as vulnerable to her as she was to him. There was harmony between them and the mutual need to make the music real and full. Before, he had guided her, but now she was ready to experiment with her own skill. She wanted to toy with tempos, to take the lead. She wanted to flow *pianissimo,* savoring each touch, each taste. Now it was her turn to teach him as he had taught her.

His skin was hot under her tongue. He was moving beneath her, but the first wave of desperation had passed into a drugged pleasure. Her fingers weren't shy but rather sought curiously, stroking over him to find what excited, what pleased. His taste was something she knew now she would starve without. She could feel his fingers in her hair tightening as his passion built. As she had the night before, she sensed his control, but now the challenge of breaking it excited her.

His stomach was taut and tightened further when

she glided over it. She heard his breathing catch. Finding the snap to his jeans, she undid it, then began to tug them down over his hips. The rhythm was gathering speed.

Then her mouth was on his, ripping them both far beyond the gentle pace she had initiated. She was suddenly starving, trembling with the need. Pushing herself up, Raven let the robe fall from her shoulders. Her hair tumbled forward to drape her breasts.

"Touch me." Her eyes were heavy but locked in his. "Touch me now."

Brand's fingers tangled in her hair as they sought her flesh. When she would have swayed back down to him, he held her upright, wanting to watch the pleasure and passion on her face. Her eyes were blurred with it. The need built fast and was soon too great.

"Raven." There was desperate demand in his voice as he took her hips.

She let him guide her, then gave a sharp gasp of pleasure. Their bodies fused in a soaring rhythm, completely tuned to each other. Raven shuddered from the impact. Then, drained, she lowered herself until she lay prone on him. He brought his arms around her to hold her close as the two of them flowed from passion to contentment.

Tangled with him, fresh from loving in a room quiet and warm, Raven gave a long, contented sigh. "Brandon," she murmured, just wanting to hear the sound of his name.

"Hmm?" He stroked her hair, seemingly lost somewhere in a world between sleep and wakefulness.

"I never knew it could be like this."

"Neither did I."

Raven shifted until she could look at his face. "But you've been with so many women." She curled up at his side, preparing to rest her head in the curve of his shoulder.

Brand rose on his elbow, then tilted her face up to his. He studied her softly flushed cheeks, the swollen mouth and drowsy eyes. "I've never been in love with my lover before," he told her quietly.

For a moment there was silence. Then she smiled. "I'm glad. I suppose I've never been sure of that until now."

"Be sure of it." He kissed her, hard and quick and possessively.

She settled against him again but shivered, then laughed. "A few moments ago I'd have sworn I'd never be cold again."

Grinning, Brand reached for her robe. "I seriously doubt we'll get any work done unless you get dressed. In fact, I'd suggest unattractive clothes."

After tugging her arms through the sleeves, Raven put her hands on his shoulders. Her eyes were light and full of mischief. "Do I distract you, Brandon?"

"You might put it that way."

"I'll probably be tempted to try all the time, now that I know I can." Raven kissed him, then gave a quick shrug. "I won't be able to help myself."

"I'll hold you to that." Brand lifted a brow. "Would you like to start now?"

She gave his hair a sharp tug. "I don't think that's

very flattering. I'm going to go see about those unattractive clothes."

"Later," he said, pulling her back when she started to rise.

Raven laughed again, amazed with what she saw in his eyes. "Brandon, really!"

"Later," he said again and pressed her back gently to the floor.

Chapter 12

Summer came to Cornwall in stages. Cool mornings turned to warm afternoons that had bees humming outside the front windows. The stinging chill of the nights mellowed. The first scent of honeysuckle teased the air. Then the roses, lush wild roses, began to bloom. And all through the weeks the countryside blossomed, Raven felt that she, too, was blooming. She was loved.

Throughout her life, if anyone had asked her what one thing she wanted most, Raven would have answered, "To be loved." She had starved for it as a child, had hungered as an adolescent when she had been shuffled from town to town, never given the opportunity to form lasting friendships and affections. It was this need, in part, that had made her so successful as a performer. Raven was willing to let the audience love her. She never felt herself beyond their reach when she stood in the spotlight. And they knew it. The love she had gained from her audiences had filled an enormous need. It had filled her but had not satisfied her as much, she discovered, as Brand's love.

As the weeks passed, she forgot the demands and responsibilities of the performer and became more and more in tune with the woman. She had always known herself; it had been important early that she grasp an identity. But for the first time in her life Raven focused on her womanhood. She explored it, discovered it, enjoyed it.

Brand was demanding as a lover, not only in the physical sense but in an emotional one as well. He wanted her body, her heart, her thoughts, with no reservations. His need for an absolute commitment was the only shadow in the summery passing of days. Raven found it impossible not to hold parts of herself in reserve. She'd been hurt and knew how devastating pain could be when you loved without guard. Her mother had broken her heart too many times to count, with always a promise of happiness after the severest blow. Raven had learned to cope with that, to guard against it to some extent.

She had loved Brand before, naively perhaps, but totally. When he had walked out of her life, Raven had thought she would never be whole again. For five years she had insulated herself against the men who had touched her life. They could be friends—loving friends—but never lovers. The wounds had healed, but the scar had been a constant reminder to be careful. She had promised herself that no man would ever hurt her as Brand Carstairs had. And Raven discovered the vow she had made still held true. He was the only man who would ever have the power to hurt her. That realization was enough to both exhilarate and frighten.

There was no doubt that he had awakened her physically. Her fears had been swept away by the tides of love. Raven found that in this aspect of their relationship she could indeed give herself to Brand unreservedly. Knowing she could arouse him strengthened her growing confidence as a woman. She learned her passions were as strong and sensitive as his. She had kept them restricted far too long. If Brand could heat her blood with a look, Raven was aware he was just as susceptible to her. There was nothing of the cool, British reserve in his lovemaking; she thought of him as all Irish then, stormy and passionate.

One morning he woke her at dawn by strewing the bed with wild rosebuds. The following evening he surprised her with iced champagne while she bathed in the ancient footed tub. At night he could be brutally passionate, waking and taking her with a desperate urgency that allowed no time for surprise, protest or response. At times he appeared deliriously happy; at others she would catch him studying her with an odd, searching expression.

Raven loved him, but she could not yet bring herself to trust him completely. They both knew it, and they both avoided speaking of it.

Seated next to Brand at the piano, Raven experimented with chords for the opening bars of a duet. "I really think a minor mode with a raised seventh." She frowned thoughtfully. "I imagine a lot of strings here, a big orchestration of violins and cellos." She played more, hearing the imagined arrangement rather than the solitary piano. "What do you think?" Raven turned her head to find Brand looking down at her.

"Go ahead," he suggested, drawing on a cigarette. "Play the lot."

She began, only to have him interrupt during a bridge. "No." He shook his head. "That part doesn't fit."

"That was your part," she reminded him with a grin.

"Genius is obliged to correct itself," he returned, and Raven gave an unladylike snort. He looked down his very straight British nose. "Had you a comment, then?"

"Who, me? I never interrupt genius."

"Wise," he said and turned back to spread his own fingers over the keys. "Like this." Brand played the same melody from the beginning, only altering a few notes on the bridge section.

"Did you change something?"

"I realize your inferior ear might not detect the subtlety," he began. She jammed her elbow into his ribs. "Well said," he murmured, rubbing the spot. "Shall we try again?"

"I love it when you're dignified, Brandon."

"Really?" He lifted an inquiring brow. "Now, where was I?"

"You were about to demonstrate the first movement from Tchaikovsky's Second Symphony."

"Ah." Nodding, Brand turned back to the keys. He

ran through the difficult movement with a fluid skill that had Raven shaking her head.

"Show-off," she accused when he finished with a flourish.

"You're just jealous."

With a sigh she lifted her shoulders. "Unfortunately, you're right."

Brand laughed and put his hand palm to palm with hers. "I have the advantage in spread."

Raven studied her small, narrow-boned hand. "It's a good thing I didn't want to be a concert pianist."

"Beautiful hands," Brand told her, making one of his sudden and completely natural romantic gestures by lifting her fingers to his lips. "I'm quite helplessly in love with them."

"Brandon." Disarmed, Raven could only look at him. A tremble of warmth shot up her spine.

"They always smell of that lotion you have in the little white pot on the dresser."

"I didn't think you'd notice something like that." She shivered in response when his lips brushed the inside of her wrist.

"There's nothing about you I don't notice." He kissed her other wrist. "You like your bath too hot, and you leave your shoes in the most unexpected places. And you always keep time with your left foot." Brand looked back up at her, keeping one hand entwined with hers while he reached up with the other to brush the hair from her shoulder. "And when I touch you like this, your eyes go to smoke." He ran a fingertip gently over the point of her breast and watched her irises darken and cloud. Very slowly he leaned over and touched his lips to hers. Lazily he ran his finger back and forth until her nipple was taut and straining against the fabric of her blouse.

Her mouth was soft and opened willingly. Raven tilted her head back, inviting him to take more. Currents of pleasure were already racing along her skin. Brand drew her closer, one hand lingering at her breast.

"I can feel your bones melt," he murmured. His mouth grew hungrier, his hand more insistent. "It drives me crazy." His fingers drifted from her breast to the top button of her blouse. Even as he loosened it, the phone shrilled from the table across the room. He swore, and Raven gave a laugh and hugged him.

"Never mind, love," she said on a deep breath. "I'll remind you where you left off this time, too." Slipping out of his arms, she crossed the room to answer. "Hello."

"Hello, I'd like to speak with Brandon Carstairs, please," a voice said.

Raven smiled at the musical lilt in the voice and wondered vaguely how one of Brand's fans had gotten access to his number. "Mr. Carstairs is quite busy at the moment." She grinned over at him and got both a grin and a nod of approval before he crossed to her. He began to distract her by kissing her neck.

"Would you ask him to call his mother when he's free?"

"I beg your pardon?" Raven stifled a giggle and tried to struggle out of Brand's arms.

"His mother, dear," the voice repeated. "Ask him to

call his mother when he has a minute, won't you? He has the number."

"Oh, please, Mrs. Carstairs, wait! I'm sorry." Wide-eyed, she looked up at Brand. "Brandon's right here. Your mother," Raven said in a horrified whisper that had him grinning again. Still holding her firmly to his side, he accepted the receiver.

"Hullo, Mum." Brand kissed the top of Raven's head, then chuckled. "Yes, I was busy. I was kissing a beautiful woman I'm madly in love with." The color rising in Raven's cheeks had him laughing. "No, no, it's all right, love, I intend to get back to it. How are you? And the rest?"

Raven nudged herself free of Brand's arm. "I'll make some tea," she said quietly, then slipped from the room.

Mrs. Pengalley had left the kitchen spotlessly clean, and Raven spent some time puttering around it aimlessly while the kettle heated on the stove. She found herself suddenly hungry, then remembered that she and Brand had worked straight through lunch. She got out the bread, deciding to make buttered toast fingers to serve with the tea.

Afternoon tea was one of Brand's rituals, and Raven had grown fond of it. She enjoyed the late afternoon breaks in front of the fireplace with tea and biscuits or scones or buttered toast. They could be any two people then, Raven mused, two people sitting in front of a fireplace having unimportant conversations. The kettle sang out, and she moved to switch off the flame.

Raven went about the mechanical domestic tasks of brewing tea and buttering toast, but her thoughts kept

drifting back to Brand. There had been such effortless affection in his voice when he had spoken to his
mother, such relaxed love. And Raven had felt a swift
flash of envy. It was something she had experienced
throughout childhood and adolescence, but she hadn't
expected to feel it again. Raven reminded herself she
was twenty-five and no longer a child.

The chores soothed her. She loaded the tray and
started back down the hall with her feelings more settled. When she heard Brand's voice, she hesitated, not
wanting to interrupt his conversation. But the weight
of the tray outbalanced her sense of propriety.

He was sunk into one of the chairs by the fire when
Raven entered. With a smile he gestured her over so
that she crossed the room and set the tray on the table
beside him. "I will, Mum, perhaps next month. Give
everyone my love." He paused and smiled again, taking Raven's hand. "She's got big gray eyes, the same
color as the dove Shawn kept in the coop on the roof.
Yes, I'll tell her. Bye, Mum. I love you."

Hanging up, Brand glanced at the ladened tea tray,
then up at Raven. "You've been busy."

She crouched down and began pouring. "I discovered I was starving." She watched with the usual shake
of her head as he added milk to his tea. That was one
English habit Raven knew she would never comprehend. She took her own plain.

"My mother says to tell you you've a lovely voice
over the phone." Brand picked up a toast finger and
bit into it.

"You didn't have to tell her you'd been kissing me,"

Raven mumbled, faintly embarrassed. Brand laughed, and she glared at him.

"Mum knows I have a habit of kissing women," he explained gravely. "She probably knows I've occasionally done a bit more than that, but we haven't discussed that particular aspect of my life for some time." He took another bite of toast, studying Raven's face. "She wants to meet you. If the score keeps going along at this pace, I thought we might drive up to London next month."

"I'm not used to families, Brandon," she said. Raven reached for her cup, but he placed his hand over hers, waiting until she looked back up at him.

"They're easy people, Raven. They're important to me. You're important to me. I want them to know you."

She felt her stomach tighten, and lowered her eyes.

"Raven." Brand gave a short, exasperated sigh. "When are you going to talk to me?"

She couldn't pretend not to understand him. She could only shake her head and avoid the subject a little while longer. The time when they would have to return to California and face reality would come soon enough. "Please, tell me about your family. It might help me get used to being confronted with all of them if I know a bit more than I've read in the gossip columns." Raven smiled. Her eyes asked him to smile back and not to probe. Not yet.

Brand struggled with a sense of frustration but gave in. He could give her a little more time. "I'm the oldest of five." He gestured toward the mantel. "Michael's the distinguished-looking one with the pretty blond wife. He's a solicitor." Brand smiled, remembering the pleasure it had given him to send his brother to a good university. He'd been the first Carstairs to receive that sort of education. "There was nothing distinguished about him at all as a boy," Brand remarked. "He liked to give anyone within reach a bloody nose."

"Sounds like a good lawyer," Raven observed dryly. "Please go on."

"Alison's next. She graduated from Oxford at the top of her class." He watched Raven glance up at the photo of the fragile, lovely blonde. "An amazing brain," Brand continued, smiling. "She does something incomprehensible with computers and has a particular fondness for rowdy rugby matches. That's where she met her husband."

Raven shook her head, trying to imagine the delicate-looking woman shouting at rugby games or programming sophisticated computers. "I suppose your other brother's a physicist."

"No, Shawn's a veterinarian." Affection slipped into Brand's voice.

"Your favorite?"

He tilted his head as he reached for more tea. "If one has a favorite among brothers and sisters, I suppose so. He's simply one of the nicest people I know. He's incapable of hurting anyone. As a boy he was the one who always found the bird with the broken wing or the dog with a sore paw. You know the type."

Raven didn't, but she murmured something and continued to sip at her tea. Brand's family was beginning to fascinate her. Somehow, she had thought that people raised in the same house under the same circumstances would be more the same. These people seemed remarkably diverse. "And your other sister?"

"Moray." He grinned. "She's in school yet, claims she's going into finance or drama. Or perhaps," he added, "anthropology. She's undecided."

"How old is she?"

"Eighteen. She thinks your records are smashing, by the way, and had them all the last time I was home."

"I believe I'll like her," Raven decided. She let her gaze sweep the mantel again. "Your parents must be very proud of all of you. What does your father do?"

"He's a carpenter." Brand wondered if she was aware of the wistful look in her eyes. "He still works six days a week, even though he knows money isn't a problem anymore. He has a great deal of pride." He paused a moment, stirring his tea, his eyes on Raven. "Mum still hangs sheets out on a line, even though I bought her a perfectly good dryer ten years ago. That's the sort of people they are."

"You're very lucky," Raven told him and rose to wander about the room.

"Yes, I know that." Brand watched her move around the room with her quick, nervous stride. "Though I doubt I thought a great deal about it while I was growing up. It's very easy to take it all for granted. It must have been very difficult for you."

Raven lifted her shoulders, then let them fall. "I survived." Walking to the window, she looked out on the cliffs and the sea. "Let's go for a walk, Brandon. It's so lovely out."

He rose and walked to her. Taking her by the shoulders, Brand turned her around to face him. "There's more to life than surviving, Raven."

"I survived intact," she told him. "Not everyone does."

"Raven, I know you call home twice a week, but you never tell me anything about it." He gave her a quick, caring shake. "Talk to me."

"Not about that, not now, not here." She slipped her arms around him and pressed her cheek to his chest. "I don't want anything to touch us here—nothing from the past, nothing from tomorrow. Oh, there's so much ugliness, Brandon, so many responsibilities. I want time. Is that so wrong?" She held him tighter, suddenly possessive. "Can't this be our fantasy, Brandon? That there isn't anybody but us? Just for a little while."

She heard him sigh as his lips brushed the crown of her head. "For a little while, Raven. But fantasies have to end, and I want the reality, too."

Raven lifted her face, then framed his with her hands. "Like Joe in the script," she reflected and smiled. "He finds his reality in the end, doesn't he?"

"Yes." Brand bent to kiss her and found himself lingering over it longer than he had intended. "Proving dreams come true," he murmured.

"But I'm not a dream, Brandon." She took both of his hands in hers while her eyes smiled at him. "And you've already brought me to life."

"And without magic."

Raven lifted a brow. "That depends on your point of view," she countered. "I still feel the magic." Slowly she lifted his hand to the neckline of her blouse. "I think you were here when we left off."

"So I was." He loosened the next button, watching her face. "What about that walk?"

"Walk? In all that rain?" Raven glanced over to the sun-filled window. "No." Shaking her head, she looked back at Brand. "I think we'd better stay inside until it blows over."

He ran his finger down to the next button, smiling at her while he toyed with it. "You're probably right."

Chapter 13

Mrs. Pengalley made it a point to clean the music room first whenever Raven and Brand left her alone in the house. It was here they spent all their time working— if what show people did could be considered work. She had her own opinion on that. She gathered up the cups, as she always did, and sniffed them. Tea. Now and again she had sniffed wine and occasionally some bourbon, but she was forced to admit that Mr. Carstairs didn't seem to live up to the reputation of heavy drinking that show people had. Mrs. Pengalley was the smallest bit disappointed.

They lived quietly, too. She had been sure when Brand had notified her to expect him to be in residence for three months that he would have plans to entertain. Mrs. Pengalley knew what sort of entertainment show business people went in for. She had waited for the fancy cars to start arriving, the fancy people in their outrageous clothes. She had told Mr. Pengalley it was just a matter of time.

But no one had come, no one at all. There had been no disgraceful parties to clean up after. There had only been Mr. Carstairs and the young girl with the big gray eyes who sang as pretty as you please. But of course, Mrs. Pengalley reminded herself, she was in *that* business, too.

Mrs. Pengalley walked over to shake the wrinkles from the drapes at the side window. From there she could see Raven and Brand walking along the cliffs. Always in each other's pockets, she mused and sniffed to prevent herself from smiling at them. She snapped the drape back into place and began dusting off the furniture.

And how was a body supposed to give anything a proper dusting, she wanted to know, when they were always leaving their papers with the chicken scratchings on them all over everywhere? Picking up a piece of staff paper, Mrs. Pengalley scowled down at the lines and notes. She couldn't make head nor tail out of the notations; she scanned the words instead.

Loving you is no dream/I need you here to hold on to/Wanting you is everything/Come back to me.

She clucked her tongue and set the paper back down. Fine song, that one, she thought, resuming her dusting. Doesn't even rhyme.

Outside, the wind from the sea was strong, and Brand slipped his arm around Raven's shoulders. Turning her swiftly to face him, he bent her backward and gave

her a long, lingering kiss. She gripped his shoulders
for balance, then stared at him when his mouth lifted.

"What," she began and let out a shaky breath, "was
that for?"

"For Mrs. Pengalley," he answered easily. "She's
peeking out the music room window."

"Brandon, you're terrible." His mouth came down
to hers again. Her halfhearted protest turned into total
response. With a quiet sound of pleasure, Brand deepened the kiss and dragged her closer to him. Raven
could feel the heat of the sun on her skin even as the
sea breeze cooled it. The wind brought them the scent
of honeysuckle and roses.

"That," he murmured as his mouth brushed over her
cheeks, "was for me."

"Have any other friends?" Raven asked.

Laughing, Brand gave her a quick hug and released
her. "I suppose we've given her enough to cluck her
tongue over today."

"So that's what you want me for." Raven tossed her
head. "Shock value."

"Among other things."

They wandered to the sea wall, for some moments
looking out in comfortable silence. Raven liked the
cliffs with their harsh faces and sheer, dizzying drop.
She liked the constant, boiling noise of the sea, the
screaming of the gulls.

The score was all but completed, with only a few
minor loose ends and a bit of polishing to be done. Copies of completed numbers had been sent back to California. Raven knew they were drawing out a job that

could be finished quickly. She had her own reasons for procrastinating, though she wasn't wholly certain of Brand's. She didn't want to break the spell.

Raven wasn't sure precisely what Brand wanted from her because she hadn't permitted him to tell her yet. There were things, she knew, that had to be settled between them—things that could be avoided for the time being while they both simply let themselves be consumed by love. But the time would come when they would have to deal with the everyday business of living.

Would their work be a problem? That was one of the questions Raven refused to ask herself. Or if she asked it, she refused to answer. Commitments went with their profession, time-consuming commitments that made it difficult to establish any sort of a normal life. And there was so little privacy. Every detail of their relationship would be explored in the press. There would be pictures and stories, true and fabricated. The worst kind, Raven mused, were those with a bit of both. All of this, she realized, could be handled with hard work and determination if the love was strong enough. She had no doubt theirs was, but she had other doubts.

Would she ever be able to rid herself of the nagging fear that he might leave her again? The memory of the hurt kept her from giving herself to Brand completely. And her feelings of responsibility to her mother created yet another barrier. This was something she had always refused to share with anyone. She couldn't even bring herself to share it with the person she cared for most in the world. Years before, she had made a decision to control her own life, promising herself she would never depend too heavily on anything or anyone. Too often she had watched her mother relinquish control and lose.

If she could have found a way, Raven would have prolonged the summer. But more and more, the knowledge that the idyll was nearly at an end intruded into her thoughts. The prelude to fantasy was over. She hoped the fantasy would become a reality.

Brand watched Raven's face as she leaned her elbows on the rough stone wall and looked out to sea. There was a faraway look in her eyes that bothered him. He wanted to reach her, but their time alone together was slipping by rapidly. A cloud slid across the sun for a moment, and the light shifted and dimmed. He heard Raven sigh.

"What are you thinking?" he demanded, catching her flying hair in his hand.

"That of all the places I've ever been, this is the best." Raven tilted her head to smile up at him but didn't alter her position against the wall. "Julie and I took a break in Monaco once, and I was sure it was the most beautiful spot on earth. Now I know it's the second."

"I knew you'd love it if I could ever get you here," Brand mused, still toying with the ends of her hair. "I had some bad moments thinking you'd refuse. I'm not at all sure I could have come up with an alternate plan."

"Plan?" Raven's forehead puckered over the word. "I don't know what you mean. What plan?"

"To get you here, where we could be alone."

Raven straightened away from the wall but continued looking out to sea. "I thought we came here to write a score."

"Yes." Brand watched the flight of a bird as it swooped down over the waves. "The timing of that was rather handy."

"Handy?" Raven felt the knot start in her stomach. The clouds shifted over the sun again.

"I doubt you'd have agreed to work with me again if the project hadn't been so tempting," he said. Brand frowned up at a passing cloud. "You certainly wouldn't have agreed to live with me."

"So you dangled the score in front of my nose like a meaty bone?"

"Of course not. I wanted to work with you on the project the moment it was offered to me. It was all just a matter of timing, really."

"Timing and planning," she said softly. "Like a chess game. Julie's right; I've never been any good at strategy." Raven turned away, but Brand caught her arm before she could retreat.

"Raven?"

"How could you?" She whirled back to face him. Her eyes were dark and hot, her cheeks flushed with fury. Brand narrowed his eyes and studied her.

"How could I what?" he asked coolly, releasing her arm.

"How could you use the score to trick me into coming here?" She dragged at her hair as the wind blew it into her face.

"I'd have used anything to get you back," Brand said. "And I didn't trick you, Raven. I told you nothing but the truth."

"Part of the truth," she continued.

"Perhaps," he agreed. "We're both rather good at that, aren't we?" He didn't touch her, but the look he gave her became more direct. "Why are you angry? Because I love you or because I made you realize you love me?"

"Nobody *makes* me do anything!" She balled her hands into fists as she whirled away. "Oh, I detest being maneuvered. I run my own life, make my own decisions."

"I don't believe I've made any for you."

"No, you just led me gently along by the nose until I *chose* what was best for myself." Raven turned back again, and now her voice was low and vibrant with anger. "Why couldn't you have been honest with me?"

"You wouldn't have let me anywhere near you if I'd been completely honest. I had experience with you before, remember?"

Raven's eyes blazed. "Don't tell me what I would've done, Brandon. You're not inside my head."

"No, you've never let me in there." He pulled out a cigarette, cupped his hands around a match and lit it. Before speaking, he took a long, contemplative drag. "We'll say I wasn't in the mood to be taking chances, then. Will that suit you?"

His cool, careless tone fanned her fury. "You had no right!" she tossed at him. "You had no right to arrange my life this way. Who said I had to play by your rules, Brandon? When did you decide I was incapable of planning for myself?"

"If you'd like to be treated as a rational adult, perhaps you should behave as one," he suggested in a deceptively mild tone. "At the moment I'd say you're being remarkably childish. I didn't bring you here under false pretenses, Raven. There was a score to be written, and this was a quiet place to do it. It was also a place I felt you'd have the chance to get used to being with me again. I wanted you back."

"*You* felt. *You* wanted!" Raven tossed back her hair. "How incredibly selfish! What about *my* feelings? Do you think you can just pop in and out of my life at your convenience?"

"As I remember, I was pushed out."

"You left me!" The tears came from nowhere and blinded her. "Nothing's ever hurt me like that before. Nothing!" Tears of hurt sprang to her eyes. "I'll be damned if you'll do it to me again. You went away without a word!"

"You mightn't have liked the words I wanted to say." Brand tossed the stub of his cigarette over the wall. "You weren't the only one who was hurt that night. How the hell else could I be rational unless I put some distance between us? I couldn't have given you the time you seemed to need if I'd stayed anywhere near you."

"Time?" Raven repeated as thoughts trembled and raced through her mind. "You gave me time?"

"You were a child when I left," he said shortly. "I'd hoped you'd be a woman when I came back."

"You had hoped…" Her voice trailed off into an astonished whisper. "Are you telling me you stayed away, giving me a chance to—to grow up?"

"I didn't see I had any choice." Brand dug his hands into his pockets as his brows came together.

"Didn't you?" She remembered her despair at his

going, the emptiness of the years. "And of course, why should you have given me one? You simply took it upon yourself to decide for me."

"It wasn't a matter of deciding." He turned away from her, knowing he was losing his grip on his temper. "It was a matter of keeping sane. I simply couldn't stay near you and not have you."

"So you stayed away for five years, then suddenly reappeared, using my music as an excuse to lure me into bed. You didn't give a damn about the quality of *Fantasy*. You just used it—and the talent and sweat of the performers—for your own selfish ends."

"That," he said in a deadly calm voice, "is beyond contempt." Turning, he walked away. Within moments Raven heard the roar of an engine over the sound of the sea.

She stood, watching the car speed down the lane. If she had meant to deal a savage blow, she had succeeded. The shock of her own words burned in her throat. She shut her eyes tightly.

Even with her eyes closed, she could see clearly the look of fury on Brand's face before he had walked away. Raven ran a shaking hand through her hair. Her head was throbbing with the aftereffects of temper. Slowly she opened her eyes and stared out at the choppy green sea.

Everything we've had these past weeks was all part of some master plan, she thought. Even as she stood, the anger drained out of her, leaving only the weight of unhappiness.

She resented the fact that Brand had secretly placed a hand on the reins of her life, resented that he had offered her the biggest opportunity in her career as a step in drawing her to him. And yet... Raven shook her head in frustration. Confused and miserable, she turned to walk back to the house.

Mrs. Pengalley met her at the music room door. "There's a call for you, miss, from California." She had watched the argument from the window with a healthy curiosity. Now, however, the look in the gray eyes set her maternal instincts quivering. She repressed an urge to smooth down Raven's hair. "I'll make you some tea," she said.

Raven walked to the phone and lifted the receiver. "Yes, hello."

"Raven, it's Julie."

"Julie." Raven sank down in a chair. She blinked back fresh tears at the sound of the familiar voice. "Back from the isles of Greece?"

"I've been back for a couple weeks, Raven."

Of course. She should have known that. "Yes, all right. What's happened?"

"Karter contacted me because he wasn't able to reach you this morning. Some trouble on the line or something."

"Has she left again?" Raven's voice was dull.

"Apparently she left last night. She didn't go very far." Hearing the hesitation in Julie's voice, Raven felt the usual tired acceptance sharpen into apprehension.

"Julie?" Words dried up, and she waited.

"There was an accident, Raven. You'd better come home."

Raven closed her eyes. "Is she dead?"

"No, but it's not good, Raven. I hate having to tell you over the phone this way. The housekeeper said Brand wasn't there."

"No." Raven opened her eyes and looked vaguely around the room. "No, Brandon isn't here." She managed to snap herself back. "How bad, Julie? Is she in the hospital?"

Julie hesitated again, then spoke quietly. "She's not going to make it, Raven. I'm sorry. Karter says hours at best."

"Oh, God." Raven had lived with the fear all her life, yet it still came as a shock. She looked around the room again a little desperately, trying to orient herself.

"I know there's no good way to tell you this, Raven, but I wish I could find a better one."

"What?" She brought herself back again with an enormous effort. "No, I'm all right. I'll leave right away."

"Shall I meet you and Brand at the airport?"

The question drifted through Raven's mind. "No. No, I'll go straight to the hospital. Where is she?"

"St. Catherine's, intensive care."

"Tell Dr. Karter I'll be there as soon as I can. Julie…"

"Yes?"

"Stay with her."

"Of course I will. I'll be here."

Raven hung up and sat staring at the silent phone.

Mrs. Pengalley came back into the room carrying a cup of tea. She took one look at Raven's white face and set it aside. Without speaking, she went to the liquor cabinet and took out the brandy. After pouring out two fingers, she pressed the snifter on Raven.

"Here now, miss, you drink this." The Cornish burr was brisk.

Raven's eyes shifted to her. "What?"

"Drink up, there's a girl."

She obeyed as Mrs. Pengalley lifted the glass to her lips. Instantly Raven sucked in her breath at the unexpected strength of the liquor. She took another sip, then let out a shaky sigh.

"Thank you." She lifted her eyes to Mrs. Pengalley again. "That's better."

"Brandy has its uses," the housekeeper said righteously.

Raven rose, trying to put her thoughts in order. There were things to be done and no time to do them. "Mrs. Pengalley, I have to go back to America right away. Could you pack some things for me while I call the airport?"

"Aye." She studied Raven shrewdly. "He's gone off to cool his heels, you know. They all do that. But he'll be back soon enough."

Realizing Mrs. Pengalley spoke of Brand, Raven dragged a hand through her hair. "I'm not altogether certain of that. If Brandon's not back by the time I have to go to the airport, would you ask Mr. Pengalley to drive me? I know it's an inconvenience, but it's terribly important."

"If that's what you want." Mrs. Pengalley sniffed. Young people, she thought, always flying off the handle. "I'll pack your things, then."

"Thank you." Raven glanced around the music room, then picked up the phone.

An hour later she hesitated at the foot of the stairs. Everything seemed to have happened at once. She willed Brand to return, but there was no sign of his car in the driveway. Raven struggled over writing a note but could think of nothing to say on paper that could make up for the words she had thrown at him. And how could she say in a few brief lines that her mother was dying and she had to go to her?

Yet there wasn't time to wait until he returned. She knew she couldn't risk it. Frantically she pulled a note pad from her purse. "Brandon," she wrote quickly, "I had to go. I'm needed at home. Please, forgive me. I love you, Raven."

Dashing back into the music room, she propped the note against the sheet of staff paper on top of the pile on the piano. Then, hurrying from the room, she grabbed her suitcases and ran outside. Mr. Pengalley was waiting in his serviceable sedan to drive her to the airport.

Chapter 14

Five days passed before Raven began thinking clearly again. Karter had been right about there only being a matter of hours. Raven had had to deal not only with grief but also with an unreasonable guilt that she hadn't been in time. The demand of details saved her from giving in to the urge to sink into self-pity and self-re-buke. She wondered once, during those first crushing hours, if that was why people tied so many traditions and complications to death: to keep from falling into total despair.

She was grateful that Karter handled the police himself in a way that ensured the details would be kept out of the papers.

After the first busy days there was nothing left but to accept that the woman she had loved and despised was gone. There was no more she could do. The disease had beaten them, just as surely as if it had been a cancer. Gradually she began to accept her mother's death as the result of a long, debilitating illness. She didn't cry, knowing she had already mourned, knowing it was time to put away the unhappiness. She had never had control of her mother's life; she needed the strength to maintain control of her own.

A dozen times during those days Raven phoned the house in Cornwall. There was never an answer. She could almost hear the hollow, echoing sounds of the ring through the empty rooms. More than once she considered simply getting on a plane and going back, but she always pushed the thought aside. He wouldn't be there waiting for her.

Where could he be? she wondered again and again. *Where would he have gone? He hasn't forgiven me.* And worse, she thought again and again, *he'll never forgive me.*

After hanging up the phone a last time, Raven looked at herself in her bedroom mirror. She was pale. The color that had drained from her face five days ago in Cornwall had never completely returned. There was too much of a helpless look about her. Raven shook her head and grabbed her blusher. Borrowed color, she decided, was better than none at all. She had to start somewhere.

Yes, she thought again, still holding the sable brush against her cheek. I've got to start somewhere. Turning away from the mirror, Raven again picked up the phone.

Thirty minutes later she came downstairs wearing a black silk dress. She had twisted her hair up and was setting a plain, stiff-brimmed black hat over it as she stepped into the hall.

"Raven?" Julie came out of the office. "Are you going out?"

"Yes, if I can find that little envelope bag and my car keys. I think they're inside it." She was already poking into the hall closet.

"Are you all right?"

Raven drew her head from the closet and met Julie's look. "I'm better," she answered, knowing Julie wouldn't be satisfied with a clichéd reply. "The lecture you gave me after the funeral, about not blaming myself? I'm trying to put it into practice."

"It wasn't a lecture," Julie countered. "It was simply a statement of facts. You did everything you could do to help your mother; you couldn't have done any more."

Raven sighed before she could stop herself. "I did everything I knew how to do, and I suppose that's the same thing." She shook off the mood as she shut the closet door. "I *am* better, Julie, and I'm going to be fine." She smiled, then, glimpsing a movement, looked beyond Julie's shoulder. Wayne stepped out of the office. "Hello, Wayne, I didn't know you were here."

He moved past Julie. "Well, I can definitely approve of that dress," he greeted her.

"And so you should," Raven returned dryly. "You charged me enough for it."

"Don't be a philistine, darling. Art has no price." He flicked a finger over the shoulder of the dress. "Where are you off to?"

"Alphonso's. I'm meeting Henderson for lunch."

Wayne touched Raven's cheek with a fingertip. "A bit heavy on the blush," he commented.

"I'm tired of looking pale. Don't fuss." She placed a hand on each of his cheeks, urging him to bend so that she could kiss him. "You've been a rock, Wayne. I haven't told you how much I appreciate your being here the last few days."

"I needed to escape from the office."

"I adore you." She lowered her hands to meet his arms and squeezed briefly. "Now, stop worrying about me." Raven shot a look past his shoulder to Julie. "You, too. I'm meeting Henderson to talk over plans for a new tour."

"New tour?" Julie frowned. "Raven, you've been working nonstop for over six months. The album, the tour, the score." She paused. "After all of this you need a break."

"After all this the thing I need least is a break," Raven corrected. "I want to work."

"Then take a sabbatical," Julie insisted. "A few months back you were talking about finding a mountain cabin in Colorado, remember?"

"Yes." Raven smiled and shook her head. "I was going to write and be rustic, wasn't I? Get away from the glitter-glamour and into the woods." Raven grinned, recalling the conversation. "You said something about not being interested in anything more rustic than a margarita at poolside."

Julie lifted a thin, arched brow. "I've changed my mind. I'm going shopping for hiking boots."

Wayne's comment was a dubious *"hmmm."*

Raven smiled. "You're sweet," she said to Julie as she kissed her cheek. "But it isn't necessary. I need to do something that takes energy, physical energy. I'm going to talk to Henderson about a tour of Australia. My records do very well there."

"If you'd just talk to Brand..." Julie began, but Raven cut her off.

"I've tried to reach him; I can't." There was something final and flat in the statement. "Obviously he doesn't want to talk to me. I'm not at all sure I blame him."

"He's in love with you," Wayne said from behind her. Raven turned and met the look. "A few thousand people saw the sparks flying the night of your concert in New York."

"Yes, he loves me, and I love him. It doesn't seem to be enough, and I can't quite figure out why. No, please." She took his hand, pressing it between both of hers. "I have to get my mind off it all for a while. I feel as if I had been having a lovely picnic and got caught in a landslide. The bruises are still a bit sore. I could use some good news," she added, glancing from one of them to the other, "if the two of you are ever going to decide to tell me."

Raven watched as Wayne and Julie exchanged glances. She grinned, enjoying what she saw. "I've been noticing a few sparks myself. Isn't this a rather sudden situation?"

"Very," Wayne agreed, smiling at Julie over Raven's head. "It's only been going on for about six years."

"Six years!" Raven's brows shot up in amazement.

"I didn't choose to be one of a horde," Wayne said mildly, lighting one of his elegant cigarettes.

"And I always thought he was in love with you," Julie stated, letting her gaze drift from Raven to Wayne.

"With *me?*" Raven laughed spontaneously for the first time in days.

"I fail to see the humour in that," Wayne remarked from behind a nimbus of smoke. "I'm considered by many to be rather attractive."

"Oh, you are," she agreed, then giggled and kissed his cheek. "Madly so. But I can't believe anyone could think you were in love with me. You've always dated those rather alarmingly beautiful models with their sculpted faces and long legs."

"I don't think we need bring all that up at the moment," Wayne retorted.

"It's all right." Julie smiled sweetly and tucked her hair behind her ear. "I haven't any problem with Wayne's checkered past."

"When did all this happen, please?" Amused, Raven cut into their exchange. "I turn my back for a few weeks, and I find my two best friends making calf's eyes at each other."

"I've never made calf's eyes at anyone," Wayne remonstrated, horrified. "Smoldering glances, perhaps." He lifted his rakishly scarred brow.

"When?" Raven repeated.

"I looked up from my deck chair the first morning out on the cruise," Julie began, "and who do you suppose is sauntering toward me in a perfectly cut Mediterranean white suit?"

"Really?" Raven eyed Wayne dubiously. "I'm not certain whether I'm surprised or impressed."

"It seemed like a good opportunity," he explained, tapping his expensive ashes into a nearby dish, "if I could corner her before she charmed some shipping tycoon or handy sailor."

"I believe I charmed a shipping tycoon a few years ago," Julie remarked lazily. "And as to the sailor..."

"Nevertheless," Wayne went on, shooting her a glance. "I decided a cruise was a very good place to begin winning her over. It was," he remarked, "remarkably simple."

"Oh?" Julie's left brow arched. "Really?"

Wayne tapped out his cigarette, then moved over to gather her in his arms. "A piece of cake," he added carelessly. "Of course, women habitually find me irresistible."

"It would be safer if they stopped doing so. I might be tempted to wring their necks," Julie cooed, winding her arms around his neck.

"The woman's going to be a trial to live with." Wayne kissed her as though he'd decided to make the best of it.

"I can see you two are going to be perfectly miserable together. I'm so sorry." Walking over, Raven slipped an arm around each of them. "You will let me give you the wedding?" she began, then stopped. "That is, are you having a wedding?"

"Absolutely," Wayne told her. "We don't trust each other enough for anything less encumbering." He gave Julie a flashing grin that inexplicably made Raven want to weep.

Raven hugged them both again fiercely. "I needed to hear something like this right now. I'm going to leave you alone. I imagine you can entertain yourselves while I'm gone. Can I tell Henderson?" she asked. "Or is it a secret?"

"You can tell him," Julie said, watching as Raven adjusted her hat in the hall mirror. "We're planning on taking the plunge next week."

Raven's eyes darted up to Julie's in the mirror. "My, you two move fast, don't you?"

"When it's right, it's right."

Raven smiled in quick agreement. "Yes, I suppose it is. There's probably champagne in the refrigerator, isn't there, Julie?" She turned away from the mirror. "We can have a celebration drink when I get back. I'll just be a couple of hours."

"Raven." Julie stopped her as she headed for the door. Raven looked curiously over her shoulder. "Your purse." Smiling, Julie retrieved it from a nearby table. "You won't forget to eat, will you?" she demanded as she placed it in Raven's hand.

"I won't forget to eat," Raven assured her, then dashed through the door.

Within the hour Raven was seated in the glassed-in terrace room of Alphonso's toying with a plate of scampi. There were at least a dozen people patronizing the restaurant whom she knew personally. A series of greetings had been exchanged before she had been able to tuck herself into a corner table.

The room was an elaborate jungle, with exotic plants and flowers growing everywhere. The sun shining through the glass and greenery gave the terrace a warmth and glow. The floor was a cool ceramic tile, and there was a constant trickle of water from a fountain at the far end of the room. Raven enjoyed the casual elegance, the wicker accessories and the pungent aromas of food and flowers that filled the place. Now, however, she gave little attention to the terrace room as she spoke with her agent.

Henderson was a big, burly man whom Raven had always thought resembled a logjammer rather than the smooth, savvy agent he was. He had a light red thatch of hair that curled thinly on top of his head and bright merry blue eyes that she knew could sharpen to a sword's point. There was a friendly smattering of freckles over his broad, flat-featured face.

He could smile and look genial and none too bright. It was one of his best weapons. Raven knew Henderson was as sharp as they came, and when necessary, he could be hard as nails. He was fond of her, not only because she made him so rich, but because she never resented having done so. He couldn't say the same about all of his clients.

Now Henderson allowed Raven to ramble on about ideas for a new tour, Australia, New Zealand, promotion for the new album that was already shooting up the charts a week after its release. He ate his veal steadily, washing it down with heavy red wine while Raven talked and sipped occasionally from her glass of white wine.

He noticed she made no mention of the *Fantasy* score or of her time in Cornwall. The last progress report he had received from her had indicated the project was all but completed. The conversations he had had with Jarett had been enthusiastic. Lauren Chase had approved each one of her numbers, and the choreography had begun. The score seemed to be falling into place without a hitch.

So Henderson had been surprised when Raven had returned alone so abruptly from Cornwall. He had expected her to phone him when the score was completed, then to take the week or two she had indicated she and Brand wanted to relax and do nothing. But here she was, back early and without Brand.

She chattered nervously, darting from one topic to another. Henderson didn't interrupt, only now and again making some noncommittal sounds as he attended to his meal. Raven talked nonstop for fifteen minutes, then began to wind down. Henderson waited, then took a long swallow of wine.

"Well, now," he said, patting his lips with a white linen napkin. "I don't imagine there should be any problem setting up an Australian tour." His voice suited his looks.

"Good." Raven pushed the scampi around on her plate. She realized she had talked herself out. Spearing a bit of shrimp, she ate absently.

"While it's being set up, you could take yourself a nice little vacation somewhere."

Raven's brows rose. "No, I thought you could book me on the talk-show circuit, dig up some guest shots here and there."

"Could do that, too," he said genially. "After you take a few weeks off."

"I want gigs, not a few weeks off." Her brows lowered suspiciously. "Have you been talking to Julie?"

He looked surprised. "No, about what?"

"Nothing." Raven shook her head, then smiled. "Gigs, Henderson."

"You've lost weight, you know," he pointed out and shoveled in some more veal. "It shows in your face. Eat."

Raven gave an exasperated sigh and applied herself to her lunch. "Why does everyone treat me like a dimwitted child?" she mumbled, swallowing shrimp. "I'm going to start being temperamental and hard to get along with until I get some star treatment." Henderson said something quick and rude between mouthfuls which she ignored. "What about Jerry Michaels? Didn't I hear he was lining up a variety special for the fall? You could get me on that."

"Simplest thing in the world," Henderson agreed. "He'd be thrilled to have you."

"Well?"

"Well what?"

"Henderson." Resolutely, Raven pushed her plate aside. "Are you going to book me on the Jerry Michaels show?"

"No." He poured more wine into his glass. The sun shot through it, casting a red shadow on the tablecloth.

"Why?" Annoyance crept into Raven's tone.

"It's not for you." Henderson lifted a hand, palm up,

as she began to argue. "I know who's producing the show, Raven. It's not for you."

She subsided a bit huffily, but she subsided. His instincts were the best in the field. "All right, forget the Michaels gig. What, then?"

"Want some dessert?"

"No, just coffee."

He signaled the waiter, then, after ordering blueberry cheesecake for himself and coffee for both of them, he settled back in his chair. "What about *Fantasy?*"

Raven twirled her wineglass between her fingers. "It's finished," she said flatly.

"And?"

"And?" she repeated, looking up. His merry blue eyes were narrowed. "It's finished," she said again. "Or essentially finished. I can't foresee any problem with the final details. Brandon or his agent will get in touch with you if there are, I'm sure."

"Jarett will probably need the two of you off and on during the filming," Henderson said mildly. "I wouldn't consider myself finished with it for a while yet."

Raven frowned into the pale golden liquid in her glass. "Yes, you're right, of course. I hadn't thought about it. Well…" She shook her head and pushed the wine away. "I'll deal with that when the times comes."

"How'd it go?"

She looked at Henderson levelly, but her thoughts drifted. "We wrote some of the best music either one of us has ever done. That I'm sure of. We work remarkably well together. I was surprised."

"You didn't think you would?" Henderson eyed the blueberry cheesecake the waiter set in front of him.

"No, I didn't think we would. Thank you," this to the waiter before she looked at Henderson again. "But everything else apart, we did work well together."

"You'd worked well together before," he pointed out. "'Clouds and Rain.'" He saw her frown but continued smoothly. "Did you know sales on that have picked up again after your New York concert? You got yourself a lot of free press, too."

"Yes," Raven mumbled into her coffee. "I'm sure we did."

"I've had a lot of questions thrown at me during the last weeks," he continued blandly, even when her eyes lifted and narrowed. "From the inside," he said with a smile, "as well as the press. I was at a nice little soiree just last week. You and Brand were the main topic of conversation."

"As I said, we work well together." Raven set down her cup. "Brandon was right; we are good for each other artistically."

"And personally?" Henderson took a generous bite of cheesecake.

"Well." Raven lifted a brow. "You certainly get to the point."

"That's all right, you don't have to answer me." He swallowed the cake, then broke off another piece. "You can tell *him*."

"Who?"

"Brand," Henderson answered easily and added cream to his coffee. "He just walked in."

Raven whirled around in her chair. Instantly her eyes locked on Brand's. With the contact came a wild, swift surge of joy. Her first instinct was to spring from the table and run to him. Indeed, she had pushed the chair back, preparing to do so, when the expression on his face cut through her initial spring of delight. It was ice-cold fury. Raven sat where she was, watching as he weaved his way through the crowded restaurant toward her. There were casual greetings along the way which he ignored. Raven heard the room fall silent.

He reached her without speaking once or taking his eyes from her. Raven's desire to hold out a hand to him was also overcome. She thought he might strike it away. The look in his eyes had her blood beating uneasily. Henderson might not have been sitting two feet away.

"Let's go."

"Go?" Raven repeated dumbly.

"Now." Brand took her hand and yanked her to her feet. She might have winced at the unexpected pressure if she hadn't been so shocked by it.

"Brandon…"

"Now," he repeated. He began to walk away, dragging her behind him. Raven could feel the eyes following them. Shock, delight, anxiety all faded into temper.

"Let go of me!" she demanded in a harsh undertone. "What's the matter with you? You can't drag me around like this." She bumped into a lunching comedian, then skirted around him with a mumbled apology as Brand continued to stalk away with her hand in his. "Brandon, stop this! I will not be dragged out of a public restaurant."

He halted then and turned so that their faces were very close. "Would you prefer that I say what I have to say to you here and now?" His voice was clear and cool in the dead silence of the room. It was very easy to see the violence of temper just beneath the surface. Raven could feel it in the grip of his hand on hers. They were spotlighted again, she thought fleetingly, but hardly in the manner in which they had been in New York. She took a deep breath.

"No." Raven struggled for dignity and kept her voice lowered. "But there isn't any need to make a scene, Brandon."

"Oh, I'm in the mood for a scene, Raven," he tossed back in fluid British tones that carried well. "I'm in the mood for a bloody beaut of a scene."

Before she could comment, Brand turned away again and propelled her out of the restaurant. There was a Mercedes at the curb directly outside. He shoved her inside it, slamming the door behind her.

Raven straightened in the seat, whipping her head around as he opened the other door. "Oh, you're going to get one," she promised and ripped off her hat to throw it furiously into the back seat. "How *dare* you..."

"Shut up. I mean it." Brand turned to her as she started to speak again. "Just shut up until we get where we're going, otherwise I might be tempted to strangle you here and be done with it."

He shot away from the curb, and Raven flopped back against her seat. I'll shut up, all right, she thought on wave after wave of anger. I'll shut up. It'll give me time to think through exactly what I have to say.

Chapter 15

By the time Brand stopped the car in front of the Bel-Air, Raven felt she had her speech well in order. As he climbed out of his side, she climbed out of hers, then turned to face him on the sidewalk. But before she could speak, he had her arm in a tight grip and was pulling her toward the entrance.

"I told you not to drag me."

"And I told you to shut up." He brushed past the doorman and into the lobby. Raven was forced into an undignified half-trot in order to keep up with his long-legged stride.

"I will *not* be spoken to like that," she fumed and gave her arm an unsuccessful jerk. "I will *not* be carted through a hotel lobby like a piece of baggage."

"I'm tired of playing it your way." Brand turned, grabbing both of her shoulders and dragging her against him. His fingers bit into her skin and shocked her into silence. "My game now, my rules."

His mouth came down hard on hers. It was a kiss of rage. His teeth scraped across her lips, forcing them open so that he could plunder and seek. He held her bruisingly close, as if daring her to struggle.

When Brand pulled away, he stared at her for a long, silent moment, then swore quickly, fiercely. Turning, he pulled her to the elevators.

Though she was no longer certain if it was fear or anger, Raven was trembling with emotion as they took the silent ride up. Brand could feel the throbbing pulse as he held her arm. He swore again, pungently, but she didn't glance at him. As the doors slid open, he pulled her into the hall and toward the penthouse.

There were no words exchanged between them as he slid the key into the lock. He released her arm as he pushed the door open. Without protest, Raven walked inside. She moved to the center of the room.

The suite was elegant, even lush, in a dignified, old-fashioned style with a small bricked fireplace and a good, thick carpet. Behind her the door slammed— a final sound—and she heard Brand toss the key with a faint metallic jingle onto a table. Raven drew a breath and turned around.

"Brandon…"

"No, I'll do the talking first." He crossed to her, his eyes locked on hers. "My rules, remember?"

"Yes." She lifted her chin. Her arm throbbed faintly where his fingers had dug into it. "I remember."

"First rule, no more bits and pieces. I won't have you

closing parts of yourself off from me anymore." They were standing close. Now that the first dazed shock and surprise were passing, Raven noticed signs of strain and fatigue on his face. His words were spilling out so quickly, she couldn't interrupt. "You did the same thing to me five years ago, but then we weren't lovers. You were always holding out, never willing to trust."

"No." She shook her head, scrambling for some defense. "No, that's not true."

"Yes, it's true," he countered and took her by the shoulders again. "Did you tell me about your mother all those years ago? Or how you felt, what you were going through? Did you bring me into your life enough to let me help you, or at least comfort you?"

This was not what she had expected from him. Raven could only press her hand to her temple and shake her head again. "No, it wasn't something..."

"Wasn't something you wanted to share with me." He dropped her arms and stepped away from her. "Yes, I know." His voice was low and furious again as he pulled out a cigarette. He knew he had to do something with his hands or he'd hurt her again. He watched as she unconsciously nursed her arm where he had gripped her. "And this time, Raven, would you have told me anything about it if it hadn't been for the nightmare? If you hadn't been half asleep and frightened, would you have told me, trusted me?"

"I don't know." She made a small sound of confusion. "My mother had nothing to do with you."

Brand hurled the cigarette away before he lit it. "How can you say that to me? How can you stand there and say that to me?" He took a step toward her, then checked himself and stalked to the bar. "Damn you, Raven," he said under his breath. He poured bourbon and drank. "Maybe I should have stayed away," he managed in a calmer tone. "You'd already tossed me out of your life five years ago."

"*I* tossed you out?" This time her voice rose. "You walked out on me. You left me flat because I wouldn't be your lover." Raven walked over to the bar and leaned her palms on it. "You walked out of my house and out of my life, and the only word I had from you was what I read in the paper. It didn't take you long to find other women—several other women."

"I found as many as I could," Brand agreed and drank again. "As quickly as I could. I used women, booze, gambling—anything—to try to get you out of my system." He studied the dregs of liquor in his glass and added thoughtfully, "It didn't work." He set the glass down and looked at her again. "Which is why I knew I had to be patient with you."

Raven's eyes were still dark with hurt. "Don't talk to me about tossing you out."

"That's exactly what you did." Brand grabbed her wrist as she turned to swirl away from him. He held her still, the narrow, mahogany bar between them. "We were alone, remember? Julie was away for a few days."

Raven kept her eyes level. "I remember perfectly."

"Do you?" He arched a brow. Both his eyes and voice were cool again. "There might be a few things you don't remember. When I came to the house that night I was going to ask you to marry me."

Raven could feel every thought, every emotion, pour out of her body. She could only stare at him.

"Surprised?" Brand released her wrist and again reached in his pocket for a cigarette. "Apparently we have two differing perspectives on that night. I *loved* you." The words were an accusation that kept her speechless. "And God help me, all those weeks we were together I was faithful to you. I never touched another woman." He lit the cigarette, and as the end flared, Raven heard him say softly, "I nearly went mad."

"You never told me." Her voice was weak and shaken. Her eyes were huge gray orbs. "You never once said you loved me."

"You kept backing off," he retorted. "And I knew you were innocent and afraid, though I didn't know why." He gave her a long, steady look. "It would have made quite a lot of difference if I had, but you didn't trust me."

"Oh, Brandon."

"That night," he went on, "you were so warm, and the house was so quiet. I could feel how much you wanted me. It drove me crazy. Good God, I was trying to be gentle, patient, when the need for you was all but destroying me." He ran a tense hand through his hair. "And you were giving, melting, everywhere I touched you. And then—then you were struggling like some terrified child, pushing at me as if I'd tried to kill you, telling me not to touch you. You said you couldn't bear to have me touch you."

He looked back at her, but his eyes were no longer

cool. "You're the only woman who's ever been able to hurt me like that."

"Brandon." Raven shut her eyes. "I was only twenty, and there were so many things…"

"Yes, I know now; I didn't know then." His tone was flat. "Though there really weren't so many changes this time around." Raven opened her eyes and started to speak, but he shook his head. "No, not yet. I've not finished. I stayed away to give you time, as I told you before. I didn't see any other way. I could hardly stay, kicking my heels in L.A., waiting for you to make up your mind. I didn't know how long I'd stay away, but during those five years I concentrated on my career. So did you."

Brand paused, spreading his long, elegant hands on the surface of the bar. "Looking back, I suppose that's all for the best. You needed to establish yourself, and I had a surge of productivity. When I started reading about you regularly in the gossip columns I knew it was time to come back." He watched her mouth fall open at that, and her eyes heat. "Get as mad as you damn well like when I've finished," he said shortly. "But don't interrupt."

Raven turned away to search for control. "All right, go on," she managed and faced him again.

"I came to the States without any real plan, except to see you. The solid idea fell into my lap by way of *Fantasy* when I was in New York. I used the score to get you back," he said simply and without apology. "When I stood up in that recording booth watching you again, I knew I'd have used anything, but the score did nicely." He pushed his empty glass aside with his fingertip. "I wasn't lying about wanting to work with you again for professional reasons or about feeling you were particularly right for *Fantasy*. But I would have if it had been necessary. So perhaps you weren't so far wrong about what you said on the cliffs that day." He moved from the bar to the window. "Of course, there was a bit more to it in my mind than merely getting you to bed."

Raven felt her throat burn. "Brandon." She swallowed and shut her eyes. "I've never been more ashamed of anything in my life than what I said to you. Anger is hardly an excuse, but I'd hoped—I'd hoped you'd forgive me."

Brand turned his head and studied her a moment. "Perhaps if you hadn't left, it would have been easier."

"I had to. I told you in the note..."

"What note?" His voice sharpened as he turned to face her.

"The note." Raven was uncertain whether to step forward or back. "I left it on the piano with the music."

"I didn't see any note. I didn't see anything but that you were gone." He let out a long breath. "I dumped all the music into a briefcase. I didn't notice a note."

"Julie called only a little while after you'd left to tell me about the accident."

His eyes shot back to hers again. "What accident?"

Raven stared at him.

"Your mother?" he said, reading it in her eyes.

"Yes. She'd had an accident. I had to get back right away."

He jammed his hands into his pockets. "Why didn't you wait for me?"

"I wanted to; I couldn't." Raven laced her fingers together to prevent her hands from fluttering. "Dr. Karter said it would only be a matter of hours. As it was…" She paused and turned away. "I was too late, anyway."

Brand felt the anger drain from him. "I'm sorry. I didn't know."

Raven didn't know why the simple, quiet statement should bring on the tears she hadn't shed before. They blinded her eyes and clogged her throat so that speech was impossible.

"I went a bit crazy when I got back to the house and found you'd packed and gone." Brand spoke wearily now. "I don't know exactly what I did at first; afterwards I got roaring drunk. The next morning I dumped all the music together, packed some things and took off for the States.

"I stopped off for a couple of days in New York, trying to sort things out. It seems I spend a great deal of time running after you. It's difficult on the pride. In New York I came up with a dozen very logical, very valid reasons why I should go back to England and forget you. But there was one very small, very basic point I couldn't argue aside." He looked at her again. Her back was to him, her head bent so that with her hair pulled up he could see the slender length of her neck. "I love you, Raven."

"Brandon." Raven turned her tear-drenched face toward him. She blinked at the prisms of light that blinded her, then shook her head quickly when she saw him make a move to come to her. "No, please don't. I won't be able to talk if you touch me." She drew in a deep breath, brushing the tears away with her finger-tips. "I've been very wrong; I have to tell you."

He stood away from her, though impatience was beginning to simmer through him again. "I had my say," he agreed. "I suppose you should have yours."

"All those years ago," she began. "All those years ago there were things I couldn't say, things I couldn't even understand because I was so—dazzled by everything. My career, the fame, the money, the perpetual spotlight." The words came quickly, and her voice grew stronger with them. "Everything happened at once; there didn't seem to be any time to get used to it all. Suddenly I was in love with Brandon Carstairs." She laughed and brushed at fresh tears. "*The* Brandon Carstairs. You have to understand, one minute you were an image, a name on a record, and the next you were a man, and I loved you."

Raven moistened her lips, moving to stare from the window as Brand had. "And my mother—my mother was my responsibility, Brandon. I've felt that always, and it isn't something that can be changed overnight. You were the genuine knight on a charger. I couldn't—wouldn't talk to you about that part of my life. I was afraid, and I was never sure of you. You never told me you loved me, Brandon."

"I was terrified of you," he murmured, "of what I was feeling for you. You were the first." He shrugged. "But you were always pulling back from me. Always putting up No Trespassing signs whenever I started to get close."

"You always seemed to want so much." She hugged

her arms. "Even this time, in Cornwall, when we were so close. It didn't seem to be enough. I always felt you were waiting for more."

"You still put up the signs, Raven." She turned, and his eyes locked on hers. "Your body isn't enough. That isn't what I waited five years for."

"Love should be enough," she tossed back, suddenly angry and confused.

"No." Brand shook his head, cutting her off. "It isn't enough. I want a great deal more than that." He waited a moment, watching the range of expressions on her face. "I want your trust, without conditions, without exceptions. I want a commitment, a total one. It's all or nothing this time, Raven."

She backed away. "You can't own me, Brandon."

A quick flash of fury shot into his eyes. "Damn it, I don't want to own you, but I want you to belong to me. Don't you know there's a difference?"

Raven stared at him for a full minute. She dropped her arms, no longer cold. The tension that had begun to creep up the back of her neck vanished. "I didn't," she said softly. "I should have."

Slowly she crossed to him. She was vividly aware of every detail of his face: the dark, expressive brows drawn together now with thought, the blue-green eyes steady but with the spark of temper, the faint touch of mauve beneath them that told her he'd lost sleep. It came to her then that she loved him more as a woman than she had as a girl. A woman could love without fear, without restrictions. Raven lifted her fingertip to his cheek as if to smooth away the tension.

Then they were locked in each other's arms, mouth to mouth. His hands went to her hair, scattering pins until it tumbled free around them. He murmured something she had no need to understand, then plunged deep again into her mouth. Hurriedly, impatiently, they began to undress each other. No words were needed. They sought only touch, to give, to fulfill.

His fingers fumbled with the zipper of her dress, making him swear and her laugh breathlessly until he pulled her with him to the rug. Then, somehow, they were flesh to flesh. Raven could feel the shudders racing through him to match her own as they touched. His mouth was no more greedy than hers, his hands no less demanding. Their fire blazed clean and bright. Need erupted in them both so that she pulled him to her, desperate to have him, frantic to give.

Raw pleasure shot through her, rocking her again and again as she moved with him. His face was buried in her hair, his body damp to her touch. Air was forcing its way from her lungs in moans and gasps as they took each other higher and faster. Then the urgency passed, and a sweetness took its place.

Time lost all meaning as they lay together. Neither moved nor spoke. Tensions and angers, ecstasies and desperations, had all passed. All that was left was a soft contentment. She could feel his breath move lightly against her neck.

"Brandon," Raven murmured, letting her lips brush his skin.

"Hmm?"

"I think I still had something to say, but it's slipped my mind." She gave a low laugh.

Brand lifted his head and grinned. "Maybe it'll come back to you. Probably wasn't important."

"You're right, I'm sure." She smiled, touching his cheek. "It had something to do with loving you beyond sanity or some such thing and wanting more than anything in the world to belong to you. Nothing important."

Brand lowered his mouth to hers and nipped at her still tender lip. "You were distracted," he mused, seeking her breast with his fingertip.

Raven ran her hands down his back. "I was in a bit of a hurry."

"This time…" He began to taste her neck and shoulder. "This time we'll slow down the tempo. A bit more orchestration, don't you think?" His fingers slid gently and teasingly over the point of her breast.

"Yes, quite a bit more orchestration. Brandon…" Her words were lost on a sound of pleasure as his tongue found her ear. "Once more, with feeling," she whispered.

* * * * *

Sullivan's Woman

Chapter 1

Cassidy waited. Mrs. Sommerson tossed a third rejected dress into her arms.

"Simply won't do," the woman muttered and scowled at a midnight-blue linen. After a moment's consideration this, too, was dumped into the pile over Cassidy's arms. Valiantly Cassidy held on to her patience.

After three months as a sales clerk in The Best Boutique, she felt she'd learned patience, but it hadn't been easy. Dutifully she followed the solid bulk of Mrs. Sommerson to another display of dresses. After twenty-seven minutes of standing around like a clothes rack, Cassidy thought, shifting the weight on her arms, her hard-earned patience was sorely strained.

"I'll try these," Mrs. Sommerson finally announced and marched back to the changing room. Mumbling only a little, Cassidy began to replace unsuitable dresses.

She jammed a loose hairpin into her scalp in irritation. Julia Wilson, The Best's owner, was a stickler for neatness. No hair was allowed to tumble over the shoulders of her clerks. Neat, orderly and unimaginative, Cassidy concluded, and wrinkled her nose at the midnight-blue linen. It was unfortunate that Cassidy was disorganized, imaginative, and not altogether neat. Her hair seemed to epitomize her personality. There were shades from delicate blond to rich brown melding into a tone like gold in an old painting. It was long and heavy and protested against the confines of pins by continuously slipping through them. Like Cassie herself, it was unruly and stubborn yet soft and fascinating.

It had been the appeal of Cassidy's slightly unconventional looks that had prompted her hiring. Experience had not been among her qualifications. Julia Wilson had recognized a potential advertisement for her merchandise and knew that Cassidy's long, supple body would set off the bold colors and styles of her more adventurous line. The face was undoubtedly a plus, too. Julia hadn't been certain it was a beautiful face, but she'd known it was striking. Cassidy's features were sharp and angular, undeniably aristocratic. Her brows arched over long, lidded eyes that seemed oversized in her narrow face and were a surprising violet.

Julia had seen Cassidy's face, figure and her well-pitched voice as references but had insisted on having her pin up her hair. With it down around her shoulders, it lent a distressingly wanton quality to the aristocratic features. She was pleased with Cassidy's youth, with her intelligence and with her energy. Soon after hiring her, however, Julia had discovered she was not as pliable as her age had suggested. She had, Julia felt, an unfortunate tendency to forget her place and become overly friendly with the customers. More than once, she'd come upon Cassidy as she asked customers impertinent questions or gave unwarranted advice. From time to time her smile suggested she was enjoying some private joke. And often, far too often, she daydreamed. Julia had begun to have serious doubts about Cassidy St. John's suitability.

After returning Mrs. Sommerson's rejected choices to their proper place, Cassidy took up her post by the changing room. From inside she could hear the faint rustle of materials. Idle, her mind did what it invariably did when given the opportunity. It drifted back to the manuscript that lay spread over her desk in her apartment. Waiting.

As far back as memory took her, writing had been her dream. For four years of college she had studied the craft seriously. At nineteen she'd been left without family and with little money. She had continued to work her way through college in various odd jobs while learning the discipline and art of her chosen profession. Between her education and employment, Cassidy had been left with meager snatches of free time. Even these had been set aside for work on her first novel.

To Cassidy writing was not a career but a vocation. Her entire life had been guided toward it, leaving her room for few other attachments. People fascinated her, but there were few with whom she was deeply involved. She wrote of complex relationships, but her knowledge of them came almost entirely secondhand. What gave her work quality and depth were her sharp talent for observation and her surprising depth of emotion. For the greater part of her life, her emotions had found their release in her work.

Now, a full year after graduation, she continued to take odd jobs to pay the rent. Her first manuscript worked its way from publishing house to publishing house while her second came slowly to life.

As Mrs. Sommerson opened the door of the changing room, Cassidy's mind was deep into the reworking of a dramatic scene. Seeing her standing with proper handmaidenly reserve, Mrs. Sommerson nodded approvingly. She preened ever so slightly.

"This should do nicely. Don't you agree?"

Mrs. Sommerson's choice was a flaming-red silk. The color, Cassidy noted, accented her florid complexion but was an attractively sharp contrast to her fluffy black mane of hair. The dress might have been more appropriate if Mrs. Sommerson had been a few pounds lighter, but Cassidy saw possibilities.

"You'll draw eyes, Mrs. Sommerson," she announced after a moment's deliberation. With the proper accessories, she decided, Mrs. Sommerson might very likely look regal. The silk, however, strained over her ample hips. A sterner girdle, Cassidy diagnosed, or a larger dress. "I think we have this in the next size," she murmured, thinking aloud.

"I beg your pardon?"

Preoccupied, Cassidy failed to note the dangerous arch of Mrs. Sommerson's brows. "The next size," she repeated helpfully. "This one's a bit snug through the hips. The next size up should fit you perfectly."

"This is my size, young woman." Mrs. Sommerson's bosom lifted then fell. It was an awe-inspiring movement.

Deep into solving the accessory problem, Cassidy smiled and nodded. "A splashy gold necklace, I should think." She tapped her fingertip against her bottom lip. "Just let me find your size."

"This," Mrs. Sommerson stated in a tone that arrested Cassidy's full attention, "*is* my size." Indignation seethed in every syllable. Recognizing her mistake, Cassidy felt a sinking sensation in her stomach.

Whoops, she said silently then pulled her scattered wits together. Before she could begin soothing Mrs. Sommerson's ruffled ego, Julia stepped from behind her.

"A stunning choice, Mrs. Sommerson," she stated in her well-modulated contralto. With a noncommittal smile, she glanced from her customer to her clerk then back again. "Is there a problem?"

"This young woman…" Mrs. Sommerson heaved another deep breath. "Insists I've made a mistake in my size."

"Oh, no, ma'am," Cassidy protested, but subsided when Julia arched a penciled brow in her direction.

"I'm certain what Miss St. John meant to say was that this particular style is cut a bit oddly. The sizes simply do not run true."

I should've thought of that, Cassidy admitted to herself.

"Well." Mrs. Sommerson sniffed and eyed Cassidy

with disapproval. "She might have said so, rather than suggesting that *I* was a larger size. Really, Julia." She turned back to the changing room. "You should train your staff better."

Cassidy's eyes kindled and grew dark at the tone. She watched the seams of the red silk protest against Mrs. Sommerson's generous posterior. The quick glare from Julia had her swallowing retorts.

"I'll fetch the dress myself, Mrs. Sommerson," Julia soothed, slipping her personable smile back into place. "I'm certain it will be perfect for you. Wait for me in my office, Cassidy," she added in an undertone before gliding off.

With a sinking heart, Cassidy watched Julia's retreat. She recognized the tone all too well. Three months, she mused, then sighed. Oh, well. With one backward glance at Mrs. Sommerson, she moved down the narrow hallway and into Julia's small, smartly decorated office.

She surveyed the square, windowless room, then chose a tiny, straight-backed, bronze cushioned chair. It was here, she remembered, I was hired. And it's here I'll be fired. She jammed another rebellious pin into place and scowled. In a few minutes she'll walk in, lift her left brow and sit behind her perfectly beautiful rosewood desk. She'll look at me a moment, gently clear her throat and begin.

"Cassidy, you're a lovely girl, but your heart isn't in your work."

"Mrs. Wilson," Cassidy imagined herself saying, "Mrs. Sommerson can't wear a size fourteen. I was—"

"Of course not." Cassidy pictured Julia interrupting her with a patient smile. "I wouldn't dream of selling her one, but—" here Cassidy envisioned Julia lifting up one slender, rose-tipped finger for emphasis "—we must allow her illusions *and* her vanity. Tact and diplomacy are essential for a salesperson, Cassidy. I'm afraid you've yet to fully develop these qualities. In a shop such as this—" Julia would fold her hand on the desk's surface "—I must be able to depend, without reservation, on my staff. If this were the first incident, of course, I'd make allowances, but…" Here Cassidy imagined Julia would pause and give a small sigh. "Just last week you told Miss Teasdale the black crepe made her look like a mourner. This is not the way we sell our merchandise."

"No, Mrs. Wilson." Cassidy decided she would agree with an apologetic air. "But with Miss Teasdale's hair and her complexion—"

"Tact and diplomacy," Julia would reiterate with a lifted finger. "You might have suggested that a royal-blue would match her eyes or that a rose would set off her skin. The clientele must be pampered while the merchandise moves. Each woman who walks out the door should feel she has acquired something special."

"I understand that, Mrs. Wilson. I hate to see someone buy something unsuitable; that's why—"

"You have a good heart, Cassidy." Julia would smile maternally then drop the ax. "You simply have no talent for selling…at least, not the degree of talent I require. I shall, of course, pay you for the rest of the week and give you a good reference. You've been prompt and dependable. Perhaps you might try clerking in a department store."

Cassidy wrinkled her nose at this point in her scenario, then quickly smoothed her features as the door behind her opened. Julia closed it quietly then lifted her left brow and moved to sit behind her rosewood desk. She studied Cassidy a moment then gently cleared her throat.

"Cassidy, you're a lovely girl, but…"

Cassidy's shoulders lifted and fell with her sigh.

An hour later, unemployed, she wandered Fisherman's Wharf, enjoying its cheerful shabbiness, its traveling carnival atmosphere. She loved the cornucopia of scents and sound and color. Here there was always a crowd. Here there was life in ever-changing flavors. San Francisco was Cassidy's concept of a perfect city, but Fisherman's Wharf was the end of the rainbow. Make-believe and reality walked hand in hand.

She passed through the emporiums, poking idly through barrels of trinkets, fingering newly imported silk scarfs and soaking up the noise. But the bay drew her. She moved toward it at an easy, meandering pace as the afternoon gave way to evening. The scent of fish dominated the air. Beneath it were the aromas of onions and spice and humanity.

She listened to the vendors hawk their wares and watched as a crab was selected and boiled in a sidewalk cauldron. The wharf was rimmed with restaurants and crammed with stores. Without apology, its ambience was vaguely dilapidated and faintly tawdry.

Cassidy adored it. It was old and friendly and content to be itself.

Nibbling on a hot pretzel, she moved through stalls of hanging Chinese turnips, fresh abalone and live crabs. Wisps of fog began to curl at her feet, and the sun sank lower. She was grateful for her plum-colored quilted jacket as the breeze swept in from the bay.

If nothing else, she thought ruefully, I acquired some nice clothes at a tidy discount. Cassidy frowned and took a generous bite of her pretzel. If it hadn't been for Mrs. Sommerson's hips, I'd still have a job. After all, I did have her best interests at heart. Annoyed, she pulled the pins from her hair then tossed them into a trash can as she passed. Her hair tumbled to her shoulders in long, loose curls. She breathed a sigh of relief.

Rats. She chewed her pretzel aggressively and headed for the watery front yard of Fisherman's Wharf. I needed that job. I really needed that stupid job. Depression threatened as she walked the dock between lines of moored boats. She began a mental accounting of her finances. The rent was due the following week, and she needed another ream of typing paper. According to her shaky calculations, both of these necessities could be met if she didn't put too much emphasis on food for the next few days.

I won't be the first writer to have to tighten her belt in San Francisco, she decided. The four basic food groups are probably overrated anyway. With a shrug she finished off the pretzel. That could be my last full meal for some time. Grinning, she stuck her hands in her pockets and strolled to the rail at the edge of the dock.

Like a gray ghost, the fog rolled in over the bay. It crept closer to land, swallowing up the water along the way. It was thin tonight, full of patches, not the thick mass that often coated the bay and blinded the city. To the west the sun dipped into the sea and shot spears of flame over the rim of the water. Cassidy waited for the last flash of gold. Already her mood was lifting. She was a creature of hope and optimism, of faith and luck. She believed in destiny. It was, she felt, her destiny to write. The sale of articles and occasional short stories to magazines kept the dream alive. For four years of college her life had revolved around perfecting her craft. Jobs kept a roof over her head and meant nothing more. Dating had been permitted only when her schedule allowed and was kept casual. As yet, Cassidy had met no man who interested her seriously enough to make her veer from the straight path she had chosen. There were no curves in her scheme of things. No detours.

The loss of her current job distressed her only temporarily. Even as the evening sky darkened and the lights of the wharf fluttered on, her mood shifted. She was young and resilient.

Something would turn up, she decided as she leaned over the rail. Wavelets slapped gently against the hull of a fishing boat beside her. She had no need for a great deal of money; any job would do. Clerking in a department store might be just right. Perhaps something in home appliances. It would be difficult to step on anyone's vanity while selling a toaster. Pleased with the thought, Cassidy pushed worries out of her head and watched the fog tumble closer. Its fingers reached toward her.

There was a chill in the air now as the breeze picked up. She let it wash over her, tossing her hair and waking up her skin. The sounds and calls from the stands became remote, muffled by the mist. It was nearly dark. She heard a bird call out as it flew overhead and lifted her face to watch it. The first thin light of the moon fell over her. She smiled, dreaming a little. Abruptly she drew in her breath as a hand gripped her shoulder. Before she could make a sound, she'd been turned around and was staring up into a stranger's face.

He was tall, several inches taller than Cassidy, with a shock of black curls around a lean, raw-boned face. Her mind worked quickly to categorize the face, rejecting handsome in favor of dangerous. Perhaps it was her surprise and the creeping fog and darkening sky that caused the adjective to leap into her mind. But she thought, as she looked up at him, that his features were more in tune with the Barbary Coast than Fisherman's Wharf. His eyes were a deep, intense blue under black, winged brows, and his forehead was high under the falling black curls. His nose was long and straight, his mouth full, and his chin faintly cleft. It was a compelling, hard-hitting face with no softening features. He had a rangy build accentuated by snug jeans and a black pullover. After her initial shock passed, Cassidy gripped her purse tight and squared her shoulders.

"I've only got ten dollars," she told him, keeping her chin fearlessly lifted. "And I need it at least as badly as you."

"Be quiet," he ordered shortly and narrowed his eyes. They were oddly intent on her face, searching, probing in a manner that made her shiver. When he cupped her chin in his hand, Cassidy's courage slipped away again. Without speaking, he turned her head from one side to the other, all the while studying her with absolute concentration. His eyes were hypnotic. She watched him, speechless, as his brows lowered in a frown. There was speculation in the look. She tried to jerk away.

"Be still, will you?" he demanded. His deep voice sounded annoyed, and his fingers were very firm.

Cassidy swallowed. "Now listen," she said with apparent calm. "I've a black belt in karate and will certainly break both your arms if you try to molest me." As she spoke she glanced past his shoulder and was dismayed to see the lights of the restaurants behind them had dimmed in the fog. They were alone. "I can break a two-by-four in half with my bare hand," she added when his expression failed to register terror and respect. She noted that the fingers on her chin were strong, and that despite his rangy build his shoulders were broad. "And I can scream very loudly," she continued. "You'd better go away."

"Perfect," he murmured and ran his thumb along her jawline. Cassidy's heart thudded with alarm. "Absolutely perfect. Yes, you'll do." All at once the intensity cleared from his eyes, and he smiled. The transformation was so rapid, so startling, Cassidy simply stared. "Why would you want to do that?"

"Do what?" Cassidy asked, astonished by his metamorphosis.

"Break a two-by-four in half with your bare hand."

"Do *what?*" Her own bogus claim was forgotten.

Confused, she frowned at him. "Oh, well, it's—it's for practice, I suppose. You have to think right through the board, I believe, so that—" She stopped, realizing she was standing on a deserted dock in the fog holding an absurd conversation with a maniac who still had her chin in his hand. "You'd really better let me go and be on your way before I have to do something drastic."

"You're exactly what I've been looking for," he told her but made no attempt to act on her suggestion. She noted there was a slight cadence to his speech that suggested an ethnic background, but she did not pause to narrow the choices.

"Well, I'm sorry. I'm not interested. I have a husband who's a linebacker for the 49ers. He's six feet five, two hundred and sixty-three pounds and *very* jealous. He'll be along any minute. Now let me go and you can have the blasted ten dollars."

"What the devil are you babbling about?" His brows lowered again. With the fog swirling thinly at his back, he looked fierce. Abruptly, one black brow flew up to disappear beneath the careless curls. "Do you think I'm going to mug you?" A flash of irritation crossed his face. "My dear child, I've no designs on your ten dollars or on your honor. I'm going to paint you, not ravish you."

"Paint me?" Cassidy was intrigued. "Are you an artist? You don't look like one." She considered his dashing, buccaneer's features. "What sort of an artist are you?"

"An excellent one," he replied easily and tilted her face a tad higher. A splash of moonlight found it. "I'm

Nora Roberts

famous, talented and temperamental." The charming smile was back in his face, and the cadence was Irish. Cassidy responded to both.

"I'm desperately impressed," she said. He was obviously a lunatic but an appealing one. She forgot to be afraid.

"Of course you are," he agreed and turned her head to left profile. "It's only to be expected." He freed her chin at last, but the tingle of his fingers remained on her skin. "I've a houseboat just outside the city. We'll go there and I can start sketching you tonight."

Cassidy's eyes lit with wary amusement. "Aren't you supposed to offer to show me sketches, or is this a variation on an old theme?" She no longer considered him dangerous, merely persistent.

He sighed, and she watched the quick annoyance flash over his face. "The woman has a one-track mind. Listen...what is your name?"

"Cassidy," she answered automatically. "Cassidy St. John."

"Oh, no, half Irish, half English. We'll have trouble there." He stuck his hands into his pockets. His eyes seemed determined to know every inch of her face. "Cassidy, I have no need for your ten dollars, and no plans to tamper with your virtue. What I want is your face. I've a sketch pad and so forth on my houseboat."

"I wouldn't go on Michelangelo's boat if he handed me that line." Cassidy relaxed the grip on her purse and pushed her hair from her shoulders. Though he made a swift sound of exasperation, she grinned.

"All right." She sensed the impatience in his stance

as he glanced behind him. "We'll get a cup of coffee in a well-lit, crowded restaurant. Will that suit you? If I try anything improper, you can break the table in half with your famous bare hand and draw attention."

Cassidy's lips trembled into a fresh grin. "I think I could agree to that." Before she could say anything else, he had her hand in his and was pulling her toward the cluster of restaurants. She felt an odd intimacy in the gesture along with a sense of his absolute control and determination. He was a man, she decided, who wouldn't take no for an answer. He walked quickly. She wondered if he were perpetually in a hurry. His stride was smooth, loose-limbed.

He pulled her into a small, rather dingy café and found a booth. The moment they were seated he again fixed her with his intent stare. His eyes, she noted, were even more blue than they had seemed in the dim light. Their color was intensified by his thick black lashes and bronze-toned skin. Cassidy met him stare for stare as she wondered what sort of man lived behind that incredible shade of blue. It was the waitress who broke her attention.

"What'll ya have?"

"Oh…coffee," she said when her companion made no move to speak or cease his staring. "Two coffees." When the waitress clomped away, Cassidy turned back to him. "Why do you stare at me like that?" she demanded. It annoyed her that her nerves responded to the look. "It's very rude," she pointed out. "And very distracting."

"The light's dreadful in here, but it's some improvement over the fog. Don't frown," he ordered. "It gives you a line right here." Before she could move he had lifted a finger and traced it down between her brows. "You have a remarkable face. I can't decide whether the eyes are an advantage or a drawback. One tends to disbelieve violet."

As Cassidy attempted to digest this, the waitress returned with their coffee. Glancing up, he plucked the pencil from her pocket and gave her one of his lightning smiles. "I need this for a few minutes. Drink your coffee. Relax," he directed with a careless gesture of his hand. "This won't hurt a bit."

Cassidy obeyed as he began to sketch on the paper placemat in front of him. "Do you have a job we'll need to work around or does your fictitious husband support you with his football prowess?"

"How do you know he's fictitious?" Cassidy countered and forced her eyes away from the planes of his face.

"The same way I know you'd have a great deal of trouble with a two-by-four." He continued to sketch. "Do you have a job?"

"I was fired this afternoon," she muttered into her coffee.

"That simplifies matters. Don't frown, I'm not a patient man. I'll pay you the standard sitting fee." He glanced up as Cassidy's brows lifted. "What I have in mind should take no more than two months, if all goes well. Don't look so shocked, Cassidy, my intentions were pure and honorable from the beginning. It was only your lurid imagination—"

"My imagination is not that lurid," she tossed back indignantly. She shifted in her seat as she felt her cheeks warm. "When people come looming up out of the fog and seizing other people—"

"Looming?" he interrupted and stopped sketching long enough to give her a dry look. "I don't believe I did any looming or seizing tonight."

"It seemed a great deal like looming and seizing from my perspective," she grumbled before she sipped her coffee. Her eyes dropped to the sketch he made. She set down the cup, her eyes widening with surprised admiration. "That's wonderful!"

In a few bold strokes he had captured her. She saw not just the shape of her own hair, but an expression she recognized as essentially her own. "It's really wonderful," she repeated as he began another sketch. "You really *are* talented. I thought you were bragging."

"I'm unflinchingly honest," he murmured as his borrowed pencil moved across the placemat.

Recognizing the quality of his work, Cassidy became more enthusiastic. Her mind raced ahead. Steady employment for two months would be a godsend. By the end of that time she should have heard from the publishing house that had her manuscript under consideration. Two months without having to sell toasters! She would have her evenings free to work on her new plot. The benefits began to mount and multiply. Destiny must have sent Mrs. Sommerson in search of a dress that afternoon.

"Do you really want me to sit for you?"

"You're precisely what I need." His manner sug- ·

gested that the matter was already settled. The second sketch was nearly completed. His coffee cooled, untouched. "I want you to start in the morning. Nine should be early enough."

"Yes, but—"

"Keep your hair down, and don't pile on layers of makeup, you'll just have to wash it off. You might smudge up your eyes a bit, but little else."

"I haven't said I'd—"

"You'll need the address, I suppose," he continued, ignoring her protests. "Do you know the city well?"

"I was born here," she told him with a superior sniff. "But I—"

"Well then, you shouldn't have any trouble finding my studio." He scrawled an address on the bottom of the placemat. Abruptly he lifted his eyes and captured hers again.

They stared at each other amid the clatter of cutlery and chatter of voices. What Cassidy felt in that brief moment she could not define, but she knew she had never experienced it before. Then, as quickly as it had occurred, it passed. He rose, and she was left feeling as if she had run a very long race in a very short time.

"Nine o'clock," he said simply; then as an afterthought he dropped a bill on the table for the coffee. He left without another word.

Reaching over, Cassidy picked up the placemat with the sketches and the address. For a moment she studied her face as he had seen it. Was her chin really shaped that way? she wondered and lifted her thumb and finger to trace it. She remembered his hand holding it in precisely the same fashion. With a shrug she dropped her hand then carefully folded the placemat. It wouldn't do any harm to go to his studio in the morning, she decided as she slipped the paper into her purse. She could get a look at things and then make up her mind if she wanted to sit for him or not. If she had any doubts, all she had to do was say no and walk out. Cassidy remembered his careless dominance and frowned. All I have to do, she repeated to herself sternly, is to say no and walk out. With this thought she rose and strolled out of the café.

Chapter 2

The morning was brilliantly clear, with a warmth promising more before afternoon. Cassidy dressed casually, not certain what was *de rigueur* for a prospective artist's model. Jeans and a full-sleeved white blouse seemed appropriate. As instructed she had left her hair loose, and her makeup was light enough to appear non-existent. She had yet to decide if she would sit for the strange, intriguing man she had met in the fog, but she was curious enough to keep the appointment.

With the address safely copied onto her own notepad and tucked in her purse, Cassidy grabbed a cable car that would take her downtown. The scribbled address had surprised her, as she had recognized the exclusiveness of the area. Somehow she'd expected her artist to have his studio near her own apartment in North Beach. There the atmosphere was informal and enduringly bohemian. Traditionally, clutches of writers and artists and musicians inhabited that section of the city and maintained its flavor. She wondered if perhaps he had a patron who had set him up in an expensive studio. He hadn't fit her conception of an artist. At least, she corrected herself, until she had seen his hands. They were, Cassidy recalled, perhaps the most beautiful hands she had ever seen, long and narrow with lean, tapering fingers. The bones had been close to the surface. Sensitive hands. And strong, she added, remembering the feel of his fingers on her skin.

His face remained clear in her mind, and she brooded over its image for several moments. Something about it tugged at a vague memory, but she couldn't bring her recollection into focus. It was a distinctive face, unique in its raw appeal. She thought if she were an artist, it would be a face she would be compelled to paint. There were good bones there and shadows and secrets, dominated by the terrifying blue of his eyes.

The trolley's bells clanged and snapped Cassidy out of her reverie. Stupid, she thought and lifted her face to the breeze. I didn't even get his name, and I'm obsessed with his face. He's supposed to be obsessed with mine, not the other way around. She jumped from the trolley and stepped onto the sidewalk. She scanned the street numbers looking for the address. I was right, she mused, about the quality of the neighborhood.

Still, like all of the city, it was a fascinating mixture of the exotic and the cosmopolitan, the romantic and the practical. San Francisco's dual personality was as prevalent here as it was in Chinatown or on Telegraph

Hill. There remained a blending of the antique and the revolutionary. Cassidy could hear the clang of the old-fashioned trolley as she looked up at a radically new steel-and-glass skyscraper.

The day was fine and warm, and her body enjoyed it while her mind drifted back to the plot that sat on her desk at home. She brought her attention back to the present when she reached the number corresponding to the address in her purse. She stood frowning.

The Gallery. Cassidy scanned the number on the door for confirmation, and her frown deepened. She'd browsed through The Gallery only a few months before, and she remembered quite well when it had opened five years ago. Since its opening it had gained an enviable reputation as a showcase for the finest art in the country. A showing at The Gallery could make a fledgling artist's career or enhance that of a veteran. Collectors and connoisseurs were known to gather there to buy or to admire, to criticize or simply to be seen. Like much of the city it was a combination of the elegant and the unconventional. The architecture of the building was simple and unpretentious, while inside was a treasure trove of paintings and sculpture. Cassidy was also aware that one of The Gallery's biggest draws was its owner, Colin Sullivan. She searched her memory for what she had read of him, then began to put the bits and pieces into order.

An Irish immigrant, he had lived in America for more than fifteen years; his career had taken off when he had been barely twenty. Oil was his usual medium, and a unique use of shading and light his trademark.

He had a reputation for impatience and brilliance. He would be just past thirty now and unmarried, though there had been several women linked romantically with him. There had been a princess once, and a prima ballerina. His paintings sold for exorbitant sums, and he rarely took commissions. He painted to please himself and painted well. As she stood in the warmth of the morning sunlight piecing together her tidbits of gossip and information, Cassidy recalled why the face of her artist had jarred a memory. She'd seen his picture in the newspaper when The Gallery had opened five years before. Colin Sullivan.

She let out a long breath then lifted her hands to either side of her head to push at her hair. Colin Sullivan wanted to paint her. He had once flatly refused to do a portrait of one of Hollywood's reigning queens, but he wanted to paint Cassidy St. John, an unemployed writer whose greatest triumph to date was a short story printed in a woman's magazine. All at once she remembered that she'd thought he'd been a mugger, that she had said absurd things to him, that she had told him with innocent audacity that his sketches were good. In annoyance and humiliation she chewed on her lip.

He might have introduced himself, she thought with a frown, instead of sneaking up behind me and grabbing me. I behaved quite naturally under the circumstances. I've nothing to be embarrassed about. Besides, she reminded herself, he told me to come. He's the one who arranged the entire thing. I'm only here to see if I want to take the job. Cassidy shifted her purse on her shoulder, wished briefly she had worn something more dignified or more exotic and moved to the front door of The Gallery. It was locked.

She pushed against the door again then concluded with a sigh that it was too early for The Gallery to be open. Perhaps there was a back entrance. He had spoken of a studio; surely it would have its own outside door. With this in mind Cassidy strolled around the side of the building and tried a side door, which refused to budge. Undaunted, she continued around the square brick building to its rear. When another door proved uncooperative, she turned her attention to a set of wooden steps leading to a second level.

Craning her neck, she squinted against the sun and scanned the ring of windows. The glass tossed back the light. If I were an artist with a studio, she reflected, it would definitely be up there. She began to climb the L-shaped staircase. The treads were open and steep. Faced with another door at the top, she started to test the knob, hesitated and opted to knock. Loudly. She glanced back over her shoulder and discovered the ground was surprisingly far below. A tiny sound of alarm escaped her when the door swung open.

"You're late," Colin stated with a frown of impatience and took her hand, pulling her inside before she could respond. Her senses were immediately assailed with the scents of turpentine and oils. He looked no less formidable in broad daylight than he had in the murky fog. In precisely the same manner he had employed the night before, he caught her chin in his hand.

"Mr. Sullivan..." Cassidy began, flustered.

"Ssh!" He tilted her head to the left, narrowed his

eyes and stared. "Yes, it's even better in decent light. Come over here, I want some proper sketches."

"Mr. Sullivan," Cassidy tried again as he yanked her across a high, airy room lined with canvases and cluttered with equipment. "I'd like to know a little more about all this before I commit myself."

"Sit here," he commanded and pushed her down on a stool. "Don't slouch," he added as he turned away.

"Mr. Sullivan! Would you please listen to me?"

"Presently," he replied as he picked up a wide pad and a pencil. "For now be quiet."

Totally at a loss, Cassidy sighed gustily and folded her hands. It would be simpler, she decided, to let him get his sketches out of his system. She allowed her eyes to wander and search the room.

It was large, barnlike, with wide windows and a skylight that pleased her enormously. The expanses of glass let in all the available sunlight. The floor was wood and bare, except for splatters of paint, and the walls were a neutral cream. Unframed canvases were stacked helter-skelter, facing the walls. Easels were propped here and there, and a large table was scattered with paints and brushes and rags and bottles. There was a couch at the far end of the room, sitting there as if added in afterthought. Three wooden chairs were placed at odd intervals as if pushed aside by an impatient hand and left wherever they landed. There were two other stools, two inside doors and a large goosenecked high-intensity lamp.

"Look out the window," Colin ordered abruptly. "I want a profile."

She obeyed. The vague annoyance she felt slipped away as she spotted a sparrow building a nest in the crook of an oak. The bird moved busily, carrying wisps of this and that in her beak. Patient and tenacious, she swooped and searched and built, then swooped again. Her wings caught the sun. Enchanted, Cassidy watched her. A quiet smile touched her lips and warmed her eyes.

"What do you see?" Colin moved to her, and her absorption was so deep she neither jolted nor turned.

"That bird there." She pointed as the sparrow made another quick dive. "Look how determined she is to finish that nest. The whole thing built from bits of string and grass and whatever other treasures sparrows find. We need bricks and concrete and prefabricated walls, but that little bird can build a perfectly adequate home out of next to nothing, without hands, without tools, without a union representative. Marvelous, don't you think?" Cassidy turned her head and smiled. He was closer than she had imagined, his face near hers in order for him to follow her line of vision. As she turned, he shifted his eyes from the window and caught hers. She felt a sudden jolt, as if she had stood too quickly and lost her inner balance.

"You might be even more perfect than I had originally thought," Colin said. He brushed her hair behind one shoulder.

She suddenly remembered her resolve to be businesslike. "Mr. Sullivan—"

"Colin," he interrupted. He continued to arrange her hair. "Or just Sullivan, if you like."

"Colin, then," she said patiently. "I had no idea who you were last night. It didn't occur to me until I was standing outside The Gallery." She shifted, faintly disturbed that he remained standing so close. "Of course, I'm flattered that you want to paint me, but I'd like to know what's expected of me, and—"

"You're expected to hold a pose for twenty minutes without fidgeting," he began while he pushed her hair forward again then back over her other shoulder. His fingers brushed Cassidy's neck and caused her to frown. He appeared not to notice. "You're expected to follow instructions and keep quiet unless I tell you otherwise. You're expected to be on time and not to babble about leaving early so you can meet your boyfriend."

"I was on time," Cassidy retorted and tossed her head so that his arrangement of her hair flew into confusion. "You didn't tell me to come to the back, and I wandered around until I found the right door."

"Bright, too," he said dryly. "Your eyes darken dramatically when your Irish is up. Who named you Cassidy?"

"It's my mother's family name," she said shortly. She opened her mouth to speak again.

"I knew some Cassidys in Ireland," he commented as he lifted her hands to examine them.

"I don't know any of my mother's family," Cassidy murmured, disconcerted by the feel of his hands on hers. "She died when I was born."

"I see." Colin turned her palms up. "Your hands are very narrow-boned. And your father?"

"His family was from Devon. He died four years ago. I don't see what this has to do with anything."

"It has to do with everything." He lifted his eyes from her hands but kept them in his. "You get your eyes and hair from your mother's family, and your skin and bone structure from your father's. It's a face of contradictions you have, Cassidy St. John, and precisely what I need. Your hair must have a dozen varying shades and it looks as though you've just taken your head from a pillow. You're wise not to attempt to discipline it. Your eyes go just past Celtic-blue into violet and add a touch of the exotic with the shape of them. They tend to dream. But your bones are all English aristocracy. Your mouth tips the balance again, promising a passion the cool British complexion denies. Pure skin, just a hint of rose under the ivory. You haven't walked through life without having to scale a few walls, yet there's a definite aura of the ingenue around you. The painting I want to do must have certain elements. I need very specific qualities in my model. You have them." He paused and inclined his head. "Does that satisfy your curiosity?"

She was staring at him, transfixed, trying to see herself as he described. Did her heritage so heavily influence her looks? "I'm not at all certain that it does," Cassidy murmured. She sighed, then her eyes found him again. "But I'm vain enough to want Colin Sullivan to paint me and destitute enough to need the job." She smiled. "Shall I be immortal when you've finished? I've always wanted to be."

Colin laughed, and the sound was warm and free in

the big room. He squeezed her hands, then surprisingly brought them to his lips. "You'll do me, Cass."

Cassidy's fumbling reply was interrupted as the studio door swung open.

"Colin, I need to—" The woman who swirled into the room halted abruptly and fixed sharp eyes on Cassidy. "Sorry," she said as her gaze drifted to their joined hands. "I didn't know you were occupied."

"No matter, Gail," Colin returned easily. "You know I lock the door when I'm working seriously. This is Cassidy St. John, who'll be sitting for me. Cassidy, Gail Kingsley, a very talented artist who manages The Gallery."

Gail Kingsley was striking. She was tall and thin as a reed with a long, triangular face set off by a spiky cap of vivid red hair. Everything about her was vital and compelling. Her eyes were piercingly green and darkly accented, her mouth was wide and slashed in uncompromising scarlet. Gold hoops poked through the spikes of vibrant hair at her ears. Her dress was flowing, without a definite line, a chaotic mix of greens washed over silk. The effect was bold and breathtaking. She moved forward, and her entire body seemed charged with nervous energy. Even her movements were quick and sharp, her eyes probing as they rested on Cassidy's face. There was something in the look that made Cassidy instantly uncomfortable. It was a purposeful intrusion while it remained completely impersonal.

"Good bones," Gail commented in a dismissing tone. "But the coloring's rather dull, don't you think?"

Cassidy spoke with annoyed directness. "We can't all be redheads."

"True enough," Colin said and, lifting a brow at Cassidy, turned to Gail. "What was it you needed? I want to get back to work."

There is a certain aura around people who have been intimate, Cassidy thought. It shows in a look, a gesture, a tone of voice. In the moment Gail's eyes left Cassidy to meet Colin's, she knew they were, or had been, lovers. Cassidy felt a vague sense of disappointment. Uncomfortable, she tried vainly to pull her hands from Colin's. She received an absentminded frown.

"It's Higgin's *Portrait of a Girl*. We've been offered five thousand, but Higgin won't accept unless you approve. I'd like to have it firmed up today."

"Who made the offer?"

"Charles Dupres."

"Tell Higgin to take it. Dupres won't haggle and he's fair. Anything else?" There was a simple dismissal in the words. Cassidy watched Gail's eyes flare.

"Nothing that can't wait. I'll go give Higgin a call."

"Fine." Colin turned back to Cassidy before Gail was halfway across the room. He was frowning at her hair as he pushed it back from her face. Over his shoulder, Cassidy watched Gail's glance dart back when she reached the door. Gail shut it firmly behind her. Colin stepped away and scanned Cassidy from head to toe.

"It won't do," he announced and scowled. "It won't do at all."

Confused by his statement, shaken by what she had

recognized in Gail's eyes, Cassidy stared at him then ran her fingers through her hair. "What won't?"

"That business you have on." He made a gesture with his hand, a quick flick of the wrist, which encompassed her blouse and jeans and sandals.

Cassidy looked down and ran her palms over her hips. "You didn't specify how I should dress, and in any case I hadn't decided to sit for you." She shrugged her shoulders, annoyed with herself for feeling compelled to justify her attire. "You might have given me some details instead of scrawling down the address and bounding off."

"I want something smooth and flowing—no waist, no interruptions." He ignored Cassidy's comments. "Ivory, not white. Something long and sleek." He took her waist in his hands, which threw her into speechless shock. "You haven't any hips to speak of, and the waist of a child. I want a high neck so we won't worry about the lack of cleavage."

Blushing furiously, Cassidy slipped down from the stool and pushed him away. "It's my body, you know. I don't care for your observations on it or your—your hands on it, either. My cleavage or the lack of it has nothing to do with you."

"Don't be a child," he said briskly and set her back on the stool. "At the moment, your body only interests me artistically. If that changes, you'll know quickly enough."

"Now just a minute, Sullivan." Cassidy slipped off the stool again, tossing back her head as she prepared to put him neatly in his place.

"Spectacular." He grabbed a handful of her hair to keep her face lifted to his. "Temper becomes you, Cass, but it's not the mood I'm looking for. Another time, perhaps." The corners of his mouth lifted as his fingers moved to massage her neck. His smile settled lazily over his face, and though Cassidy suspected the calculation, it was no less effective. She was conscious of his fingers on her skin. The essential physicality of the sensation was novel and intrigued her into silence. This was something new to be explored. His voice lowered into a caress no less potent than the hand on her skin. The faint lilt of Ireland intensified. "It's an illusion I'm looking for, and a reality. A wish. Can you be a wish for me, Cass?"

In that moment, with her face inches from his, their bodies just touching, the warmth of his fingers on her skin, Cassidy felt she could be anything he asked. Nothing was impossible. This was where his power over women lay, she realized: in the quick charm, the piratical features, the light hint of an old country in his speech. Added to this was an undiluted sexuality he turned on at will and an impatience in the set of his shoulders. She knew he was aware of his power and used it shamelessly. Even this was somehow attractive. She felt herself submitting to it, drawn toward it while her emotions overshadowed her intellect. She wondered what his mouth would feel like on hers, and if the kiss would be as exciting as she imagined. Would she lose or find herself? Would she simply experience? As a defense against her own thoughts, she placed her hands on his chest and pushed herself to safety.

"You're not an easy man, are you, Colin?" Cassidy took a deep breath to steady her limbs.

"Not a bit." There was careless agreement in his answer. She defined what flicked over his face as something between annoyance and curiosity. "How old are you, Cassidy?"

"Twenty-three," she answered, meeting his eyes levelly. "Why?"

He shrugged, stuck his hands in his pockets then paced the room. "I'll need to know all there is to know about you before I'm done. What you are will creep into the portrait, and I'll have to work with it. I've got to find the blasted dress quickly—I want to start. The time's right." There was an urgency in his movements that contrasted sharply with the man who had seduced her with his voice only moments before. Who was Colin Sullivan? Cassidy wondered. Though she knew finding out would be dangerous, she felt compelled to learn.

"I think I know one that might do," she hazarded while his mood swirled around the room. "It's more oyster than ivory, actually, but it's simple and straight with a high neck. It's also horribly expensive. It's silk, you see—"

"Where is it?" Colin demanded and stopped his pacing directly in front of her. "Never mind," he continued even as she opened her mouth to tell him. "Let's go have a look."

He had her by the hand and had passed through the back door before she could say another word. Cassidy took care to go along peacefully down the stairs, not wishing to risk a broken neck. "Which way?" he demanded as he marched her to the front of the building.

"It's just a few blocks that way," she said and pointed to the left. "But, Colin—" Before she could finish her thought, she was being piloted at full speed down the sidewalk. "Colin, I think you should know... Good grief, I should've worn my track shoes. Would you slow down?"

"You've got long legs," he told her and continued without slackening his pace. Making a brief sound of disgust, Cassidy trotted to keep up. "I think you should know the dress is in the shop I was fired from yesterday."

"A dress shop?" This appeared to interest him enough to slow him down while he glanced at her. With a gesture of absent familiarity, he tucked her hair behind her ear. "What were you doing working in a dress shop?"

Cassidy sent him a withering stare. "I was earning a living, Sullivan. Some of us are required to do so in order to eat."

"Don't be nasty, Cass," he advised mildly. "You're not a professional dress clerk."

"Which is precisely why I was fired." Amused by her own ineptitude, she grinned. "I'm also not a professional waitress, which is why I was fired from Jim's Bar and Grill. I objected to having certain parts of my anatomy pinched and dumped a bowl of coleslaw on a paying customer. I won't go into my brief career as a switchboard operator. It's a sad, pitiful story, and it's such a lovely day." She tossed back her head to smile at Colin and found him watching her.

"If you're not a professional clerk or waitress or switchboard operator, what are you, Cass?"

"A struggling writer who seems singularly inept at holding a proper job since college."

"A writer." He nodded as he looked down at her. "What do you write?"

"Unpublished novels," she told him and smiled again. "And an occasional article on the effects of perfume on the modern man. I have to keep my hand in."

"And are you any good?" Colin skirted another pedestrian without taking his eyes from Cassidy.

"I'm positively brimming with fresh, undiscovered talent." She tossed her hair behind her shoulders then pointed. "There we are, The Best Boutique. I wonder what Julia will have to say about this. She'll probably think you're keeping me." She bit her lip to suppress a giggle then slid her glance back to his. "Have you any smoldering looks up your sleeve, Colin?" Mischief danced in her eyes as she paused outside the front door of the shop. "You could send me a few and give Julia something to talk about for weeks." She swung through the door, her lovely face flushed with laughter.

True to form, Julia greeted Colin with scrupulous politeness and only the faintest glimmer of curiosity. There was a speculative glance for her former clerk, then recognition of Colin widened her eyes. She lifted a brow at Cassidy's request for the oyster silk dress then proceeded to wait on them personally.

In the changing room Cassidy stripped off her jeans and marveled at the irony of life. Little more than twenty-four hours before, she had been standing out-

side that very room with discarded dresses heaped over
her arms...without a thought of Colin Sullivan in her
head. Now he seemed to dominate both her thoughts
and her actions. The thin, cool silk was slipping over
her head because he wished it. Her heart beat just a
fraction quicker because he waited to see the results.
Cassidy fastened the zipper, held her breath and turned.
Her reflection stared back at her with undisguised awe.

The dress fell from a severely high neck in a straight
line, softened by the fragility of the material. Her arms
and shoulders gleamed under the thin transparency of
its full sleeves. Her hair glowed with life against the
delicacy of color. Cassidy let out her breath slowly. It
was a wish of a dress, as romantic as the material, as
practical as its line. In it she not only looked both elegant and vulnerable but felt it. With taut nerves she
moistened her lips and stepped from the changing room.

Colin was charming Julia into blushes. The incon-
gruity of flirtatious color in the cool, composed face
turned Cassidy's nerves into amusement. There was
the devil of a smile in Colin's eyes as he lifted Julia's
hand and brushed his lips over her knuckles. Cassidy
schooled her features to sobriety. A hint of a smile
lurked on her lips.

"Colin."

He turned as she called his name. The smile that lit
his face and brightened his eyes faded then died. Releasing Julia's hand, he took a few steps closer but kept
half the room between them. Cassidy, who had been
about to grin and spin a circle for inspection, stood still,
hypnotized by his eyes.

Very slowly, his eyes left her face to travel down the length of her then back again. Cassidy's cheeks grew warm with the flurry of her emotions. How could he make her feel so vitalized then so enervated with just a look? She wanted to speak, to break her own trance, but the words were jumbled and uncooperative. She found she could only repeat his name.

"Colin?" There was the faintest hint of invitation in the word, a question even she did not understand.

Something flashed in his eyes and was gone. The intense concentration was inexplicably replaced by irritation. When he spoke it was brisk and dismissive.

"That will do very well. Have it packed up and bring it with you tomorrow. We'll start then."

Cassidy's mind raced with a hundred questions and a hundred demands. His tone stiffened her pride, however, and hers was cool when she spoke. "Is that all?"

"That's all." Temper hovered in his voice. "Nine o'clock tomorrow. Don't be late."

Cassidy took a deep breath and let it out carefully. In that moment she was certain she despised him. They watched each other for another minute while the air crackled with tension and something more volatile. Then she turned her back on him and glided into the changing room.

Chapter 3

Cassidy spent most of the night lecturing herself. By morning she felt she had herself firmly in hand. There had been absolutely no reason for her to be annoyed with Colin. His brisk, impersonal attitude over the dress was only to be expected. As she rode the trolley across town, she shifted the dress box into her other arm and determined to preserve a cool, professional distance from him.

He's simply my employer. He's an artist, obviously a temperamental one. She added the modifier with a sniff. Deftly she jumped from the cable car to finish the trip on foot. He's a man who sees something in my face he wants to paint. He has no personal feelings for me, nor I for him. How could I? I barely know Colin Sullivan. What I felt yesterday was simply the over-flow of his personality. It's very strong, very magnetic.

I only imagined that there was an immediate affinity between us. Things don't happen that way, not that fast. All there is between us is the bond between artist and subject. I was writing scenes again.

Cassidy paused at the base of the stairs that led to Colin's studio. Still, he might have thanked me for finding the dress he was looking for, she thought. Never mind. She made an involuntary gesture with her hand as she climbed the steps. He's so self-absorbed he probably forgot I suggested the shop in the first place. With a quick toss of her head, Cassidy knocked, prepared to be brisk and professional in her new employ. Her resolve wavered a bit when Gail Kingsley opened the door.

"Hello," she said and smiled despite the cool assessment in Gail's eyes. For an answer Gail made a sweeping arm gesture into the room that would have seemed overdone on anyone else. Flamboyance suited her.

Gail was just as striking today in a shocking-pink jumpsuit no other redhead would have had the courage to wear. Colin was nowhere in sight. Cassidy was torn between admiration for the redhead's style and disappointment that Colin hadn't answered the door. She felt juvenile and ragged in jeans and a pullover.

"Am I too early?"

Gail placed her hands on her narrow hips and walked around Cassidy slowly. "No, Colin's tied up. He'll be along. Is that curl in your hair natural or have you a perm?"

"It's natural," Cassidy replied evenly.

"And the color?"

"Mine, too." Gail's bold perfume dominated the

scents of paint. When she came back to stand in front of her, Cassidy met her eyes levelly. "Why?"

"Just curious, dear heart. Just curious." Gail flashed a quick, dazzling smile that snapped on and off like a light. It was momentarily blinding, then all trace of it vanished. "Colin's quite taken with your face. He seems to be drifting into a romantic period. I've always avoided that sort of technique." She narrowed her eyes until she seemed to be examining the pores of Cassidy's skin.

"Want to count my teeth?" Cassidy invited.

"Don't be snide." Gail touched a scarlet-tipped finger to her lips. "Colin and I often share models. I want to see if I can use you for anything."

"I'm not a box lunch, Miss Kingsley," retorted Cassidy with feeling. "I don't care to be shared."

"A good model should be flexible," Gail reproved, stretching her slender arms to the ceiling in one long, luxurious movement. "I hope you don't make a fool of yourself the way the last one did."

"The last one?" Cassidy responded then immediately wanted to bite off her tongue.

"She fell desperately in love with Colin." Gail gave her quick light-switch smile again. Her sharp, rapid gestures skittered down Cassidy's nerves. She was a cat looking for something to stalk. "Worse, she imagined Colin was in love with her. It was really quite pathetic. A lovely little thing—milky skin, dark gypsy eyes. Naturally Colin was beastly to her in the end. He tends to be when someone tries to pin him down.

There's nothing worse than having someone mooning and sighing over you, is there?"

"I wouldn't know," Cassidy returned in mild tones. "But you needn't worry that I'll be mooning and sighing over Colin. He needs my face, I need a job." She paused a moment. Perhaps, she thought, it's best to be clear from the start. "You won't have any trouble from me, Gail. I'm too busy to orchestrate a romance with Colin."

Gail stopped her pacing long enough to fix her with a speculative frown. The frown vanished, and she moved swiftly to the door. "That simplifies matters, doesn't it? You can change through there." She flung out an arm to her left and was gone.

Cassidy took time to inhale deeply. She shook her head. Artists, she decided, were all as mad as hatters. Shrugging off Gail's behavior, she moved to the door indicated and found a small dressing room. Closeting herself inside, Cassidy began to change. As before, the gown made her feel different. Perhaps, she thought as she pulled a brush through her hair, it's the sensation of real silk against my skin, or the elegant simplicity of the line and color. Or is it because it's the image of what Colin wants me to be?

Whatever the reason, Cassidy couldn't deny that she felt heightened when she wore the gown—more alive, more aware, more a woman. After giving herself one last quick glance in the mirror, she opened the door and stepped into the studio.

"Oh, you're here," she said foolishly when she saw Colin scowling at a blank canvas. She had only a side view of him, and he didn't turn at her entrance. His hands were stuffed in his pockets, and his weight was distributed evenly on both legs. There was an impression of sharp vitality held in check—waiting, straining a bit for release. He was dressed casually, as she was now accustomed to seeing him, and the clothes seemed to suit his rangy, loose-limbed build. His face was in a black study: brows lowered, eyes narrowed, mouth unsmiling. The thought crossed Cassidy's mind that he was unscrupulously attractive and would be a terrifying man to care for. She remained where she was, certain he had not even heard her speak.

"I'm going to start on canvas straight away," he said. Still he did not turn to acknowledge her. "There're violets on the table." With one shoulder he made a vague gesture. "They match your eyes."

Cassidy looked over and saw the small nosegay tossed amid the artistic rubble. Her face lit with instant pleasure. "Oh, they're lovely!" Moving to the table, she took them then buried her face in their delicate petals. The fragrance was subtle and sweet. Touched and charmed, Cassidy lifted her smile to thank him.

"I want a spot of color against the dress," Colin murmured. His preoccupation was obvious and complete. He did not glance at her or change expression.

Pleasure shattered, Cassidy stared down at the tiny flowers and sighed. It's my fault, she thought ruefully. He bought them for the painting, not for me. It was ridiculous to think otherwise. Why in the world should he buy me flowers? With a shake of her head and a wry smile, she moved over to join him. "Do you see me there already?" she asked. "On the empty canvas?"

He turned then and looked at her, but the frown of his concentration remained. He lifted the hand that held the flowers. "Yes, they'll do. Stand over here, I want the light from this window."

As he propelled her across the room, Cassidy twisted her head to look up at him. "Good morning, Colin," she said in the bright, cheerful voice of a kindergarten instructor.

He lifted a brow as he stopped by the window. "Manners are the least of my concerns when I'm working."

"I'm awfully glad you cleared that up," Cassidy replied, smiling broadly.

"I've also been known to devour young, smart-tongued wenches for breakfast."

"Wenches!" Cassidy's smile became a delighted grin. "How wonderfully anachronistic. It sounds lovely when you say it, too. I do wish you'd said lusty young wenches, though. I've always loved that phrase."

"The description doesn't fit you." Colin lifted her chin with one finger and brushed her hair over her shoulder with his other hand.

"Oh." Cassidy felt vaguely insulted.

"Once I've set the pose, don't fidget. I just might throw an easel at you if you do." While he spoke, he moved her face and body with his hands. His touch was as impersonal as a physician's. *I might as well be a still-life arrangement*, Cassidy thought. By his eyes, she saw that his mind had gone beyond her and into his art. She recognized his expression of absolute concentration from her own work. She, too, had a tendency to block out her surroundings and step into her own mind.

At length he stood back and studied her in silence. It was a natural pose and simple. She stood straight, with the nosegay cupped in both hands and held just below her right hip. Her arms were relaxed, barely bent at the elbows. He had left her hair tumbled free, without design, over both shoulders. "Lift your chin a fraction higher." He held up a hand to stop the movement. "There. Be still and don't talk until I tell you."

Cassidy obeyed, moving only her eyes to watch him as he strode behind the easel again. He lifted a piece of charcoal. Minutes passed in utter silence as she watched the movements of his arms and shoulders and felt the probing power of his eyes. They returned again and again to her face. She knew he could look into her eyes and see directly into her soul, learning more perhaps than she knew herself. The sensation made her not nervous so much as curious. What would he see? How would he express it?

"All right," Colin said abruptly. "You can talk for the moment, but don't move the pose. Tell me about those unpublished novels of yours."

He continued to work with such obsessed concentration that Cassidy assumed he had invited her to talk only to keep her relaxed. She doubted seriously if her words made more than a surface impression. If he heard them at all, he would forget them moments later.

"There's only one actually, or one and a half. I'm working on a second novel while the first bounces from rejection slip to rejection slip." She started to shrug but caught herself in time. "It's about a woman's coming of age, the choices she makes, the mistakes. It's rather sentimental, I suppose. I like to think she makes the right choices in the end. Do you know it's very difficult to talk without your hands? I had no idea mine were so necessary to my vocabulary."

"It's your Gaelic blood." Colin frowned deeply at the canvas then lifted his eyes to hers. By the movement of his shoulders she knew he continued to work. "Will you let me read your manuscript?"

Surprised, Cassidy stared a moment before gathering her wits. "Well, yes, if you'd like. I——"

"Good," he interrupted and slashed another line on the canvas. "Bring it with you tomorrow. Be quiet now," he commanded before Cassidy could speak again. "I'm going to work the face."

Silence reigned until he put down the charcoal and shook his head. "It's not right." He scowled at Cassidy then paced. Unsure, she held the pose and her tongue. "You're not giving me the right mood. Do you know what I want?" he demanded. There was impatience and a hint of temper in his voice. She opened her mouth then closed it again, seeing the question had been rhetorical. "I want more than an illusion. I want passion. You've passion in you, Cassidy, more, by heaven, than I need for this painting." He turned to face her again, and she felt the room vibrate with his tension. Her heart began to quicken in response. "I want a promise. I want a woman who invites a lover. I want expectation and the freshness that springs from innocence. Untouched but not untouchable. It's that you have to give me. That's the essence of it." In his frustration, the cadence of his native land became more obvious. The fire of his talent flickered in his eyes. Fascinated, Cassidy watched him, not speaking even when he stopped directly in front of her. "There would be a softness in your eyes and just a trace of heat. There would be a giving in the set of your mouth that comes from having just been kissed, from waiting to be kissed again. Like this."

His mouth took hers quickly, stunningly. He framed her face with his hands, thumbs brushing her cheeks while he took the kiss into trembling intimacy with terrifying speed. His lips were warm and soft and experienced. His tongue plundered without warning. Somewhere deep within her came an answer. Passion, long overlooked, smoldered then kindled then licked tentatively into flame. She tasted the flavor of power. As quickly as his mouth had taken, it liberated.

Though she was unaware of it, her expression was exactly what he'd demanded of her—expectant, inviting, innocent. Fleetingly he dropped his gaze to her mouth; then, taking his time, he removed his hands from her face. Impatience flickered in his eyes before he turned and strode to his easel.

Cassidy tried to steady her spinning brain. Reason told her the kiss had meant nothing, a means to an end, but her heart thudded in contradiction. In a few brief seconds he had stirred up a hunger she hadn't been aware of having, had stirred up desires she hadn't been aware she had. It was more a revelation, she thought bemusedly, than a kiss. Forcing her breathing to slow, she tried to keep the quick encounter in perspective.

She was a grown woman. Kisses were more common than handshakes. It was her treacherous imagination that had turned it into something else. *Only my imagination,* she decided as she calmed, and his utter effrontery. He'd taken her totally by surprise. He'd kissed her when he'd had no right to do so, and in a way that had been both proprietary and intimate. No man had ever been permitted either of the privileges, and his seizure of them had left her shaken. Cassidy could justify her reaction to Colin by intellectually dissecting the scene, its cause and results. She turned her emotions over to her mind and plotted the scene. She examined motivations. Still, something lingered inside her that could not quite be rationalized or explained away. Disturbed, she tried to ignore it.

"We'll stop now," Colin stated abruptly and put aside the charcoal. He glanced up as he cleaned his hands on a paint rag. She thought perhaps he saw Cassidy St. John again for the first time since he had set the pose. "Relax."

When Cassidy obeyed, she was surprised to find her muscles stiff. "How long have I been standing there?" she demanded as she arched her back. "A good bit more than twenty minutes."

Colin shrugged, his eyes back on the canvas. "Perhaps. It's moving nicely. Do you want coffee?"

Cassidy scowled at his casual dismissal of the time. "Twenty minutes is quite long enough to stand in one position. I'll bring a kitchen timer with me from now on, and yes, I want coffee."

He ignored the first two-thirds of her statement and headed for the door. "I'll fix some."

"Am I allowed to look?" She gestured toward the canvas as he drew back the bolt.

"No."

She made a sound of disgust. "What about the others?" Her gesture took in the canvases against the wall. "Are they a secret, too?"

"Help yourself. Just stay away from the one I'm working on." Colin disappeared, presumably to fetch the promised coffee.

Making a face at the empty doorway, Cassidy set down the nosegay and wandered toward the neglected canvases. They were stacked here and tilted there, without order or design. Some were small while others were large enough to require some effort on her part to turn them around. Within moments, whatever minor irritation she'd felt was eclipsed by admiration for his talent. She saw why Colin Sullivan was considered a master of color and light. Moreover she saw the sensitivity she had detected in his hands and the strength she had felt there. There was insight and honesty in his portraits, vitality in his city scenes and landscapes. A play of shadows, a splatter of light, and the paintings breathed his mood. She wondered if he painted what he saw or what he felt, then understood it was a marriage of both. She decided that he saw more than the average mortal was entitled to see. His gift was as much in his perception as in his hands. The paintings moved her almost as deeply as the man had.

Carefully she turned another canvas. The subject

was beautiful. The woman's undraped body lounged negligently on the couch that now sat empty at the far end of the studio. There was a lazy smile on her face and a careless confidence in the attitude of her naked limbs. From the milky skin and gypsy eyes, Cassidy recognized the model Gail had spoken of that morning.

"A lovely creature, isn't she?" Colin asked from behind. Cassidy started.

"Yes." She turned and accepted the proffered mug. "I've never seen a more beautiful woman."

Colin's brow arched as he moved his shoulders. "Of a type, she's nearly perfect, and her body is exquisite."

Cassidy frowned into her coffee and tried to pretend the stab of irritation didn't exist.

"She has a basic sexuality and is comfortable with it."

"Yes." Sipping her coffee, Cassidy spoke mildly. "You've captured it remarkably well."

Her tone betrayed her. Colin grinned. "Ah, Cass, it's an open book you are and surely the most delightful creature I've met in years." The thickened brogue rolled easily off his tongue. Better women than she, Cassidy was certain, had fallen for the Gaelic charm.

She tossed her head, but the glare she had intended to flash at him turned of its own volition into a smile. "I can't keep up with you, Sullivan." She studied him over the rim of her mug. Sunlight shot through her hair and shadowed the silk of the dress. "Why did you settle in San Francisco?" she asked.

Colin straddled one of the abandoned wooden chairs, keeping his eyes on her. She wondered if he saw her as a person now or still as a subject. "It's a cross section of the world. I like the contrasts and its sordid history."

"And that it trades on that sordid history rather than apologizing for it," Cassidy concluded with an agreeing nod. "But don't you miss Ireland?"

"I go back now and then." He lifted his coffee and drank deeply. "It feeds me, like a mother's breast. Here I find passion, there I find peace. The soul requires both." He glanced up at her again and searched her face. The violet of her eyes had darkened. Her expression revealed her thoughts. They were all on him. Colin turned away from the innocent candor of her eyes. "Finish your coffee. I want to perfect the preliminary outline today. I'll start in oil tomorrow."

The morning passed almost completely in silence while she took advantage of Colin's absorption to study him. She had read of the dark devil looks and fiery blue eyes of the volatile black Irish, and now she found them even more compelling in the flesh. She wondered at the strange quirk in her own personality that caused her to find moodiness appealing.

With only the barest effort she could feel the swift excitement of his lips on hers. Warmed, she drifted with the sensation. For a moment she imagined what it would be like to be held by him in earnest. Though her experience with men had been limited, her instincts told her Colin Sullivan was dangerous. He interested her too much. His dominance challenged her, his physicality attracted her, his moodiness intrigued her.

Gail Kingsley's scathing comment about Cassidy's

predecessor came back to her. She had a quick mental picture of the redhead's demanding beauty and the model's sultry allure. Cassidy St. John, she mused, is at neither end of the spectrum. She isn't strikingly vivid nor steamily sexy. Feminine extremes apparently appeal to Colin both as an artist and as a man. She caught herself, annoyed with the train of her own thoughts. It would not do to get involved or form any personal attachments with a man like Colin Sullivan. Don't get too close, she cautioned herself. Don't open any doors. *Don't get hurt.* The last warning came from nowhere and surprised her.

"Relax."

Cassidy focused on Colin and found him staring down at the canvas. His attention was concentrated on what only he could see. "Go change," he directed without glancing up. Cassidy's thoughts darkened at his tone. Rude, she decided, was a mild sort of word for describing Sullivan the artist. Controlling her temper, Cassidy went back to the dressing room.

My worries are groundless, she told herself and closed the door smartly. No one could possibly get close enough to that man to be hurt.

A few moments later Cassidy emerged from the dressing room in her own clothes. Colin stood, facing the window, his hands jammed into his pockets, his eyes narrowed on some view of his own.

"I've left the dress hanging in the other room," Cassidy said coldly. "I'll just be off, since you seem to be done." She snatched up her purse from the chair. Even as she swung it over her shoulder and turned for the door, Colin took her hand in his.

"You've that line between your brows again, Cass." He lifted a finger to trace it. "Smooth it out and I'll buy you some lunch before you go."

The line deepened. "Don't use that patronizing tone on me, Sullivan. I'm not an empty-headed art groupie to be patted and babied into smiles."

His brow lifted a fraction. "Quite right. Then again, there's no need to go off in a tiff."

"I'm not in a tiff," Cassidy insisted as she tried to jerk out of his hold. "I'm simply having a perfectly normal reaction to rudeness. Let go of my hand."

"When I'm through with it," he replied evenly. "You should mind your temper, Cass my love. It does alluring things to your face, and I'm not one for resisting what appeals to me."

"It's abundantly clear the only appeal I have for you is on that canvas over there." Cassidy wriggled her hand in an attempt to free it. With a quick flick of the wrist, Colin tumbled her into his chest. Mutinous and glowing, her face lifted to his. "Just what do you think you're doing?"

"You challenge me to prove you wrong." There was amusement in his eyes now and something else that made her heart beat erratically.

"I don't challenge you to anything," she corrected with a furious toss of her head. Her hair swung and lifted with the movement then settled into its own appealing disarray.

"Oh, but you do." His free hand tangled in her hair

and found the base of her neck. "You threw down the gauntlet the night I found you in the fog. I think it's time I picked it up."

"You're being ridiculous." Cassidy spoke quickly. She realized her temper had carried her into territory she would have been wise to avoid. As she began to speak again, he caught her bottom lip between his teeth. The movement was sudden, the pressure light, the effect devastating.

Though she made a tiny sound of confused protest, her fingers clutched at his shirt instead of pushing him away. The tip of his tongue traced her lip as if experimenting with its flavor. When he released it, she stood still. Her eyes locked with his.

"This time when I kiss you, Cass, it's to pleasure myself," he said as his mouth lowered to take hers. Knowing he would meet no resistance, he circled her waist to mold her against him. Cassidy responded as if she'd been waiting for the moment all of her life. Her body seemed to know his already and fitted its soft, subtle curves to his firm, taut lines. Her hands traveled from his neck to tangle in his hair, while her mouth grew more mobile under his. For one brief instant, he crushed her to him with staggering force, ravishing her conquered mouth. Just as swiftly, her lips were freed. Her breath came out in a quick rush as she gripped him for balance. He held her close, keeping their bodies as one, his eyes boring into hers. Only the sound of their mixed breathing disturbed the silence.

The weakness Cassidy felt was a shock to her. Her knees trembled beneath her and she shook her head in a quick attempt to deny what he had awakened. Something deep and secret was struggling for release. The strength of it alarmed and fascinated her. Still, her fear outweighed her curiosity. Instinct warned her it was not yet time. Even as she found the will to draw away, Colin pulled her closer.

"No, Colin, I can't." She swallowed as her hands pushed against his chest. She watched his eyes darken as his lips lingered just over hers.

"I can," he murmured, then crushed her mouth. She swirled back into the storm.

Nothing in her experience had ever prepared her for the new demands of her own body. With innocent allure, she moaned against his mouth. She felt his lips move against hers as he murmured something. Then he plundered, pulling her down into a world of heat and darkness. A quickening fear rose with her passion. When he released her mouth, her breath came in short gasps. Her eyes clouded with desire and confusion.

"Please, Colin, let me go. I think I'm frightened."

He was capable of taking her, she knew, and of making her glad that he had. His eyes were blazing blue, and she kept hers locked on them. To let her eyes drift to his mouth would have been her downfall. The fingers at her neck tightened, then relaxed and dropped away. Seizing the moment, Cassidy stepped back. The narrowness of her escape shook her, and she dragged her hand through her hair.

Colin watched her, then folded his arms across his chest. "I wonder if you had more difficulty fighting yourself or me."

"So do I," Cassidy replied with impulsive candor.

He tilted his head at her response and studied her. "You're an honest one, Cassidy. Mind how honest you are with me—I'd have few qualms about taking advantage."

"No, I'm sure you wouldn't." After blowing out a long breath, Cassidy straightened her shoulders. "I don't suppose that could have been avoided forever," she began practically. "But now that it hasn't been, and it's done, it shouldn't happen again." Her brow furrowed as Colin tossed back his head and roared with laughter. "Did I say something funny?"

"Cass, you're unique." Before she could respond, he had moved to her and had taken her shoulders in his hands. He kneaded them quickly in a friendly manner. "That streak of British practicality will always war with the passionate Celt."

"You're romanticizing," she claimed and lifted her chin.

"The door's been opened, Cassidy." She frowned because his words reminded her of her earlier thoughts. "Better for you perhaps if we'd kept it locked." He shook her once, rapidly. "Yes, it's done. The door won't stay closed now. It'll happen again." He released her then stepped back, but their eyes remained joined. "Go on now, while I'm remembering you were frightened."

The strong temptation to step toward him alarmed her. In defense against it, she turned swiftly for the door. "Nine o'clock," he said, and she turned with her hand on the knob.

He stood in the room's center, his thumbs hooked

in his front pockets. The sun fell through the skylight, silhouetting his dark attraction. It occurred to Cassidy that if she were wise, she would walk out and never come back.

"Not a coward, are you, Cass?" he taunted softly, as if stealing her thoughts from her brain.

Cassidy tossed her head and snapped her spine straight. "Nine o'clock," she stated coolly then slammed the door behind her.

Chapter 4

As the days passed Cassidy found herself more at ease in the role of artist's model. As for Colin himself, she felt it would be a rare thing for anyone to remain relaxed with him. His temperament was mercurial, with a wide range of degrees. Fury came easily to him, but Cassidy learned humor did as well. As she began to uncover different layers of the man, he became more fascinating.

She justified her concentrated study of Colin Sullivan as a writer's privilege. It was a personality like his—varied, unpredictable, bold—that she needed as grist for her profession. There was nothing between them, she told herself regularly, but an artistic exchange. She reminded herself that he hadn't touched her again, except to set the pose, since the first day he had begun work on the canvas. The stormy kiss was a vivid memory, but only that...a memory.

Sitting at her typewriter in her apartment, Cassidy told herself she was fortunate—fortunate to have a job that kept the wolf from the door, and fortunate that Colin Sullivan was absorbed in his work. Cassidy was honest enough to admit she was more than mildly attracted to him. It was much better, she mused, that he was capable of pouring himself into his work to the extent that he barely noticed she was flesh and blood. *Unless I move the pose.* She frowned at the reflection of her desk lamp in the window.

Being attracted to him is perfectly natural, she decided. I'm not behaving like my predecessor with the milky skin and falling in love with him. I'm much too sensible. *Don't be so smug,* a voice whispered inside her head. Cassidy's frown became a scowl. I *am* sensible. I won't make a fool of myself over Colin Sullivan. He has his art and his Gail Kingsley. I have my work. Cassidy glanced down at the blank sheet of paper in her typewriter and sighed. But he keeps interfering with it. No more, she vowed then shifted in her seat until she was comfortably settled. I'm going to finish this chapter tonight without another thought of Sullivan.

At once the keys on her typewriter began to clatter with the movement of her thoughts. Once begun, she became totally involved, lost in the characters of her own devising. The love scene developed on her pages as she unconsciously called on her own feelings for her words. The scene moved with the same lightning speed as had the embrace with Colin. Now Cassidy was in control, urging her characters toward each other, propelling their destinies. It was as she wanted, as she planned, and she never noticed the influence of the man she had vowed to think no more about. The scene was nearly finished when a knock sounded on her door. She swore in annoyance.

"Who is it?" she called out and stopped typing in midsentence. She found it simpler to pick up her thoughts when returning to them that way.

"Hey, Cassidy." Jeff Mullans stuck his friendly, red-bearded face through her door. "Got a minute?"

Because he was her neighbor and she was fond of him, Cassidy pushed away the urge to sigh and smiled instead. "Sure."

He eased himself, a guitar and a six-pack of beer through the door. "Can I put some stuff in your fridge? Mine's busted again. It's like the Mojave Desert in there."

"Go ahead." Cassidy spun her chair until she faced him, then quirked her brow. "I see you brought all your valuables. I didn't know your six-string needed refrigeration."

"Just the six-pack," he countered with a grin as he marched back into her tiny kitchen. "And you're the only one in the building I'd trust with it. Wow, Cassidy, don't you believe in real food? All that's in here's a quart of juice, two carrots and half a stick of oleo."

"Is nothing sacred?"

"Come next door and I'll fix you up with a decent meal." Jeff came back into the room holding only his guitar. "I got tacos and stale doughnuts. Jelly-filled."

"It sounds marvelous, but I really have to finish this chapter."

Jeff's fingers pawed at his beard. "Don't know what

you're missing. Heard anything from New York?" After glancing at the papers scattered over her desk, he settled Indian-fashion on the floor. He cradled his guitar in his lap.

"There seems to be a conspiracy of silence on the East Coast." Cassidy sighed, shrugged and tucked up her feet. "It's early days yet, I know, but patience isn't my strong suit."

"You'll make it, Cassidy, you've got something." He began to strum idly as he spoke. His music was simple and soothing. "Something that makes the people you write about important. If your novel is as good as that magazine story, you're on your way."

Cassidy smiled, touched by the easy sincerity of the compliment. "You wouldn't like to apply for a job as an editor in a New York publishing house, would you?"

"You don't need me, babe." He grinned and shook back his red hair. "Besides, I'm an up-and-coming songwriter and star performer."

"I've heard that." Cassidy leaned back in her chair. It occurred to her suddenly that Colin might like to paint Jeff Mullans. He'd be the perfect subject for him—the blinding red hair and beard, the soft contrast of gray eyes, the loving way the long hands caressed the guitar as he sat on her wicker rug. Yes, Colin would paint him precisely like this, she decided, in faded, frayed jeans with a polished guitar on his lap.

"Cassidy?"

"Sorry, I took a side trip. Have you got any gigs lined up?"

"Two next week. What about your gig with the

artist?" Jeff tightened his bass string fractionally, tested it then continued to play. "I've seen his stuff…some of it, anyway. It's incredible." He tilted his head when he smiled at her. "How does it feel to be put on canvas by one of the new masters?"

"It's an odd feeling, Jeff. I've tried to pin it down, but…" She trailed off and brought her knees up, resting her heels on the edge of the chair. "I'm never certain it's me he's seeing when he's working. I'm not certain I'll see myself in the finished portrait." She frowned then shrugged it away. "Maybe he's only using part of me, the way I use parts of people I've met in characterizations."

"What's he like?" Jeff asked, watching her eyes drift with her thought. The glow of her desk lamp threw an aura around her head.

"He's fascinating," she murmured, all but forgetting she was speaking aloud. "He looks like a pirate, all dashing and dangerous with the most incredible blue eyes I've ever seen. And his hands are beautiful. There's no other word for them; they're perfectly beautiful."

Her voice softened, and her eyes began to dream. "He exudes a thoughtless sort of sensuality. It seems more obvious when he's working. I suppose it's because he's being driven by his own power then, and is somehow separate from the rest of us. He tells me to talk, and I talk about whatever comes into my head." She moved her shoulders then rested her chin on her knees. "But I don't know if he hears me. He has a dreadful temper, and when he rages his speech slips back to Ireland. It's almost worth the storm to hear it. He's outrageously selfish and unbearably arrogant and utterly charming. Each time I'm with him I find a bit more, uncover another layer, and yet I doubt I'd really know him if I had years to learn."

There was silence for a moment, with only Jeff's music. "You're really hung up on him," he observed.

Cassidy snapped back with a jolt. Her violet eyes widened in surprise as she straightened in the chair. "Why, no, of course not. I'm simply...simply..." *Simply what, Cassidy?* she demanded of herself. "Simply interested in what makes him the way he is," she answered and hugged her knees. "That's all."

"Okay, babe, you know best." Jeff stood in an easy fluid motion, the guitar merely an extension of his arm. "Just watch out." He smiled, leaned over and cupped her chin. "He might be a great artist, but if the gossip columns are to be believed, he's very much a man, too. You're a fine-looking lady, and you might as well be fresh from the farm."

"I'd hardly call four years at Berkeley fresh from the farm," Cassidy countered.

"Only someone utterly naive could evade every pass I make and still make me like her." Jeff closed the distance and gave her a gentle invitation of a kiss. It was as pleasant and as soothing as his music. Cassidy's heartbeat stayed steady. "No dice, huh?" he asked when he lifted his head. "Think of the rent we could save if we moved in together."

Cassidy tugged on his beard. "You're only lusting after my refrigerator."

"A lot you know," he scoffed and headed for the door. "I'm going home to write something painfully sad and poignant."

"Good grief, I'm always inspiring someone these days."

"Don't get cocky," Jeff advised then closed the door behind him.

Cassidy's smile faded as she stared off into space. Hung up on, she repeated mentally. What a silly phrase. In any case, I'm not hung up on Colin. Can't a woman express an interest in a man without someone reading more into it? Thoughtfully she ran her fingertip over her bottom lip and brought back the feel of Jeff's kiss. Easy, undisturbing, painless. What sort of chemistry made one man's kiss pleasant and another's exhilarating? The smart woman would go for the pleasant, Cassidy decided, knowing Jeff would be basically kind and gentle. Only an idiot would want a man who was bound to bring hurt and heartache.

With a quick shake of her head she swung back to her typewriter and began to work. Her fingers had barely begun to transfer her thoughts when a knock sounded again. Cassidy rolled her eyes to the ceiling.

"You can't possibly be finished writing a painfully sad and poignant song," she called out and continued to type. "And the beer certainly isn't cold yet."

"I can't argue with either of those statements."

Cassidy spun her chair quickly and stared at Colin. He stood in her opened doorway, negligently leaning against the jamb and watching her. There was light amusement on his face and male appreciation in his eyes as they roamed over her skin. It was scantily covered in brief shorts and a T-shirt that had shrunk in the basement laundry. His lazy survey brought out a blush before she found her tongue.

"What are you doing here?"

"Enjoying the view," he answered and stepped inside. He closed the door at his back then lifted a brow. "Don't you know better than to keep your door unlatched?"

"I'm always losing my key and locking myself out, so I..." Cassidy stopped because she realized how ridiculous she sounded. One day, she promised herself, I'll learn to think before I speak. "There isn't anything in here worth stealing," she said.

Colin shook his head. "How wrong you are. Wear your key around your neck, Cass, but keep your door locked." Her brain formed an indignant retort, but before she could vocalize it he spoke again. "Who did you think I was when I knocked?"

"A songwriter with a faulty refrigerator. How did you know where I lived?"

"Your address is on your manuscript." He gestured with the thick envelope before setting it down.

Cassidy glanced at the familiar bundle with some surprise. She had assumed Colin had forgotten her manuscript as soon as she'd given it to him. Suddenly it occurred to her why she hadn't asked him before if he had read it, or what he'd thought of it. His criticism would be infinitely harder to bear than an impersonal rejection slip from a faceless editor. Abruptly nervous, she looked up at him. Any critique she was expecting wasn't forthcoming.

Colin wandered the room, toying with an arrangement of dried flowers, examining a snapshot in a silver frame, peering out of the window at her view of the city.

"Can I get you something?" she asked automatically then remembered Jeff's inventory of her refrigerator. She bit her lip. "Coffee," she added quickly, knowing she could provide it as long as he took it black.

Colin turned from the window and began to wander again. "You have a proper eye for color, Cass," he told her. "And an enviable way of making a home from an apartment. I've always found them soulless devices, lacking in privacy and character." He lifted a small mirror framed with sea shells. "Fisherman's Wharf," he concluded and glanced at her. "It must be a particular haunt of yours."

"Yes, I suppose. I love the city in general and that part of it in particular." She smiled as she thought of it. "There's so much life there. The boats are all crammed in beside each other, and I like to imagine where they've been or where they're going." As soon as the words were spoken Cassidy felt foolish. They sounded romantic when she had been taking great pains to prove to Colin she was not. He smiled at her, and her embarrassment became something more dangerous. "I'll make coffee," she said quickly and started to rise.

"No, don't bother." Colin laid a hand on her shoulder to keep her seated then glanced at her desk. It was cluttered with papers and notes and reference books. "I'm interrupting your work. Intolerable."

"It seems to be the popular thing to do tonight." Cassidy shook off her discomfort and smiled as he continued to pace the room. "It's all right because I was nearly done, otherwise I suppose I'd behave as rudely as you do when you're interrupted." She enjoyed the look he gave her, the ironical lift of his brow, the light tilt of a smile on his mouth.

"And how rudely is that?"

"Abominably. Please sit, Colin. These floors are thin, you'll wear them through." She gestured to a chair, but he perched on the edge of her desk.

"I finished your book tonight."

"Yes, I thought perhaps that's why you brought the manuscript back." She spoke calmly enough, but when he made no response she moaned in frustration. "Please, Colin, I'm no good with torture. I'd confess everything I knew before they stuck the first bamboo shoot under my fingernail. I'm a marshmallow. No, wait!" She held up both hands as he started to speak. She rose and then took a quick turn around the room. "If you hated it, I'll only be devastated for a short time. I'm certain I'll learn to function again...well, nearly certain. I want you to be frank. I don't want any platitudes or cushioned letdowns." She pushed her mane of hair back with both hands, letting her fingers linger on her temples a moment. "And for heaven's sake, don't tell me it was interesting. That's the worst. The absolute worst!"

"Are you finished?" he asked mildly.

Cassidy blew out a long breath, tugged her hand through her hair and nodded. "Yes, I think so."

"Come here, Cass." She obeyed instantly because his voice was quiet and gentle. Their eyes were level, and he took her hands in his. "I haven't mentioned the book until now because I wanted to read it when I wouldn't be interrupted. I thought it best not to talk about it until I finished." His thumbs ran absently over the back of her hands. "You have something rare, Cass, something elusive. Talent. It's not something they taught you at Berkeley, it's something you were born with. Your college years polished it, perhaps, disciplined it, but you provided the raw material."

Cassidy released her breath. Astonishing, she thought, that the opinion of a man known barely a week should have such weight. Jeff's opinion had pleased her; Colin's had left her speechless.

"I don't know what to say." She shook her head helplessly. "That sounds trite, I know, but it's true." Her eyes drifted past him to the disorder of papers on her desk. "Sometimes you just want to chuck it all. It just isn't worth the pain, the struggle."

"And you would choose to be a writer," Colin said.

"No, I never had any choice." She brought her eyes back to his. The violet glowed almost black in the shadowed light. "If anything, it picked me. Did you choose to be an artist, Colin?"

He studied her a moment, then shook his head. "No." He turned her hands, palms up, and looked at them with lowered brows. "There are things that come to us whether we ask for them or not. Do you believe in destiny, Cass?"

She moistened her lips, finding them suddenly dry, then swallowed. "Yes." The single syllable was little more than a breath.

"Of course, I was certain you did." He lifted his eyes and locked them on hers. Cassidy's heartbeat jumped skittishly. "Do you think it's our destiny to be lovers, Cassidy?" Her mouth opened but no words came out. She shook her head in mute denial. "You're a poor liar," he observed; then, cupping her chin in his palm, he moved his lips to hers. In direct contrast to the ease and pleasantness of Jeff's kiss, this brought a pain that seemed to vibrate in every cell of her body. Defensively Cassidy jerked her head back.

"Don't!"

"Why?" he countered, and his voice was soft. "A kiss is a simple thing, a meeting of lips."

"No, it's not simple," Cassidy protested, feeling herself being pulled to him by his eyes only. "You take more."

He kissed one cheek, then the other, barely touching her skin. Cassidy's eyelids fluttered down. "Only as much as you'll give me, Cass. That much and no more." His lips moved over hers, teasing, persuading, until her blood thundered in her brain. His fingers were gentle on her face. "You taste of things I'd forgotten," he murmured. "Fresh, young things. Kiss me, Cass, I've a need for you."

With a moan, half despair, half wonder, she answered his need.

The flames that leapt between them were intense and wild. Her brain sent out quick, desperate protests and was ignored. A hunger for him drove her; her mouth became urgent and searching as his hands began to explore her soft curves. The fear she felt only added to her excitement, the exquisite terror of losing control. She was overwhelmed by a primitive need, an ageless necessity. When their lips parted and met again, hers ached for the joining.

Abruptly he tore his mouth from hers and buried it against her neck. Cassidy shuddered from the onslaught even as she tilted back her head to offer him more. With his teeth he brought her skin alive with delicious pain. His hands found their way under her shirt, running up her rib cage. With his thumbs he stroked the sides of her breast while she strained against him.

Her joints went fluid, leaving her helpless but for his support. For a moment, when their lips met again, there was nothing she had that was not his. The offer was complete and unconditional. Slowly, with his hands on her shoulders, Colin drew her away. Her lashes fluttered up then down, before she found the strength to open her eyes. His expression was dark and forbidding. Briefly his hands tightened.

"It seems you were right," he began in a voice thick with desire. "A kiss isn't a simple thing. I want you, Cass, and you'd best know nothing in heaven or hell will keep me from taking you when I've a mind to." His hands relaxed, the grip becoming a caress. "When the painting's finished, we'll have no choice but to meet our destinies."

"No." Frightened, disturbed by feelings that were too intense, Cassidy pulled out of his arms. She dragged a trembling hand through her hair, and her breath came quickly. "No, Colin, I won't be the latest in your string of lovers. I won't! I think more of myself than that.

That's something you'd best understand." She stepped away from him, her shoulders straightening with inherent pride.

Colin's eyes narrowed. She could see his temper rising. "It should be an interesting contest." He took a step forward and grabbed a handful of her hair. With a quick jerk he brought her face to his, then gave her a hard, brief kiss. Cassidy's breath trembled out, but she kept her eyes steady. "Time will tell, Cass my love. Now it's late, nearly midnight, and I'd best be on my way." Lifting her hand, he brushed her fingers with his lips. "Sinning is much more appealing after midnight." With another careless smile, he turned for the door. Reaching it, he pushed the latch so that it would engage when he shut it. "Find your keys," he ordered and was gone.

Chapter 5

Another week passed without any clash between Colin and Cassidy. She had returned to his studio the day after his visit to her apartment determined to resist him. She'd spoken the truth when she'd told him she wouldn't be one of his lovers.

All her life she had waited for a relationship with depth and permanence. Her own ideals and her dedication to her studies had kept her aloof from men, and her aloofness had prolonged her naiveté. She'd grown up with only a father and had never closely witnessed the commitment of a man and a woman to each other. She had watched her father enjoy several light relationships as she'd grown up, but none of the women in his life had become important to him. Watching him drift through life with only his work, Cassidy had vowed she would find someone one day to share hers.

She didn't consider her vow romantic, but as necessary to her soul as food was to her body. Until she found what she searched for, she would wait. Before Colin there had never been any temptation to do otherwise. Still, when she returned to his studio, she was prepared to stand firm against him. Her preparation proved unnecessary.

Colin spoke to her only briefly, and when he set the pose his touch was impersonal. But there seemed to be some surge of emotion just under the surface of his face, something that just stirred the air. Whether it was temper or passion or excitement, Cassidy had no way of knowing. She knew only she was vitally aware of it…and of him.

They passed the days with only what needed to be said, and long gaps of silence filled the sessions. By the end of the week Cassidy's nerves were stretched taut. She wondered if Colin felt the tension, or if it was simply within her. He seemed intent only on the painting.

The sun fell over Cassidy warmly, but her muscles were growing stiff from holding the pose. Colin stood behind his easel, and she watched his brush move from palette to canvas. He could work for hours without a moment's rest. Cassidy tried to imagine how he had painted her.

Will I hang in The Gallery or face the wall in a corner up here until he decides what to do with me? she thought. Will I be sold for some astronomical price and hang in a manor house in England? What will he title me? *Woman in White. Woman with Violets.* She tried to imagine being discussed and pondered over by an art class in a university. A century from now, will someone see me in some dusty gallery and wonder who I was or what I was thinking when he painted me?

The idea gave Cassidy an odd feeling, one she was not certain wholly pleased her. How much of her soul could Colin see, and how much would be revealed with oil and canvas? Would she, in essence, be as naked as the model who'd lounged on the couch?

Colin swore roundly, snapping her attention back to him. Her eyes widened as he slammed down his palette.

"You've moved the pose." He stalked toward her as her mouth opened to form an apology. "Hold still, blast you," he ordered curtly, adjusting her shoulders with impatient hands. His brows were lowered in annoyance. "I won't tolerate fidgeting."

Cassidy's mouth snapped shut on her apology. Swift and heated, her temper rose. With one quick jerk she pulled out of his hands. "Don't you speak to me that way, Sullivan." She threw her nosegay on the windowsill and glared at him. "I was not fidgeting, and if I were, it would be because I'm human, not a—a robot or a dime-store dummy." She tossed her head, effectively destroying his arrangement of her hair. "I'm sure it's difficult to understand a mere mortal when one is so lofty and godlike, but we can't all be perfect."

"Your opinions are neither requested nor desired." Colin's voice was as cold as his eyes were heated. "The only thing I require from a model is that she hold still." He took her shoulders again, firmly. "Keep your temper to yourself when I'm working."

"Go paint a tree, then," she invited furiously. "It won't give you any back talk." Cassidy turned to stalk to the dressing room, but Colin grabbed her arm and spun her around. His face was alive with temper.

"No one walks away from me."

"Is that so?" Cassidy lifted her chin, infuriated with his arrogance. "Watch this." She turned her back on him only to be whirled around again before she had taken two steps. "Let go of me," she ordered as blood surged angrily under her skin. Nerves that had been stretched for a week strained to the breaking point. "I've nothing more to say, and I'm through holding your blasted pose for the day."

His grip on her arm tightened. "Very well, but there's more between us than painting and talking, isn't there?" He bit off the words as he dragged her against him.

Cassidy's heart jumped to her throat when she felt the violence of his fingers against her skin. She saw that temper ruled him now, a temper sharp enough to cut through any protest she could make. He was a man of passion, and she was aware that his darker side could carry them both past the turning point. In a desperate attempt to hold him off, Cassidy arched away from him. Even as she made the move, his mouth crushed hers. She tasted his fury.

Her sounds of protest were muffled, her arms pinioned by his. In her throat, her heart thudded with the knowledge that she was totally at his mercy. His lips were bruising, unyielding, as his tongue penetrated her mouth. The kiss became as intimate as it was savage. When she tried to turn her face from his, he gripped her hair tightly and held her still. His mouth was hard and hot and ruthless. Behind her closed lids, a dull red mist swirled. For the first time in her life, Cassidy feared she would faint. Her protests became slighter. Colin took more.

He was pulling her too deep too quickly, down dark corridors, beyond the border of thought and into sensation. There was no gentleness on the journey, only hard, uncompromising demand. Unable to fight him any longer, Cassidy went limp. She made no struggle when his hand moved to unfasten the dress. Her body was consumed by fire, instinctively responding to his touch. The knock on the studio door vibrated like a cannon through the room. Ignoring it, Colin continued to ravish her mouth.

"Colin." Dimly Cassidy heard Gail Kingsley's voice and the sound of another knock. "There's someone here to see you."

With a savage oath, Colin tore his mouth from Cassidy's. He released her abruptly, and freed of support she staggered and fell against him. Cursing again, he took her arms and held her away, but his words halted as he studied her wide, frightened eyes.

Her mouth was trembling, swollen by his demands. Her breath sobbed in and out of her lungs as she clung to him for balance.

"Colin, don't be nasty." Gail's voice sounded with practiced patience through the door. "You must be pretty well finished by now."

"All right, blast it!" he called out brusquely to Gail but kept his eyes on Cassidy. Leading her by the arm, he walked to the dressing room. Inside he turned her again to face him. In silence she looked up, struggling to balance her system and discipline her breathing. The need to weep was tearing at her.

An expression came and went in Colin's eyes. "Change," he said in a quiet voice. He seemed to hesitate, as if to say more, then he turned away. When he shut the door, Cassidy turned to face the wall.

She let the trembling run its course. Several minutes passed before the voices in the studio penetrated.

There was Gail's quick, nervous tone and Colin's, calm now, without any trace of the temper of passion that had dominated it before. An unfamiliar voice mixed with theirs. It was light and male with an Italian accent. Cassidy concentrated on the voices rather than the words. Turning, she stared at her own reflection. What she saw left her stunned.

Color had not yet returned to her cheeks, leaving them nearly as white as the dress she wore. Her eyes were haunted. It was the look of utter vulnerability that disturbed her the most; the look of a woman accepting defeat.

No. No, I won't. She pressed her palm over the face in the glass. *He'll win nothing that way, and we both know it.* Quickly she stripped out of the dress and began to pull on her clothes. The straight, uncompromising lines of her khakis and button-down shirt made her appear less frail, and she began a careful repair of her face. The conversation in the outer room started to penetrate her thoughts. The first moments of eavesdropping were unconscious.

"An interesting use of color, Colin. You seem to be working toward a rather dreamlike effect." Hearing Gail's comment, Cassidy realized they were discussing the painting. She frowned as she applied blusher to her cheeks. He lets her look at it, she thought resentfully. Why not me? "It seems almost sentimental. That should be a surprise to the art world."

"Sentimental, yes." The Italian voice cut in while Cassidy now eavesdropped shamelessly. "But there is passion in this play of color here, and a rather cool practicality in the line of the dress. I'm intrigued, Colin—I can't figure out your intention."

"I have more than one," Cassidy heard him answer in his dry, ironic tone.

"How well I know." The Italian chuckled then made a sound of curiosity. "You have not begun the face."

"No." Cassidy recognized the dismissal in the word, but the Italian ignored it.

"She interests me...and you, too, it appears. She would be beautiful, of course, and young enough to suit the dress and the violets. Still, she must have something more." Cassidy waited for Colin's reply, but none came. The Italian continued, undaunted. "Will you keep her hidden, my friend?"

"Yes, Colin, where is Cassidy?" Gail's question held an undertone of amusement that made Cassidy's eyes narrow. "You know she'd adore meeting Vince." She gave a light laugh. "She is rather a sweet-looking thing. Don't tell me we ran her off?"

Thoroughly annoyed with the condescending description, Cassidy turned and opened the door. "Not at all," she said and gave the trio by the easel a brilliant smile. "And of course I'd adore meeting Vince." She saw Gail's eyes glitter with a quick fury then shifted her gaze to Colin. His face told her nothing, and again her gaze shifted.

The man beside Colin was nearly a head shorter, but his lean build and proud carriage gave the illusion of height. His hair was as dark as Colin's, but straight, and his eyes were darkly brown against the olive of his skin. He had smooth, handsome features, and when he smiled he was all but irresistible.

"Ah, *bella.*" The compliment was a sigh before he crossed the room to take both of Cassidy's hands in his. "*Bellisima.* But of course, she is perfection. Where did you find her, Colin?" he demanded as his eyes caressed her face. "I will go and set up camp there until I find a prize of my own."

Cassidy laughed, amused by his undisguised flirtation. "In the fog," she told him when Colin remained silent. "I thought he was a mugger."

"Ah, my angel, he is much worse than that." Vince turned to Colin with a grin but retained Cassidy's hand. "He is a black Irish dog whose paintings I buy because I have nothing better to do with my money."

Colin lifted a brow as he moved to join them. "Vince, Cassidy St. John. Cass, Vincente Clemenza, the duke of Maracanti."

At the introduction Cassidy's eyes grew wide. "Ah, now you have impressed her with my title." Vince's teeth flashed into a grin. "How accommodating of you." With perfect charm he lifted both of Cassidy's hands to his lips. "My pleasure, *signorina*. Will you marry me?"

"I've always thought I'd make a spectacular duchess. Do I curtsy?" she asked, smiling at him over their joined hands. "I'm not certain I know how."

"Vince normally requires that one kneel and kiss his ring." At the comment, Cassidy let her eyes drift to Colin. His gaze was dark and brooding on her face. Fractionally, she lifted her chin. Though he said nothing, she sensed his acknowledgment of the gesture.

"You exaggerate, my friend." Vince released Cassidy's hands then laid his own on Colin's shoulder. "As never before, I envy you your gift. You will give me first claim on the portrait."

Colin's eyes remained fixed on Cassidy's face. "There's been a prior claim."

"Indeed." Vince shrugged. The movement was at once elegant and foreign. "I shall have to outbid my competition." There was an inflection in his tone of a man used to having his own way. Hearing it Cassidy wondered how he and Colin dealt together with such apparent amiability.

"Vince wanted to see *Janeen,*" Gail cut in and moved across the room to a stack of canvases.

"If you'll excuse me, then," Cassidy began, but Vince scooped up her hand again.

"No, *madonna,* stay. Come peruse the master's work with me." Without waiting for her assent he urged her across the room.

Gail took a canvas then propped it on an easel. It was

the portrait of the nude with the milky skin. Cassidy glanced up to see Gail smiling.

"Cassidy's predecessor," she announced then stepped back to stand with Colin. Cassidy recognized the proprietary nature of the gesture. She turned her attention back to the portrait without looking at Colin.

"An exquisite animal," Vince murmured. "One would say a woman without boundaries. There is quite an attractive wickedness about her." He turned his head to smile at Cassidy. "What do you think?"

"It's magnificent," she replied immediately. "She makes me uncomfortable, and yet I envy her confidence in her own sexuality. I think she would intimidate most men…and enjoy it."

"Your model appears to be an astute judge of character." Vince rubbed his thumb absently over Cassidy's knuckles. "Yes, I want it. And the Faylor Gail showed me downstairs. He shows promise. Now, madonna…" He turned to face Cassidy again. His eyes were dark and appreciative. "You will have dinner with me tonight? The city is a lonely place without a beautiful woman."

Cassidy smiled, but before she could speak Colin laid a hand on her shoulder. "The paintings are yours, Vince. My model isn't."

"Ah." Vince's one syllable was ripe with meaning. Cassidy's eyes narrowed with fury. Smoothly Colin turned to take the painting from the easel.

"Have someone package this and the Faylor for Vince," he told Gail as he handed her the canvas. "I'll be down shortly and we'll discuss terms."

Without a word Gail crossed the studio and swung through the door. Vince watched her with a thoughtful eye then turned back to Cassidy.

"*Arrivederci,* Cassidy St. John." He kissed her hand then sighed with regret. "It seems I must find my own dream in the fog. I will expect a bargain price to soothe my crushing disappointment, my friend." He shot a look at Colin as he moved to the door. "If you are ever in Italy, madonna…" With a final smile he left them.

Trembling with rage, Cassidy turned on Colin the moment the door closed. "How *dare* you?" Now she had no need of blusher to bring color to her cheeks. "How dare you imply such a thing?"

"I merely told Vince he could have the paintings but not my current model," Colin countered. Carelessly he moved across the room and covered Cassidy's portrait. "Any implication was purely coincidental."

"Oh, no!" Cassidy followed him, propelled by fury. "That was no coincidence. You knew precisely what you were doing. I won't tolerate that sort of interference from you, Sullivan." She took a finger and poked him in the chest. "I'm perfectly free to see whomever I choose, whenever I choose, and I won't have you implying otherwise."

Colin hooked his hands in his pockets. For a moment he studied her face in silence. When he spoke it was with perfect calm. "You're very young and remarkably naive. Vince is an old friend and a good one. He's also a charming rake, if you'll forgive the archaic term. He has no scruples with women."

"And you do?" Cassidy retorted in an instant of blind

heat. She saw Colin stiffen, saw his eyes flare and the muscles in his face tense. For the first time she witnessed his calculated control of his temper.

"Your point, Cass," he said softly. "Well taken." His hands stayed in his pockets as he watched her. "Don't come back until Thursday," he told her and turned to walk to the door. "I need a day or two."

Cassidy stood alone in the empty studio. I may have scored a point, she thought wretchedly, but this victory isn't sweet. She was drained, physically as well as emotionally. She returned to the dressing room for her purse. Colin wasn't the only one who needed a day or two.

"Oh, what luck, I've caught you." Gail swept into the studio just as Cassidy emerged from the dressing room. "I thought we might have a little chat." Gail shot her a quick, flashing smile and leaned back against the closed door. "Just us two," she added.

Cassidy sighed with undisguised weariness. "Not now," she said and shifted her purse to her shoulder. "I've had enough temperament for one day."

"I'll make it brief, then, and you can be on your way." Gail spoke pleasantly enough, but Cassidy felt the antagonism just below the surface.

It's best not to argue, Cassidy decided. It's best to hear her out, agree with everything she says and go quietly. That's the sensible thing to do.

She gave her what she hoped was an inoffensive smile. "All right, go ahead, then."

Gail took a quick, sweeping survey. "I'm afraid perhaps I haven't made myself clear…about myself and

Colin." Her voice was patient—teacher to student. Cassidy ignored a surge of annoyance and nodded.

"Colin and I have been together for quite some time. We meet a certain need in each other. Over the years he's had his share of flirtations, which I'm quite capable of overlooking. In many cases these relationships were intensified for the press." She shrugged a gauze-covered shoulder. "Colin's romantic image helps maintain the mystique of the artist. I'll sanction anything when it helps his career. I understand him."

As if unable to remain still for more than short spurts, Gail began to roam the room.

"I'm afraid I don't see why you're telling me this," Cassidy began. The last thing she needed to hear at the moment was how experienced Colin Sullivan was with women.

"Let's you and I understand each other, too." Gail stopped pacing and faced Cassidy again. Her eyes were hard and cold. "As long as Colin's doing this painting, I have to tolerate you. I know better than to interfere with his work. But if you get in my way…" She wrapped her fingers around the strap of Cassidy's purse. "I can find ways of removing people who get in my way."

"I'm sure you can," Cassidy returned evenly. "I'm afraid you'll find I don't remove easily." She pried Gail's fingers from her strap. "Your relationship with Colin is your own affair. I've no intention of interfering with it. Not," she added as a satisfied smile tilted the corner of Gail's mouth, "because you threaten me. You don't intimidate me, Gail. Actually, I feel rather sorry for you."

Cassidy ignored Gail's harsh intake of breath and continued. "Your lack of confidence where Colin is concerned is pathetic. I'm no threat to you. A blind man could see he's only interested in what he puts on that canvas over there." She flung out a hand and pointed to the covered portrait. "I interest him as a *thing,* not as a person." She felt a quick slash of pain as her own statement came home to her. She continued to speak, though the words rushed out in desperation. "I won't interfere with you because I'm not in love with Colin, and I have no intention of ever being in love with him."

Whirling, she darted through the back door of the studio, slamming it at her back. Only after she had gulped in enough air to steady her nerves did Cassidy realize she had lied.

Chapter 6

For the next two days Cassidy buried herself in her work. She was determined to give herself a time of peace, a time of rest for her emotions. She knew she needed to cut herself off from Colin to accomplish it. The disruption of their day-to-day contact wasn't enough. She knew she needed to block him from her mind. In addition, Cassidy forced herself not to consider the knowledge that had come to her after the scene with Gail. She wouldn't think of being in love with Colin or of the circumstances that made her love impossible. For two days she would pretend she'd never met him.

Cassidy wrote frantically. All her fears and pain and passion were expressed in her words. She worked late into the night, until she could be certain there would be no dreams to haunt her. When she slept, she slept deeply, exhausted by her own drive. More than once she forgot to eat.

On the second day it began to rain. There was a solid gray wall outside Cassidy's window of which she remained totally unaware. Below, pedestrians scrambled about under umbrellas.

Cassidy's concentration was so complete that when a hand touched her shoulder, she screamed.

"Wow, Cassidy, I'm sorry." Jeff tried to look apologetic but grinned instead. "I knocked and called you twice. You were totally absorbed."

Cassidy held a hand against her heart as if to keep it in place. She took two deep breaths. "It's all right. We all need to be terrified now and again. It keeps the blood moving. Is it your refrigerator?"

Jeff grimaced as he ran a finger down her nose. "Is that where you think my heart is? In your refrigerator? Cassidy, I'm a sensitive guy, my mother'll tell you." Cassidy smiled, leaning back in her chair.

"I've got that gig in the coffeehouse down the street tonight. Come with me."

"Oh, Jeff, I'd love to, but—" She began to make her excuses with a gesture at the papers on her desk. Jeff cut her off.

"Listen, you've been chained to this machine for two days. When are you coming up for air?"

She shrugged and poked a finger at her dictionary. "I've got to go back to the studio tomorrow, and—"

"All the more reason for a break tonight. You're pushing yourself, babe. Take a rest." Jeff watched her face carefully and pressed his advantage. "I could use a friendly face in the audience, you know. We rising stars are very insecure." He grinned through his beard.

Cassidy sighed then smiled. "All right, but I can't stay late."

"I play from eight to eleven," he told her then ruffled her hair. "You can be home and tucked into bed before midnight."

"Okay, I'll be there at eight." Cassidy glanced down at her watch, frowned then tapped its face with her fingertips. "What time is it? My watch stopped at two-fifteen."

"A.M. or P.M.?" Jeff asked dryly. He shook his head. "It's after seven. Hey." He gave her a shrewd look. "Have you eaten?"

Cassidy cast her mind back and recalled an apple at noon. "No, not really."

With a snort of disgust Jeff hauled her to her feet. "Come on with me now, and I'll spring for a quick hamburger."

Cassidy pushed her hair back out of her face. "Golly, I haven't had such a generous offer for a long time."

"Just get a coat," Jeff retorted, stalking to her door. "In case you haven't noticed, it's pouring outside."

Cassidy glanced out her window. "So it is," she agreed. She pulled a yellow slicker out of the closet and dragged it on. "Can I have a cheeseburger?" she asked Jeff as she breezed past him.

"Women. Never satisfied." He closed the door behind them.

The rain didn't bother Cassidy. It was refreshing after her hibernation. The hurried cheeseburger and soft drink were a banquet after the scant meals of the past two days. The smoky, crowded coffeehouse gave her a taste of humanity that she relished after her solitude.

Seated near the back, she drank thick café au lait and listened to Jeff's soothing, introspective music. The evening had grown late when she realized she had relaxed her guard. Colin had slipped over her barrier without her being aware. He stood clearly in her mind's eye. Once he had breached her defenses, Cassidy knew it was useless to attempt to force him out again. She closed her eyes a moment, then opened them, accepting the inevitable. She could not avoid thinking of him forever.

Colin Sullivan was a brilliant artist. He was a confident man who twisted life to suit himself. He had wit and charm and sensitivity. He was selfish and arrogant and totally dedicated to his work. He was thoughtless and domineering and capable of violence.

And I love him completely.

Cassidy trembled with a sigh, then stared into her coffee. I'm an idiot, a romantic fool who knew the pitfalls then fell into one anyway. I see he has a lover, I understand he sees me as important only as a subject for his painting. I'm aware he would make love to me without his heart ever being touched. I know there've been dozens of women in his life, and none of them have lasted.

No, not even Gail, she mused, for all her claims. She's just another woman who's touched the corners of his life. Colin's never made a commitment to a woman.

Knowing all this, and wanting a healthy, one-to-one relationship with a man, I fall in love with him. Brilliant.

It's insane. He'll trample me. So what do I do? Slowly
Cassidy lifted her coffee and sipped. She drifted away
from her surroundings.

I have to finish the portrait; I gave my word. It would
be impossible to be in the studio together day after day
and not speak. I'm not capable of feuding in any case.
Her elbows were propped on the table, the cup held
between her hands, but her eyes were staring over the
rim and into the distance.

Fighting with him is too dangerous because it brings
the emotions to the surface. I don't know how deeply
inside me he's capable of seeing. I won't humiliate myself or embarrass him with the fact that I've been stupid
enough to fall in love with him. The only thing to do is
to behave naturally. Hold the pose for him, talk when
he asks me to talk and be friendly. The painting seems
to be moving well; it should be finished in a few more
weeks. Surely I can behave properly for that amount
of time. And when it's finished…

Her thoughts trailed off into darkness. And when
the painting's finished, what? I pick up the pieces, she
answered. For a moment her eyes were lost and sad.
When the painting's finished and Colin drops out of
my life, the universe will still function. What a small
thing one person's happiness is, she reflected. What a
tiny, finite slice of the whole.

With a sigh Cassidy shook off her thoughts and finished the coffee. Setting down the cup she let herself
be stroked by Jeff's quiet music.

* * *

Cassidy pulled her jacket closer as she stood outside the studio door and searched her bag for the key Colin had given her.

Blasted key, she grumbled silently as she groped for it. She blew her hair from her eyes then pulled out a notepad, three pencils and a linty sourball.

"How did that get in there?" she mumbled. Her eyes flew up when Colin opened the door. "Oh. Hello."

He inclined his head at the greeting then dropped his eyes to her laden hands. "Looking for something?"

Cassidy followed his gaze. Embarrassed, she dumped everything back into her bag and fumbled for poise. "No, I…nothing. I didn't think you'd be here so early." She shifted her purse back to her shoulder.

"It appears it's fortunate I am. Have you lost your key, Cass?" There was a smile on his face that made her feel foolish and scatter-brained.

"No, I haven't lost it," she muttered. "I just can't find it." She walked past him into the studio. Her shoulder barely brushed his chest and she felt a jolt of heat. It wasn't going to be as easy as she'd thought. "I'll change," she said briefly then went directly to the dressing room.

When she emerged, Colin was setting his palette and gave her not so much as a glance. His ignoring of her brought a wave of relief. There, you see, she told herself, there's nothing to worry about.

"I'm going to do some work on the face today," Colin stated, still mixing paints. His use of the impersonal pronoun was further proof his thoughts were not on

Cassidy St. John. She denied the existence of the ache in her chest. Keeping silent, she waited until he was finished then stood obligingly while he set the pose. She would, she determined, give him absolutely no trouble. But when he cupped her chin in his hand, she stiffened and jerked away.

Colin's eyes heated. "I need to see the shape of your face through my hands." He set the pose again with meticulous care, barely making contact. "It's not enough to see it with my eyes. Do you understand?"

She nodded, feeling foolish. Colin waited a moment then took her chin again, but lightly, with just his fingertips. Cassidy forced herself to remain still. "Relax, Cassidy, I need you relaxed." The patient tone of the order surprised her into obeying. He murmured his approval as his fingers trailed over her skin.

To Cassidy it was an agony of delight. His touch was gentle, though he frowned in concentration. She wondered if he could feel the heat rising to her skin. Colin traced her jawline and ran his fingers over her cheekbones. Cassidy focused on bringing air in and out of her lungs at an even pace. She tried to tell herself that his touch was as impersonal as a doctor's, but when his hand lingered on her cheek she brought her eyes warily to his.

"Hold steady," he commanded briskly, then turned to go to his easel. "Look at me," he ordered as he picked up his palette and brush.

Cassidy obeyed, trying to put her mind on anything but the man who painted her. Even as her eyes met his, she realized it was hopeless. She could not look at him and not see him. She could not be with him and not be aware of him. She could not block him out of her mind with any more success than she could block him out of her heart.

Would it be wrong, she wondered, to let myself dream a little? Would it be wrong to look for some pieces of happiness in the time I have left with him? Unhappiness will come soon enough. Can't I just enjoy being near him and pay the price after he's gone? It seemed a small thing.

Cassidy watched him work, memorizing every part of him. There would come a time, she knew, when she would want the memories. She studied the dark fullness of the hair falling on his forehead and curling over his collar. She studied the black arched brows which were capable of expressing so many moods. The planes of his face fascinated her. His eyes lifted again and again to her face as he painted. There was a fierce concentration in them, an urgency that intensified an already impossible blue.

She couldn't see his hands, but she envisioned them, long and narrow and beautiful. She could feel them learning her face, seeing what perhaps she herself would never see, understanding what she might never understand. If one has to fall foolishly in love, she decided, there couldn't be a more perfect man.

They worked for hours, taking short breaks for Cassidy to stretch her muscles. Colin was always impatient to begin again. She sensed his mood, his excitement, and knew something exceptional was being created.

The studio was alive with it. Eagerness, anticipation, tingled in the air.

"The eyes," he muttered and set down his palette. Quickly he stalked over to her. "Come, I need to see you closer." He pulled her to just behind the easel. "The eyes can be the soul of a portrait."

Colin took her by the shoulders, and his face was barely an inch from hers. The smell of paint and turpentine was sharp in her nostrils. Cassidy knew she would never smell them again without thinking of him.

"Look at me, Cass. Straight on."

She obeyed, though the look of his eyes nearly undid her. It was deep, intruding, reaching past what was offered and seeking the whole. Reflected in his eyes, she saw herself.

I'm a prisoner there, she thought. His. Their breaths mingled, and her lips parted, inviting his to close the minute distance. Something flickered and nearly caught flame. Abruptly he stepped back to his canvas.

Cassidy spoke without thinking. "What did you see?"

"Secrets," Colin murmured as he painted. "Dreams. No, don't look away, Cass, it's your dreams I need."

Helplessly Cassidy brought her eyes back. It was far too late for resistance. Setting down his palette and brush, Colin frowned at the canvas for several long moments, then he stepped toward Cassidy and smiled.

"It's perfect. You gave me what I needed."

Cassidy felt a tiny thrill of alarm. "Is it finished?"

"No, but nearly." He lifted her hands and kissed them one at a time. "Soon."

"Soon," she repeated and thought it an ugly word.

Quickly she shoved back depression. "Then it must be going well."

"Yes, it's going well."

"But you're not going to let me see it yet."

"I'm superstitious." He gave her hands a gentle squeeze. "Humor me."

"You let Gail see it." Unable to prevent herself, Cassidy let resentment slip into her tone.

"Gail's an artist," Colin pointed out. He released her hands then patted her cheek. "Not the model."

With a sigh of defeat Cassidy turned to wander the room. "You must have painted her...at one time or other," she commented. "She's so striking, so vital."

"She can't hold a pose for five minutes," Colin said. He began to clean his brushes at the worktable.

Smiling, Cassidy leaned on the windowsill. "Do you have a hard time with your seascapes?" she asked him. "Or do you simply command the water and clouds to stop fidgeting? I believe you could do it." She stretched then lifted the weight of her hair from her neck. With an expansive sigh, she let it fall again to tumble as it chose. The sun shimmered through its shades.

When she turned her head to smile at Colin again, she found him watching her, the brush he was cleaning held idly in one hand. Something pulled at her, urging her to go to him. Instead, she walked to the other end of the room.

"The first painting of yours I ever saw was an Irish landscape." Cassidy kept her back to him and tried to speak naturally. "It was a small, exquisite work bathed in evening light. I liked it because it helped me imagine my mother. Isn't that odd?" She turned back to him as the thought eclipsed her nerves. "I have several pictures of her, but that painting made her seem real. She rarely seems real to me." Her voice softened with the words; then, suddenly, she smiled at him. "Are your parents alive, Colin?"

His eyes held hers for a moment. "Yes." He went back to cleaning his brushes. "Back in Ireland."

"They must miss you."

"Perhaps. They've six other children. I don't imagine they find much time to be lonely."

"Six!" Cassidy exclaimed. Her lips curved at the thought. "Your mother must be remarkable."

Colin looked over again, flashing a grin. "She had a razor strap that could catch three of us at one time."

"No doubt you deserved it."

"No doubt." He scrutinized the sable of his brush. "But I recall wishing a time or two her aim hadn't been so keen."

"My father lectured," Cassidy remembered, taking a long breath in and out. "I'd often wish he'd whack me a time or two and be done with it. Lectures are a great deal more painful, I think, than a razor strap."

"Like Professor Easterman's at Berkeley?" Colin asked with a grin. Cassidy blinked at him.

"How did you know about him?"

"You told me yourself, Cass my love. Last week, I think it was. Or perhaps the week before."

"I never thought you were listening," she murmured. Cassidy tried to remember all she had rambled about since the sittings had begun. Her teeth began to worry her bottom lip. "I can't think of half the things I talked about."

"That's all right, I do…well enough." After wiping his hands on a rag, Colin turned back to her. She was frowning, displeased. "You've got those lines between your brows again, Cass," he said lightly and smiled when she smoothed them out. "Well now, I've made you miss lunch, and that's a crime when you're already thin enough to slip under the door. Shall I poison you with whatever's in the kitchen, or will you settle for coffee?"

"I think I'll pass on both those gracious invitations." She swung around and glided toward the dressing room. "I'll take my chances at home. I have a neighbor who hoards stale doughnuts."

Cassidy closed the door behind her and smiled. That wasn't so bad, she told her reflection. The ground was only shaky a couple of times. Now that the worst of it's over, the rest of the sittings should be easy.

Humming lightly, she began to strip out of the gown. Everything's going to be all right. After all, I'm a grown woman. I can handle myself.

After she had slipped out of the dress, Cassidy held it aloft to shake out the folds. When the door opened, her humming turned to a shriek. In a quick jerk she pressed the dress against her naked skin and held on with both hands.

"What about dinner?" Colin asked and leaned against the open door.

"Colin!"

"Yes?" he asked in a pleasant tone.

"Colin, go away. I'm not dressed." She hugged the dress close and hoped she was somewhat covered.

"Yes, so I see, but you haven't answered my question."

Cassidy made an anxious sound and swallowed. "What question?"

"What about dinner?" he repeated. His eyes skimmed over her bare shoulders.

"*What* about dinner?" she demanded.

"You can't eat stale doughnuts for dinner, Cass. It's not healthy." He smiled at the incredulity on her face. She shifted the dress a bit higher.

"He keeps tacos as well," she said primly. "Now, would you mind shutting the door on your way out?"

"Tacos? Oh, no, that won't do." Colin shook his head and ignored her request. "I'll have to feed you myself."

Cassidy began to demand her privacy again then stopped. For a moment she studied him thoughtfully. "Colin, are you asking me for a date?"

"A date?" he repeated. For a moment he said nothing as he appeared to consider the matter. One brow arched as he studied her. "It certainly seems that way."

"To dinner?" Cassidy asked cautiously.

"To dinner."

"What time?"

"Seven."

"Seven," she repeated with a nod as she shut her ears on her practical side. "Now, close the door so I can get dressed."

"Certainly." A wicked gleam shot into his eyes, making her clutch the dress with both hands. She took one wary step in retreat. "By the way, Cass, you'd never've been a successful general."

"What?"

"You forgot to cover your flank," he told her as he shut the door behind him.

Twisting her head, Cassidy caught the full rear length of herself in the mirror.

Chapter 7

As Cassidy dressed that evening she blessed her short skip into the boutique business. The wisteria crepe de chine was worth all the hours she had practiced patience. It was a thin, dreamlike dress with floating lines. Her shoulders were left bare as the bodice was caught with elastic just above her breasts. The material nipped in at the waist then fell fully to the knees. She slipped on the cap-sleeved matching jacket and tied it loosely at the waist. The color was good for her eyes, she decided, bringing out the uniqueness of their shade. This was a night she didn't want to feel ordinary.

You shouldn't even be going. Cassidy brought the brush through her hair violently in response to the nagging voice. I don't care. I am going. *You'll get hurt.* I'll be hurt in any case. Moving quickly, she fastened small gold lover's knots to her ears. Doesn't everyone deserve one special moment? Aren't I entitled to a glimpse of real happiness? I'll have my one evening with him without that blasted painting between us. I'll have my moment when he's looking at me, seeing me, and not whatever it is he sees when we're in the studio.

She lifted her scent and sprayed a cloud as delicate as the wisteria. I won't think about tomorrow, only tonight. The painting's almost finished and then it'll be over. I have to have something. One evening isn't too much to ask. I'll pay the price later, but I'm going to have it. After tossing her hair behind her shoulders, Cassidy glanced at her watch.

"Oh, good grief, it's already seven!" Frantically she began to search for her key. She was on her hands and knees, peering under the convertible sofa that doubled as her bed, when the knock came. "Yes, yes, yes, just a minute," she called out crossly and stretched out for something shiny in the dark beneath the sofa.

She pulled it out with an "Aha!" of triumph, then sighed when she saw a quarter and not a key in her fingers.

"I said I'd buy," Colin told her, and Cassidy's head shot up. He stood inside her door, looking curiously at the woman on her hands and knees. Cassidy straightened up, blew her hair from her eyes and studied him.

He wore a slimly tailored black suit. Its perfect cut accentuated the width of his shoulders and leanness of his build. His shirt was a splash of white in contrast and opened at the throat. Cassidy concluded Colin Sullivan would never restrict himself with a tie. She leaned back on her heels.

"I've never seen you in a suit before," she commented. The lamplight fell softly on her upturned face. "But you don't look too conventional. I'm glad."

"You're an amazing creature, Cassidy." He held out a hand to help her up, touching the other to her hair as she rose.

Standing, she tilted her head back and smiled at him. "Do you think so?"

A smile was his answer as he stepped back, keeping her hand in his. "You look lovely." The survey he made was quick and thorough. "Perfectly lovely." Taking her other hand, he turned it palm up and revealed the quarter. "Cab fare?" he asked. "It won't take you far."

Cassidy frowned down at her own hand. "I thought it was my key."

"Of course." Colin took the quarter and examined it critically. "It looks remarkably like one."

"It did in the dark under the sofa," Cassidy retorted then resumed her search. "It has to be here somewhere," she muttered as she shuffled through papers on her desk. "I've looked everywhere, positively everywhere."

"Where's the bedroom?" Colin asked, watching her shake out the pages of a dictionary.

"This *is* the bedroom," Cassidy informed him and poked through the leaves of a fern. "And the living room, and the study and the parlor. I like things all in one place, it saves steps." She found an eraser under a pile of notebooks and scowled at it. "I looked all over for this yesterday." With a long sigh she set it down.

"All right, just a minute," she said to the room in general as she leaned back on the desk. "I'll get it."

Her eyes closed as she rubbed the tip of her finger over the bridge of her nose. "Last time I had it, I'd been to the market. I came in," she said, pointing to the door, "and I took the bag into the kitchen. I put a can of juice into the freezer, and…" Her eyes widened before she scrambled into the next room.

When she came back, she bounced the key from palm to palm. "It's cold," she explained and flushed under Colin's amused glance. "I must have been thinking of something else when I left it in there." Picking up a small gold bag, Cassidy dropped the frozen key inside. "That should do it." She moved to the door and engaged the lock. Gravely, Colin walked to her then cupped her face in his hands.

"Cass."

"Yes?"

"You don't have any shoes on."

"Oh." She lifted her shoulders then let them fall. "I suppose I'll need them."

He kissed her forehead and let her go. "It's best to be prepared for anything." A grin accompanied the gesture of his arm. "They seem to be by your desk."

In silence, Cassidy walked to the desk and slipped into her shoes. Her eyes were smiling as she returned to Colin. "Well, have I forgotten anything else?"

He took her hand, interlocking their fingers. "No."

"Do you like organized people particularly, Colin?" She tilted her head with the question.

"Not particularly."

"Good. Shall we go?"

* * *

Cassidy's first surprise of the evening was the Ferrari that sat by the curb. It was red and sleek and flashy. "That must be yours," she murmured, taking her eyes from bumper to bumper then back again. "Or my neighbor has suddenly inherited a fortune."

"One of Vince's bribes." Colin opened the door on the passenger side. "For this I did a portrait of his niece. A remarkably plain creature with an overbite. Shall I put the top up?"

"No, don't." Cassidy settled into the seat as she watched him round the hood. Cinderella never had a pumpkin like this, she thought and smiled. "I thought you didn't paint anyone unless you were particularly interested in the subject."

"Vince is one of the few people I have difficulty refusing." The Ferrari roared into life. Excitement vibrated under Cassidy's feet.

"Did you know you can buy a three-bedroom brick rambler in New Jersey for what this car costs? With a carport and five spreading junipers."

Colin grinned and swung away from the curb. "I'd make a lousy neighbor."

Colin drove expertly through the city. They skirted Golden Gate Park, and avoided the labyrinthine stretches of freeway. They took side roads, narrow roads, and he maneuvered through traffic with smooth skill.

Cassidy could smell the varied scents from the sidewalk flower vendors and hear the brassy clang of the trolley bell. Tilting her head back, she could see the peak of a slender skyscraper. "Where're we going?" she asked but cared little as the breeze fluttered over her cheeks. It was enough to be with him.

"To eat," Colin returned. "I'm starving."

Cassidy turned to face him. "For an Irishman, you're not exactly talkative. Look." She sat up and pointed. "The fog's coming in."

It loomed over the bay, swallowing the bridge with surprising speed. As Cassidy watched, only the pinnacles of the Golden Gate speared the tumbling cloud.

"There'll be foghorns tonight," she murmured then looked at Colin again. "They make such a lonely sound. It always makes me sad, though I never know why."

"What sound makes you happy?" He glanced over to her, and she brushed wisps of flying hair from her face.

"Popping corn," she answered instantly then laughed at herself.

Leaning her head back, Cassidy looked up at the sky. It was piercingly blue. How many cities could have tumbling fog and blue skies? she wondered. When Colin pulled to the curb, her gaze traveled down until it encountered the huge expanse of the hotel. Her lips parted in surprise as she recognized the area. Nob Hill. She had paid no attention to their direction.

Her door was opened by a uniformed doorman who offered his hand to help her alight. She waited while Colin passed him a bill then joined her.

"Do you like seafood?" He took her hand and moved toward the entrance.

"Why, yes, I—"

"Good. They have rather exceptional seafood here."

"So I've heard," Cassidy murmured.

In a few steps she walked from a world she knew into one she had only read of.

The restaurant was huge and sumptuous. High, iridescent glass ceilings crowned a room dripping with chandeliers. The carpet was rich, the tables many and elegantly white clothed. The maître d' was immediately attentive, and as Colin called him by name Cassidy realized the artist was no stranger there.

The secluded corner table set them apart from the vastness of the restaurant yet left Cassidy with a full view of the splendor. Jeff's cheeseburger seemed light-years away. Having gawked as much as she deemed proper, Cassidy turned to Colin.

"It seems I'm going to do better than tacos after all."

"I'm a man of my word," he informed her. "That's why I give it as seldom as possible. Wine?" he asked and smiled at her in his masterfully charming fashion. "You don't look the cocktail type."

"Oh?" Her head tilted. "Why not?"

"Too much innocence in those big violet eyes." He brushed her hair behind her shoulder. "It almost makes me consider doing something bourgeois like cutting the wine with water."

A black-coated waiter stood respectfully at Colin's elbow. "A bottle of Château Haut-Brion blanc," he ordered, keeping his eyes on Cassidy. With a slight bow the waiter drifted backward and away. She watched him then took another long look around the room, trying to absorb every detail. "I noticed by your desk that you've been working. Is it going well?"

Cassidy studied Colin with some surprise. Perhaps he saw more than she assumed he did. "Yes, actually, I think it is. I'm having one of those periods when everything falls into place. They don't last long, but they're productive. Does it work like that with painting?"

"Yes. Times when everything seems to flow without effort, and times when you scrape the canvas down again and again." He smiled at her, and his long fingers traced her wrist. "Somewhat like you tearing up pages, I imagine."

The waiter returned with their wine, and the ritual of opening and tasting began. Gratefully, Cassidy remained silent. The pulse in her wrist had leapt at Colin's casual touch, and she used the time to quiet its skittish rhythm. When her glass was filled, she was able to lift it with complete composure. The wine was lightly chilled and exquisite.

"To your taste?" Colin asked as he watched her sip.

Cassidy's eyes smiled into his. "It could become a habit."

"Tell me what you're writing about." He, too, lifted his glass, but his free hand covered hers.

"It's about two people and their life together and apart from each other."

"A love story?"

"Yes, a complex one." She frowned a moment at their joined hands then brought her eyes to Colin's again. The flame of the candle threw gold among the violet. She reminded herself to enjoy the moment, not to think of tomorrow. A smile lifted her lips as she touched the glass to them. "They both seem to be volatile characters and get away from me sometimes. There's a fierce determination in them both to stand separate, yet they're drawn together. I'd like to think love allows them to remain separate in some aspects."

"Love makes its own rules, depending on who's playing." His finger trailed over her knuckles then down to her nails before they traveled back. The simple gesture quickened her heartbeat. "Will they have a happy ending?"

Cassidy allowed herself to absorb the pure blue of his eyes. "Perhaps they will," she murmured. "Their destinies are in my hands."

Watching her, Colin brought her hand to his lips. "And for tonight, Cass," he said softly, "is yours in mine?"

Her eyes were dark and steady on his. "For tonight."

He smiled then, with the flash of the pirate. Lifting his glass, he toasted her. "To the long evening ahead."

It was a luxuriously lengthy meal. Wine sparkled in crystal. Even after endless courses, they lingered long over coffee. Cassidy savored each moment. If she was to have only one evening with the man she loved, she would relish each morsel of time. Perhaps by the force of her own will, she could slow the hands of the clock.

The candle flickered low when they rose from the table. Her hand slipped into his. Just as they reached the lobby Cassidy heard Colin's name called. Looking up, she saw a round, balding man in an impeccably cut suit coming toward them. He had a full smile and an extended hand. On reaching Colin, he pumped it enthusiastically while his other thumped on Colin's shoulder. Cassidy saw a large diamond flash from the ring on his hand.

"Sullivan, you rascal, it's good to see you."

"Jack." An easy grin spread over Colin's face. "How've you been?"

"Getting by, getting by. Have a little job in town." His eyes drifted to Cassidy and lingered.

"Cass, this is Jack Swanson, a perfect reprobate. Jack, Cassidy St. John, a perfect treasure."

Cassidy was torn between pleasure at Colin's description and astonishment as she put Swanson's face and name together. Over the past twenty-five years he had produced some of the finest motion pictures in the industry. As he took her hand and squeezed it, she struggled to conceal her feelings.

"Reprobate?" Swanson snorted and kept possession of Cassidy's hand. "You can't believe half the things this Irishman says. I'm a pillar of the community."

"There's a plaque in his den that says so," Colin added.

"Never did have an ounce of respect. Still…" Swanson's eyes roamed over Cassidy's face. There was appreciation in the look. "His taste is flawless. Not an actress, are you?"

"Not unless you count being a mushroom in the fourth-grade pageant." Cassidy smiled.

Swanson chuckled and nodded. "I've dealt with actresses who had lesser credits."

"Cassidy's a writer," Colin put in. He draped an arm around her shoulders, running his hand lightly down her arm. "You warned me to stay away from actresses."

"Since when have you listened to my sage advice?"

Swanson scoffed. He pursed his lips as he studied Cassidy. Appreciation became speculation. "A writer. What sort of writer are you?"

"Why, a brilliant one, of course," she told him. "Without a scrap of ego or temperament."

Swanson patted her hand. "I've a late meeting or I'd steal you away from this young scamp now. We'll have dinner before I leave town." He cast an eye at Colin. "You can bring him along if you like." With another slap for Colin's shoulder, he lumbered away.

"Quite a character, isn't he?" Colin asked as he steered Cassidy toward the door again.

"Marvelous." It occurred to her that since meeting Colin, she had held hands with an Italian duke and one of Hollywood's reigning monarchs.

They stepped outside into the soft light of evening. The sun was gone, but some of its light still lingered. Cassidy slipped into the Ferrari with a contented sigh. She watched the first star flicker into life. With surprise she noted that Colin was headed away from the direction of her apartment.

"Where are we going?"

"There's this little place I know." He turned a corner and eased into traffic. "I thought you'd enjoy it." He shot her a glance and a smile. "Not tired, are you?"

Cassidy's lips curved. "No, I'm not tired."

The nightclub was dimly lit and smoky. Tables were small and crowded together. Jeans sat next to elegant evening dresses and splashy designer outfits. Brassy music blared from a band near a postage-stamp dance floor. Couples swayed together as they moved to the beat.

Colin escorted Cassidy to a dark table at the side of the room. His name was called now and again, but he only made a gesture of acknowledgment and continued until they were seated.

"This is wonderful! I'm certain it's a front for gun running or jewel smuggling," Cassidy exclaimed.

Colin laughed, taking both her hands. "You'd like that, would you?"

"Of course." She grinned, and her eyes lit with mischief.

A waitress had pushed her way over to them and stood, impatient, with her weight on one hip. "The lady needs champagne," Colin told her.

"Who doesn't," she mumbled and shoved her way back through the tables.

Cassidy laughed with unbridled delight. "No deferential bows for Mr. Sullivan in here," she commented.

"It's all a matter of atmosphere. I'm rather fond of sassy waitresses in the right setting. And," he added softly, turning her hand over and kissing the inside of her wrist, "crowded tables that require very close contact. Poor lighting," he continued, pressing his lips to her palm. "Where I can enjoy the taste of your skin in relative privacy." With a slight movement of his head, he kissed the sensitive skin behind her ear.

"Colin," she said breathlessly and lifted her hand to his lips in defense. He merely took it in his and kissed her fingers.

The bottle of champagne came down on the table

with a bang. Colin pulled out a bill and handed it to the waitress. Shoving it in her pocket, she stalked away.

"Annoyingly speedy service tonight," he murmured as he opened the bottle. The pop was drowned out by the loud horns of the band. Cassidy accepted the wine and took a long, slow sip in the hope of stabilizing her pulse.

They drank champagne in quiet companionship, watching the raucous nightlife revolve around them. Cassidy's mood grew mellow and dreamy. Reality and make-believe became too difficult to separate. When Colin stood and took her hand, she rose to go with him to the dance floor.

The music had turned low and bluesy. He slipped both arms around her waist, and in response she lifted hers to circle his neck. Their bodies came together. The air was thick with smoke and clashing perfumes. Other couples were little more than shadows in the dim light. Their movement was only a slow swaying with their bodies pressed close.

Cassidy tilted back her head to look at him. Their eyes joined, their lips tarried less than a whisper apart. She felt a quick surge of desire. If they had been on an island without a trace of humanity, she could not have felt more alone with him. The music ended on a haunted bass note.

Silently Colin took her hand and led her from the crowd.

The moon was a white slice. Cooler air blew some of the heat from Cassidy's blood and some of the clouds from her brain. The Ferrari climbed a hill then descended. Cassidy smiled to herself. There was nothing in the evening she would have changed. No regrets.

Fog curled in twisting fingers on the road ahead. As she glanced to the side Cassidy saw the solid mass of clouds over the bay below them. Again she turned to Colin.

"To my houseboat," he told her before she could form the question. "I have something for you."

Warning lights flashed on and off in her brain. The bittersweet taste of danger was in her mouth. Cassidy looked out on the fog-choked bay and told herself she should ask Colin to take her home. But the night isn't over, she reminded herself. I promised myself tonight.

Fog swirled more thickly as they drove toward sea level. Now and again, from somewhere deep in the mist, came the low warning horns. She'd lost all sense of time when Colin stopped the car. Once again she was in a make-believe world. This one had drifting mists and the sigh of lapping water. Colin led her toward a shrouded shape. The high, maniacal call of a loon speared the silence. A narrow rope bridge swayed lightly under her feet as they crossed it. A breeze blew aside a curtain of fog, and the houseboat jumped into the opening.

"Oh, Colin." She stopped to stare at it with delight and surprise. "It's wonderful."

She saw a wide structure of aged wood in two levels with a high deck on the bow. Fog misted over again as they approached.

Inside Cassidy shook the dampness from her hair

as Colin switched on a light. They walked down two steps and into the living room. It was a large square room with a low, inviting couch and tables scattered for convenience. To the right another short set of stairs led to the galley.

"How marvelous to live on the water." Cassidy spun to Colin and smiled.

"On a clear night the city's all prisms and crystals. In the fog it's brooding and wrapped in mystery." He came to her and, with a habitual gesture, brushed her hair behind her shoulder. His fingers lingered. "Your hair's damp," he murmured. "Do you know how many shades of gold and brown I used to paint your hair? It changes in every light, daring someone to define its color." Colin frowned suddenly and dropped his hand. "You should have a brandy to ward off the chill."

He turned away and walked to a cabinet. Cassidy watched him pour brandy into snifters while she dealt with the effect the intimate tone of his voice and the touch of his hand had had on her.

After accepting the brandy she turned to wander around the room. On a far wall was a painting of the bay at sunrise. The sky was molten with color, reds and golds at their most intense. There was a feeling of frenzied motion and brilliance. Even before she looked for the signature, Cassidy knew it was a Kingsley.

"She's immensely talented," Colin commented from behind.

"Yes," Cassidy agreed with sincerity. The painting gripped her. "It makes the start of a day demand your attention. A sunrise like this would be exciting, but

I don't think I could begin each morning with such violence, however beautiful."

"Are you speaking of the painting or of the artist?"

Realizing his question had followed her thoughts, Cassidy shrugged and stepped away. "Strange," she began again. "One would think an artist would cover his walls with paintings. You have relatively few." She began to examine his collection, moving slowly from one to the next. Abruptly she stopped, staring at a small canvas. It was the Irish landscape she had told him of that morning.

"I wondered if you'd remember it." He stood behind her again, but this time his hands came to her shoulders. There was something casually possessive in the gesture.

"Yes, of course I do."

"I was twenty when I painted that. On my first trip back to Ireland."

"How odd that I should have spoken of it just this morning," Cassidy murmured.

"Destiny, Cass," Colin claimed and kissed the top of her head. Stepping around her, he took the canvas from the wall. "I want you to have it."

Cassidy's eyes flew to his. "No, Colin, I couldn't." Distress and amazement mingled in her voice.

"No?" His brow arched under his fall of hair. "You appeared to like it."

"Oh, Colin, you know I do. It's beautiful, it's wonderful." Her distress deepened, reflecting clearly on her face. "I can't just take one of your paintings."

"You're not taking it, I'm giving it to you," he countered. "That's one of the privileges of the artist."

"Colin." Her eyes went back to the painting then lifted to his. "You wouldn't have kept it all this time if it hadn't meant something special to you. You'd have sold it."

"Some things you don't sell. Some things you give." He held the small canvas out to her. "Please."

Tears thickened in her throat. "I've never heard you say 'please' before."

"I save it for special occasions."

Cassidy looked back at him. He had given her more than the painting; it was a bond—between herself and a woman she had never known. Her smile came slowly. "Thank you."

Colin traced her lips with a fingertip. "This is one of the loveliest things about you," he murmured. "Come," he said abruptly. "Sit down and drink your brandy." He took the canvas and set it aside, then led Cassidy to the sofa.

"Do you paint here, too?" she asked as she sipped her brandy.

"Sometimes."

"I remember the night I met you, your wanting me to come back here for sketches."

"And you threatened me with a husband in a football helmet."

"It was the best I could think up on the spur of the moment." She turned her head to grin at him and found his face dangerously close. His fingers tangled in her hair before she could ease away. Slowly he leaned closer until his lips brushed her cheek. Feather light, the kiss moved to her other cheek, lingering over her lips without touching. Still, she could taste the kiss on them.

"Colin," Cassidy whispered. She put a hand to his chest as his lips moved to her temple. She knew the warmth she felt was not from the brandy.

"Cassidy." He trailed his mouth down to her jawline then drew away. His eyes were grave as he looked down at her, his hand light on her shoulder. "The last time I kissed you, I hurt you. I regret that."

"Please, Colin." Cassidy shook her head to halt his words. "We were both angry."

"You've already forgiven me, because it's your nature to do so. But I remember the look on your face." He ran his hand down her arm until it linked with hers. "I want to kiss you again, Cass, the way you should be kissed." He took his hand and gently circled her neck. "But I need you to tell me it's what you want."

It would be so easy to refuse. She had only to form the word "no," and she knew he'd let her go. But she was as truly his prisoner now as if she were chained to him. "Yes," she said and closed her eyes. "Yes."

His mouth touched hers lightly, and her lips parted. His kisses were soft and gentle, lingering before one ended and another began. She felt him slip the light jacket from her shoulders and enjoyed the warmth of his hands on her skin. Slowly the kisses grew deeper. Her arms found their way around him. The languor that spread through her went far beyond the effects of the wine. Her limbs were pliant, her mind clouded as her senses grew sharper.

When their lips parted, Colin loosened his hold. "Cass."

With a sigh she snuggled against him, brushing his neck with a kiss. She ran a hand experimentally up the silk of his shirt. "Yes?" she murmured, lifting her face to his. Her eyes were slumberous, her lips a temptation. Colin swore under his breath before he crushed his mouth to hers.

Cassidy's response was instantaneous. Her passion went from languid to flaming in the space of a heartbeat. Blood pounded thickly in her brain as she found herself falling backward onto the cushions of the sofa. Colin's body was taut. His hands caressed the bare skin of her shoulders as the kiss deepened. At the base of her throat he found more pleasure, and his mouth lingered there as her pulse beat wildly beneath it.

The elastic of her bodice slid down at his insistence, freeing her breasts to his searching hands. Unbridled, her passion raced through her, bringing a moan that spoke of longing and delight. His mouth trailed down through the valley between her breasts, devouring her heated skin. His fingers brushed over the peak of her breasts, exploring, learning, until his mouth replaced them. Cassidy gave a shuddering moan as he brought his lips back to hers, accepting the fierce, final urgency that flared before he ended the kiss. Her eyes opened to meet the dark fire of his.

Seeing the tumble of his hair over his brow, she lifted

a hand to push it back. She murmured his name. Colin caught her hand in his as she took it to his cheek. Carefully he drew the bodice of her dress into place then pulled her with him to a sitting position.

"I make few noble gestures, Cassidy." His voice was husky, and under her palm she could feel the rapid beat of his heart. "This is one of them." Rising, he drew her to her feet then draped her jacket over her shoulders. "I'll take you home."

"Colin," she began, knowing only that she wanted to be his.

"No, don't say anything." He dropped his hands from her shoulders and put them in his pockets. "You put your destiny in my hands for tonight. I'll take you home. Next time the decision will be in your hands."

Chapter 8

The sun was high and bright. Cassidy watched it spear through her window as she lay in bed. It fell in a patch on the floor and shimmered. Her eyes drifted to the painting that hung to her left. It had hung there for only two days, but she knew every minute detail of the canvas. She knew the very texture of the brush strokes. Sighing, she stared up at the ceiling.

She remembered every moment of her evening with Colin, from the instant she had looked up from her hands and knees by her couch to the brief good-bye at the door.

When she had returned to the studio the morning after their date, Colin had fallen into his work pattern with apparent ease. Whatever had been between them, Cassidy decided, had been for that night. For him, it was over. For me, she thought, studying the painting again, it's forever.

I should be grateful to him for taking me home when he did. If I had stayed... If I had stayed, she repeated after a long breath, I would have become one of his lovers. And then he would have picked up his life exactly where he left off, and I would be even more alone than I am now. As it is, I have one exceptional evening to remember. Wine and candlelight and music.

"Romantic fool," she muttered abruptly then rolled over and punched her pillow.

"Cassidy." The knock sounded as a brief concession before Jeff burst through the door. "Hey, Cassidy." He stopped and gave her a look of disgust. "Still in bed? It's eleven o'clock."

Cassidy pulled the sheet up to her chin and scrambled to sit up. "Yes, I'm still in bed. I worked till three-thirty." She frowned past him. "I thought I'd remembered to lock that door."

"Uh-uh." Jeff hurried over and plopped on the bed while she flushed with embarrassed amusement.

"Make yourself at home," she said with a grand gesture of her free arm. "Don't mind me."

"Take a look at this! You got yourself in the paper."

"What?" Cassidy glanced down at the newspaper Jeff had clutched in his hand. "What are you talking about?"

"I splurged on a Sunday paper," he began then his lips spread in a grin. He touched her nose with a fingertip. "And who do I see when I take a look at the society section, but my friend and neighbor, Cassidy St. John."

"You're making that up," Cassidy accused and tossed

back her sleep-tumbled hair. "What would I be doing on the society page?"

"Dancing with Colin Sullivan," Jeff informed her as he waved the paper under her nose.

Cassidy grabbed his wrist to stop the movement, then her mouth fell open in astonishment. She stared, unbelievingly, at the picture. In two quick moves she had dropped the sheet and grabbed the paper from Jeff's hand. "Let me see that."

"Help yourself," he said amiably. He settled back on one elbow to watch myriad expressions cross her face. The flush sleep had put into her cheeks grew deeper. "Seems you were seen together in some hot spot. A picture gets snapped, and they add a bit of interesting speculation of who Sullivan's latest flame is." He pulled on his beard and chuckled. "Little do they know she's sitting right here in a number fifty-three football jersey that looks a lot better on her than it would on a right tackle." He chuckled again then peered down at the newspaper. "You look real good in there, too."

"This is all—all drivel!" Cassidy slammed down the paper then scrambled to her knees. Pushing Jeff aside she stepped over him to the floor. "Did you read that story?" she demanded and kicked a stray tennis shoe into a corner. "How dare they imply such things?"

Jeff sat back up, watching her spin around the room. "Hey, Cassidy, it's just a story, nothing to get all worked up about. Besides…" He picked up the discarded paper and smoothed it out. "They're really pretty complimentary where you're concerned. Listen, they call you a…" He paused while he searched down the phrase.

"Oh, yeah, here it is. A 'nubile young beauty.' Sounds pretty good."

Cassidy made a low sound in her throat then kicked the mate to the tennis shoe into an opposing corner. "That's just like a man," she stormed back at him. Turning away, she pulled open a drawer and yanked out a pair of cutoffs; then, spinning around, she waved them at him. "Toss out a few compliments and it makes everything all right." Cassidy dove back into the drawer and came up with a crimson scoop-necked T-shirt. "Well, it's not, it's absolutely not." She pushed her hair out of her face and drew in a deep breath. "Can I keep that?" she asked in more controlled tones.

"Sure." Warily, Jeff rose and handed her the paper. He cleared his throat. "Well, I guess I'll just go read the rest of the paper," he told her, but she was already scowling down at the picture again. Taking advantage of her preoccupation, he slipped out the door.

Less than an hour later Cassidy was stalking down the pier toward Colin's houseboat. Gripped in her hand was the folded page of the Sunday paper. Filled with righteous indignation, she crossed the narrow swaying bridge then pounded on the door. There was silence and the lapping of waves. She glanced around then scowled at the Ferrari.

"Oh, you're home all right, Sullivan," she muttered darkly then pounded again.

"What the devil are you banging about?" Colin's voice boomed over her head. Cassidy backed away from the door, looked up and was blinded by the sun. Furious, she flung up a hand to shade her eyes.

She saw him leaning over the rail of the top deck. He was bare-chested, his cutoffs a slight concession to modesty. He held a paint brush tipped in blue in his hand.

"I've got to talk to you!" Cassidy shouted and waved the paper at him.

"All right then, come up, but stop that idiotic banging." He disappeared from the rail before she could speak again. Cassidy walked toward the bow until she spotted a steep set of stairs. After climbing them, she stood on the upper deck with her hands on her hips. She scowled at his back.

He was on a three-legged stool in front of a canvas, painting with sure, rapid strokes. Glancing over, she saw the sailboats he was recreating. They skimmed over the bay with spinnakers billowing in a riot of color.

"Well, what brings you rapping at my door, Cass?" His voice was muffled as he held the stem of a brush between his teeth like a pirate's saber. Another glided over the canvas. Cassidy stomped over and fearlessly waved the paper in front of his face.

"This!"

With surprising calm, Colin put down both of his brushes, cast her a raised-brow look, then took the paper from her. "It's a good likeness," he said after a moment.

"Colin!"

"Ssh. I'm reading." He lapsed into silence, eyes on the paper, while Cassidy ground her teeth and stalked around the deck. Once he laughed outright but held up a hand when she started to speak. She shut her mouth on something like a growl and turned her back on him. "Well," he said at length. "That was highly entertaining."

Cassidy whirled around. "Entertaining? *Entertaining?!* Is that all you have to say about this—this trash?"

Colin shrugged. "It could be better written, I suppose. Do you want coffee?"

"Did you *read* that?" she demanded and stormed forward until she stood in front of him. The wind tugged at her hair, and she pushed it back, annoyed. "Did you read the things it said, the things…" Cassidy sputtered to a halt, stomped her foot in frustration then gave him a firm rap on the chest with her fist. "I am not your latest flame, Sullivan."

"Ah."

Her eyes kindled. "Don't you use that significant 'ah' on me. I am *not* your latest flame, or your flame of any sort, and I resent the term. I resent all the little insinuations and innuendos in that article. I resent the unstated fact that you and I are lovers." She tossed back her head. "What sort of logic is it that because we dance together, we have to be lovers?"

"You have to admit the idea is appealing." He chuckled at her smoldering glare. The breeze rolling in from the bay continued to blow her hair around her face. Absently Colin brushed it back then laid a hand on her shoulder. "Would you like to sue the paper?"

She heard the soft amusement in his voice and stuck

her hands in her pockets. "I want a retraction," she said stubbornly.

"For what?" he countered. "For snapping a picture? For writing a bit of gossip? My dear child, the picture's enough all by itself." He held it out, drawing her eyes to it. "These two people appear to be totally absorbed in each other."

Cassidy turned away and walked to the rail. She knew it had been the picture that had set her off. Their bodies were close, her arms around his neck, their eyes locked. The dark, smoky nightclub was a backdrop. No words were needed to complete the picture. She remembered the moment, the feeling that had rushed through her, the utter intimacy they had shared.

The picture was an invasion of her private self, and she hated it. She detested the chatty little column beside it that linked her so casually with Colin. Without even having learned her name, they had titled her his woman, his woman of the moment...until the next one. Cassidy frowned out at the water, watching the gulls swoop.

"I don't like it," she muttered. "I don't like being splashed in print for speculation over cornflakes and coffee. I don't like being made into something I'm not by someone's lively imagination. And I don't like being described as a..."

"'Nubile young beauty'?" Colin provided.

"I see nothing funny in that grand little phrase. It makes me feel absurd." She folded her arms over her chest. "It's not a compliment, whatever you and Jeff might think."

"Who the devil is Jeff?"

"He thought the article was just peachy," she continued, working up to a high temper again. "He sat on my bed this morning, telling me I should be flattered, that I should—"

"Perhaps," Colin interrupted and walked to her, "you'd tell me who Jeff is and why he was in your bed this morning?"

"Not in, *on,*" Cassidy corrected impatiently. "And stick to the point, Sullivan."

"I'd like this matter cleared up first." He took a final step toward her then captured her chin. His fingers were surprisingly firm. "In fact, I insist."

"Will you stop it?" she demanded and jerked away. "How can I get anywhere when you're constantly badgering and belittling me."

"Badgering and belittling?" Colin repeated then tossed back his head and roared with laughter. "Now *that's* a grand little phrase. Now, about Jeff."

"Oh, leave him out of it, would you?" Cassidy blew out a frustrated breath, making a wide sweep with her arms. Her eyes began to glitter again. "He brought me the article this morning, that's all. I'm telling you, Colin, I won't be lumped in with all your former and future flames. And I won't be used to sustain the romantic mystique of the artist."

His brows drew together. "Now what precisely is the meaning of that last sentence, for those of us who missed the first installment?"

"I think it's clear, a simple declarative sentence in the first person. I mean it, Colin."

"Yes." He studied her curiously. "I can see you do."

They watched each other in silence. She was painfully aware of the lean attraction of his build, of the bronzed skin left bare but for low-slung cutoffs. Thrown off balance by her own thoughts, Cassidy turned away again and leaned over the rail. For a moment she listened to the gentle slap of water against the wood of the boat. Her shoulders moved with her sigh.

"I'm basically a simple person, Colin. I've never been out of the state and scarcely been more than a hundred miles from the city. I don't have a fascinating background. I'm not a woman of mystery." Composed again, she turned back to him. The breeze picked up her hair and tossed it behind her. "I don't like being misrepresented." She lifted her hands a moment then dropped them to her sides. "I'm not the sort of woman they made me seem in that paper."

Colin folded the paper then tucked it in his back pocket before he crossed to her. "You are infinitely more fascinating than the sort of woman they made you seem in that paper."

Cassidy shook her head. "I wasn't fishing for a compliment."

"A simple statement of fact." He kissed her before she could decide whether to accept or evade him. "Feel better now?"

Cassidy frowned at him. "I'm not a child having a temper tantrum."

His brow lifted. "A nubile young beauty, then."

Cassidy narrowed her eyes at him then glanced down at herself. "I'm nubile enough, I should think."

"And certainly young."

Bringing her eyes back up, she gave him a provocative look. "Don't you think I'm beautiful?"

"No."

"Oh."

Colin laughed then captured her face with his hands. "That face," he said as his eyes roamed over her, "has superb bones, exquisite skin. There's strength and frailty and vivacity, and you're totally unaware of it. A unique, expressive face. *Beautiful* is far too ordinary a word."

Color warmed Cassidy's cheeks. She wondered why, after so many close examinations, her blood still churned when he studied her face. "A charming way to make up for an insult," she said lightly. "It must be the Irish in you."

"I've a much better way."

The kiss was so quickly insistent, Cassidy had no time for thought, only response. A sound of pleasure escaped her as she moved her hands up the taut, bare skin of his chest. She felt the heat of the sun and her own instant need. Her mouth became avid. Desire swirled through her blood, causing her to demand rather than surrender. The passion he released in her ruled her, changing submission to aggression. She felt Colin's arms tighten around her and heard his low moan of approval.

"Cassidy," he murmured as his lips roamed over her face. "You bewitch me."

With a curiosity of their own, her hands explored the long line of his torso, the wiry muscles of his arms and back. His heart hammered against hers as she touched him. Here was a whole new world, and her mouth searched his ravenously as she tested it.

"Oh, dear, I seem to be interrupting."

Startled, Cassidy pulled her mouth from Colin's but was unable to break his hold. Twisting her head, she stared at Gail Kingsley. She stood just at the top of the stairs, one hand poised on the railing. An emerald silk scarf rippled at her throat and trailed in the breeze.

"That seems obvious enough," Colin returned evenly. Flushing to the roots of her hair, Cassidy wriggled for freedom.

"I do apologize, Colin darling. I had no idea you had company. So rare for you on a Sunday, after all." She gave him a smile that established her knowledge of his habits. "I needed to pick up those Rothchild canvases, you remember? And we do have one or two things to discuss. I'll just wait downstairs." She crossed the deck as she spoke and opened a door that led inside. "Shall I make coffee for three?" she added then disappeared without waiting for an answer.

Cassidy twisted her head back to Colin, pressing her hands against his chest. "Let me go," she demanded between her teeth. "Let me go this minute."

"Why? You seemed happy enough to be held a moment ago."

She threw back her head as she shoved against him. The muscles she had just tested made her movements useless. "A moment ago I was blinded by animal lust. I see perfectly now."

"Animal lust?" Colin repeated. He grinned widely

in appreciation. "How interesting. Does it come over you often?"

"Don't you grin at me, Sullivan. Don't you dare!"

Colin released her without sobering his features. "At times it's difficult not to."

"I won't have you holding me while Gail stands there with her superior little smile." With a sniff, she brushed at her T-shirt and shorts.

"Why, Cass, are you jealous?" His grin grew yet wider. "How flattering."

Her head snapped up, her breathing grew rapid. "Why you smug, insufferable—"

"You were perfectly willing to suffer me when you were blinded by animal lust."

A sound of temper came low in her throat. Tested past her limit, Cassidy took an enthusiastic swing at him that carried her in a complete circle. He dodged it, catching her neatly by the waist.

"Women are supposed to slap," he instructed. "Not punch."

"I never read the rules," she snapped then jerked away. Cassidy turned, intending to leave in the same manner she had arrived. Colin caught her hand and spun her back until she collided with his chest. He smiled then kissed the tip of her nose.

"What's your hurry?"

"There's an old Irish saying," she told him as she pushed away again. "Three's a crowd."

He chuckled, patting her cheek. "Cass, don't be a fool."

She rolled her eyes to the sky and prayed for will-power. Screaming wouldn't solve anything. She took several deep breaths. "Oh, go...go paint your spinnakers," she suggested and stalked down the steps to the lower deck.

"Sure and it's a fine-looking woman you are, Cassidy St. John," Colin called after her in an exaggerated brogue. She glanced back over her shoulder with eyes blazing. He leaned companionably over the rail. "And it's the truth it's no more hardship watching your temper walking away than it is watching it coming ahead. Next time I'll be wanting to paint you in a pose that shows your more charming end."

"When pigs fly," she called back and doubled her pace. His laughter raced after her.

Chapter 9

Cassidy knew the painting was nearly finished. She had the frantic, hollow sensation of one living on borrowed time. Though she sensed the end would be almost a relief, a release from the tension of waiting, she tried to hold it off by sheer force of will. As she held the pose, she sensed Colin was perfecting, polishing, rather than creating fresh. His quick impatience had relaxed.

He made no mention of her Sunday visit, and she was grateful. In retrospect, with her temper at a reasoning degree, she knew she had overreacted. She was also forced to admit that she had made a fool of herself. A complete fool.

It's not the first time, she mused. And perhaps, in a way, excusable. All I could see was a very public picture revealing my very private feelings. Then that silly little article... Then remembering Gail's spouting off about romantic press and Colin's image. Cassidy caught herself before she scowled. Well, I won't have to listen to her much longer. I'd better start picking up the pieces. It's time to start thinking about tomorrow. A new job, she concluded dismally. A new start, she corrected. New experiences, new people. Empty nights.

"Fortunately, I finished the face yesterday," Colin commented. "Your expression's altered a dozen times in the last ten minutes. Amazing what a range you have."

"I'm sorry. I was…" She searched for a word and settled on an inanity. "Thinking."

"Yes, I could see." His eyes caught hers. "Unhappy thoughts."

"No, I was working out a scene."

"Mmm," Colin commented noncommittally then stepped back from the easel. "Not a particularly joyful one."

"No. They can't all be." She swallowed. "It's finished, isn't it?"

"Yes. Quite finished." Cassidy let out a quiet sigh as she watched his critical study. "Come, have a look," he invited. He held out his hand, but his eyes remained on the canvas.

It surprised her that she was afraid. Colin glanced up at her and lifted a brow.

"Come on, then."

Her fingers tightened around the nosegay, but she walked toward him. Obediently she slipped her hand into his extended one. She turned and looked.

Cassidy had tried to imagine it a hundred times, but it was nothing like what she'd thought. The background was dark and shadowy, playing on shading and depth. In its midst, she stood highlighted in the oyster-white dress. Her nosegay was a surprising splash of color calling attention to the frailty of her hands. Pride was in the stance, in the tilt of her head. Her hair was thick and gloriously tumbled, offsetting the quiet innocence of the dress. It was hair that invited passion. There was a delicacy in the bones of her face she had been unaware of, a fragility competing with the strength of the features. She had been right in thinking he would see her as she had never seen herself.

Her lips were parted, unsmiling but waiting to smile. The smile would be to welcome a lover. The knowledge was in her expression, along with the anticipation of something yet to come. The eyes told everything. They were the eyes of a woman consumed by love...the eyes of innocence waiting to be surrendered. No one could look at it and remain unaware that the woman in the painting had loved the man who painted it.

"So silent, Cass?" Colin murmured and slipped an arm around her shoulders.

"I can't find the word," she whispered then drew a trembling breath. "Nothing's adequate, and anything less would sound platitudinous." She leaned against him a moment. "Colin." Cassidy tried to forget for a moment that the eyes in the painting were naked with love. She tried to see the whole and not the revelation of her emotions. Secrets, he had said. Dreams.

Colin kissed her neck above the silk of the dress then released her. "Rarely, an artist steps back from his work and is astonished that his hands have created something extraordinary." She could hear the excitement in his voice, a wonder she had not expected him to be capable of feeling. "This is the finest thing I've ever done." He turned to her then. "I'm grateful to you, Cassidy. You're the soul of it."

Unable to bear his words, Cassidy turned away. She had to cling to some rags of pride. Desperately she kept her voice calm. "I've always felt the artist is the soul of a painting." Cassidy dropped the nosegay on the worktable then continued to wander around the room. The silk whispered over her legs. "It's your—your imagination, your talent. How much of me is really in that painting?"

There was silence for a long moment, but Cassidy didn't turn back to him. "Don't you know?" Cassidy moistened her lips and struggled to keep her tone light as she turned around.

"My face," she agreed; then, gesturing down the dress, she added, "My body. The rest is yours, Colin, I can't take credit for it. You set the mood, you drew out of me what you already saw. You had the vision. It was a wish you asked me to be, and that's what you've made. It's your illusion." Saying the words caused her more pain than she had believed possible. Still, she felt they had to be said.

"Is that how you see it?" Colin's look was speculative, but she sensed the anger just beneath the surface. "You stood, and I pulled the strings."

"You're the artist, Colin." She shrugged and answered lightly. "I'm just an unemployed writer."

After a long, silent study, he crossed to her. There

was a steady calculation about the way his hands took her shoulders. She had felt that seeking, probing look before and stiffened her defenses against it. His fingers tightened on her skin. "Has the woman in that portrait anything to do with you?" He asked the question slowly.

Cassidy swallowed the knot in her throat. "Why, of course, Colin, I've just told you—"

He shook her so quickly, the words slid back down her throat. She saw the fury on his face, the vivid temper she knew could turn violent. "Do you think it was only your face I wanted? Just the shell? Is there nothing that's inside you in that painting?"

"Must you have everything?" she demanded in despair and anger. "Must you have it all?" Her voice thickened with emotion. "You've drained me, Colin. That's drained me." She flung a hand toward the canvas. "I've given you everything, how much more do you want?"

She pushed him away as a tidal wave of anguish engulfed her. "You never looked at me, thought of me, unless it was because of that painting." She pushed her hair back with both hands, pressing her fingers against her temples. "I won't give you anymore. I can't, there isn't any. It's all there!" She gestured again, and her voice shook. "Thank God it's over."

With a quick jerk, she was out of his hold and running from the studio.

Cassidy spent the next two weeks in the apartment of vacationing friends. Leaving a brief note for Jeff, she packed up her typewriter and buried herself in work. She unplugged the phone, bolted the door and shut herself in. For two weeks she tried to forget there was a world outside the people and places of her imagination. She lost herself in her characters in an attempt to forget Cassidy St. John. If she didn't exist, she couldn't feel pain. At the end of the interlude, she'd shed five pounds, produced a hundred pages of fresh copy and nearly balanced her nerves.

As she returned, hauling her typewriter back up the steps to her apartment, she heard Jeff's guitar playing through his door. For a moment she hesitated, thinking to stop and tell him she was back, but she passed into her own apartment. She wasn't ready to answer questions. She considered calling Colin at The Gallery to apologize, then decided against that as well. It was best that their break had been complete. If they parted on good terms, he might be tempted to get in touch with her from time to time. Cassidy knew she could never bear the casual friendliness.

She packed up the dress she had worn on her flight from the studio. Her fingers lingered on the material as she placed it back in the dress box. So much had happened since she had first put it on. Quickly she smoothed the tissue over it and closed the lid. That part of her life was over. Turning, she went to the phone to call The Gallery. The clerk who answered referred her immediately to Gail.

"Why, hello, Cassidy. Where did you run off to?"

"I have the dress from the portrait and the key to the studio," Cassidy told her. "I'd like someone to come pick them up."

"I see." There was a brief hesitation before Gail continued. "I'm afraid we're just terribly busy right now, dear. I know Colin particularly wanted that dress. Be sweet and drop it by? You can just let yourself into the studio and leave everything there. Colin's away, and we're just swamped."

"I'd rather not—"

"Thank you, darling. I must run." The phone clicked. With a quick oath of annoyance, Cassidy hung up.

Colin's away, she thought as she picked up the dress box. Now's the time to finish it completely.

A short time later Cassidy pushed open the back door of Colin's studio. The familiar scents reached out and brought him vividly to her mind. Resolutely she pushed him away. Now is not the time, she told herself and walked briskly to his worktable to set down the dress and key.

For a moment she stood in the room's center and looked about her. She had spent hours there, days. Every detail was already etched with clarity on her memory. Yet she wanted to see it all again. A part of her was afraid she would forget something, something small and insignificant and vital. It surprised her that the portrait still stood on the easel. Forgetting her promise to leave quickly, Cassidy walked over to study it one last time.

How could he look at that, she wondered as she gazed into her own eyes, and believe the things I said? I can only be grateful that he did. I can only be grateful he believed what I said rather than what he saw. Reaching out a hand, she touched the painted violets.

When the door of the studio opened, Cassidy jerked her hand from the painting and whirled. Her heart flew to her throat.

"Cassidy?" Vince strolled into the room with a wide smile. "What a surprise." In seconds, her hands were enveloped by his.

"Hello." Her voice was a trifle unsteady, but she managed to smile at him.

He heard the breathlessness in her voice and saw there was little color in her face. "Did you know Colin has been looking for you?"

"No." She felt a moment's panic and glanced at the door. "No, I didn't. I've been away, I've been working. I just..." She drew her hands away and clasped them together as she heard herself ramble. "I just brought back the dress I wore for the portrait."

Vince's dark eyes became shrewd. "Were you hiding, madonna?"

"No." Cassidy turned and walked to a window. "No, of course not, I was working." She saw the sparrow, busily feeding three babies with gaping mouths. "I didn't realize you were going to be in America this long." Say anything, she told herself, but don't think until you're out of here.

"I have stayed a bit longer in order to convince Colin to sell me a painting he was reluctant to part with."

Cassidy gripped the windowsill tightly. *You knew he would sell it.* You knew from the beginning all that would be left would be dollars and cents. Did you expect him to keep it and think of you? Shaking her head, she made a quiet sound of despair.

"Cassidy." Vince's hand pressed lightly on her shoulder.

"I shouldn't have come here," she whispered, shaking her head again. "I should've known better." She started to flee, but he tightened his grip and turned her to face him. As he studied her, he lifted a hand to brush her cheek. "Please…" She closed her eyes. "Please don't be kind to me. I'm not as strong as I thought I was."

"And you love him very much."

Cassidy's eyes flew open. "No, it's only that I—"

"Madonna." Vince stopped her with a finger to her lips. There was a wealth of understanding in his eyes. "I've seen the portrait. It speaks louder than your words."

Lowering her head, Cassidy pressed the heel of her hand between her brows. "I don't want to… I'm trying so very hard not to. I have to go," she said quickly.

"Cassidy." Vince held her shoulders. His voice was gentle. "You must see him…speak to him."

"I can't." She placed her hands on his chest, shaking her head in desperation. "Please, don't tell him. Please, just take the portrait and let it be over." Her voice broke, and when she found herself cradled against Vince's chest she made no protest. "I always knew it was going to be over." She closed her eyes on the tears, but allowed herself to be held until the need to release them faded. He stroked her hair and kept silent until he felt her breathing steady. Gently he kissed the top of her head then tilted her face to his.

"Cassidy, Colin is my friend—"

"Interesting." Cassidy's eyes darted to the doorway... and to Colin. "I'd thought so myself." His voice was quiet. "It appears I've been mistaken about more than one person recently." Even before he crossed the room, Cassidy felt the danger. "Gail told me I'd find you up here," he said when he stood directly in front of them. "With my *friend*."

"Colin..." Vince began, only to be cut off with a fierce look.

"Take your hands off her, and keep out of this. When I've finished, you can pick up where you left off."

Hearing the fury in his words, Cassidy nudged out of Vince's hold. "Please," she murmured, not wanting to cause any trouble between them. "Leave us alone for a moment." When Vince's hand stayed on her arm, she turned her eyes to him. "Please," she repeated.

Reluctantly Vince dropped his hand. "Very well, *cara*." He turned briefly to Colin. "I've never known you to be mistaken about anyone, my friend." He walked across the room then closed the door quietly behind him. Cassidy waited an extra moment before she spoke.

"I came to return the dress and the key." She moistened her lips when he only stared down at her. "Gail told me you were away."

"How convenient the studio was available for you and Vince."

"Colin, don't."

"Setting yourself up as a duchess?" he asked coldly.

"I should warn you, Vince is known for his generosity, but not his constancy." His eyes raked her face. "Still, a woman like you should do very well for herself in a week or two."

"That's beneath you, Colin." She turned and took a step away, but he grabbed a handful of her hair. With a small sound of surprise and pain, she stared up at him.

His eyes were shadowed and dark, as was his chin with at least a day's growth of beard. It occurred to her suddenly that he looked exhausted. Thinking back, she knew he had never shown fatigue after hours of painting. His fingers tightened in her hair.

"Colin." In defense, she lifted a hand to his.

"Such innocence," he said softly. "Such innocence. You're a clever woman, Cassidy." His hands came to her shoulders, quickly, ruthlessly. She stared up at him in silence, tasting fear. "It's one thing to lie with words, but another to lie with a look, to lie with the eyes day after day. That takes a special kind of cheat."

"No." She shook her head as his words brought back the tears she had stemmed. "No, Colin, please." She wanted to tell him she had never lied to him, but she couldn't. She had lied the very last time they had been together. She could only shake her head and helplessly let the tears come.

"What is it you want from me?" he demanded. His voice became more infuriated as tears slipped down her cheeks. The sun fell through the skylight and set them glinting. "Do you want me to forget that I looked at you day after day and saw something that was never there?"

"I gave you what you wanted." Tears became sobs

and she struggled against him. "Please, let me go now. I gave you what you wanted. It's finished."

"You gave me a shell, a mask. Isn't that what you told me?" He pulled her closer, forcing her head back until she looked at him. "The rest was my imagination. Finished, Cass? How can something be finished when it never was?" His hand went back to her hair as she tried to lower her head. "You said that I'd drained you. Have you any idea what these past weeks have done to me?" He shook her, and her sobs grew wilder.

"You were right when you told me that painting was nothing more than your face and body. There's no warmth in you. I created the woman in that painting."

"Please, Colin. Enough." She pressed her hands over her ears to shut out his words.

"Do you cringe from the truth, Cassidy?" He tore her hands away, forcing her face back to his again. "Only you and I will know the painting's a lie, that the woman there doesn't exist. We served each other's needs after all, didn't we?" He pushed her aside with a whispered oath. "Get out."

Freed, Cassidy ran blindly for escape.

Chapter 10

It was late afternoon when Cassidy approached her apartment building. She had walked for a long time after her tears had dried. The city had been jammed with people, and she had sought the crowd while remaining separate. The pain had become numbed with fatigue. She was two blocks from home when the rain started, but she didn't increase her pace. It was cool and soft.

Inside her building she began an automatic search for her mailbox key. Her movements were mechanical, but she forced herself to perform the routine task. She would not crawl into a hole of despair. She would function. She would survive. These things she had promised herself during the long afternoon walk.

With the key at last in the lock, Cassidy lifted the cover on the narrow slot and pulled out her mail. She riffled through the advertisements and bills automatically as she started for the stairs. Her feet came to an abrupt halt as she spotted the return address on one of the envelopes. *New York*.

For several minutes she merely studied it, turning it over then back again. Walking back to her mailbox, she pushed the rest of her mail back inside then leaned against the wall. A rejection slip? she reflected, nibbling her bottom lip. Then where was the manuscript? She turned the envelope over again and swallowed.

"Oh, the devil with it," she muttered and ripped it open. She read the letter twice in absolute silence. "Oh, why now?" she asked and hated herself for weeping again. "I'm not ready for it now." She forced back the tears and shook her head. "No, it's the perfect time," she corrected then made herself read the letter again. There couldn't be a better time.

She stuffed the letter into her pocket and ran back into the rain. In ten minutes she was banging on Jeff's door.

Guitar in hand, he pulled open the door. "Cassidy, you're back! Where've you been? We were ready to call out the marines." Stopping, he took his eyes from the top of her head to her feet. "Hey…you're drenched."

"I am not drenched," Cassidy corrected as she dripped on the hall floor. She hoisted up a bottle of champagne. "I'm much too extraordinary to be drenched. I've been accepted into the annals of literature. I shall be copywritten and printed and posted in your public library."

"You sold your book!" Jeff let out a whoop and hugged her. His guitar pressed into her back.

Laughing, Cassidy pulled away. "Is that any way to express such a momentous occurrence? Peasant." She pushed back her sopping hair with her free hand. "However, I'm a superior person, and will share my bottle of champagne with you in my parlor. No dinner jacket required." Turning, she walked to her own door, pushed it open then gestured. Grinning, Jeff set down his guitar and followed her.

"Here," he said after he had closed the door and taken the bottle from her. "I'll open it, you go get a towel and dry off or else you'll die of pneumonia before the first copy hits the stands."

When she came back from the bathroom wrapped in a terry-cloth robe and rubbing a towel over her hair, Jeff was just releasing the cork. Champagne squirted out in a jet.

"It's good for the carpet," he claimed and poured. "I could only find jelly glasses."

"My crystal's been smashed," Cassidy told him as she picked up her glass. "To a very wise man," she said solemnly.

"Who?" Jeff raised his glass.

"My publisher," she announced, then grinned and drank. "An excellent year," she mused, gazing critically into the glass. The wine fizzed gently.

"What year is it?" Jeff lifted the bottle curiously.

"This one." Cassidy laughed and drank again. "I only buy new champagne."

They drank again then Jeff leaned over and kissed her. "Congratulations, babe." He pulled the damp towel from her shoulders. "How does it feel?"

"I don't know." She threw her head back and closed her eyes. "I feel like someone else." Quickly she filled her glass again. She knew she had to keep moving, had to keep talking. She couldn't think seriously about what she had won that day or she would remember what she had lost. "I should've bought two bottles," she said, spinning a circle. "This is definitely a two-bottle occasion." She drank, feeling the wine rise to her head. "The last time I had champagne…" Cassidy stopped, remembering, then shook her head. Jeff eyed her in puzzlement. "No, no." She gestured with her hand as if to wipe the thought away. "I had champagne at Barbara Seabright's wedding in Sausalito. One of the ushers propositioned me in the cloakroom."

Jeff laughed and took another sip. A knock sounded. Cassidy called out, "Come in, there's enough for—" Her words were cut off as Colin opened the door.

Cassidy's color drained slowly. Her eyes darkened. Jeff looked quickly from one to the other, then set down his glass.

"Well, I gotta be going. Thanks for the champagne, babe. We'll talk later."

"No, Jeff," Cassidy began. "You don't have to—"

"I've got a gig," he announced, lifting her restraining hand from his arm. She saw him exchange one long look with Colin before he slipped through the door.

"Cass." Colin stepped forward.

"Colin, please go." Shutting her eyes, she pressed her fingers between her brows. There was a pressure in her chest and behind her lids. Don't cry. Don't cry, she ordered herself.

"I know I haven't any right to be here." There was a low harshness in his tone. "I know I haven't the right to ask you to listen to me. I'm asking anyway."

"There isn't anything to say." Cassidy forced herself to stand straight and face him. "I don't want you here," she said flatly.

He flinched. "I understand, Cassidy, but I feel you have a right to an apology…an explanation."

Her hands were clenched, and slowly she spread her fingers and stared down at them. "I appreciate the offer, Colin, but it isn't necessary. Now—" she lifted her eyes to his "—if that's all…"

"Oh, Cass, for pity's sake, show more mercy than I did. At least let me apologize before you shut me out of your life."

Unable to respond, Cassidy merely stared at him. He stooped to pick up the bottle of champagne. "I seem to have interrupted a celebration." He set the bottle back and looked at her. "Yours?"

"Yes." Cassidy swallowed and tried to speak lightly. "Yes, mine. My manuscript was accepted for publication. I had a letter today."

"Cass." He moved toward her, lifting a hand to touch her cheek.

Cassidy stiffened and took a quick step back. Catching the look that crossed his face, she knew she had hurt him. Colin slowly dropped his hand.

"I'm sorry," Cassidy began.

"Don't be." His voice had a quiet, final quality. "I can hardly expect you to welcome my touch. I hurt you." He paused, looking down at his hand a moment before bringing his gaze back to her face. His eyes searched hers. "Because I know you as well as I know myself, I'm aware of how badly I hurt you. I have to live with that. I haven't the right to ask you to forgive me, but I'll ask you to hear me out."

"All right, Colin, I'm listening," Cassidy said wearily. She drew a deep breath and tried to speak calmly. "Why don't you sit down."

He shook his head and, turning, moved back to the window and looked out, resting his hands in the sill. "The rain's stopped and there's fog. I still remember how you looked that night, standing in the fog looking up at the sky. I thought you were a mirage." He murmured the last sentence, as if to himself. "I had an image in my mind of a woman. My own idea of perfection, a balance of qualities. When I saw you, I knew I had found her. I had to paint you."

For a moment he lapsed into silence, brooding out at the gloom. "After we'd started, I found everything in you I'd ever looked for—goodness, spirit, intelligence, strength, passion. The longer I painted you, the more you fascinated me. I told you once you bewitched me; I almost believe it. I've never known a woman I've wanted more than I've wanted you."

He turned then and faced her. The play of the light threw his features into shadows. "Each time I touched you, I wanted more. I didn't make love to you that night on the houseboat because I wouldn't have you think of yourself as just one of my lovers. I couldn't take advantage of your being in love with me."

At his words, Cassidy's eyes closed. She made a soft sound of despair.

"Please, don't turn away. Let me finish. The day the painting was finished, you denied everything. You said the things I'd seen had been in my own imagination. You were so cool and dispassionate. You very nearly destroyed me.... I had no idea anyone had such power over me," he continued softly. "It was a revelation, and it hurt a great deal. I wanted more from you, I needed more, but you told me you had nothing left. I was angry when you ran away, and I let you go. When I came here later, you were gone.

"I've been out of my mind for over two weeks, not knowing where you were or when—worse, *if*—you were coming back. Your friend next door had your cryptic little note and nothing else."

"You saw Jeff?" she asked.

"Cassidy, don't you understand? You disappeared. The last time I saw you, you were running away from me, and then you were gone. I didn't know where you were, or how to find you, if something had happened to you. I've been going slowly mad."

She took a step toward him. "Colin, I'm sorry. I had no idea you'd be concerned...."

"Concerned?" he repeated. "I was frantic! Two weeks, Cassidy. Two weeks without a word. Do you know what a helpless feeling it is to simply have to wait? Not to know. I've haunted Fisherman's Wharf, been everywhere in the city. Where in heaven's name were you?" he demanded furiously then held up a hand before she could answer. She watched him take a deep breath be-

fore turning away from her. "I'm sorry. I haven't had much sleep lately, and I'm not completely in control."

His movements became restless again. He stopped and lifted Cassidy's discarded glass of champagne. Thoughtfully, he studied the etchings on the side. "An interesting concept in a wineglass," he murmured. Turning back, he toasted her. "To you, Cass. To only you." He drank then set down the empty glass.

Cassidy dropped her eyes. "Colin, I am sorry you were worried. I was working, and—"

"Don't." The word stopped her, and her eyes shot back to his. "Don't explain to me," he said in more controlled tones. "Just listen. When I walked into the studio today and saw you with Vince, something snapped. I can give you excuses—pressure, exhaustion, madness, take your pick. None of them make up for the things I said to you." His eyes were eloquent on hers. "I despise myself for making you cry. I hated the things I said to you even as I said them. Finding you there, with Vince, after looking for you everywhere for days..." He stopped, shaking his head, then moved back to the window.

"Gail arranged the timing very well," he said. "She knew what I'd been through the past two weeks and knows me well enough to predict how I'd react finding you alone with Vince. She sent him up to the studio on a fictitious errand before I got back to The Gallery. She told me the two of you were meeting up there. She made the suggestion, but I grabbed on to it with both hands." He rubbed his fingers over the back of his neck as if to release some tension.

"We'd been occasional lovers up until about a year

ago when things got a bit complicated. I should have re-membered whom I was dealing with, but I wasn't think-ing too clearly. Gail's decided to take a long—perhaps permanent—sabbatical on the East Coast." He paused a moment then turned to study her. "I'd like to think you could understand why I behaved so abominably."

In the silence Cassidy could just hear Jeff's guitar through the thin walls of the apartment. "Colin." Her eyes searched his face then softened. "You look so tired."

His expression altered, and for a moment she thought he would cross to her. He stood still, however, keeping the distance between them. "I don't know when I fell in love with you. Perhaps it was that first night in the fog. Perhaps it was when you first wore that dress. Per-haps it was years before I met you. I suppose it doesn't matter when."

Cassidy stared at him, robbed of speech. "I'm not an easy man, Cassidy, you told me that once."

"Yes," she managed. "I remember."

"I'm selfish and given to temper and black moods. I have little patience except with my work. I can promise to hurt you, to infuriate you, to be unreasonable and impatient, but no one will love you more. No one." He paused, but still she could only stare at him, transfixed. "I'm asking you to forget what makes sense and be my wife and my lover and mother my children. I'm asking that you share your life with me, taking me as I am." He paused again, and his voice softened. "I love you, Cass. This time, my destiny's in your hands."

She watched him as he spoke, heard the cadence of

his native land grow stronger in his speech. Still he made no move toward her, but stood across the room with shadows playing over his face. Cassidy remembered how he had looked when she had flinched away from his touch.

Slowly she walked to him. Reaching up, she circled his neck with her arms then buried her face against his shoulder. "Hold me." His arms came gently around her as his cheek lowered to the top of her head. "Hold me, Sullivan," she ordered again, pressing hard against him. She turned her head until her mouth found his.

His arms drew tight around her, and she murmured in pleasure at their strength. "I love you," she whispered as their lips parted then clung again. "I've needed to tell you for so long."

"You told me every time you looked at me." Colin buried his face in her hair. "I refused to believe I'd fallen in love with you, that it could have happened so quickly, so effortlessly. The painting was nearly finished when I admitted to myself I'd never be able to live without you."

His voice lowered, and he drew her closer. "I've been crazy these last two weeks, staring at your portrait and not knowing where you were or if I'd ever see you again."

"Now you have me," she murmured, making no objection when his hands slipped under the terry cloth to roam her skin. "And Vince will have the portrait."

"No, I told you once some things can't be sold. The portrait has too much of both of us in it." He shook his head, breathing in the rain-fresh fragrance of her hair. "Not even for Vince."

"But I thought…" She realized that she had only assumed Vince had been speaking of her portrait. There was a new wealth of happiness in the knowledge that Colin had not intended to sell what was to her a revelation of their love.

"What did you think?"

"No, it's nothing." She pressed her lips against his neck. "I love you." Her mouth roamed slowly up his jawline, savoring what she knew now was hers.

"Cass." She felt his heart thud desperately against hers as his fingers tightened in her hair. "Do you know what you do to me?"

"Show me," she whispered against his ear.

With a groan, Colin kissed her again. She could taste his need for her and wondered at the strength of it. Her answer was to offer everything.

"We'll get married quickly," Colin murmured then took her lips again, urgently. Inside her robe, his hands ran in one long stroke down her sides, then roamed to her back to bring her closer. "Very quickly."

"Yes." Cassidy closed her eyes in contentment as his cheek rested against hers. "I already have the perfect dress." She sighed and nestled against him. "What will you title the painting, Colin?"

"I've already titled it." He smiled into her eyes. *"Sullivan's Woman."*

* * * * *

Get ready to meet the MacKade family...

'The most successful author on planet Earth'
—*Washington Post*

www.millsandboon.co.uk

BL/267/CRF

Introducing
the Stanislaskis...

**Fall under the spell of *New York Times*
bestselling author**

Nora Roberts

www.millsandboon.co.uk